THE STENCH OF BURNED FLESH
SCORCHED THE AIR

Some of the smaller corpses had been tossed outside; scavengers had been at work. The bodies left inside were blackened, unrecognizable. It was some time before Egan discovered Mary's body on the bloodied blanket.

The men buried their dead in silence. The tiny body of Mary's infant son was placed beside her.

Five graves held eleven mutilated small corpses. Egan stood numbly in the growing darkness.

"Reckon we ought to say some words," the other man said.

"I only say this," Egan said, his voice shaking, tears streaming down his face. "For each of them, no fewer than ten of their people. This I swear, and this vow will only be broken by death."

The White Indian Series
Ask your bookseller for the books you have missed

The White Indian Series
Book XVIII

FATHER OF WATERS

Donald Clayton Porter

Created by the producers of
The First Americans, **Wagons West**,
and **Children of the Lion**.

Book Creations Inc., Canaan, NY · Lyle Kenyon Engel, Founder

BANTAM BOOKS
NEW YORK · TORONTO · LONDON · SYDNEY · AUCKLAND

FATHER OF WATERS

*A Bantam Book / published by arrangement with
Book Creations, Inc.*

PRINTING HISTORY

Bantam edition / December 1989

*Produced by Book Creations, Inc.
Lyle Kenyon Engel, Founder*

ISBN 0-553-28285-9

Published simultaneously in the United States and Canada

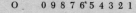

PRINTED IN THE UNITED STATES OF AMERICA

O   0 9 8 7 6 5 4 3 2 1

This is a work of fiction. While the general
outlines of history have been faithfully followed,
certain details involving setting, characters,
and events may have been simplified.

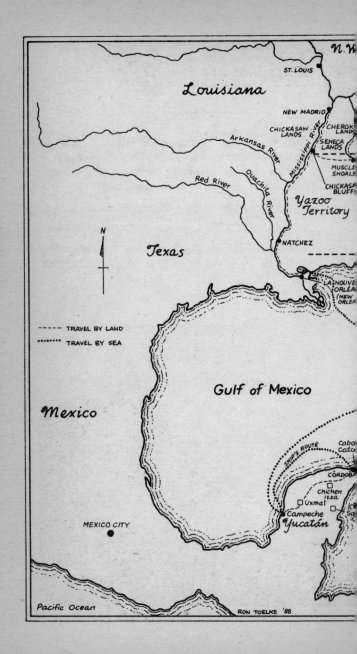

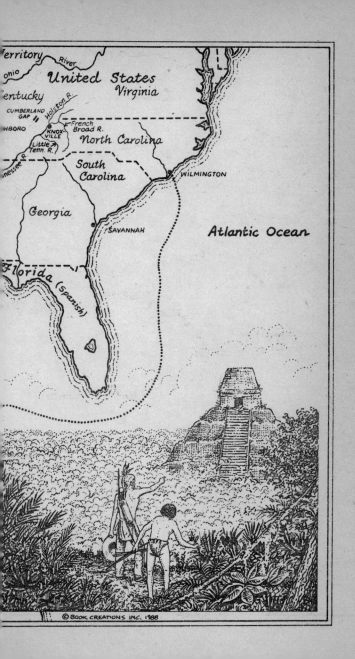

© BOOK CREATIONS INC. 1988

Chapter I

The Kirk homestead occupied a small clearing on the southern slope of a wooded ridge twenty miles west of Knoxville. There were two log cabins connected by a covered breezeway. The larger cabin was more weathered and had been enlarged as John Kirk's family grew, by the addition of shedlike rooms. A tiny, gurgling brook sparkled its way from a crystal spring above the cabin and past the house to the clear creek at the foot of the slope. The neat, narrow valley, with its carefully tended crops, extended into the distance, toward the Tennessee River.

The Cumberland frontier had been peaceful for years, but John Kirk and his oldest son, eighteen-year-old Egan, had cleared away the trees to give unobstructed fields of fire from each of the slotted windows of the cabins.

Kirk had carved his holding from virgin forest in what had once been Cherokee land. The nearest neighbors were of that tribe, and relations between the Kirk family and their neighbors were good. Rusog, principal chief of the Cherokee, was a friend of the white man, a man who believed in peace.

John and Egan Kirk put fresh meat on the table with their hunting skills, just as Daniel Boone and the earliest settlers had done and just as the Indian had done for untold generations before the white man came across the mountains through the Cumberland Gap. For the Kirks, with thirteen mouths to feed, hunting was not a sport but a necessary chore. The need for fresh meat was one reason why John and Egan were miles away to the northwest when a minor Cherokee chief known to the Kirks as Slim Tom stepped into the clearing from the forest and in good English called out, "Hello, the house."

Egan's sixteen-year-old wife, Mary, was stirring the wash as it boiled in a huge, cast-iron caldron over an open fire in the front yard. When she saw Slim Tom she lifted one hand to wave, then looked over her shoulder to see her mother-in-law, Margaret, standing inside the doorway just below the loaded musket that hung on its rack over the sill.

"It's Slim Tom," Mary called.

The older woman relaxed, stepped out onto the rough, hand-hewn planks of the porch, and sat wearily in a cane rocker made by her husband. As the Cherokee approached he carried his musket loosely cradled in one arm.

Slim Tom had been a village chief before his people moved away to put more land between them and the settlements that expanded from Knoxville. He was small for a Cherokee, and wiry. He wore a mixture of Cherokee and white man's clothing.

"You are working too hard," he commented pleasantly as he looked down at Mary's wash pot.

"I wouldn't object to someone helping me carry this here tub of clothes to the line," Mary said.

Slim Tom grasped one handle of the tub and helped. The woman smelled of lye soap mixed with that distinctive aroma of the white settler. As Mary started hanging the wet wash on the clothesline, Margaret came to stand nearby.

"It's good to see you, Slim Tom," Margaret said.

"I have come to speak with John Kirk," the Cherokee replied, his dark eyes taking in the younger children as they spilled out of the two cabins to see what was going on. Visitors were rare. The children ranged in age from Mary's infant son, who was just beginning to crawl, to fourteen-year-old Eliza, John and Margaret's oldest daughter. Margaret's youngest, also a girl, was only months older than her grandson.

"Well," Margaret said, looking around warily, seeing only the enclosing forest, the greening corn crop in the little valley, and the sparkling water, "the mister's not here right now." She studied Slim Tom's face. Seeing no reaction, she added quickly, "We 'spect him back any minute now."

Mary looked up at the sun. "It's close to noon. I reckon Slim Tom would take victuals with us."

"My pleasure." Slim Tom inclined his head.

Eleven Kirks laced into the midday meal of corn dodgers, fried potatoes, and salt pork. The younger ones carried their plates to the breezeway. Slim Tom, the two adult women, and Eliza sat at the table. The Cherokee ate in silence, then pushed his plate away and rose.

"Do you suppose that John Kirk has been delayed?" he asked.

"'Spect so," Margaret said. "He won't be long, though, and Egan's just up the hill." Even with a friendly Indian one was cautious. The forests west of the mountains were extensive, reaching toward the Mississippi into a land peopled only by Indians. There was the Cherokee Nation, a nation only in name, held loosely together by a common language and tribal traditions. Margaret had met the principal chief, and she agreed with her husband that Rusog was a man to be trusted. But in that wide wilderness were countless villages ruled by minor chieftains, some of whom did not necessarily agree with Rusog.

It also paid to be careful because a war raged in the west—a war without sieges or great battles. It was fought in fearful isolation by settlers whose land hunger had driven them to clear an acre or two in the wilderness and to plant their crops with one eye on the encroaching forest and one hand near a loaded rifle. To the north the Shawnee and the Miami and other Ohio tribes had vowed eternal hostility. From the south Creek war parties urged the isolated village chiefs to join the war that had never ended.

"Thank you for the meal," Slim Tom said. "Now I will go."

For some minutes Margaret sat in the rocker, within quick reach of the loaded musket over the door. When a mockingbird perched on the leaning post of the clothesline and offered a splendid repertoire of melodies, Margaret went to help Mary finish the washing. They soon had it hanging in the afternoon sun to dry.

It was Mary who noticed the movement in the trees to the west—a hint of sun reflecting on metal . . . a shadow. "I think we'd better go inside, Mother Kirk," she said quietly.

It was stifling in the main cabin with all the doors closed and the shutters covering all but the rifle slits in the windows. The afternoon wore on. Both women realized that John and Egan were not coming back before nightfall. They were on a long hunt to the northwest, scouting good areas to set traps during the winter. Probably they would not return for at least another day, maybe two, for on the way back they would kill and butcher at least two young, tender does.

From Spanish New Orleans to the little village that had grown up around an Indian trading post at New Madrid, the Father of Waters that the Ojibwa had named Misi Sipi, "great river," was a watery way that cut into the heart of the North American continent; in the late eighteenth century the Mississippi was an artery of the Spanish Empire.

Due to the windings of the channels, travel by the

Mississippi was often dangerous, a challenge that could be met only sporadically by sail. The Spanish relied mainly on man-powered poles and oars to make their infrequent trips to their far northern outposts such as New Madrid. It was aboard such a riverboat that Alexander McGillivray, called king of the Creek, arrived at New Madrid for a parlay with a few select chiefs from the Ohio Valley tribes.

The meeting, arranged by Esteban Miró, the Spanish governor, was not intended to be a general council of chiefs. Miró, who knew well McGillivray's persuasive powers, wanted the Creek and just one or two of the war leaders of the northern tribes to explore the possibilities of closer cooperation between the Creek and the Spanish in the south and the hostile tribes in the north.

McGillivray, like many prominent Indian leaders, was of mixed blood, actually more white than Indian. He was the son of a wealthy Scots merchant and an Indian woman, called a princess, who was herself half-French. Boren to wealth, the king of the Creek was as much at home in an English or a Charleston salon as he was as he faced two Indians over a campfire outside New Madrid. McGillivray's father had been a Loyalist during the War of the Revolution, and his holdings in Georgia had been confiscated by the rebels. McGillivray had never forgotten and would never forgive the state of Georgia for that injustice. He himself had fought on the side of the British, and after the war the Creek National Council elected him chief and head warrior, and he had used all his influence to stir unrest along the Georgia border.

McGillivray was a wealthy man, a silent partner in a prosperous English trading company. He was well educated and had extravagant tastes. His unwavering hatred for all Georgians—and white men in general—fed his determination to keep war simmering all along the western frontier of the United States. Hopeful of aiding the Indians in their war, he had courted the Spanish, promising war against the United States in exchange for weapons and supplies.

The two Indians who sat across from the highly civilized McGillivray offered an interesting study in contrasts. He had been disappointed to find that he had made the long, grueling trip up the Father of Waters to speak with lesser chiefs; he had expected to meet with the man whose leadership and vision was legendary on the frontier, the Miami war chief Little Turtle. Instead he faced Little Turtle's best war leaders: Blue Jacket, so named for his choice of clothing as a young man, and a tall, hooded shaman who kept his face hidden and said nothing. The conversation was in English, McGillivray speaking with a fine, upper-class British accent, Blue Jacket with the tongue of the frontier. Blue Jacket spoke for Little Turtle, assuring McGillivray that as long as the time of new beginning put forth fresh, green leaves on the trees each year, as long as the streams ran and the sun gave light, then the Miami, the Shawnee, the Wyandot, the Delaware, and others would fight to hold that sweet and fruitful land north of the Ohio River.

"The Spanish governor is your friend," McGillivray assured Blue Jacket, "and your tribes will benefit from being a friend of the Spanish king. Many boatloads of weapons and the gold and silver coins of the white man to buy powder and shot will come up the great river to you."

"It is said that the Spanish, like the Americans, hunger for our lands," Blue Jacket pointed out.

McGillivray laughed. "And your red-coated friends the British do not?"

"Better the evil we know," Blue Jacket retorted.

"Of all the three, who, my brother, can put the most armed soldiers in the field against us?" McGillivray asked.

Blue Jacket was silent. The other man, an odd one, spoke in a low, grating voice, his imperfectly articulated words made eerie by a hissing sound. McGillivray winced involuntarily when he saw that the man's tongue was split, like that of a snake. "Your point is well made, King of the Creek," said the shaman.

"I am pleased that you understand, Spirit Man," Mc-

Gillivray said. "We must stand together against the Americans, who are most numerous. We must accept any help from the jealous Spanish and English. And then, when the Americans are defeated, it will be but the work of a moment to drive the Spanish and the English from our lands."

"The great spirit man Hodano is right," Blue Jacket remarked, "but only if the British or Spanish kings do not choose to send their soldiers in countless numbers across the great waters."

"The European countries have problems of their own at home," McGillivray said. "Did the British send a sufficient number of redcoats to defeat those who rebelled against them? No. Nor will they when we have pushed the Americans back across the Ohio, back across the mountains, and to the coastal plain in my land, in the south. Take what help the Spanish governor wants to give you, my friends, and be assured that as you fight here in your northern lands, the Creek will be fighting in the south."

"And the others?" the shaman asked. "The Choctaw, the Chickasaw?"

"Women," McGillivray said, spitting. "The Choctaw want only to be left alone to plant their corn and pretend to be white men. The Chickasaw, who were once among the fiercest of warriors, talk only of peace. Among the Cherokee, however, there are those who shed white blood."

"There is one who influences them to keep the peace," Hodano said. "A Seneca."

McGillivray nodded. "I have heard of this sachem. He is called Renno, and he is related by marriage to the Cherokee Rusog."

Hodano hissed, and the wolverine cowl fell back. His fire-ruined face showed white scars in the flickering light. One eye gleamed redly; the other existed only under a mass of tangled tissue. "The Seneca you name fought with the United States, and he will fight against his brothers if his white masters wish him to do so."

"Perhaps you are wrong, Spirit Man," McGillivray said. "When victory is evident, all Indians will join us."

Hodano hissed. "There is only one way to handle the Seneca. An arrow in the back."

McGillivray raised one eyebrow. "I, for one, face my enemies."

With a snarl Hodano raised his cowl, stood, and stalked away.

"Who is that man?" McGillivray asked. The shaman made him shiver in spite of himself, and McGillivray was afraid of no man.

"He lives with the spirits," Blue Jacket explained uncomfortably. "His advice is valued by Little Turtle. With his magic he can smell a white man from miles away."

"I am pleased that I will not have to fight with him at my side," McGillivray admitted. "He is Seneca, is he not? Does that explain his hatred for this Renno?"

"They have faced each other more than once, and the outcome was never to Hodano's liking," Blue Jacket said. "The Seneca Renno is a mighty warrior, and his counsel is heard by the white man, including the great white chief Washington. He, like you, has the blood of the white man in his veins. Perhaps if you met with him—"

"How many warriors can he field?"

Blue Jacket shrugged. "Two hundred. No more."

McGillivray laughed. "I can field two hundred warriors from one or two Creek villages. I think I will not concern myself with a Seneca who can do so little."

"Add to his two hundred the strength of the main body of the Cherokee, under Rusog," Blue Jacket continued.

"Ah." McGillivray nodded. "Perhaps one day I will talk with this Seneca. On my way downriver I will try to meet with those Cherokee who fight with us. Perhaps from them I can learn more of the Seneca and his Cherokee brother-by-marriage."

Hodano had returned to stand near the fire. He spoke in his low, sibilant voice. "There is one. I have taught him. He has few men at this time, but he is a *warrior*. His name is Atarho, and I think you will hear of him, for even now he is shedding white blood in the settlements in the Cumberland."

"Atarho?" McGillivray echoed. "Is that a Cherokee name?"

"It is the name of a warrior," Hodano replied forcefully. "Remember it."

In the never-ending war along the western frontiers of the United States, attack came with a cruel suddenness that often left behind bloody scenes of torture to be discovered by some distant neighbor coming to see why his friend had not been in contact. No section of the frontier was immune—not even the usually peaceful lands where white settlement met Cherokee lands.

At dusk Mary Kirk heard sounds on the roof at the same time that her mother-in-law lifted a musket, pushed its muzzle through a firing slit, and dropped an Indian in the front yard with a skill that would have been envied by many men.

"They're coming," Margaret said.

Fourteen-year-old Eliza saw an Indian run whooping across the clearing toward the cabins. She sighted down the length of her long rifle, squeezed the trigger, and closed her eyes at the sound of the shot. When she opened her eyes, the Indian was falling limply. She felt giddy and faint, for she had never shot a man before. The younger girls were loading while Margaret, Mary, and Eliza kept up a fire that held the main body of the attackers away from the cabins. But the footsteps on the roof were louder now, and a shower of soot fell from the chimney into the glowing embers in the fireplace.

"They're trying to come down the chimney," Mary said calmly. She moved quickly to gather two feather pillows and an ax. She ripped open the pillowcases, and as soot showered down from the wide chimney, she spread the feathers over the coals. A choking smoke rose, and from the chimney came a cry of alarm followed by desperate coughing. A singed, half-suffocated Indian plummeted into the coals, rolled out, bringing fire with him, to meet the ax, wielded by Mary. His skull split with frightening loudness.

Mary jerked the ax away in time to see a second Indian plunge into the smoldering feathers. This time she caught the warrior on the back of his neck, swinging the ax with all her strength.

The younger ones looked on wide-eyed and silent. There was a lull in the firing. The Indians, with three men killed outside, were presenting no targets.

Mary's eyes jerked toward the door as the stout wood reverberated from a hard blow. The sound repeated.

"Someone's using an ax on the door," Margaret said.

"Mama," Eliza whispered. "They're Cherokee."

"Renegades," Margaret corrected, keeping her voice calm. "Children, stack anything you can move in front of the door."

Eliza led by example, pushing a chest of drawers toward the door. But before she could move the chest into place, the door splintered and a gaping hole appeared. A dark hand thrust through, fumbling for the sturdy bar that secured it shut. Mary swung her ax, and four fingers fell to the floor. One of the young Kirk girls screamed. With more blows the door shattered. Margaret's musket took one last payment in blood, and a warrior sprawled half-in, half-out of the doorway. But others poured through.

Eliza fired but missed. Mary lifted her ax, and a warrior leaped forward, his tomahawk cutting her hand badly, causing her to drop the ax. A blow with the flat side of the tomahawk sent her sprawling to the floor, dazed.

"Slim Tom!" Margaret gasped. "You?"

"White men gave me that name," the Cherokee snarled, his mouth twisted with loathing. "Now hear the name *I* have chosen, the name that speaks of my hatred. I am Atarho."

Now Margaret recognized another face. "And *you*, Simon Purdy! A white man!"

For most it would have required a second look to see that the man to whom Margaret spoke was not an Indian. He was dressed as a Cherokee, and his face and hands were darkened by the sun.

"Why do you do this?" Margaret demanded. "We have been your friends."

"There can be no friendship with those who steal our lands," Atarho said.

"Enough talk," Simon Purdy snarled, reaching for Mary, who cringed away.

"Listen," Margaret said quickly. "I reckon you'll do what you want, and I reckon there's nothing we can do about it. But in the name of mercy let the young ones go. They can find their way into Knoxville."

Purdy grinned, winking at Atarho. "Now that's a reasonable request, ain't it?"

"Quite reasonable," Atarho agreed.

Purdy moved swiftly, jerking Mary's infant son from the arms of an eight-year-old girl. "We'll let this 'un go first," he said, dangling the boy by the heels to meet the blade of a tomahawk in his other hand. The blow severed neck, spinal cord, and arteries. The tiny head fell to the floor with a thud and rolled, spilling blood, to within two inches of Mary's dilated eyes. She screamed and leaped to her feet. Purdy dropped the infant's body and hit her in the face with his fist. A warrior lunged forward to bury his tomahawk into Margaret's belly. Another sent Eliza to the floor, gray matter and blood spilling from a cracked skull.

"Damn it!" Purdy yelled. "That one was mine!" He looked around. Already the next oldest girl was dead. He stood over the fallen Mary, glaring at anyone who came near. "This one's mine," he said repeatedly.

The Cherokee warriors looked at Purdy with open contempt as, having finished their bloody work, they stood, scalps in hand.

"Burn," Atarho ordered.

"Now wait a minute!" Purdy shouted. "Give a man a chance to enjoy himself in a proper bed."

"If you must act like a rutting animal," Atarho said, "do so outside."

Purdy seized a blanket from a bed and dragged the dazed Mary into the yard. The cabin was already beginning to blaze, so he pulled her a comfortable distance from the growing fires and spent a few minutes with her before, sated, he sliced her throat and then lifted her scalp.

When John and Egan Kirk returned on the evening of the next day, a stench of burned flesh and feathers hung over the clearing. Some of the smaller corpses had been tossed outside; scavengers had been at work. The bodies left inside were merely blackened, unrecognizable, diminished things. It was some time before Egan discovered Mary's body on the bloodied blanket, dashing his hopes that she may have survived. She was naked, and it was evident that she had been used sexually before being murdered.

The two men buried their dead in eerie silence, both digging, lifting the burned, blackened remains from the ruins of the cabin, then, lastly, lowering the blanket-wrapped body of Mary into a grave. The tiny body of her infant son was placed beside her. The boy's head had been left inside the cabin to be burned, so the whiteness of the little corpse contrasted horribly with the blackened skull that Egan placed in its proper position relative to the torso.

Five graves held eleven mutilated small corpses. John Kirk stood numbly in the growing darkness. "Reckon we ought to say some words," he croaked.

"I say this," Egan said, his voice shaking, tears running down his face. "For each of them, no fewer than ten will die. This I swear, and this vow will only be broken with my death."

The news of the massacre at the Kirk place spread quickly. In Knoxville, settlers gathered to recount with hate and horror the Kirks' description of what they had found upon their return to the homestead. There were those who demanded war, but they were in the minority. Most pointed out that the murders had been done by renegades and that only a few Cherokee had taken to the warpath. There was warmth in the greetings given to the chief of the

Cherokee, Rusog, when he arrived in Knoxville with his wife, Ena; his brother-in-law Renno; and senior warriors from both the Cherokee and the Seneca.

Rusog spoke to the gathered villagers. "These killers of women and children are not Cherokee warriors but renegades who would just as easily kill other Cherokee. Of this I assure you: The Cherokee Nation wishes only to live in peace. The Cherokee themselves will seek out those who have killed and punish them."

"You'd kill your own people?" a man called out skeptically.

"These animals are not our people," Rusog answered. "They are outlaws, as much despised in our society as in yours."

"Well, we won't leave punishment of these killers to other Indians!" a settler shouted.

A sturdily built man in buckskins stepped to Rusog's side. He was half a head taller than the Cherokee, and his piercing blue eyes silenced the crowd. "I am Renno, sachem of the Seneca. Many of you know me, and you know that my word is as unbending as steel. You doubt that my brothers the Cherokee will punish members of their own tribe." He lifted his head high. His hair was light, and tied at the back of his neck with a leather thong. "Let no man call me liar when I say that the guilty ones will be punished. Let us not break the peace that has existed between us, because of the actions of a small band of renegades."

Renno looked around, his blue eyes meeting the stares until Knoxville's mayor stepped forward to offer the white Indian his hand. "I know what Roy Johnson would say if he were here, Renno. He'd say that if Renno says it, it will be done. I think I can speak for everyone here when I say that we'll keep the peace."

"So," Renno acknowledged. But he was wishing that Roy Johnson was present. Johnson had been Renno's father-by-marriage, and although Emily had died years before, the two men were still close. As a former frontier militia colonel, Johnson's opinions would have carried weight. Roy would have spoken with the voice of reason. But he wasn't here, and eleven women and children had been killed, mutilated, raped, and burned, and word of the massacre was spreading like wildfire over the country.

Roy's cabin was boarded up since just after the death of his wife, Nora. He had left no word, had given no one—not even Renno, father of Roy's grandchildren—any clue as to his intentions. He had set out from Knoxville without anyone seeing him leave. Renno knew that Roy would return and thought that he understood the man's reasons for going off alone—Roy had lost both his beloved daughter, Emily, and his wife within a relatively short period of time. Renno himself had wanted to disappear into the wilderness, to be alone, when he returned from a long journey to find his Emily dead.

After the conference in Knoxville both Renno and Rusog were eager to be away from the town. They started homeward even though it was late and marched well into the night before making camp.

"There will be more trouble," Rusog observed glumly.

Renno agreed.

The trouble had already begun. John Sevier was not noted for restraint. Indian fighter, onetime governor of the would-be state of Franklin, Sevier had called for volunteers to put down what he considered to be an Indian uprising. One of the first volunteers was Egan Kirk. Egan, frustrated and disgusted with the attitude of the men in Knoxville, had ridden to Nashboro just in time to hear that old Sevier was going after the murderers.

Egan joined a small group of men under the command of one of Sevier's lieutenants, James Hubbard. Hubbard was not too many years older than Egan, and he lacked John Sevier's wilderness experience, but he was eager and ready to go into the forest to start hunting for Indians. Egan Kirk was willing to ride with any man who wanted to kill Indians.

Two days out of Nashboro the force of militiamen trotted into a pretty little valley that was the site of at least two

Cherokee villages. Egan Kirk was riding out on point as the force neared the first village. He saw five Cherokee men walk from the village under a white flag of truce. His finger itched as it pressed against the trigger of his musket, but he forced himself to honor the truce. He waited until the Cherokee were near enough for the leader, a stringy old man, to call out a peaceful greeting.

"Speak," Egan told the old Indian.

"I am Old Tassel. I and these four chiefs who stand with me wish to speak with John Sevier."

"Might be pretty hard to do," Egan said. "Sevier's back in Nashboro."

"Then we will speak with the commander of your force," Old Tassel offered.

Egan heard the beat of a horse's hooves at a trot and looked over his shoulder to see Hubbard riding up, the militia force not far behind.

"What we got here, Egan?" Hubbard looked disdainfully at the five Cherokee and their white flag.

"They want to talk with Sevier," Egan answered.

"We know why you ride," Old Tassel began. "We come to meet you in peace. You must know that those who killed the white women and children are not of us. They have been cast out. They are renegades. The people of our villages have only goodwill for their white brothers."

"What the hell?" Hubbard said under his breath. He longed for action, wanted to hear the muskets barking, wanted to see Indians falling to moisten the earth with their blood. He turned to Egan. "I need to think about this." He looked around. Nearby, on the outskirts of the village, was a log cabin. "See if that place is empty."

Egan rode to the house, dismounted, opened the door cautiously, and looked into the one room. "Empty," he shouted back.

Hubbard ordered a few of the men to escort Old Tassel and the other four village chiefs to the cabin and saw them shoved roughly through the door. Then he dismounted, took off his hat, and ran his fingers through his sweat-

moistened shock of black hair. "Flag of truce, hell," he
muttered. He lifted a Cherokee tomahawk from his belt,
spun it in the air, caught it by the blade, and extended the
handle toward Egan Kirk.

"Isn't it time you started getting back a little of your own,
Egan?" Hubbard asked.

As the young man walked slowly to the door of the cabin
he saw Mary's face as it had been contorted in death,
remembered the ravages that had been done to her body,
and smelled the stench of the corpses in the burned cabin.

Old Tassel looked up when the door opened to see death
in the eyes of the strong young white man. The other four
joined him as he stood facing Egan.

"There are five of you," Egan said.

"We have no weapons," Old Tassel told him.

"I have only this," Egan said, brandishing the tomahawk.
"Maybe you can take it from me."

"We will not despoil a flag of truce," Old Tassel replied
quietly.

The words did not register with Egan. A madness
overtook him as he saw in his mind's eye the mutilated body
of his wife, the pitiful little lumps that had once been his
son. He was not fully sane as he leaped forward and aimed
a killing blow at the head of the nearest chief. The man
looked him in the eye to the last second before the
tomahawk thudded into his temple.

One by one, the other four silently died, Old Tassel the
last, each honoring the flag of truce by offering no resistance.

James Hubbard waited for a long time before opening the
door to the cabin. He saw Egan standing head down, the
bloody tomahawk hanging loosely at his side. Blood had
spread in wide circles on the rough planks of the floor.

"Come on," Hubbard urged.

Egan trailed behind as the militia rode through the
deserted Cherokee village. Hubbard, in the lead, kept his
eyes open. A dog barked, then ran away in fright. Other-

wise there was silence. Hubbard considered burning the
village but decided against it. Cherokee women and children hadn't killed the Kirk family; he would not make war
against women and children, only against Cherokee warriors. He yelled out in protest when the man just behind
him raised his musket and fired at a movement in the
bushes near the outskirts of the village, for he had seen the
movement himself and had recognized a bent, ancient
Cherokee woman.

The shot rang out and echoed from the ridges on either
side of the valley. The old woman pitched forward, out of
the bushes.

"Looky here," a militiaman said, standing over the fallen
woman. "Someone killed Grandma."

The shot had been true, taking the old woman on the
bridge of the nose, smashing her face.

"Who killed Grandma?" someone yelled. The others
laughed.

For the balance of the day the young militiaman who had
killed the old Cherokee woman was ribbed good-naturedly
by his companions, and the last words heard in the camp
that night were "Who killed Grandma?"

In council, Rusog told of the murders of Old Tassel and
the four other village chiefs while they had been under a
flag of truce. One by one senior warriors of the two
adjoining villages, Cherokee and Seneca, had their say. The
long peace between the white settlers and the Cherokee
was obviously at risk, and the fires of hate were burning.
Renno's stepfather, Ha-ace the Panther, suggested that
Rusog send runners to all Cherokee villages with a message
advising all village chiefs to exercise restraint. Some discussion followed, enough to delay a decision, for it was
growing late. And before the council could be reconvened
the next day, emissaries from Knoxville and Nashboro
arrived, white men of goodwill who assured Rusog and
Renno that the settlers did not want a general war and that
the self-appointed avengers, Sevier and Hubbard, would
be controlled.

Rusog spoke in a bitter voice. "I think we have little to fear from these avengers, since they seem to kill only unarmed men who do not resist and the occasional old woman. We protest these unthinkable atrocities, but we will not break the peace."

The youngest male of the blood of the white Indian had furnished meat for the evening meal, and he had eaten his share of the stewed rabbit and cornmeal dumplings prepared by his grandmother, Toshabe.

"That last one," Little Hawk said, speaking to all but with his eyes on his father, Renno, "was a sly one. He was the largest of the lot, and I had to stalk him for hours."

Ha-ace winked at Toshabe, while Renno nodded seriously. It was a warrior's pleasure and prerogative to tell stories about a good hunt. Today his son took rabbits with the small bow that Renno had made for him. Soon Little Hawk would be coming back to the village with a full-grown deer thrown over his shoulder.

"I cleaned and cut the corn for the pudding," Renna piped in her sweet voice.

"And you did very well," Renno said to his daughter. "It was very good pudding. I don't know of anyone who makes corn pudding better and sweeter than your grandmother."

Toshabe smiled in pleasure. The manitous, she felt, had indeed blessed her in her children. One was a sachem in the tradition of his father, grandfather, and great-grandfather, the original white Indian for whom the present Renno was named. The second son, El-i-chi, was the tribe's shaman, a brave warrior and skilled in magic and the healing arts. And the daughter, Ena, warrior and scout, was now the mother of twins. Ah, no woman had been more blessed than Toshabe. She was only sorry that the father of her children, the great Ghonkaba, was not alive to see his expectations met fully in his children and to be blessed with the joy of watching his grandchildren develop. Thinking of her first husband, however, did not lessen her respect for her second, the senior warrior Ha-ace.

"I know where a raccoon dens," Little Hawk continued. "I have not been able to take him yet."

"You must be careful, for the raccoon has large teeth," Toshabe urged.

"I will be very careful," Little Hawk promised. "When I take this one, Grandmother, I will clean him for you, removing all of the layers of fat and the scent glands."

"I should hope," Toshabe said.

"And then you will please make raccoon pie?"

"*Hmm*," Toshabe said, finger to her chin. "I'll need some coltsfoot ashes and some maple syrup—"

"And potatoes and green peppers," Little Hawk interrupted eagerly, almost tasting the raccoon pie.

Renno chuckled. Renna came to settle into his lap sleepily. She often slept in Toshabe's longhouse while Renno and Little Hawk went across the village square to Renno's own house. Renna was very fond of Ah-wa-o, daughter of Ha-ace, daughter-by-marriage to Toshabe and, thus, sister to Renno, Ena, and El-i-chi. That last relationship, in which Ah-wa-o was sister-by-marriage to El-i-chi, was a problem, for El-i-chi and the little Rose were very much in love and wanted very badly to be married.

So, in addition to his concern about the fragile peace in the land, Renno, as sachem, had more personal problems, having to do with his family and his people. He had promised El-i-chi that he would speak in his behalf and make every effort to extract a favorable ruling from the matrons of the tribe, for it was the clans' women who made the decisions pertaining to custom and to marriage.

Fortunately, Ah-wa-o was not in Toshabe's longhouse that night but was eating the evening meal with her best friend, An-da, sister of the young warrior Tor-yo-ne. Renno had finally been able to enjoy a meal in peace without Ah-wa-o's large, liquid eyes beseeching him to speak to the matrons. And, for once, little An-da had not been present to try to anticipate Renno's every wish and to stare at him with adoring eyes. It had been a good evening.

Now, with Renna asleep in his arms and Little Hawk, having repeated once more the tale of the great rabbit hunt, nodding off, Renno decided to leave. He put Renna in her bed, picked up his son, and said, "Come, great hunter, it is time for warriors to rest."

It was a night of perfection, cool enough with a slight breeze for good sleeping. The lights in the sky were brilliant and sparkling, so close that with perhaps only a bit of help from the manitous, a man could reach up and touch one. Renno was content.

Chapter II

The leader of a desperate band of mighty heroes raiding deep into enemy territory stood on the high bank of a sandy-bottomed gully and surveyed the dangerous situation. There was only one way to cross the chasm and go on to glory. That way was a single grapevine as thick as Little Hawk's wrist.

The leader said to his men, "Follow me, brothers," and grabbing the vine, made a running leap out over the fearful drop. His momentum carried him to the far side, and he stood there panting and bright eyed, looking back expectantly. "Hurry!" he shouted. "All life depends upon our venture!"

One by one the other courageous heroes made the daring

crossing. There was one loss. The warrior—he was only four years old, after all—lost his grip on the grapevine and fell down, down into the sand to be devoured by the fierce, wild animals inhabiting the Gorge of Death. The leader, Little Hawk, helped his fallen companion back up the bank of the gully.

"I don't want to be dead," the fallen one protested.

"Those are the rules," replied the leader. "There are always rules, always."

"Well, it isn't fair," the small warrior persisted. "Only yesterday we were all dropping from the vine into the soft sand and no one was killed then."

"Come," Little Hawk soothed. "Now you can be a manitou, and in the time of need you can advise us."

That prospect brightened the little warrior's mood, and so the pack of heroes crept onward toward the well-traveled track that led toward Knoxville. A large enemy band would soon be coming down the trail, unaware of the ambush being laid for them. The heroes would be vastly outnumbered, but with the aid of the manitous—the newly appointed one already offering advice to the leader at every turn—the cause of truth and justice would prevail.

Little Hawk positioned his men and waited. If they were lucky, *someone* would come—a hunter, perhaps even maidens out for a stroll—and then the attack would be quick, loud, and, if the object of the assault was girls, momentarily frightening.

"I hear something," whispered the small manitou.

"We all hear something," Little Hawk said.

The sound was distant but quickly recognized as the squeak of a wagon wheel in need of grease. Then came the thud of hooves, the voices of men speaking in English, and the low rumble of heavily laden wagons on the trail.

"Quiet! Be very quiet," Little Hawk commanded his force as a horseman followed by several wagons came into view. Little Hawk counted eleven adult men plus two young men. The total of thirteen outnumbered his band only by two to one, but there comes a time in the career of every leader when he must fall back and regroup. In addition to the men there were six females ranging in age from the lower teens, Little Hawk guessed, to full maturity. They sat in open wagons that carried cargo unfamiliar to Little Hawk.

"We will tell my father of this," the boy said. He looked around, knowing that the small manitou would not be able to keep up on the run back to the village. He quickly designated three, including the manitou, to stay with the wagon train and observe it, thus giving the other, older boys and himself freedom to run at full speed and reach the village in advance of the visitors.

Little Hawk ran lithely, easily, his legs pumping in a steady rhythm. He tried to match his running style to that of his father, for his father, he knew, could cover fifty miles at a tireless pace and fight at the end of the run.

The group of boys found Renno and El-i-chi sitting in the sun in front of the sachem's longhouse. The white Indian looked up, and when he saw his well-formed son leading a race down the village square, a smile crossed his face. El-i-chi and he had been discussing the lack of success of all the Cherokee villages in finding the renegades who had killed the Kirk women and children, and Renno was not displeased to have an excuse to drop the subject. El-i-chi, always fiery and impatient, had been advocating that Renno and he go after the renegades.

Little Hawk panted to a halt directly in front of his father and gave a traditional Seneca greeting politely and in full. It was not appropriate for him, with the blood of sachems in his veins, to blurt out the news he was carrying. When, in due time and with formality, Little Hawk did get around to telling the sachem that the village was to have visitors, their exact number, and enough of a description to yield a good estimation of the situation, Renno thanked him formally, rose languidly, stretched, and walked slowly to the outskirts of the village.

The horseman who led the train was a large man with a huge beard. Streaks of gray in his hair told Renno his approximate age—middle or late forties—and the man's dress and manner told him more.

"I speak with Renno, sachem of the Seneca?" the man asked.

Renno nodded.

"My name is Brown, sir, James Brown. May I climb down, sir?"

"Please do," Renno invited. "If you are ready to make camp for the night, water is beyond that grove, and you can tether your horses and mules on that meadow where the grass is fresh and green."

"I thank you, sir," Brown said, getting down after having signaled the wagon drivers to their stopping places. "We will ask your permission, Sachem, to travel through your lands and the lands of your brothers the Cherokee, toward the south."

Renno nodded but said nothing. South meant either Choctaw or Creek lands, either choice unwise.

Brown laughed. "I think I note disapproval, Sachem."

"Your God gave you freedom of choice, just as did ours," Renno replied.

"But you think I'm foolish?" Brown asked.

"I don't know how far you intend to travel," Renno answered. "I don't know your intentions."

"Come with me, sir," Brown said, leading the way to the heavily laden wagons. They carried construction parts that would fit together neatly. "You see here, Sachem, the constituent parts of a unique boat with a shallow bottom, masts for sails, and oarlocks. It is designed for easy assembling, disassembling, and for portage."

"You plan, then, to go down the Tennessee," Renno remarked.

"Exactly."

"Into Chickasaw lands?"

"Indeed. For two reasons, sir. First, to bring the word of God to the Chickasaw—"

"There have been missionaries to the Chickasaw before," Renno warned.

"Yes, yes, but God has spoken to me, Sachem," Brown

said, taking off his hat and looking skyward. "He has told me to go into the lands of the Chickasaw to preach the true gospel. He has told me that there, in those far lands beyond the big bend of the Tennessee, I will find the acreage that was promised to me for fighting for the liberty of my country."

El-i-chi, who had come up behind Renno in time to hear Brown's plans, made a derisive sound.

"My brother, El-i-chi," Renno introduced. "Mr. Brown."

"I think, sir," El-i-chi said, "that the Chickasaw will not take kindly to either of your purposes. They feel they have heard enough of the white man's preachings, and I assure you that they will kill any white man who tries to settle in the heart of their hunting grounds."

"God is my protection," Brown intoned. "I only do as He has commanded. Now, if you'll excuse me, Sachem, El-i-chi, I must help get my people settled in for the night. It being the Sabbath tomorrow, I trust you will not object to our resting here?"

"No," Renno said. "Feel free to stay as long as you like."

"Kind of you," Brown responded. "Matter of fact, we do need to make some repairs, and the animals could use the graze and the rest. If you'll bear with us, Sachem, we will spend perhaps the better part of a week here before setting out toward the Tennessee."

When the Brown party gathered for Sunday-morning worship service, they had an audience. The sachem of the Seneca himself sat on a grassy bank overlooking the area where Brown had erected his carved, walnut pulpit in the open air. Beside Renno sat his children, Little Hawk and Renna, their faces scrubbed, both wearing clean buckskins. Renno was very familiar with the Bible; the mother of his children had often read to him from the Book, and he frequently turned to it, especially the Old Testament with its tales of kings and battles.

As the Brown party sang to the accompaniment of a concertina played by one of Brown's sons, Renno joined in, for the hymn was a rousing one, and it was pleasant to hear the strong, melodious chords and the inspiring words drift toward the clean, blue sky and the morning sun. When Brown began to preach, however, his voice full but not overbearing, Little Hawk became restless.

"Sit and hear," Renno whispered into his son's ear. Now that Emily and her mother were dead, there was no one to fulfill Emily's wish that her children know of her God as well as that of the Seneca, often called the Master of Life.

"They have pretty dresses," Renna whispered. Renno felt a stab of guilt, for this one, this little blond Renna, was the image miniaturized of his dead Emily, with Emily's eyes and Emily's way of moving and speaking. Not long past Renna had been clothed in "pretty dresses" by Beth Huntington, in Wilmington, and Renno had taken his daughter away from that influence. True, Renna was Seneca, but she was white as well, and there were promises about exposing the children to both cultures, promises, both spoken and implied, made to the dead, to the children's mother and their white grandmother.

To Renno's pleasure, Brown related one of Renno's favorite Bible stories—the tale of David and Goliath. This story was not new to them, but the missionary told it well, with a new twist that captured even Little Hawk's attention. "Did David fight the giant only for God and country?" Brown asked.

Renno had never given the matter much thought, although he had read the story many times.

"Sachem," Brown asked, looking up at Renno, "you are a brave man, and you have—as have I—fought for God and country. But did we fight for God and country alone?"

Renno lifted his hands, palms up, indicating an inability to answer Brown's question without a modicum of consideration.

"I think not," Brown continued. "I fought for freedom! I fought for myself! I fought because I did not want my family to live forever under the rule of British royalty. I did not want my sons to have to bow and scrape to some petty British popinjay simply because he had a title from a king.

And I fought for personal gain, for the land that was promised to all who fought alongside George Washington."

Renno nodded. If one looked at the matter that way, he, too, had fought for personal reasons.

"And so David fought not only for God but for personal gain. And I tell you, there is nothing wrong with that. God knew what He was doing. Picture this: The entire Israelite army, King Saul's army, is camped in front of the enemy, the Philistines. And out there is Goliath of Gath, big and mean, daring any man to fight him. All the men of Israel are afraid until David comes along, to bring food to his older brother in the army's camp.

"He hears the roars of Goliath and sees the soldiers' shame when no one will fight. Then David hears a soldier say that the man who kills this giant who defies Israel will get great riches from King Saul, will marry a princess, and will never pay taxes in Israel."

Brown looked around and nodded, smiling. "Not a bad offer, is it? After all, the giant's spear was only as big as a small tree. So what did David do? Did he cry out, 'Lord, our men are shamed, but I will fight and restore pride to Israel.' Did he do that? No. He spoke to a group of soldiers and he said, 'Who is this uncircumcised Philistine, that he should defy the armies of the living God?' You know the rest. David killed the giant, then went to Saul to claim his reward.

"Did David have great riches? Did he marry a princess? Did Saul make his house free in Israel? Not exactly—or at least not at that time. But that's another story, and it's getting on to time to see what our ladies have made up in the way of a Sunday meal."

"When I am a man," Little Hawk declared, "I will fight bravely for my people and without thought of personal gain."

"You will," Renno agreed, running his hand fondly through his son's scalp lock. "But when your uncle El-i-chi and I, along with your aunt Ena and Rusog and others fought the Spanish in the far west, the victory was made sweeter by gold, which was well spent on our people."

"Well, I guess it wouldn't hurt anything to pick up some gold now and then," Little Hawk allowed.

"I liked the singing," Renna said. "Did my mother sing like that?"

"As sweet as the mockingbird," Renno said.

"Beth sang well, too," Renna went on. "I remember."

"I will sing for you," Renno offered, unwilling on such a glorious day to dwell for long on a love dead and a love lost. He lifted his head and burst into the words of a hymn, and as the three of them walked back into the village, his voice thundered out the old words of hope and promise. The women, curious, thrust their heads out of longhouses, and men turned their faces toward the sachem and his children.

Renno finished the hymn just as they reached the door to Toshabe's longhouse. Renna clapped her hands. Renno pushed his daughter into the dwelling first, then bent to follow Little Hawk. The boy, prepared to greet his grand-mother, froze into shy immobility when he saw that in addition to Toshabe, Ah-wa-o, her best friend, An-da, and Ha-ace, others were present. Two white girls sat between Ah-wa-o and An-da.

Renno sighed. These days, his mother's house always seemed to be full of young women. He knew that his mother believed that Little Hawk and Renna should have a woman to look after them but did not like Toshabe's hinting that An-da or some other Seneca girl would make a good wife for a sachem. He immediately realized, however, that the presence of the two white girls was not a part of Toshabe's plot to introduce him to a likely wife. Having had two white daughters-by-marriage, she would not be push-ing another one at her son.

"Sachem," Ah-wa-o said respectfully, "here are two sis-ters, Mandy and Tess, who were lonely, so Toshabe kindly gave us permission to invite them to a meal."

"You are welcome to our village," Renno said with great formality. Little Hawk and Renna took their seats next to Toshabe's. Renno sat at the right of Ha-ace, with Ah-wa-o to his left, the older of the two white girls just beyond

Ah-wa-o. The young maiden looked disappointed that El-i-chi had not come in with his brother.

The main dish was a game stew, which blended the wild taste of squirrel with the mildness of turkey. The stew was seasoned with bay leaves, wild onions, and other native herbs, and given body with corn and lima beans. It was one of Little Hawk's favorite meals. He did his duty by it, as did the others, including the sisters, Mandy and Tess.

Mandy, who told the gathering that she was seventeen, was attractive in spite of the plainness of her clothing. She had dark-brown hair and eyes, a pleasant, regular face, and a slim but well-rounded form that could not be entirely concealed under her heavy clothing. Tess, the younger, was of the same mold but just beginning to show the curves of womanhood.

"Renno," Ah-wa-o said, "I thought that only people of dark skin could be made slaves."

Renno raised one eyebrow, indicating that he needed more information before commenting.

"Mandy and Tess were forced to come west with Colonel Brown," Ah-wa-o explained.

Renno looked to the older white girl for elaboration.

"We are bond servants," Mandy told him.

"It is true that indenture is a form of slavery," Renno said, nodding toward Ah-wa-o.

"I don't understand," An-da said. "The whites make slaves of other whites?"

"May I explain?" Mandy asked. Renno nodded assent. "We are not slaves, actually. Indenture is a common practice. A young boy can be apprenticed to a craftsman for a number of years, say five, in payment for his training. At the end of that time he has learned a trade and is free to practice it. The craftsman, in his turn, has had free labor from the apprentice for five years as his reward for teaching the boy a trade."

"And is Colonel Brown teaching you and Tess a trade?" Ah-wa-o asked.

Tess laughed. "The trade of drudge work," she said. "Cleaning, washing, and cooking."

"Please, Tess," Mandy said. "You will make our new friends think that Colonel Brown does us wrong. Actually, he is within his rights."

"But Tess has told me that she is fearful of going into strange lands," Ah-wa-o said. She looked at Renno. "He's taking them into Chickasaw lands. Can't you and El-i-chi stop him?"

"How did you come to be indentured to Colonel Brown?" Renno wanted to know.

"It's a long story. Are you sure you want to hear it?" Mandy asked.

"Actually, there's nothing an Indian likes more than a long, well-told story," Toshabe encouraged.

"I will try to tell the story well, then," Mandy said. "Our family lived in Norfolk, not in great luxury but in comfort. Our father was a clerk in a bank, a well-respected man. Tess and I were in school. Then our mother became seriously ill, and I stayed home to tend her. Her sickness lasted for well over a year, and it seemed as if she was being devoured by the disease. As she grew thin and wasted, it was obvious that she was going to die. My father became desperate. I didn't know at that time that the cost of medicines and doctors had used up all my family's savings.

"Father started drinking heavily toward the last, for his heart was breaking to see Mother suffering such fearful pain." She paused for a deep breath. "The end came suddenly. But when Mother died, my father refused to go to work. He lay on his bed drinking until the constables took him to prison."

"Whatever for?" An-da asked.

"He had been stealing money from the bank," Mandy said. "To recover a portion of what had been embezzled, a judge allowed the bank to take our house and everything in it except for the clothes that Tess and I were wearing."

"I don't think I would like to live in the white man's world," Ah-wa-o said fervently.

"What did you do?" An-da asked, her lovely eyes wide.

"Our father would not be released from prison until he had repaid the rest of the money he'd stolen from the bank," Mandy answered. "And, of course, he had no way of getting money while in prison. Tess and I did the only thing we could do."

Tess giggled and said, "Tell them about our first offer."

Mandy blushed. "I don't think—"

"Please," Ah-wa-o urged.

"We were offered jobs in a house of ill repute," Tess said.

An-da gasped and put her hand over her mouth. Toshabe frowned in disapproval of such talk in front of the maidens and the two children.

"Of course we refused," Mandy said. "We indentured ourselves to a family friend—a very pleasant old man who lived near our house. He had an aged wife who could not do housework, so when I offered to sell my sister and myself to him, he agreed. We signed papers of indenture for five years, took the money, gave it to the bank, and our father was released from prison." Mandy paused, her eyes downcast. "Our father died the night he was released from prison. Some said it was his heart; some said he simply drank himself to death."

"How sad!" Ah-wa-o sympathized, and Toshabe reached out to pat Mandy's hand.

"You sold yourself into indenture for nothing," An-da said.

"We settled a debt for the sake of our family's dignity." Mandy spoke firmly. "That was important. But misfortune was not yet finished with us. Shortly after our father was buried, our benefactor died suddenly, and his wife followed him to the grave within two days. A son came to the house, sold it and everything in it. In the process he sold our indenture papers to Colonel Brown. Mistress Brown is frail and needs help with packing, cooking, and cleaning. So here we are."

"Renno," Ah-wa-o begged, "you must not let the colonel take them into danger."

"It is not my son's business," Toshabe said.

"In addition to Colonel Brown there are seven other men," Ha-ace pointed out. "Such numbers will provide some safety."

"Renno?" Ah-wa-o asked.

"A man is free to do as he pleases," the sachem said.

"But not to force others into danger," Ah-wa-o insisted.

"You have a good heart, but enough is enough, Daughter," Ha-ace scolded, and Ah-wa-o fell silent.

"Don't worry," Mandy reassured them. "God will protect us. Colonel Brown is a devout and a good man. He has been very kind to us."

Tess giggled again. "Mandy thinks that Colonel Brown bought our papers not only to have servants for his wife but eventually to have wives for his sons."

Mandy blushed hotly.

Renno nodded. "I have looked at the Brown boys. They have the makings of good, strong men."

For a week James Brown's party camped near the Seneca village. Mandy and her sister were often in company with Ah-wa-o and An-da, and many Seneca and Cherokee, all of whom had heard the preachings of the white man before, attended Brown's nightly services, primarily to join in the spirited singing.

Toward the end of the week, when it was obvious that the repairs to the wagons and harness had been completed, that the animals were well rested and well fed, Rusog came to Renno in the Seneca village.

"Soon the colonel will take himself, his two sons, five men and six women and children to their deaths," the Cherokee chief said grimly.

Renno nodded.

"There is hate and restlessness in our land," Rusog continued, "from the Kirk killings and the murder of Old Tassel and others of our people. I would not want the Cherokee to be blamed for the deaths of this fool and those who follow him."

"Nor would I," Renno agreed. "I have planned, my brother, to have warriors follow until Colonel Brown and his party are well out of the lands of the Cherokee."

"My brother is always wise," Rusog approved. He smiled

fleetingly. "I should have known that you would have thought the same as I."

"Yes," Renno said.

"Who will go, then?" Rusog asked.

"Someone whose word will be beyond doubt," Renno answered.

"I myself could use a stretching of the legs," Rusog suggested.

Renno smiled. "My sister would scalp both of us if I took you away with two young ones in the lodge."

"You speak true," Rusog said, "and I must admit that I enjoy watching those two little wildcats."

"I, too, would stretch my legs," Renno said, "but I have been away too long, and so recently. *My* two wildcats also are a pleasure to watch."

"Se-quo-i's reputation and word counts well with the whites," Rusog pointed out.

"And El-i-chi's," Renno added.

"So it is settled," Rusog stated, for with both of the men named, the word of their chiefs would be accepted without question.

Se-quo-i and El-i-chi accepted the orders from their chiefs enthusiastically, each for a different reason: Se-quo-i had been too long sequestered with his books and his efforts to create written symbols for the various sounds that made up the Cherokee language. He was ready to put his studies aside and become one with nature for a time.

El-i-chi's eagerness to get away from the village was rooted in sheer frustration. For months now he had known that the woman he wanted to rule his longhouse was Ah-wa-o. She was of age. She returned his love and had consented to be his wife. He had held her in his arms, had kissed her smiling lips, had sampled her very womanly curves with his hands until the lynx of desire raged in his blood. And still the matter was unresolved.

"I go, Sachem," he told Renno, "with the expectation of hearing good news when I return."

Renno turned away, making a face of distaste. He did not look forward to pleading the case of El-i-chi's love before a

group of the matrons of the tribe, including the prime
matron, their mother, Toshabe. He would not admit to
El-i-chi that the delay was from apprehension of what the
women would decide. Already many Seneca traditions had
been abandoned or blended with the customs of the
Cherokee, so that the older women were very, very
protective of those rules and traditions that remained.
Renno was sorely afraid that El-i-chi's petition to marry the
girl who was his sister-by-marriage would be denied, and to
that date the sachem had postponed the decision on one
pretext or the other lest he be proved right. He feared the
decision of the women, but he feared more his brother's
reaction to a negative decision.

"You will speak for us while I am away?" the shaman
pressed.

"I will," Renno agreed. "Or, at worst, shortly after you
return, for it would be better to have you present in case
the women want to question you."

"How far do we accompany these people who are so
determined to be killed?"

"Follow them to the river, and then downriver until the
lands on both sides are Chickasaw," Renno answered.

"Both Se-quo-i and I would prefer to travel apart from
the Brown party," El-i-chi said.

"I see no reason for the colonel to know that he is being
observed," Renno replied. "When you return, however, I
want a statement in Colonel Brown's own handwriting that
he was escorted safely through the land of the Cherokee
into Chickasaw country."

"Then we will make ourselves known when it is time to
get such a written statement."

"Including a description of the site and an account of
their travels to prove, should it become necessary, that they
passed safely through Cherokee hunting grounds."

In the early evening, in that time between sunset and
darkness, it was not unusual for a young maiden to walk out
from the village alone or in pairs to meet the warrior of her
choice. Such meetings were condoned by the customs of

both the Cherokee and the Seneca. Alone, the young lovers were free to touch, to kiss, and to fondle one another with a certain familiarity. The touching could go only so far, however, with disgrace coming to both the male and the female who went beyond the bounds of traditional propriety.

Such freedom of association was not approved for El-i-chi and Ah-wa-o because in the eyes of the tribe they were brother and sister. But over the weeks they had developed a system of communication. A certain movement of El-i-chi's hand, while visiting in his mother's longhouse, would tell Ah-wa-o the place, another movement the time. On the evening before the Brown party was to set out toward the south, the place was a wooded knoll north of the village, the time sunset.

Ah-wa-o made her way to the knoll by way of the stream, where others walked and eager young ones hurried to enjoy just one more plunge into the clear water before darkness. She made sure that she was not seen or followed, and then she was running up a familiar slope and into the arms of her tall, strong, handsome young shaman. Her heart pounded in joy, her lips warmed by his own. To El-i-chi the curve of her waist and that delicate hollow of her back above her womanly hips was a delight and the feel of her both a joy and a torment.

"You are going with the Brown party," Ah-wa-o said, after a long, long time of breathless kisses and caresses.

"I would never leave you if you were mine," El-i-chi said, "but it is torture to be near you and not have you."

"I understand," she whispered. "Take me with you."

"You know I can't. Se-quo-i and I travel alone."

"I could run away. There are times when I fear that we will never be allowed to be one, El-i-chi. Should that happen, I would want to run away so we could be alone in the wilderness forever."

"Ummm," El-i-chi said, thrilling to think of being alone with her in their own home somewhere far from the tribe; but then he sobered, for exile from his people was a serious matter. "That will not be necessary. Renno will state our case to the matrons while I am gone, or as soon as I have returned."

"I will pray that the manitous pour golden sweetness on his tongue," she said, clinging to him, pressing her soft breasts against his chest, and lifting her face so that, for a long time, there was no more talk. When El-i-chi pushed her forcefully away from him, his blood was on fire, and she was flushed, her limbs molten with her own desire.

"Go," he whispered weakly.

"Must I?"

"Toshabe will be asking for you."

"Will you eat with us tonight?" she implored.

"Perhaps." He laughed and looked down at the front of his breechclout. "If thoughts of you do not continue to make me unsuitable to appear before others."

Ah-wa-o blushed but did not turn her eyes away. Soon, soon, she would be his, and nothing would be forbidden to them, and she would see to it that his manhood would never be rampant and unsatisfied again. And, with fire in her own loins, she turned and ran down the slope toward the village.

Once again that night Toshabe's dwelling was filled with young women. Mandy and Tess were there. Ah-wa-o's eyes seldom left El-i-chi's face—a fact that was not lost on Toshabe. An-da, a bit more subtle, made a point of offering every dish of the meal to Renno.

"You have been so kind to us, Toshabe," Mandy said as Little Hawk and Renna nibbled on sweet balls—nuts mixed in honey and spices—and the adults sat contentedly, sated with good food. "We will remember all of you forever."

Ah-wa-o looked first at El-i-chi, then at Renno, for to her ears, Mandy's words seemed to be a last farewell carrying a meaning beyond what was intended.

"May the manitous go with you," Toshabe said. She felt, as did everyone else, that Colonel Brown was leading his party to their demise unless he gave up his ideas of homesteading in Chickasaw hunting grounds.

"I think I'd like living here with you all," Tess said. "You seem so happy and peaceful."

"Each has his own place in the world," Toshabe said.

"I went with An-da to pick corn today," Tess told her. "The sweet corn smelled so good, Toshabe, and it tasted so delicious the way you cooked it. We'll miss your cooking."

"I have written down some of Toshabe's recipes," Mandy said, smiling. "You won't starve, I promise." She rose, made her good-byes, and the two sisters left.

An-da and Ah-wa-o looked accusingly at Renno and El-i-chi. Renno grinned, for it was the first time that An-da's eyes had held anything but somewhat dazed approval of him.

"You're sending El-i-chi and Se-quo-i to follow the Brown party," Ah-wa-o said after the white sisters were gone. "But you do not send enough warriors to protect them against a Chickasaw attack."

"Am I to provide a permanent guard for them?" Renno asked. "Am I to send an army to help them wrest Chickasaw land from its rightful owners? That is what it would take— an army and a full-scale war."

"Oh, Renno, I'm sorry," Ah-wa-o apologized. "It's just that I've come to like Mandy and her little sister so much. It is as if I know, as if I have had the word of the manitous, that I will never see them again."

"It would not be likely," Toshabe agreed, "because they will settle far from this village."

"But if they were alive," Ah-wa-o said, "if they lived, it would be different. I would know that they were alive. Now it seems that they are already dead."

Renno spoke in a kindly voice. "In the Bible from which my Emily read to me, the man who has killed his brother asks, 'Am I my brother's keeper?' I *am* my brother's keeper, and I would lay down my life protecting my brother's life. But brotherhood must be felt two ways."

"You're saying that the white man is not your brother, so you are not responsible for his death," Ah-wa-o said with a little edge.

"He is not responsible for the stupidity of Colonel

Brown." El-i-chi spoke forcefully. "Enough. I, too, can feel sympathy for the two young white girls, but they also have a responsibility. They took value for value when they indentured themselves, and it is up to them to fulfill the terms of their agreement."

An-da made a sound of disrespect and giggled immediately. El-i-chi looked stern for a moment, then joined An-da in laughter. There were times when An-da seemed mature—at others, very young. El-i-chi liked An-da, whose name meant Sweet Day. He thought it was a shame that her brother, Tor-yo-ne, was such a pain in the rump, but he didn't hold that against her.

He and Ah-wa-o had discussed An-da's obvious infatuation with Renno and the fact that she found many excuses to be in Toshabe's home at mealtime. El-i-chi felt that he wouldn't mind having An-da as a sister-by-marriage, but his older brother looked on her as a pretty little girl and treated her in much the same way he treated his daughter, Renna.

"El-i-chi," An-da said, "don't let anything happen to them."

"Not in our own lands," El-i-chi promised, "nor in those of the Cherokee."

Renna, who had become drowsy immediately after the meal and had been placed in her bed by Toshabe, raised her little blond head. "I wish you all would be more quiet. I am trying to sleep, you know."

Chapter III

El-i-chi and Se-quo-i, Seneca and Cherokee, had traveled together before. Each young man had his own thoughts, so during the first days of their watch over the Browns' wagon train, it was not unusual for hours to pass without a word being spoken. A sign, a nod, or a look was all the communication needed to indicate who would run ahead to scout, who would hunt. Talk, when it came, was usually over the evening campfire. It was then that Se-quo-i spoke of the things he was learning about the white man through his reading; and it was then that El-i-chi voiced his fear that the women of his tribe would stand on tradition in the matter of his petition to marry Ah-wa-o.

39

"Had I a vote," Se-quo-i said, "you know how it would go."

"What about you, my friend?" El-i-chi asked. "Has the spirit of love never invaded your heart?"

Se-quo-i laughed. "I tell myself that one day I will make time to seek a wife. My mother and my other relatives keep telling me that I should be married."

"I would think," El-i-chi said, "that a book makes a cold companion in bed on a winter night."

For the first few days the wagon train rumbled through country that was very familiar to the two warriors, passing villages that were in the mainstream of Cherokee life. Peace and prosperity in Rusog's backyard created a safe environment for the Brown party. If any renegade group had tried to penetrate the area, however, their presence would have met with swift resistance.

Brown was following a trace that connected villages and intersected with the Tennessee River at a point past the narrow gorges and rapids of the upper river.

"His journey would be shorter and would be made more quickly by traveling west," El-i-chi observed. He was becoming impatient with the slow pace. The days had a sameness that left him too much time to think of Ah-wa-o and to wonder if Renno had spoken with the tribe's matrons.

"Yet," Se-quo-i said, looking with understanding at his frustrated companion, "there is something soothing to traveling by water."

The Tennessee was a Cherokee river, arising from the union of two mountain streams above Knoxville, the Holston and the French Broad. The river had taken its name from a Cherokee village near the mouth of the Little Tennessee, a village called Tennassee. Se-quo-i knew from his reading and from tribal lore that the Tennessee was not easily navigated. He explained to El-i-chi that this was a fortunate circumstance, for nothing encouraged the white settlers to penetrate an area more than easy access by water.

The river was one of the more important tributaries of the great Ohio, but it took a roundabout route in getting there, flowing southwest out of Cherokee lands into Creek territory, then swinging northwest into Chickasaw hunting grounds before flowing almost directly north into the Ohio in Kentucky.

The middle course of the river, the portion that Colonel Brown's flatboat would be traversing, was winding, often narrow, and made dangerous by rapids. The flatboat that was being carried by the extra wagons would have to be disassembled and portaged past Muscle Shoals without the benefit of wagons or mules, since the wagons and the animals would be sent back to Knoxville with the hired drivers once the flatboat was afloat. It still seemed to El-i-chi to be an odd way to travel, but then the white man often did things the hard way.

When the Brown party reached the Tennessee and began to offload the constituent parts of the barge from the wagons, El-i-chi and Se-quo-i made a semipermanent camp overlooking the scene, for it was evident that it would take a few days for the work to be done. After three days El-i-chi's impatience got the better of him. He told Se-quo-i that they might as well make their presence known and give the men a hand in putting the flatboat together, or at the rate it was going, they'd be camped on the bluff overlooking the river when the first snow came.

The two warriors approached the camp along the open riverbank, walking on a sandbar. In the wilderness one did not appear in any man's camp suddenly. Their approach was watched by several of the party. Mandy recognized El-i-chi first and reminded Colonel Brown who he was. The preacher came forward, hand outstretched.

"I had a feeling we were being observed," Brown said, after formal greetings. "You two, was it?"

El-i-chi nodded.

"Well, we appreciate the sachem's desire to give us protection, but it was unnecessary."

El-i-chi cast a quick look at Se-quo-i. At any given time

during the trip to the river, a small group of warriors could have killed the Brown party quickly and easily.

"We will help you put the boat together," Se-quo-i offered.

"Any help along that line will be greatly appreciated," Brown said.

It was hard work. The planks that made up the hull of the flatboat were heavy. The sun was working with its typical summer efficiency, and a plague of deerflies and mosquitoes did nothing to make the sweaty work more pleasant. More than once during the day each man found a reason to walk or fall into the river. When at last the barge was finished, every seam tight, the Browns' personal possessions were carried on board, piled neatly, and covered against the weather.

Se-quo-i looked at his hands ruefully. "Brother, the people of our tribes must never know that Se-quo-i the odd one and El-i-chi the great shaman worked with their hands until there were blisters atop blisters."

"Well," Colonel Brown said, smiling expansively, pleased that all was in readiness, "are you two boys going to travel with us a bit farther? Be glad to have you."

"When the river turns toward the south in half a day—a day at most—you will be in Creek lands," El-i-chi told him.

Brown looked thoughtful. "I think I get your meaning. Correct me if I'm wrong: Your sachems ordered you to see us safely out of Cherokee country. Once we are in Creek and then Chickasaw lands, any harm that might come to us would not be blamed on the Cherokee."

El-i-chi nodded unhappily. He had little use for fools, but he had come to like Brown, and he felt that it was a shame for the man to be so misguided, so trustful of his God, that he would take women and children into danger. "It is not too late to change your mind, Colonel." He grinned. "Although I would hate to have to help you take that boat apart and load it back onto the wagons, you could reverse your direction and make your settlement in those lands already ceded to the white man to the north, around the Cumberland Gap."

"I understand your concern, my boy," Brown responded. "What you suggest is impossible, of course. My decision was not made lightly, but with the help of the Lord. I take it you'll keep an eye on us until we cross into Creek hunting grounds."

El-i-chi nodded again. "My sachem would have me make a request of you."

"I'm listening."

"A paper from you, in your handwriting, stating that you and your party crossed through Cherokee lands safely."

Mandy, who had been hovering nearby, shuddered with dread.

"No problem," Brown said. "Mandy, fetch me my writing desk."

Brown sat on a driftwood log, positioned the lap desk on his knees, dipped his pen, and wrote. He lifted the paper and waved it to dry the ink, then folded it, sealed it with his signature, and handed it to the shaman. El-i-chi tucked the paper carefully into his belt pouch.

With the morning the lines securing the barge were loosed, and the vessel swung slowly into the current, straightened as Brown, his sons, and his men used poles and sweeps to steer it, and began to move downriver. The creaking wagons and their hired drivers were already making their way north, back to Knoxville.

It was not difficult for El-i-chi and Se-quo-i to keep pace with the vessel. At first they merely strolled along the river, sometimes wading in the shallows, sometimes climbing to high banks. The first day was uneventful, the river favorable to the flatboat. With the evening Brown tied up on the north shore, and El-i-chi and Se-quo-i, having encountered a careless young buck late in the day, contributed fresh deer meat to the evening meal, much to the pleasure of the Brown party.

The evening was very pleasant. For a change, as if by some miracle, a breeze discouraged the voracious mosquitoes. The campfires glowed cheerily as darkness settled. Because there was no moon, the stars shone so bright, they gave an illusion of light. El-i-chi and Se-quo-i had taken their meal with Colonel Brown and his wife, Judith. Mandy and Tess had served all, and then they had eaten with the group. Stomachs full, tired from the long day, everyone seemed content to listen silently to the call of an owl from the trees across the narrow river. Mistress Brown excused herself and went to the flatboat and her bed. The colonel rose to make one last round of inspection of the camp and the lines that secured the vessel.

"El-i-chi," Mandy said, "when you go home, will you please tell Ah-wa-o and An-da that we think of them often?"

"I will," El-i-chi agreed.

"And tell Toshabe that we do, indeed, miss her good cooking," Tess said with a girlish giggle. "I'm afraid Mandy hasn't quite mastered her recipes."

El-i-chi's heart was heavy. They were so young, so vulnerable. He had no doubt that their fate was predetermined by Brown's hardheaded insistence on going into areas guarded fiercely by the Creek and by the Chickasaw. For one moment he considered stealing them away during the night and taking them back with him to safety. Unfortunately, the white man had his own laws and customs, and those rules said that Brown had control of the lives of the two young girls.

"It's such a dark night," Mandy said. "I wish there was a moon."

"A late moon will rise tonight," Se-quo-i said. "A crescent moon that will give little light."

"The owl sounds so lonely." Mandy sighed.

"He is a creature of the dark," Se-quo-i explained, "as is the bear."

Tess shivered and scooted nearer the fire.

Se-quo-i was immediately sorry that he had frightened her by mentioning a bear. "Do you know how there came to be night and day?"

"God said 'Let there be light,'" Mandy answered.

"Yes," Se-quo-i agreed, "but there is a story."

"Tell it, please," Tess said, wanting to be diverted from thoughts of great bears lurking in the deep forests that surrounded the river and the campsite.

"In the beginning the leader of all the animals was the porcupine," Se-quo-i began. "He had many decisions to make, and he often called the other animals together to discuss how things would be. One question he asked was whether there should be darkness forever or sunshine and light."

"Good heavens," Mandy said. "Who would want it to be dark all the time?"

"The bear," Se-quo-i answered, "for he likes the night, and he made a song praising darkness. But the chipmunk, a wise animal in spite of his small size, made a song praising a division of night and day, of moons and seasons. His song was the best. He sang the day into coming and sang the sun into rising, thus making the bear angry for having lost his beloved darkness. The bear leaped toward the small chipmunk to punish him, but the chipmunk, in his quickness, narrowly escaped. The bear's paw merely grazed his back, leaving a black streak down the little animal's fur that the chipmunk carries to this day—just as night and day have alternated ever since."

"From now on, every time I see a chipmunk, I will thank him," Tess said. "To have night always would be horrible."

"It is night," El-i-chi said, "and the night is for rest and sleeping." He wanted to say something reassuring, but the words would not come. He did not lie well. Still, he wanted to do something. He removed his knife from his belt and presented it, haft first, to Mandy, who looked at it doubtfully before accepting it.

"It is always wise to have some protection in the wilderness," El-i-chi explained. "In addition to protection, the knife makes a good tool. It can be used for preparing game for food and completing many other tasks. It can be used, even by a woman, to kill a man who threatens her."

"Oh, I could never—" Mandy began, only to be silenced by El-i-chi.

"You are not surrounded by the white man's civilization, and you are not protected by the white man's law. There may well come a time when your willingness to use this knife will mean the difference between life or death for you and your sister."

"But I don't know how."

El-i-chi took her hand in his, positioned the knife, and squeezed her fingers tightly around it. "It is not an ax to be used for chopping." He moved her arm up and down in the motion that one not trained in knife fighting would naturally use. "The most effective way to kill is this: Hold the knife thus and bring it up from your hip into the enemy's stomach, here, just under the ribs. Remember that the human skin is tough, the body hard to penetrate. Should you ever have to strike, strike with all your strength, driving the knife upward under the ribs."

"I feel just a bit faint," Mandy quavered.

El-i-chi sighed. He would have liked to have more time to give the girl some basic instruction in self-protection. "Conceal the knife in your clothing, but where you can reach it without fumbling." Without waiting to see if she obeyed him, he went to his own bed.

The flatboat was under way with the sun. El-i-chi and Se-quo-i, without admitting it to each other, had been reluctant to make another farewell to the party—especially to Mandy and Tess—and had left the camp before the others were awake. They stood on a bluff and watched the boat disappear around a bend in the river.

"They will hit the first rapids sometime during the afternoon," Se-quo-i predicted.

"By midday they will be well into Creek territory," El-i-chi said.

"Perhaps it would be interesting to watch them go through the rapids," Se-quo-i suggested, unwilling to voice his belief that disaster awaited the flatboat and all those aboard her.

"So," El-i-chi agreed, setting out, leading the way down-river.

The flatboat had negotiated a narrow gorge with a speed that sent it ahead of the two warriors. They ran along the banks, their progress often impeded by undergrowth, to emerge atop a bluff. Below them, half a mile away, the barge was next to the far bank of the river. It was Se-quo-i who first noted that several canoes were being pushed into the river from the north side. He pointed.

"Cherokee," El-i-chi said.

Already Se-quo-i was moving, running hard. El-i-chi let him set the pace. They broke out onto the bank of the river a few minutes later at a point still slightly upriver from Brown's boat. They could hear the Cherokee in the canoes hailing the vessel, then heard Brown's answer. The Cherokee were speaking in a friendly manner, and the preacher was answering in kind.

"Do you recognize any of them?" El-i-chi asked.

"No," Se-quo-i responded.

"He should not let them board," El-i-chi said. He knew that he was too far away to call out a warning to the colonel. The canoes were nearing the flatboat. He and Se-quo-i would have to swim the river to reach the Brown party. He started running again, but the way was made difficult by riverside thickets.

When, once again, they had a clear field of view, the Cherokee were already aboard the barge, their canoes tied to the larger vessel. He counted fifteen Indians. Most were seated, and he could make out the features of Mandy and Tess as they and other girls offered food and water to the visitors. He chided himself for worrying over nothing. The visiting Cherokee seemed peaceful enough; no weapons were in evidence.

"We should have crossed the river upstream," he told Se-quo-i, but hindsight did not help the situation.

"It would not be wise to call out now, not with all of them aboard," Se-quo-i said.

"We will backtrack, swim across beyond that far bend, and come down unseen on the other side. I am hopeful that my concern is unnecessary."

"These are still Cherokee lands," Se-quo-i pointed out.

They swam the river, pushing their muskets and powder flasks ahead of them on driftwood floats, gained the far bank, and began to pick their way downstream. As they neared the position of the barge, they were galvanized into action by a hoarse scream.

El-i-chi, moving swiftly and silently, came to a point where he could see the flatboat. He knew instantly that he was too late. Already white men lay in their own blood on the planking of the flatboat's deck. Only Colonel Brown and one of his sons were still on their feet, surrounded by a half-dozen whooping renegades. Even as El-i-chi waited for Se-quo-i to catch up, the Brown boy fell, a tomahawk cracking his skull, and the colonel's right arm was almost severed by a sharp blade, leaving him helpless before the assault of three renegades.

Se-quo-i seized El-i-chi's arm and exerted all his strength to prevent the Seneca from dashing over the last fifty yards that separated them from the flatboat. "Wait," he whispered. "Look."

The Cherokee aboard the flatboat were tossing the bodies of the eight dead men overboard. Others were guarding the females.

"They will not kill Mistress Brown and the girls—not yet," Se-quo-i said. "It would serve no purpose to rush in now, my friend. We are two against fifteen. With the darkness we can be more effective."

Anger and self-reproach almost propelled El-i-chi into a vastly uneven battle from which he would not have emerged alive. For days now he had watched the Brown party and had traveled with them. Although he had, in his mind, given them up as dead, he had not expected their demise to come while they were in the lands of his brothers. He should have been there; he should have stayed with them until that unmarked boundary separating the lands of the Cherokee from the Creek's had been passed. Had he and Se-quo-i been aboard the flatboat, he could have advised Brown not to let the canoes approach. But he recognized the wisdom of Se-quo-i's words: With the night, two men could do some damage. Two, working swiftly and with daring, could cut the odds considerably before a final confrontation. Of one thing he was sure—

those Cherokee who were aboard the flatboat, who had killed eight men, would not escape unscathed.

"I think they were after Mistress Brown and the girls," Se-quo-i said after they had observed the renegades' actions for a few minutes. "They will be safe for a time. The warriors are no doubt in a state of purification for war and will remain celibate. If the renegades were interested in scalps only, the females would be dead already. At any rate, there is nothing we can do as long as it is light and they are alert."

Although it rankled him, El-i-chi bowed to Se-quo-i's wisdom. He withdrew into the forest and checked his powder—to be certain that the crossing of the river had not wet it—reloaded his musket, saw to its priming, and fingered the sharp edge of his tomahawk. Se-quo-i had stayed at the edge of the river to keep an eye on the barge. Only an hour had passed before El-i-chi heard the Cherokee's alerting approach signal.

"I was right in thinking that the renegades have plans for Mistress Brown and girls," Se-quo-i said. "They have cast off the lines and are drifting the flatboat downriver."

El-i-chi leaped to his feet and ran lightly to the river to see the flatboat disappearing around the bend. The two warriors followed the barge through a hot, still afternoon, crawling near to look down from the height of a riverbank.

At sunset the renegades pulled the vessel to the southern bank of the river and secured it. Now there was the matter of waiting. Someone on board had found a supply of rum, and the bottles were being passed around freely. El-i-chi smiled grimly. Unwittingly the renegades were helping his cause, for drunken men would not be at their fighting best.

Aboard the flatboat the Cherokee who called himself Atarho had limited his own drinking to a few swallows, just enough to light a pleasant fire in his belly and give him a feeling of well-being. Others, including Simon Purdy, had not been so conservative. A few Cherokee warriors had drunk themselves into a stupor. Occasionally one would writhe, moan, and empty his stomach onto the deck.

The encounter with the flatboat had been, for Atarho, a happy accident. He had led his group far to the south, to escape the concerted effort by the white settlers and the peaceful Cherokee to find and punish the perpetrators of the Kirk massacre. The spirits had led him directly to a prize so great that he took time, at dusk, to chant his thanks to the spirits of darkness, to whom he had been introduced by the great shaman of the northland, Hodano. The supplies aboard the vessel represented riches. Although the weapons taken had been disappointing—only a few old muskets and a pistol or two—the greatest prize consisted of six white females huddled at the center of the barge under the canvas awning that had been erected to protect a frail older woman from the hot summer sun.

White women represented wealth if one could get them intact to one of the Spanish settlements, for white women were scarce on the frontier, and the appetites of the isolated Spanish soldiers, far from home, were enormous. Aside from drink, the men had little opportunity to spend the silver with which they were paid for their services in the far-flung Spanish outposts.

Atarho had seen immediately that the barge offered two opportunities: One, it would get him and his renegades out of danger, to the Mississippi and the protection of the Spanish. Two, if the boat could be moved down the Tennessee to the Ohio and then to the Father of Waters with most of its cargo intact, Atarho would become a wealthy man who could buy men and weapons to continue the war that he had sworn to wage.

The price that the five white girls would bring would be impressive if they were delivered to New Madrid. The price would be even higher in New Orleans. Before Purdy had drunk so much of Colonel James Brown's "medicinal" rum that his thinking was impaired, Atarho had pointed out the possibilities to the white renegade, and Purdy had agreed that Atarho's proposal had merit.

Atarho's only concern, since the Cherokee were in purification for war and would not touch a woman for carnal purposes until they washed off the war paint, was to keep his men from becoming bloodthirsty; it was good sport to torture a white woman. To avert this possibility Atarho stationed himself near the huddled females and chewed on biscuit and cold venison left over from the last meal served aboard the flatboat.

There had been tears and screams of pure terror among the survivors while their men were being killed and their scalpless bodies thrown overboard, but now, with the coming of darkness, a tense silence prevailed among them. Mistress Brown was trying to put up a brave front, but her efforts were not convincing. She had never been overly strong, and the horror of the day had sapped her strength, leaving her lying almost helpless on a blanket. Her three daughters hovered near her, their eyes red from weeping, each knowing her own terrible fears.

Mandy and Tess sat with their arms entwined, Tess whimpering quietly, Mandy alert, observing the drunken antics of the murderers. Now and then her right hand would go to her waist where, among the folds of her skirts, she carried the knife given to her by El-i-chi such a short time before. It seemed to her the shaman had exhibited great powers of prediction, for he had foreseen the bloody deaths, and she and her sister now faced terrible danger. As she pushed her palm against the hard handle of the knife, she wondered if she could bring herself to use it—even under the direst of threats. Surely one young girl with a knife could offer little resistance to the murderers who outnumbered her.

The Indians had paid no attention to them at all since they had found the rum. Only the leader watched them, and he seemed lost in thought. Mandy could not guess what fate lay ahead of her, but she was not optimistic.

"Tess," she whispered into her sister's ear. "When they are all asleep we will slip over the side and into the water."

Tess shivered but nodded.

"We will try to find our way back to the Seneca village," Mandy said.

Tess nodded, but her small shoulders jerked with a new onset of sobbing.

"You rest now," Mandy said. "Sleep if you can."

Simon Purdy had claimed an entire bottle of rum for himself, and he had done yeoman's service by it. Now there were only a couple of swallows left and no more liquor to be found aboard the barge. He had eaten, and the food had helped still the whirling of his head and the queasiness of his stomach. Soon, he knew, the effects of the rum would fade, and he would have a long night ahead of him.

He had looked over the females carefully. One in particular interested him—one of the younger ones. He looked around. His Cherokee friends were either asleep or too drunk to care what he did. He rose and crept back toward the center of the craft where the women were grouped under the canvas canopy. Atarho lifted his head in disgust as Purdy passed, but said nothing.

"Do no visible damage to the women," Atarho said at last.

Purdy laughed. He stood for a moment looking down at the group, saw the girl he fancied, pointed his finger, and said, "You, come with me."

Mandy, seeing the drunken white man who was dressed as an Indian pointing to her sister, took a deep breath and fingered her knife.

"You heard me," Purdy said. "You come with me."

"Please, can't you leave us alone?" Mistress Brown whispered, her voice weak and frightened.

Purdy bent to reach for Tess.

Mandy leaped to her feet and put herself between Purdy and her sister. She knew—and the knowledge frightened her—what Purdy had in mind for Tess. But Tess was only thirteen, just a child—although nature and her body said that she was a functioning woman.

"*I* will go with you." Mandy had decided to use the knife given to her by El-i-chi. Not knowing the Indian customs, she expected that it would be only a matter of time before the others, sobering from their drinking, would come to the midsection of the boat for the same reason that had brought the white renegade. She had one chance. She would kill this one, and then perhaps Tess and she could slip overboard. She had thought about that possibility, and although it grieved her to think about leaving the Brown girls in the hands of the renegades, she knew that she could not hope to save them all. She had learned to like the Browns, the girls more so than their mother, but she had made the difficult choice to do her best to save her sister.

"Eager, are you?" Purdy asked, examining Mandy in the fading light.

"My sister is too young," Mandy said, her hand touching the knife.

"Come, then." Purdy grasped Mandy's arm and led her back toward the rear of the barge among the stacks of cargo. "There's no reason why I can't enjoy both you girls—you first, then your sister for the remainder of the night."

He chose a spot between two covered bales and reached out to close his hand on one of Mandy's breasts. She had freed the knife from the folds of her clothing; as she turned, she tried to remember what El-i-chi had told her. She brought the knife up from her hip, thrusting it in the direction of the man's belly, but he saw the motion and leaped backward just in time. The blade whistled upward, narrowly missed his chin, and before Mandy could recover, he struck her sharply in the face with his fist, seized her knife arm, and twisted it painfully. The knife clattered to the deck.

"Bitch!" he hissed, slapping her again and again.

The force of the first blow had stunned Mandy, leaving her feeling vague and dreamy, unable to feel pain as the man's hand made its repeated contact with her face. She scarcely realized it when her clothing was torn off. She fell heavily and tried to roll away, feeling the rough planks on her bare backside, and then she was pinioned under a weight that forced the breath from her. She felt another blow to her face as she tried to find the man's eyes with her fingernails, but after that she knew only a sharp, quick pain and the panting, heaving weight of him.

* * *

In the darkness El-i-chi and Se-quo-i crept to the top of
the bank overlooking the flatboat. A fire had been started in
the cooking pit on the deck, and the flames showed them
that most of the renegades were still sleeping off the rum.
It was a fine time to make their move. El-i-chi gestured to
indicate his mode of attack. Se-quo-i, in his turn, indicated
the men he would kill. They slid down the bank to the edge
of the water. The barge swung on its ropes some ten feet
from the bank. El-i-chi waded into the stream but halted
when he heard motion aboard the boat.

Atarho had decided that it was time to get back to
business. He was sleepy, and he did not intend to stand
guard by himself all night and let the others sleep off their
rum. He began to make the rounds, kicking, punching, and
shouting to wake the others. There were grumbling and
protests, but Atarho persisted.

Waist-deep in the river, El-i-chi and Se-quo-i waited.
El-i-chi knew that they had let the prime time for a surprise
attack pass, so he touched Se-quo-i and led the way back to
the bank. Even if the leader did awaken the renegades, he
reasoned, they would have to go back to sleep sometime
during the night.

Atarho began to address his men. His voice carried well
and could be heard easily by El-i-chi and Se-quo-i. It was
quickly evident that Atarho was an orator in the finest of
Indian tradition, which, as defined by old Casno, El-i-chi's
mentor, was a man who spoke with the voice of a panther
who had drunk oil.

"Hear me," Atarho said. "For I give voice to one who has
gone before us to the Place Across the River, the voice of
the great Atotarho."

El-i-chi's interest was aroused. Atotarho, he knew, was a
name that epitomized evil. Atotarho had been an Onondaga
chief who opposed the great Hiawatha's efforts to form the
league of the Ho-de-no-sau-nee, the League of the Iroquois. As legend had it, Atotarho had been ferocious in

appearance and had been able to call on all the dark spirits. In his battles against Hiawatha, Atotarho had been seen to turn his hair into serpents.

"For I am the reincarnation of the great Atotarho," the speaker was saying. "I am a student of Hodano, who is familiar with all of the powerful and dark spirits, and I will lead you to greatness."

There was another name that captured El-i-chi's attention—Hodano. He had faced that evil Seneca shaman once in a Seneca longhouse far to the north and had shamed Hodano's magic with some rather simple tricks taught to him by Casno; but as later events had demonstrated, his victory over Hodano had been mostly the result of surprise, for the evil shaman had proven to be an almost deadly foe of El-i-chi's brother, Renno.

The Seneca nodded. It was interesting to know that Hodano was still alive and had a disciple so far south in Cherokee lands. It would be even more interesting to ask this man who fancied himself to be a reincarnation of the evil Atotarho a few pointed questions.

"Twice now we have shown the white man that he cannot invade our lands unpunished," Atarho intoned. "We left the blood of his women and his children to tell him these things."

Se-quo-i's head jerked toward El-i-chi. "When we kill these," the Cherokee said, "we kill those who murdered the Kirks."

El-i-chi nodded.

"Remember, my friends," Atarho continued, "that we are embarked on a sacred mission, that we are purified for war against the white man. Soon many will follow our cause, for we have shown that it is right and possible to punish the white invaders of our lands. Soon the warriors of the Cherokee, the Creek, the Choctaw, and the Chickasaw will flock to us, and we will show them how to kill."

"Will he talk all night?" El-i-chi muttered.

"Remember," Atarho said. "Remember our purpose. It is good that you have taken time to enjoy yourselves briefly this night, and there will be many more rewards for those who are brave."

"Brave?" El-i-chi snorted. "They outnumber their victims two to one in a sneak attack, and he calls that brave."

"Hush, Brother," Se-quo-i whispered.

"We must be alert," Atarho said. "You, and you. You will stand guard over the white women, whom we will sell to the Spanish for much silver and gold. You take the bow, and you, the stern. And stay awake, for, as you know, we are not without enemies in this land."

El-i-chi sighed. With guards posted the job would be complicated, and the time of waiting extended. He made himself a more comfortable position on the bank and settled in for the wait. When at last the flatboat was once again quiet, El-i-chi said, "We cannot face all of them and hope to live. We must reduce the odds quietly, before any one of them awakens to give the alarm. If for any reason we fail in this, I will cry out once like a hunting hawk. If you hear that sound, break off your fight and jump into the water. We will meet downstream, atop the bank overlooking the swift waters at the bend of the river."

Within minutes Se-quo-i was drawing himself up onto the deck of the flatboat by the bowline. He crouched there, thinking that the sound of water dripping from him onto the deck was frightfully loud, until he spotted the bow sentinel sleeping on a pile of cargo. He moved silently, his moccasins leaving wet tracks on the deck. His knife hissed, then grated on bone. There was a gurgling sound as the dying sentinel tried to make his last outcry, but Se-quo-i was already moving away.

El-i-chi's boarding at the stern was not as easily accomplished. The man posted to watch was not asleep. El-i-chi had to find a new place to board, then make his way among the cargo. He saw something white and pale directly in his path, halted, saw no movement, then realized that he was looking at the naked body of a woman. He moved forward, knelt, heard the woman breathing, smelled the carnal aroma of sex. He felt deep regret when he looked into the beaten, swollen face of the woman he recognized as Mandy.

It was with anger that he approached the sentinel from the rear and sent him to his ancestors quickly, one of his hands closing over the renegade's mouth, the other slicing across the jugular with the blade of his tomahawk.

El-i-chi moved forward as silently as a spirit. Another man died in his sleep. The Seneca was now abreast of the canvas shelter where the females slept. He saw motion there and froze, poised to leap into action. He hissed a warning to the captives to be quiet, and then all of his plans were altered when one of the girls, seeing his shadowy form as she emerged from a half sleep, screamed piercingly.

Within seconds there was frantic action on the flatboat as twelve men leaped to their feet, each reaching for his weapons.

Chapter IV

Mandy felt so odd. She saw the shadowy form approaching her in the darkness, but for some reason she felt no fear. Then she recognized El-i-chi and cried out gladly, only there was no sound from her lips. She reached for him, but her hand would not move. Then he was gone, so she lay there, looking up at the stars for a long, long time. Everything seemed so peaceful. Her head did not hurt anymore. Something had happened, but she couldn't quite remember what it had been. When she heard Tess scream, the sound proved to be a key to her state of numbed shock. She sat up quickly, and pain hit her down low. Blood rushed to her head and roared in her ears as she remembered.

She was naked, but she could not take time to worry about that. Around her men were exploding into action. It was now or never for her. If she was to get Tess and herself off the flatboat, there would never be a better opportunity.

El-i-chi met two confused renegades in a grim confrontation that ended quickly in death for the two Cherokee. He sounded a great war cry and heard Se-quo-i's answer as his tomahawk clashed, steel on steel, with that of another enemy. But men were closing in on him. Leap and parry as he might, he faced no fewer than five men, Atarho among them.

Se-quo-i had also met with initial success, killing one opponent swiftly, and then he, like El-i-chi, was hemmed in by numbers. His blade struck flesh and penetrated to bone, but for a few minutes, at least, the wound merely infuriated the man to mount a more vigorous attack.

El-i-chi leaped high to avoid a low sweep of a tomahawk and came down with his arm moving downward, the blow aimed to smash into the back of an enemy's neck. He missed. There were too many of them. Out of the corner of his eye he saw a vague, white shape, and his mind registered that Mandy, naked, was up and moving.

"Mandy, get into the water and swim for the far shore!" he shouted even as he parried a serious attempt for his throat.

Mandy heard. She was ten feet from the canvas canopy where the four Brown females and her sister huddled in fear, not really able to see what was happening but hearing the grunts, cries, and curses of the battling men. Her foot struck something on the deck, and looking down, she saw that it was a tomahawk. She bent. Her knife was gone, but now she had another weapon. She would use it to make certain that her younger sister did not receive the same treatment she had suffered. She moved toward the shelter but was forced to leap aside as the fight around El-i-chi swirled her way.

El-i-chi, for the first time in his life, was fighting a purely defensive battle, using all his skill and strength merely to stay alive. He was reluctant to admit that he was in danger, but fact was fact. Five skilled fighters were determined to kill him, and that left several more of the enemy for Se-quo-i. With a surge of anger mixed with shame, El-i-chi gave the signal to abandon the fight, lifting his head, to give vent to the scream of a hunting hawk. Even as he cried out he felt a tremendous impact to the side of his head, and suddenly his arm was too heavy to hold up. His legs were no longer pillars of strength but limp, useless things. He sank to the deck.

Se-quo-i, with one renegade dead on the deck, his corpse interfering with the progress of the battling men, heard El-i-chi's signal and returned it. He began working his way toward the side of the flatboat, and with one last surge of offensive energy that left blood gushing from a slashed shoulder, he turned and leaped into the darkness, went underwater, and came up swimming strongly. He heard yells from behind him but did not look back.

Mandy saw El-i-chi fall, and her heart sank, for now there were renegades between her and the shelter. For the moment, however, they were looking down at the fallen El-i-chi. She could slip by, grab Tess, and then slide quietly into the water.

"This scalp is mine," a renegade declared, starting to bend down only to be jerked away by another who growled his own claim to El-i-chi's hair.

Mandy felt tears of sorrow spring to her eyes. She could see that El-i-chi's head was bloody. She was about to avert her eyes and move toward the shelter when she saw El-i-chi move feebly. He was not dead. That made her even more sad, for there was nothing she could do for him. She began to inch toward the canvas canopy just in time to have her way blocked by a rush of the men who had been fighting Se-quo-i at the prow of the flatboat. Her mind went blank. And then she had an idea. She ran to the bow of the boat and used the tomahawk to slash the lines holding the flatboat to the bank. The barge began to move swiftly with the current.

It took only a minute for someone to notice that the boat was moving. The men who had been wrangling over El-i-chi's scalp heard Atarho's voice: "Quickly, we must secure the boat."

To try to navigate the rapids just down the river at night would most certainly end in disaster. Atarho saw his prize slipping away, and his orders were harsh and loud. He himself led three men to the bow, leaped into the water, tried to stop the drifting of the boat. In the meantime, others were going over the side to secure the boat by the stern lines.

Mandy stood at the canvas shelter and called out her sister's name. The sound caused one of the Brown girls to scream, and the scream brought Simon Purdy on the run. Mandy fell back into the shadows, fear and hate rendering her helpless. There was the man who had hurt her. There was the man she should kill before he could do the same vile things to Tess. But she could not bring herself to move against him. He stood there, a musket in one hand, tomahawk in the other, as if daring her to attack. Instead, she fell back farther into the shadows, and her foot contacted something soft.

El-i-chi's hand went out weakly as he felt contact. His fingers closed around an ankle. It took a supreme effort to exert enough strength to yank the leg out from under his enemy. Dazed, he was thinking only that if he jerked the enemy's leg out from under him, the enemy would then fall and be on the same level—so far, far down—as El-i-chi.

Mandy fell atop El-i-chi and rolled off. His hand still clutched her ankle. His other arm lifted slowly, the light of the fire that still burned in the cooking pit sparkling off the steel of his tomahawk.

"Don't," Mandy managed to say. "It's me, Mandy." She struggled to her feet.

El-i-chi sent the message to his arm to stay the blow, and it seemed to take many moons for the message to get there.

The tomahawk flashed to one side and thudded into the planking of the deck. The world was a place of red haze for the shaman, and it was painful to think. But for some reason he was still alive, and there was no enemy near. Mandy helped him to stand. She stood facing him, undecided, when he seized her and began to push her toward the side of the flatboat.

"No, no," she whispered. "Tess! I must get Tess!"

Blood was running into El-i-chi's eyes. The water of the river would wash it away. His feet seemed to weigh tons, and the distance to the edge of the barge looked like miles, but then he felt himself falling, pushing the girl ahead of him to hit the water first, so he went in atop her. He took a deep breath and was underwater and fighting, his limbs reluctant to obey. He felt as if he were swimming in thick molasses. His lungs were burning, and a fierce pain stabbed at his forehead just as peace came in a swirl of blackness.

Atarho and his men had managed to stop the drifting of the flatboat by snugging lines around riverside trees. The vessel swung in and lay alongside the bank. Atarho saw some of the men racing to get back to the body of the fallen enemy, and then he heard whoops of frustration and shouts that the enemy was gone. He ordered torches lit for a search. He had lost six men. Two more were wounded, one badly, with a terrible cut on his shoulder. And one of the female captives was missing, the older girl, the one he had seen being taken to the rear of the boat by Simon Purdy.

"I told you not to hurt the females," Atarho seethed.

"What I did to her didn't hurt her a'tall," Purdy said. "She musta jumped overboard. We'll find her in the morning." He looked around. "Or maybe she's hiding." He thrust a torch close to the face of Mistress Brown. "Is she still on board, woman? Is she hiding?"

"Please, I don't know," Judith Brown said weakly. "It was so dark. I couldn't see anything."

"I think you're lying," Purdy snarled, thrusting the torch closer to the frail woman's head. "I think I'll just set your hair afire and see if I can get the truth out of you then."

He pushed the torch closer, and there was the smell of singed hair. She gasped and clutched at her breast, her eyes going wide. She fell forward, vomiting. Another stench joined that of her vomit as her bowels voided. Her heart, never strong, was fluttering weakly, and within a few seconds, the pain ended forever.

"She was old and stringy," Purdy rationalized. "She wouldn't have been worth much."

"Get rid of her," Atarho said.

Purdy added Mistress Brown's long hair to his collection of scalps and kicked the thin corpse overboard. The current took the body and carried it away.

Under the canvas shelter four young girls quaked, too terrified now to weep.

Se-quo-i let the current aid him as he swam away from the flatboat. When he was well hidden by the darkness he turned to look for El-i-chi. A flurry of action erupted on the barge. Se-quo-i tried to swim against the current, to go back, for it seemed evident that El-i-chi had not been able to leave the vessel. The boat was loose, drifting, and Se-quo-i believed that only El-i-chi could have cut it loose.

The current was increasingly swift as the river narrowed before plunging between two rocky ridges in a respectable rapid. Se-quo-i landed on a gravelly bar and pulled himself up to prevent being washed through the rapids. There he watched and waited. He saw torches being lit on the vessel, which had been stopped and was again moored to the bank. He waited for what seemed to be a very long time. When he heard a splashing from the dark river, he waded out waist deep and called El-i-chi's name.

Mandy heard and called, "Help us."

Se-quo-i plunged into the water and swam to her. Her fingers were buried in El-i-chi's scalp lock, and the Seneca floated behind her as she struggled toward the bank. Se-quo-i swam behind El-i-chi, pushing, until he and the girl could stand, and then the two of them dragged El-i-chi's limp body to the gravelly bar.

"He's not dead," Se-quo-i said, after putting his fingertips on El-i-chi's throat to feel a strong pulse there.

"No," Mandy confirmed.

"We've got to get away from the river," Se-quo-i warned. "They'll look for us with the morning."

El-i-chi was deadweight. Mandy carried his legs, Se-quo-i his arms. They struggled up the bank and into the trees for a hundred yards, then lowered the shaman to the ground.

"I will go back and obliterate the sign we left on the bar," Se-quo-i said. He made his way back to the river in the growing light of dawn and used a pine bough to erase their tracks. He saw the flatboat, still tied upriver.

But even as he watched from cover he saw movement aboard, and soon the vessel was being maneuvered out into the current. It took only minutes for the strength of the flow to move the flatboat past Se-quo-i's position and into the rapids, where it picked up speed and disappeared around a bend. He didn't have to worry about pursuit from the renegades.

When he rejoined Mandy and El-i-chi, the naked white girl was seated on the ground, cradling El-i-chi's head in her lap. Se-quo-i noted that her bruised face was swollen badly from a beating. He removed his buckskin jacket and went to her side.

"He's breathing well," Mandy reported. She shivered, and Se-quo-i realized that she was in shock.

"Lift your arms," he said. She obeyed meekly, and he slipped the jacket on her and knelt beside her to lace it closed up to her neck. "Better?"

"I'm cold," she said. She looked into Se-quo-i's eyes with a strange intensity. "My sister—"

"They will keep her alive," he told her. "We will go after them."

"I don't know if she can survive," Mandy said. Her expression changed, and she was overcome by a fit of weeping that shook her violently.

Se-quo-i gently lifted El-i-chi's head from the girl's lap, pulled her to her feet, and guided her to sit with her back against an outcrop of stone. "Rest while I build a fire. I'll go back upriver to the spot where we left our packs. I have a breechclout there, which I'll wear while you wear my trousers."

"My sister," Mandy said. "They will violate her."

"Not likely," Se-quo-i disagreed. "Warriors on the warpath are in a state of purification. We will have time to overtake them before they wash off the war paint."

Mandy's bitter laugh made him wonder what she was thinking, but he learned quickly enough. He felt a surge of sympathy when she said, "There is a white man among them. He was not in a state of purification when he violated me."

Se-quo-i had had little experience in comforting women. All he could think to say was, "Well, we'll have you some more clothing soon."

El-i-chi groaned, and Se-quo-i rushed to his side. There was a huge bump over the Seneca's left temple. *Thank the manitous,* Se-quo-i thought, *that the blade of the tomahawk landed on the flat side*.

As it was, there had been a loss of blood, for El-i-chi's buckskin shirt still showed bloodstains in spite of having been in the water. Se-quo-i knelt, lifted first one eyelid and then the other. One of El-i-chi's pupils was larger than the other, not a good sign. There was nothing to do but wait.

Se-quo-i turned to Mandy. "Will you be all right here alone with him? If so, I'll go get our packs."

"I'll be fine." Mandy's limbs were shaking less, and she was more acutely aware of her seminudity, the buckskin jacket coming only to the lower crease of her buttocks, exposing a long, white length of thigh and leg.

During Se-quo-i's absence she walked a few paces away into the brush, out of sight of El-i-chi, and, lifting the jacket, examined herself by sight and by feel. There seemed to be no overt damage, but she was sore. She knelt and prayed to God to spare her the additional shame of bearing the rapist's child. Then, feeling slightly better, she went back to sit on the pine needles beside El-i-chi, to touch his brow, to wipe flecks of white foam from his lips.

"Live, Shaman," she implored. "So many are dead, and
my sister is worse than dead. But you must live, do you
hear me? You must, for enough have died already."

As if in answer El-i-chi spewed vomitus, and she,
responding instinctively, turned his head and body to one
side so that he would not choke on it.

The acid stink was still in the air when Se-quo-i came
back. He knew that it was a bad sign. Fatal head injuries
often produced vomiting and then slow death.

He had changed into his breechclout and now extended
his buckskin trousers toward Mandy. She rose, took them
gratefully, and, to Se-quo-i's amusement, went behind
some bushes to don the trousers. He had seen her naked
and dressed only in his jacket, but to slip her feet and legs
into his trousers, she had to hide herself. *Well*, he thought,
women.

"I must talk with you," he said as Mandy emerged,
dressed fully except for shoes. Her hair was still wet,
hanging loose in a great, sodden mass that cascaded over
her shoulders. "El-i-chi is seriously hurt. In all frankness,
I'm not sure he'll live. Head injuries are unpredictable. I
have seen warriors with great, gaping wounds on the scalp
go on fighting while others fall from what seems to be a
mere tap. I have seen men recover from fearful blows, and
I've seen men lapse into sleep and die from what seemed to
be a lesser blow."

"He must live," Mandy responded.

"Look," Se-quo-i said, lifting El-i-chi's eyelids to show
her the unequal dilation of the pupils. "That and the fact
that he vomited are bad signs." He rose. "We will not give
up, however. I have a plan, which will require courage on
your part. I think you have that courage, for I saw you pull
him from the river when he was unconscious. I will run to
the village and organize a force to pursue the renegades.
We know, of course, that they are on the river—"

"They plan to follow the river all the way to the Mississippi," Mandy said. "I heard the one called Atarho discussing it with Simon Purdy."

"Perhaps when they realize the difficulty of navigating

the river, they will change their minds," Se-quo-i said. "At any rate, they'll stay on the river at least until they reach Muscle Shoals. If they decide to dismantle the flatboat and portage it around the shoals, we may catch them there."

"You want me to stay with El-i-chi while you run back to the village. Yes, I can do that."

"Good girl," Se-quo-i said.

"Will you leave right away?"

"The sooner the better. It may be days before El-i-chi can travel. By the time I return, the question of his condition will be answered. My trust is in the manitous that he will be waiting for me, eager to be off and away after the renegades."

Se-quo-i was not as much the endurance runner as Renno. The Cherokee could make good time, but his physical condition, diminished by the many hours he spent with his books and making jewelry, forced him to walk one-third of the distance. Even at that pace he made good headway and got to the village in a fraction of the time that it had taken the Brown wagon train to reach the Tennessee.

El-i-chi slept—or was unconscious—throughout all the rest of the day after Se-quo-i left. He did not so much as move or make a sound through a long night, and that frightened Mandy. She felt more alone than ever in her young life. Every sound and every stirring of wind startled her and sent fear flooding into her. The flutter of the wings of a passing nightbird put a swivel into her neck so that she spent the next few minutes looking first over one shoulder, then the other. Sleep was out of the question. Her eyelids had a will of their own, springing open immediately if she allowed them to close.

She had made a spot for herself near El-i-chi, and toward morning, when it grew chill, she pushed close to him to share the warmth of her body. The way his chest moved up and down was reassuring, and the sound of his breathing was promising.

With the morning she left him for a few minutes to walk to the river for water and to wash her weary eyes. She returned with El-i-chi's kerchief dampened and with a swallow or two of water in a freshwater mussel-shell half, which she had found on the bar. First she dripped water onto his closed lips from the shell. She knew a surge of hope when his tongue came out to lick his moist lips. When she managed to dribble the rest of the water into his mouth, he swallowed instinctively. Then she used the dampened kerchief to clean his face and his neck.

Mandy nibbled on a piece of jerky from El-i-chi's travel pack for breakfast and the midday meal. Throughout the morning she had made trips to the river to bring back tiny amounts of water in the mussel shell. Although El-i-chi's eyes did not open and he made no sound, he accepted all the water she could bring. She returned from another trip at midafternoon to kneel by the warrior's side. El-i-chi moved with fearful swiftness, and the blade of his tomahawk whizzed over her head. He would have killed her had he not been seeing two heads instead of one, one slightly above the other.

Mandy croaked a half scream and fell backward. El-i-chi made a feeble movement of pursuit, then collapsed. His eyes remained open, however, and his brow was knitted in his effort to focus.

"El-i-chi, it's Mandy," she said.

His throat worked but no sound came until he tried several times more. "Mandy?"

"Yes. We're safe. Se-quo-i has gone for help, to the village."

El-i-chi nodded weakly. His head was an ocean of fire, and there was a weakness in his limbs. He closed his eyes and slept.

It was dark when she heard him ask, "Is there water?"

She knelt beside him. "I have nothing to carry it in."

"Then help me get to the river," he requested, raising himself on one elbow.

"Perhaps you should just rest. I'll bring as much as I can."

"No. Help me." He pushed himself to a sitting position. Two Mandys looked at him. Then he felt her hands on his arms, and she was helping him to his feet. He swayed unsteadily. "How long?"

"The night before last."

He thought. He'd been unconscious two full days and a full night. But his vision, although still blurred, was improving. "I will not die, then."

"Thank God," Mandy whispered.

"Water." He leaned on her and found her to be strong for a young girl. Then he was lying prone, drinking slowly. He rinsed his face, and that seemed to help. He sat up. "The flatboat?"

"It went downstream. My sister is still on it."

"And Se-quo-i left?"

"With the sun, yesterday morning."

"We will follow the barge, leaving signs for those who will come."

"I think you should rest and regain your strength."

He tried to stand, and his legs turned to water. He sat down heavily and grunted. "I think you are right. We will build a fire there, atop the bank."

"What if someone sees the fire?"

"Anyone who sees it will be a friend," he answered. "The rapids below here will take the flatboat fast and far."

He had to help her strike fire with flint and metal. She blew on the tinder, for the effort made his head hurt, and soon a cheery fire was burning. El-i-chi chewed on jerky, wishing for something more substantial. With the morning he told her that he would hunt, but he made it only a few steps before he realized that he was too weak.

"Can you use a bow?" he asked.

"I'm afraid not."

"Can you shoot?"

"A little. The colonel had us all fire a musket several times during the trip to the river."

"Take the musket, then. Go into the woods until you find a grassy area with few trees. Sit there quietly, and you will soon see the rabbits come out to eat or play. Wait until one gets quite close."

Mandy did not want to be alone, but she too was hungry.

She told herself that El-i-chi needed solid food to regain his strength; she forced herself to walk in the dimness of the forest until she came to a grassy glade. She sat in shadows and was very still. Soon a pair of rabbits emerged from their dens to munch on greenery. She lifted the musket slowly, and the sound of the shot caused her to jerk and close her eyes, but when she opened them a rabbit was kicking out its life, with most of its head blown away—she had aimed for the larger area of the little animal's body. The scent of blood brought back to her the carnage aboard the flatboat, and she was trembling when she rejoined El-i-chi.

"Do you have the knife I gave you?"

She shook her head. "I tried to kill him, but he was too quick."

"Use this," he said, handing her the tomahawk. He sat with his back against a tree and gave her instructions, and soon the smell of roasting meat was in the air. He ate ravenously, and she matched him bite for bite, so when both were satisfied, nothing was left but marrowless bones. He was seeing only one and a half of her now, and his limbs felt stronger. He directed Mandy in the gathering of boughs for beds, asked her to help him to the river for a long drink and a good wash, then fell asleep almost immediately.

Se-quo-i, winded and hungry, went immediately to Rusog's lodge upon arrival in the Cherokee village. The chief was inside with Ena and the twins. When he saw that the young warrior was wet with sweat and very nearly spent, he indicated a place to sit, while Ena pushed the twins away. She came to stand with her husband in front of the young warrior as he told the story without haste and in detail. When he reached the point of telling of the attack of the renegades, Ena interrupted.

"Where is El-i-chi?" Her face showed strain.

"Hurt, but alive when I left him," Se-quo-i said.

"You left him wounded?" Ena demanded.

"Hush," Rusog said, "so that he may speak."

Se-quo-i went on to explain the situation. Ena turned

away and began to gather her weapons. "What are you doing?" Rusog asked.

"I am going," she answered.

"And these?" Rusog indicated the twins.

"My mother will care for them."

"They need their own mother," Rusog said firmly.

Motherhood had changed Ena. Before the birth of Ho-ya and We-yo she would have risked confrontation with her husband. Now, mellowed by the fine, lively little boy and girl, she paused to think. "You are right, Husband."

"Send a runner for Renno," Rusog said. "I will prepare my weapons and my kit." He turned to Se-quo-i. "Will you be fit for travel?"

"Nothing can stop me. There is a debt to be paid, and there is punishment to be dealt to those who have killed on our hunting grounds."

"Rest. Ena will give you food. We will leave very soon," Rusog said.

Renno had outdistanced the runner sent to summon him when he burst into the lodge to find Rusog applying war paint. Ena told him the essentials of the story in as few words as possible and saw a hint of pain on her brother's face when the nature of El-i-chi's injury was described.

"At least six renegades were killed?" Renno asked.

"And one wounded," Se-quo-i answered. "The nature and location of the wound will prevent him from being effective in a fight."

"So there will be no more than ten," Renno declared. "We will travel faster with a small group, Rusog."

"My thoughts, as well," the chief agreed. "We will be three."

"Four," Renno said, not willing to admit the possibility that El-i-chi was dead or incapacitated.

"Four, indeed," Rusog said. "How much time do you require?"

"I am ready," Renno said. He had his weapons: musket, pistol, the Spanish stiletto, and the good, stout English longbow that always reminded him of his friend William and the flame-haired woman who had been so much a part of his life for a time. He had decided to leave his war club behind.

Not even Rusog, fine warrior that he was, could match Renno when it came to covering ground. After striving mightily to keep up with the white Indian for half a day, with Se-quo-i often lagging behind, Rusog called a halt and, panting, said, "I understand your eagerness, Brother. But we push Se-quo-i too hard. Remember that he has already made the run one way."

"Stay with him," Renno requested. "The way can't be missed. I will wait for you in El-i-chi's camp." And, so saying, he was away, his long, powerful legs reaching for distance, his feet seeming to pick their way through the forest by magic so that his swift passage was made in near silence. He ran all out, until the pain began to surge into his body; then he continued to run until there came that magic rejuvenation, that surge of second strength that sent him speeding down the well-used trail with ground-eating speed.

He rested only for minutes at a time, this done while drinking from a clear stream or a spring, and never slept. He ran through the night and into another day, and then he drank from the Tennessee and set off down its bank. He soon smelled woodsmoke and cooking meat and slowed his pace, cautious even though he was certain that the fire came from El-i-chi's camp. He saw the girl, dressed in too-large buckskins, bending over the river, washing her face and hands. And then he was mounting the bank to appear suddenly in El-i-chi's vision. He stopped then. His chest was heaving, but his heart began to slow its beat quickly.

"You're just in time," El-i-chi said, smiling widely and pointing toward a fat turkey roasting on a spit over the fire. He stood, and Renno came to him to clasp him in his arms. No words were necessary.

After drinking deeply now that the run was over, Renno claimed his share of the turkey and listened as Mandy and El-i-chi told of the events. El-i-chi was careful to include what he had heard when the leader of the renegades was making his speech to his men.

"Hodano's influence reaches far," Renno said. The look on his face was fierce with hatred for the wicked shaman. "I thought he had died in Jamaica. He plunged into a pit, and although I heard no sound of the impact . . . to have survived such a fall, the man must be aided by evil forces you and I do not understand."

"This Atarho is no Hodano," El-i-chi said. "He is a village chief without a village, and I think that his ambitions are greater than his abilities."

"And yet he bested the great El-i-chi," Renno said, grinning.

"An accident," El-i-chi protested. "My foot slipped."

"You will take Mandy back to the village," Renno said. "A blow to the head such as you have experienced takes time to heal."

El-i-chi's face darkened, and he stood. "*You* take the girl back. This is *my* fight, *my* head that was split, not yours."

"We will travel fast and light," Renno warned. "We cannot have you holding us back."

"Stay at my heels, Brother," El-i-chi said, "and you will soon have the renegades in the sights of your musket."

"And the girl?" Renno asked.

"Please," Mandy said, "I must go. My sister is only a child. She'll be so frightened."

Renno said nothing. He walked to the river to look down toward the narrowing gorge and the rapids. By the time Rusog and Se-quo-i had arrived, his decision was made. It would not be wise to send the girl back toward the village alone, and four were better than three to fight the rene-gades once they were overtaken. It would not be necessary to travel at maximum speed, for if the renegades stayed with the flatboat and portaged it past Muscle Shoals, they could be overtaken by traveling at a walk.

"We will not waste time by taking the girl to a Cherokee village," he announced. "And we will not ask a girl unfa-miliar with the wilderness to travel alone."

"Thank you," Mandy breathed.

"Now if our invalid is prepared for travel, we will move," Renno said.

They marched along the banks of the narrow gorge. The river tumbled in swiftness, roaring and creating impressive white water. Below the rapids the river widened again, and it was possible to travel in haste along the bank, where sand and gravel bars were exposed by the shallow water. They had gone only a couple of miles past the rapids when Renno, in the lead, saw a hint of color in the shallows behind a bar that extended into the river. Upon investigation he saw that the color came from the dress that was wound wetly around the bloated legs of the deceased Judith Brown.

No one questioned the loss of time when Renno said that the woman was to be buried. El-i-chi, Rusog, and Se-quo-i went to find a suitable spot and to start the difficult task of digging a shallow grave with their tomahawks. Renno was a bit surprised when Mandy, without qualm, offered to help him carry the body; it was not a pleasant sight.

"I can do it alone," Renno said.

"Thank you for being considerate," Mandy replied. "But I've seen men die and be mutilated, and I've been a victim myself. Somehow, after that, nothing seems to have the capacity to shock me."

"A suggestion only," Renno proposed. "Her clothing seems to be in good condition. If it were washed thoroughly and dried . . ."

A shiver convulsed her for a moment, and then she said, "It will be quite useful."

Renno began to work with the clothing.

"Let me, please," Mandy said. "She was a good woman, a modest woman. It would shame her even in death to have a man see her nakedness."

And so it was that there, on a lonely sandbar on the middle Tennessee river, Mandy denuded a corpse that had been in the water for days, rinsed the clothing thoroughly, and hung it to dry over riverside bushes. Meanwhile Renno had carried the dead woman, covered by his own buckskin jacket, to place her in the grave that the others had dug.

Mandy stood over the grave when it was covered and marked by two lengths of tree limb tied together in the shape of a cross. She had donned the dead woman's clothing, so Se-quo-i had his buckskins back.

"She was a decent woman," Mandy whispered, just loud enough for everyone to hear. "She followed her husband into this frightful wilderness—without question, in obedience to her marriage vows—and here she died. But God saw her die, and God knows her name. She is with Him now, and we pray to You, Lord God, for vengeance for Judith Brown and for the others who have died, as we pray for the safety of those who have survived."

According to instructions left behind by Rusog, a runner went into Knoxville to make public the news that the Cherokee renegades had struck again and that members of the Brown party had been killed or taken captive. There were those in Knoxville who merely nodded, for they had expected such news, although not so quickly. They knew Rusog and Renno, and when the runner said that the Cherokee and the Seneca had sent a party after the renegades, they said, "Well, no need for us to do anything. If them two can't catch and kill the murderers, they won't never be caught."

Word spread rapidly along the frontier, and it was only a matter of days before a tall, gaunt, weary-looking young white man arrived in the Cherokee village asking for information about the Brown massacre. It was Ena who talked to him.

"Who are you?" she asked, not bothering to be polite, for she suspected his identity.

"My name is Egan Kirk. Those renegades killed my wife, my son, my family."

"I know," Ena fumed. "And you killed Old Tassel and four others who did not resist because *they* were under a flag of truce."

Kirk tried to stare Ena down but finally dropped his own eyes. "That was a mistake."

"It was murder," Ena retorted hotly. "And now you come

here, expecting us to tell you all. I think not. You might not be able to tell the difference between criminal renegades and the good men who will mete out punishment to them."

Egan swallowed swift anger. "Please," he begged. "My father and I dug eleven graves. My son was only a baby. I *must* be there when the murderers die."

There was an air of torment about the man—the boy, really, for he was only eighteen—that touched Ena. She could not imagine having to bury her own babies. "Perhaps you can be there," she conceded at last. "The renegades are taking the Brown flatboat down the Tennessee. By cutting across country, across the loop of the river, you might catch the boat where the river turns northward."

Chapter V

It was after Renno, Rusog, and Se-quo-i had left that Ah-wa-o learned that El-i-chi had been wounded. She had only secondhand information from Ena, who assured her that El-i-chi would be all right. Ena, basically an optimist, had great faith in the ability of both of her brothers. Ah-wa-o, younger, allowed her imagination to work overtime and cried herself to sleep for several nights, thinking of El-i-chi tossing in fever, alone in the wilderness, with only an inexperienced young white girl to tend him.

"Ena, why didn't you come to me?" she moaned. "I should be with him. I should have gone with Renno and the others."

"They would not have permitted it," Ena said. "They traveled fast."

"If he is wounded badly and needs me—" Ah-wa-o could not finish.

Ena, feeling sympathy, put her arm around the girl's shoulder. "With Renno and Rusog he will be in the best of hands. My guess is that you won't hear from them until they come home bearing the scalps of the renegades, El-i-chi leading the way."

"Oh, Ena, if anything happens to him, I will die," Ah-wa-o vowed.

"One day you will die," Ena said, "but most probably not from love." She could clearly remember how it felt to be in the first throes of love with a man, how a maiden's heart swelled with her love's nearness and shrank with his absence, for, although—thank the manitous—she had never been as overtly smitten as Ah-wa-o, she had loved Rusog fiercely during their stormy courtship. The tragedy here was that Ah-wa-o's love might never be fulfilled. Ena had heard some of the Seneca women talking, anticipating a council of clan matrons when the fate of El-i-chi and Ah-wa-o's love would be decided by an interpretation of tribal custom and taboo. It was Ena's guess that their answer would be no, that brother and sister must not marry even if they were related by marriage and not by blood. The reasoning would be that to breach the customs in the slightest way would make a larger rent in the fabric of tradition through which more serious changes would pass in the future.

Ah-wa-o spent a lot of time with Ena, and Ena welcomed her, for the twins were a pleasant burden more easily managed by two females. So it was that Ah-wa-o learned quickly of Egan Kirk's coming to the Cherokee village and of his talk with Ena. Ah-wa-o made it a point to walk near the man's campsite on the outskirts of the village, shuddering just a bit as she saw him, tall, young, and in anguish— the man who had lost his family and killed five chiefs under a flag of truce.

Egan was being treated with deliberate coldness. If he

spoke to a Cherokee, that Cherokee answered, but no one initiated conversation. He had told Ena that he would be on his way with the morning, and that, Ena felt, would be good.

When, in the evening, Egan came to her lodge, Ah-wa-o was there. Ena opened the door, looked at the white man impassively, and waited for him to speak.

"I was wondering," Egan began, "if I could get someone to go with me, to show me the trails. I'm not familiar with the country west of here."

"Perhaps you can find someone from one of the villages on your way west," Ena suggested.

"It sure would be helpful if I could get some young warrior, maybe, from here," Egan persisted.

"Not likely," Ena told him.

"Well, I thank you," Egan said, turning.

"Wait," Ah-wa-o said, coming to stand beside Ena. "You will have no problem finding the way. Just follow the setting sun. When you strike the Tennessee, you will be at the start of the northward section of the river."

"Thank you, ma'am," Egan said, surprising himself by calling an Indian girl "ma'am."

"When you meet our sachems, Renno and Rusog, and the men from our villages," Ah-wa-o continued, "there will be a young warrior, fair of skin, with them. His name is El-i-chi. Tell El-i-chi that I, Ah-wa-o, send my greetings."

"I'll do that, ma'am," Egan promised.

"Most likely he'll try to shoot El-i-chi in the back," Ena said after Kirk had walked away.

"He doesn't seem to be a cold-blooded killer," Ah-wa-o protested.

"Five unarmed chiefs stood calmly as he chopped them to pieces with his tomahawk," Ena said.

Ah-wa-o stayed until the twins had received their evening bathing and feeding, then enjoyed a cup of hot tea with Ena after the toddlers were asleep. When she left the lodge, it was dark, with only the stars to give a soft, muted light. She became aware immediately that someone was standing in the shadows near Ena's lodge, and for a moment she debated whether or not to go back inside. Then she heard a soft hiss, and her name, mispronounced slightly. She walked toward the shadow, and Egan Kirk greeted her.

"I didn't mean to scare you," he apologized.

"Nor did you," Ah-wa-o said icily.

"I needed to talk with you more, ma'am. You see, I've traveled a lot up north of here, around my homeplace, but to tell the truth I'm not the finest wilderness hand you've ever seen. I always traveled with my father, 'cause on a cloudy day I tend to lose my sense of direction. I was wondering, ma'am, if you might know a Seneca who would be willing to go along with me. I can't pay much, but I'd sure be grateful."

"I don't think I can help you," Ah-wa-o said.

"Well, that's too bad, because I understand that there are only four men from your villages going after those killers, and there's maybe sixteen or so of them. Me and a good Seneca warrior might just be able to give those men a bit of help."

Ah-wa-o had to admit that his words made sense. It frightened her to think of El-i-chi and the others facing such odds. "Let me think about it, Mr. Kirk."

"I want to leave in the morning."

"If someone has not come to your camp at first light, then I have been unable to help you," she said.

Ah-wa-o knew that what she was thinking would be considered outrageous by her father and by Toshabe, but the strain of knowing that El-i-chi had been wounded—and not knowing how seriously—was making it difficult for her to sleep or to think of anything else. She knew that Renno, Rusog, and Se-quo-i would continue their pursuit of the renegades, whether or not El-i-chi was alive. Renno would, she knew, be even more diligent in his quest for revenge if, the manitous forbid, his brother had died of the blow to his head. Either way it could be weeks, *months*, before she knew, and the uncertainty was somehow more terrible than sure knowledge would have been.

Ena had just fallen asleep when she heard a sound at the door. She waited, her hand closing on the haft of a tomahawk, as the door opened slowly. She recognized the silhouette of Ah-wa-o against the background of starlit night.

"Don't ever do that," Ena said harshly. "Don't *ever* sneak into someone's lodge at night! You might have a blade buried in your skull before you have a chance to identify yourself."

"I'm sorry," Ah-wa-o said. "I didn't want anyone to know I'm here."

Ena rose, pulled on skirt and tunic, and lit an oil lamp. She saw that Ah-wa-o was carrying a travel pack.

"I see we have some talking to do." Ena looked grim.

"You're the only one who might understand," Ah-wa-o said.

"I will not allow you to go off into the forest with that murderer."

Ah-wa-o was momentarily silenced. She took a deep breath, then slowly blew it out. "Then I will go alone and try to catch up with them by following the river."

"You will do no such thing. You will go back to my mother's longhouse, and you will go to bed, without waking Toshabe or Ha-ace, and you will wait until the men return."

"Ena," Ah-wa-o croaked, near tears. "You, of all people, should understand."

"My brother El-i-chi is not dead," Ena said. "He will come back. You, too, are his sister, little Rose, and I beg you not to build your expectations too high, for I know my brother. He is the shaman, a healer, brother of the sachem. If the matrons refuse to give him permission to marry you, then he will not marry you. Prevent a broken heart by controlling your emotions."

"It is far too late for that," Ah-wa-o replied. She turned toward the door and straightened her back. "I'm sorry I awoke you."

"Hold," Ena ordered, moving to seize Ah-wa-o's arm. "Perhaps you'd best stay here with me, after all. It will be dawn soon."

"No, I'll go home."

"Will you?" Ena looked into the younger girl's eyes and

saw a determination that answered her question. "I see."
She sighed. "If I should stop you tonight, you would sneak
away at the first opportunity."

"Yes," Ah-wa-o answered. "Ena, this Egan Kirk seems to
be a decent sort. I know he killed Old Tassel in cold blood,
but he was mourning the death of his entire family. I don't
think he's a mean killer."

"Only of Indians," Ena fumed. "I have met his type
before. John Sevier was like him. To such men the only
good Indian is a dead Indian."

"He needs someone to guide him—"

"Ha! How many times have *you* traveled the lands
between here and the Tennessee?"

"I don't lose my sense of direction on a cloudy day."

"Yes, yes," Ena said impatiently. "I don't doubt that you
could lead this man to the river." She turned and paced.
She, too, wondered about El-i-chi, and if it had not been for
the twins, she herself would have gone with Rusog and
Renno.

"I have traveled to the sea at Wilmington," Ah-wa-o put
in. "I can snare game and find water and choose the easiest
trails. I had two good teachers—your brothers."

"*Our* brothers," Ena said. She paced some more, shaking
her head. "This is insane. They will think we have both
been touched by the manitous."

Ah-wa-o held her breath.

"Your being with El-i-chi in the wilderness, even with
others present, will give the matrons something else to
gossip about," Ena warned. "Any hint of improper behavior
will carry weight with them when they consider El-i-chi's
petition to marry you."

"El-i-chi would never ask me to do anything improper,"
Ah-wa-o said.

"Yes, but others might not know that." Ena was silent for
long minutes as she paced. Then she turned and faced
Ah-wa-o with a smile. "All my life, little sister, I have
fought against those who say 'A woman should not do this.
A woman should not do that.' Whatever the form of your

love for our brother, you are his sister by the laws of the Seneca, and no one can fault you for worrying about him."

"Ena, if you were in my place, you would go, wouldn't you?"

Ena's smile softened. "Yes, I would go, and if my brother should be dead when I found myself reunited with Renno and Rusog, I would bare my blades and help them avenge him."

"Alas, I am not a warrior," Ah-wa-o said, "but I can cook for them, get food for them, and I can keep up with them during the chase."

"And if you reach the Tennessee only to find that Renno and my husband have accomplished the mission somewhere along the river to the south and east, you will be far from home and alone."

"In that case I will retrace my steps," Ah-wa-o said.

Ena nodded. "Come." She checked on the twins, who were sleeping soundly, then led Ah-wa-o to the outskirts of the village. The stars were spectacular in their brilliance, and there was a fresh feeling of the coming day in the air. Ena paused several feet away from where Egan Kirk slept, wrapped in a blanket, next to the embers of a fire. She woke him by calling softly with the voice of a mourning dove and waited until he was alert, musket in hand, before advancing toward him.

The night had begun to fade, and in the cool light of predawn Ena saw that Kirk was puzzled.

"Hear me," Ena said. "Ah-wa-o, my sister, will guide you. Guard her well, white man, and treat her with respect. Should anything happen to her through negligence or willfulness on your part, the forests are not wide enough to keep me from finding you and making your death a thing of legend."

"I had hoped for a warrior," Egan said.

"It is my sister, Ah-wa-o, or no one. She can show you the way, and she will be your spokesman with any Chero-kee or Chickasaw you might encounter—and with my brothers, as well, when you find them."

"Well . . ." Egan began doubtfully.

"Go," Ena said, "and go swiftly." She pulled Ah-wa-o aside and whispered into her ear. "I will stall any pursuit for at least a day. Travel swiftly, little sister, and should Ha-ace follow, meet him alone, lest he kill Kirk without question."

Kirk and Ah-wa-o were under way within minutes, Kirk gathering his pack quickly. Ena went back to her lodge but did not sleep. Shortly after dawn she had a visitor, her nephew, Little Hawk. She met him at the door, her finger to her lips, for the twins were still sleeping.

"Aunt," Little Hawk said, "I have been sent to inquire for Ah-wa-o."

"Go back, Nephew, and tell Ha-ace and my mother that Ah-wa-o has been with me." She did not lie.

"Come and have breakfast with us?" Little Hawk asked.

"Perhaps, if the wild ones awake in time," Ena said.

Ha-ace the Panther was angry. He was not accustomed to awakening to find that his daughter's bed had not been slept in. He knew, or he could reason, that Ah-wa-o was either with An-da or Ena, and in either case that would have been all right had she had the courtesy to inform him that she had intended to spend the night with her friend or her sister.

"I will have a word or two for that one," he said not once but several times before Little Hawk returned, and then again at breakfast.

Toshabe was not concerned. She knew that Ah-wa-o was a level-minded girl, a girl to be trusted. "Yes," she said to her husband, "she should have told you she was spending the night with Ena, but she is young, Ha-ace."

After breakfast, Ha-ace made a round of the village, pausing here and there to speak to fellow warriors, to watch the young ones at play, to admire a new baby. The life of a senior Seneca warrior was not a strenuous one in times of peace. Hunting did not occupy all of his time, and the fields were the domain of the women. Ha-ace's function was to share his wisdom with younger warriors and on occasion to take part in their training and to join the tribe's pine trees—respected elders and senior warriors—in council from time to time. In Renno's absence he was the unofficial sachem of the tribe.

The fine summer morning passed swiftly for Ha-ace, so he thought no more of his errant daughter until it was time for the midday meal.

"She has not yet returned?" he asked as he entered the longhouse to find only Toshabe and the two children.

"Ena sent word that they are taking the twins to the stream this afternoon," Toshabe said.

Thus it was just before the evening meal, with darkness approaching, that Ha-ace at last decided that it was time to bring his daughter to account.

"Will the food wait for a few minutes?" he asked Toshabe.

"I will keep it warm," she said, knowing without asking where he was going, and nodding in approval. Ah-wa-o was indeed being inconsiderate and needed to be reminded of the responsibilities of a daughter.

Toshabe served Little Hawk and Renna their food. She herself would wait to eat with Ha-ace and Ah-wa-o. It was only a few minutes before Ha-ace appeared in the door, panting from running. Without speaking he went to the end of the longhouse where his weapons were hung and began to prepare himself for a march.

"Will you tell me?" Toshabe asked as he faced her, musket in hand, pouches, bow, and tomahawk in place.

"She marches west with the white man!" Ha-ace exploded, his face grim.

Toshabe could not find words for a moment.

"Ena knew," he continued, as if he could not believe his own words. "She agreed with my daughter to deceive me, to let my daughter go into the forests with a white murderer."

"It is not because of the white man that she went," Toshabe said.

"What am I to think?" Ha-ace asked. "She is alone with a white man in the forest. Has she no thought for the honor of her father?"

Ena had entered with the twins just in time to hear this last question. "I do not doubt the honor of my sister, and if the honor of Ah-wa-o is pure, how can that sully the honor of her father?"

"You!" Ha-ace shouted. "You have disappointed me greatly, daughter of my wife."

"And you disappoint me, husband of my mother," Ena shot back, "when you doubt Ah-wa-o. I have told you that she goes because our brother is wounded, and for no other reason."

Toshabe put herself between her daughter and her husband. "In all the years of my life there have been no angry and bitter words between members of my family in my longhouse," she said quietly, scooping Ho-ya from Ena's arm. "There will be none now. We will speak quietly and reasonably of this matter and come to a conclusion, as we have always discussed matters of importance in this house."

"Forgive me for speaking harshly to you, Ha-ace," Ena said. "Hear me. Your daughter came to me for advice. If you are to blame anyone for what she is doing, blame me, for I told her that if it were not for the fact that my two young ones need the milk from my breasts, I would be with her, going to the aid of our brothers." She turned to face Toshabe. "But perhaps, Mother, all the blame is not mine, for Ah-wa-o's fears and uncertainties have a source other than the fact that we don't know how seriously El-i-chi is hurt."

"As the daughter of a Seneca sachem you are entitled to sit with the council of matrons," Toshabe said. "That is the place to state your opinions in the matter to which you refer."

"How long must the lovers wait?" Ena asked.

"We *were* considering the fact that my daughter has run away into the forests with a white man," Ha-ace said. "There has already been enough talk of it. I will go and fetch her back."

"You will have to run very fast," Ena said, "for she expects you to do just that and is, I suspect, moving very swiftly and covering her trail carefully."

"I will never understand women."

"It is very simple," Ena told him. "Ah-wa-o loves El-i-chi. She has not done and will not do anything improper, but the word of his being wounded, coming on top of the uncertainty regarding whether or not the old women will allow her to marry El-i-chi—"

"To be called old is not an insult," Toshabe said stiffly, her tone belying her words.

"—made it absolutely necessary for her to do something. I, myself, take the responsibility for her safety with the white man, Ha-ace."

Toshabe was beginning to look at the matter in a different light. Ena had obviously devoted considerable thought to the situation before, in effect, giving Ah-wa-o permission to go. Toshabe knew her daughter to be one of the most intelligent persons she had ever known, especially in a crisis. If Ena had felt it desirable—or necessary—for Ah-wa-o to go, then perhaps it was so. "It is natural for a sister to concern herself for her brother," Toshabe allowed.

"Now you both confuse me," Ha-ace grumbled. "Ena seems to be saying, 'Let her go.' Do you now say the same, Toshabe?"

"I'm thinking," Toshabe said. "True, you can go after her, and in spite of what Ena says, I think you can overtake her and bring her back. Suppose you do? What if something has happened or does happen to El-i-chi?" She looked at Ena. "I know that they share love. I would gladly have her as the wife of my son. But I think it is highly unlikely that the council of clan matrons will give tribal blessing to such a union. Thus, I am certain that Ah-wa-o faces disappointment and heartbreak. Love is such a strong force in the young! Let her spend some of that force, Ha-ace, in this quest of hers. Let her go to El-i-chi this one last time as a lover, and then, perhaps in the future, she can reconcile herself to being his sister."

"Perhaps she will not find them," Ena said. "The land is wide, the distances great. Perhaps Renno and Rusog will return to us, their mission completed, before Kirk and Ah-wa-o can reach the Tennessee. If so, there is still no harm done, for Ah-wa-o is capable of making her own way home, if necessary."

Ha-ace looked undecided.

"They travel through Cherokee lands," Ena said. "They will not even be in Chickasaw lands until they near the river."

"If any harm comes to her because of the white man . . ." Ha-ace vowed, leaving the threat unfinished but perfectly understood.

After two days of hard travel Egan had learned new respect for the delicate-looking Ah-wa-o. She set a pace that pushed him to the limit. The first night she had insisted on a cold camp, and there had been nothing to eat but jerky and a couple of nut balls. On the evening of the second day, Ah-wa-o halted on the edge of a grassy glade and told Egan to wait. She went into the glade, disappeared among the grass as she lowered herself to the ground, and came out ten minutes later with a rabbit, which she had stunned with an accurately thrown rock. That night they enjoyed a fire and hot food.

There was little talk between them for a long time as they traveled west. Ah-wa-o did the cooking without comment, and Egan collected wood for the fire and, on the third day, killed a turkey for the evening meal. Not wanting to waste time, Ah-wa-o led them around the occasional Cherokee settlement.

There came a day of low clouds and light rain that occasionally thickened into a downpour, the kind of day that worried Egan when he was alone in the wilderness. No sun filtered through the heavy clouds, but Ah-wa-o seemed not to be concerned, leading him onward even through the worst of the rain. When early darkness forced them to halt, it was still raining. Egan found an outcrop of rock that made a shallow cave. It was dry under the overhang and pleasant to sit near the fire as their clothing dried.

"I guess we're not being followed," Egan ventured.

"Ena saw to it that we were not," Ah-wa-o said.

After a while Egan asked, "Are all Indian woman like you and this Ena?"

"I do not know all Indian women," she answered, not intending to be rude but simply stating a fact.

"I mean, can any of you find your way in the wilderness?"

"I'd think so."

"Well, it is your world," he said.

"Yes, it is."

Egan was moodily silent, thinking of his dead Mary. Of late he had begun to blame himself for her death, for she, unlike this Indian girl, had not been a part of this wilderness world of savages and sudden death. His wife had gently expressed a wish to leave the frontier, to live in a town where she could go to church on Sunday and have neighbors and schools. At the time he'd laughed indulgently and asked her whatever would he do to make a living in a town. Now, if he had it to do over, he would take her to a town and shine boots for a living or shovel horse manure in the stables.

Ah-wa-o had prepared her bed—nothing but a blanket, and yet she was, Egan saw, already asleep. Mary could never have done that. If she'd had to sleep on a blanket on the hard ground in damp clothing, she would not have complained, but her discomfort would have been evident, and she would probably have come down with a fever. It was, he felt, an odd world that was inhabited by the Indian—a world with few comforts. He did not quite understand why the Indian would continue to fight to protect so little.

The white settler had little enough: a log house, maybe a few sticks of furniture carried west with great difficulty and often becoming battered in the process. But at least the settler had a goal. If he could clear enough land and plant enough crops, he could sell his produce and use the money to buy a—what? Egan looked around. The rain had abated somewhat and now fell on the forest floor as lightly as a blessing. A fresh, clean scent permeated the air, as if the rain had washed the world. He was startled by his own thoughts, for what *would* the settler buy with the money that he'd earned by his own labor and sweat? More furniture? The Indian needed no furniture. He made his

bed and his shelter from natural materials, so easily replaced that he was not tied to one spot as was the settler.
With only the weapons he could make himself—a bow, a
war club, a stone ax—the Indian had lived well for un-
counted aeons; and even now he needed little. A steel
blade or two, a cooking pot, and a musket were all that the
Indian wanted of the white man's civilization.

"Ah-wa-o," Egan asked the next morning as they started
their day's travel, "if the white man had come to the lands
of the Indians to live as an Indian, what would have
happened?"

"I don't understand the question."

"What if the first white men had not built homes of stone
and wood, had not started cutting down the trees to plant
their crops, but had adapted to the ways of the Indian?"

"Then, I suppose, the white man would have become just
another tribe. But that is not the problem with the white
man. It is the sheer numbers that make for conflict. White
women bear their young as often as rabbits—or so it
seems—and breed a sea of white faces that continually push
toward the Indian lands. And there is a basic difference in
the way the Indian and the white man look at the land. How
can you own the land?" She lifted an arm and indicated the
view. They had climbed a ridge, and from a relatively clear
spot they could see for miles over the top of the unbroken
forest that extended toward the next ridge.

"It was here before us," she went on, "and it will be here
after us. How can anyone own it, when it will outlast any
man living?"

"Well, you can own it for your lifetime and pass it along
to your children," Egan suggested.

"What gives you the right to pass it along to any one
particular child?" she asked. "It will be here for all children."

Egan laughed. "Well, I can't answer your questions,
Ah-wa-o. I guess it'd take someone smarter than me to
explain what it means to a settler to have a piece of land he
can call his own, a place to put down roots." He shaded his
eyes and looked in a full circle and saw nothing but green
and rolling ridges. "But my God, doesn't it seem that

there's enough of it for everyone? Why do we have to fight over it when there's so much? My Mary and my little son died for just a few acres, and there's so much of it."

Ah-wa-o looked at Egan with slitted eyes. This was the man who had killed Old Tassel. He represented the worst of the white race, the type who valued an Indian life no more than that of a snake or a rodent. And yet he had been very considerate of her during the journey thus far, and the pain of loss was very evident in his eyes. She shrugged mentally. Some things about human nature baffled her. "See that shape atop the next ridge," she said, "the point that reaches for the sky? That is our next landmark."

Kirk made no move to get under way again. "I've been thinking, Ah-wa-o. I'm wondering if we're not on some kind of wild-goose chase. When I talked about coming cross-country to head off the flatboat, it sounded so simple. But we've been traveling for days now and have more days to travel, and meanwhile anything could have happened. Your sachems could have caught up with the renegades. The renegades could have decided to leave the flatboat and strike out in any direction."

"No," Ah-wa-o said, "they would not leave the river once they were in Creek and then Chickasaw lands. The first Creek or Chickasaw hunting party that came along would take their loot and their female captives. Once they chose to float downriver into Creek lands, they were committed to go all the way to the Mississippi, where they can sell their captives to the Spanish. It is possible that Renno and the others caught up with them along the river, but remember this: They, too, will be moving through enemy lands as long as they are in Creek country, and they will have to travel cautiously even in Chickasaw lands. Although there is peace between Chickasaw and Cherokee, it is not good to cross another's land without permission."

"You think we should press on, then. . . ." Egan said unsurely.

"I estimate that we are more than halfway there," she answered. "A few more days, and we will be at the river and can inquire of the Chickasaw who live along the river if the flatboat has passed."

For three days El-i-chi's eagerness to travel was not matched by his endurance. He was no stranger to injury, but he had never experienced such persistent and debilitating pain as the headaches that blurred his vision and made his stomach uneasy. Renno, concerned for his brother, called off the march when it became evident that El-i-chi was moving forward on courage alone and was in great pain.

El-i-chi slept about twenty hours out of twenty-four, waking only now and then, often in the middle of the night. During his waking moments he tried to communicate with the manitous, especially with the spirit of Casno, his mentor. He was the tribe's shaman, a healer, and yet he could not heal himself. When he awakened in the night, he noted that either Renno or Mandy was awake, sitting near him.

"Is this a death watch you've mounted over me?" he asked Renno after awakening at that dim, chill, lonely time that comes a couple of hours before dawn.

"My brother speaks nonsense," Renno said lightly. "We watch to be sure that you, in your eagerness, do not leave us behind."

There came a time when El-i-chi was no longer sleepy, and after a night during which he slept little, he was the first one awake. He kindled the fire and spitted half-cooked meat from the previous night's kill so that the others were roused by the smell of cooking meat.

Renno was greatly encouraged to see El-i-chi eating with gusto, tearing at the meat like a hungry wolf. And for several hours, as they moved downriver, El-i-chi was able to keep pace well. He tired early in the afternoon, however, and Renno called a halt.

"You must go on without me," El-i-chi said in disgust.

"And leave you to be scalped by the first wandering Creek?" Rusog asked. "I wouldn't be able to face Ena and your mother after that."

"There is time," Se-quo-i said. "When the barge reaches the shoals, it will take days to move its cargo, then the parts of the boat itself, past the obstructions to clear water."

"If we don't catch them there," El-i-chi pointed out, "it will be a long chase to the Ohio and the Mississippi."

"Have you other things of importance to do?" Renno asked with a grin.

"I had hoped to become a married man before my hair turns white," El-i-chi answered. "Other than that—"

Day by day El-i-chi's strength returned. Day by day Se-quo-i became more certain that they would catch the renegades at Muscle Shoals. Then, as the Cherokee scholar was taking his turn at leading the main party, he almost lost his scalp by stumbling into the camp of a Creek hunting party. Only the preoccupation of the Creek with dressing a young male deer and their good-natured quarrel over the choice internal organs saved Se-quo-i, for he walked clear of the trees and stood, shocked, for long seconds as he watched the hunters squabble over the deer's liver. There were seven warriors, all in their prime. Slowly, slowly, he backed into the shelter of the trees and then ran silently to warn his companions.

"Seven of them?" El-i-chi asked. "My arms have been long without healthful exercise. Shall I go with Se-quo-i and clear the way of Creek?"

"We seek no war with them," Renno said. "We are not here to count coup or collect scalps—at least not the scalps of warriors who are hunting in their own lands."

To circle around the hunting party took time and care. Now Se-quo-i joined El-i-chi in fretting, for many days had passed since the flatboat disappeared downriver. Even working slowly the renegades could have portaged the flatboat and its contents to the clear water and would, by now, be making good time downriver.

The matter was complicated when members of the Creek hunting party crossed their trail by accident and began to follow.

"There are three of them," Rusog reported, coming back from a quick look at their backtrack. "Moving swiftly. We can run or stand, but if we run, we'll rouse their suspicions even more."

"So," Renno said. "You and I, Rusog."

"And I," El-i-chi volunteered.

"You and Se-quo-i and Mandy go to the river directly and make your camp there. No fire until well after dark. By that time the way will be cleared." Renno's voice was grim. He had not wanted to battle the Creek. The manitous, however, often willed odd things, and it seemed that an encounter was inevitable.

He would, he explained to Rusog, give the Creek a chance to allow his party to pass through their lands in peace. So it was that the leading Creek warrior, bent to read the signs, was within a few yards of Renno and Rusog before he lifted his face and halted in his tracks. He barked a startled cry, and his two companions, not far behind, raced forward to join him.

"We ask peace," Renno said, his right hand raised. "It is true we come into your lands without permission, but we claim the permission of the manitous, for we are on a mission to avenge crimes committed by some of our own people who flee down the river."

"There will be no need for you to continue," one of the Creek said, "for any invaders of our land will be punished by the Creek."

"Still, we ask your permission," Renno said.

"We give permission for you to leave as you came, and swiftly," the tall Creek said, reaching for his tomahawk to give force to his words.

"I am sorry," Renno replied, "but we cannot do that. We must continue our journey. We ask once again, in the spirit of peace, for your permission."

The tall Creek gave a whoop as a signal to his fellows, and the three leaped to the attack.

A grim smile stretched Rusog's lips. "These are foolish ones, Brother," he said, raising his tomahawk. It was not arrogant pride on Rusog's part—just sure knowledge that no three Creek, nor twice that number, were a match for Renno and Rusog.

"Two are mine, Brother," Renno said, dodging the attack of the tallest Creek easily and ending that warrior's life with an underhand blow that split the man's chin and smashed upward into the nasal cavities.

"You'll have to hurry," Rusog said, sending one Creek crashing to the ground limply. He pivoted quickly. The surviving Creek now faced two warriors. To his great credit, and the admiration of both Renno and Rusog, he first sang a brief song of death, a song that lasted no more than fifteen seconds, and then, with a mighty whoop, leaped to meet two tomahawks, one that took him high, under the chin, and the other in the pit of his stomach.

Chapter VI

Rusog knelt beside a fallen Creek, his knife in his hand. He lifted the dead man's head by his hair and then, with a sigh, let it rest. Renno understood. Both men had taken their share of scalps, and neither felt the need to add to his total. They knew who they were, were confident of their strength, and needed no artificial reassurance in the form of scalps to prove their manhood.

"So it has begun," Rusog said somberly as he rose.

Renno nodded. Words did not fly like swarming mayflies between him and his brother-by-marriage, but over the years they had built an understanding that did not require words to express emotions. Three brave Creek had died, and now others must die. Somewhere near here were four more Creek warriors in the hunting party, who, if allowed to live, would find the dead. And before seeking revenge they would get word to the nearest village that deadly intruders were in Creek lands. Renno and Rusog could not afford to have a good portion of the Creek Nation seeking them.

It was a bit odd for Rusog to try to put his feelings into words. "Why, Brother," he asked, speaking in a low voice, not looking at Renno, "did not the Master of Life send a Degandawida to all of the tribes?"

Renno had no immediate answer. Rusog had made a reference to the great man who had first dreamed of the League of the Ho-de-no-sau-nee and of the Great Peace that had ended warfare among the five tribes of the Iroquois. Rusog met his eye, as if expecting an answer.

"It is unfortunate that He did not," Renno said, "for we of common ancestry are brothers."

"And if we had been one people," Rusog said, "the white man would never have—" He paused, then laughed self-consciously. "Dangerous thoughts, eh? Foolish thoughts."

"No," Renno responded.

Rusog sighed. "I think they would have their camp near the river."

Renno nodded.

The four Creek had indeed made their camp near the river in a pleasant, grassy, open glade that sloped to the water. They were in their own territory, members of a great tribe, and they were confident. Their fire was burning well, and a forequarter of a young deer was broadcasting a delicious aroma as it sizzled over the flames. One man sat with his back against a tree, repairing the guiding feathers on an arrow. The other three lay on the ground, sunning.

Renno, thinking that it had to be done quickly, reached for his longbow. Rusog put his hand on Renno's arm and whispered, "They deserve to see the faces of those who will send them to the spirits."

"So," Renno agreed.

Two warriors stood, tall and silent, tomahawks in hand. It was a full minute before the Creek finished the repair to his arrow and looked up. His face went slack, and then, with a startled whoop, he dropped the arrow, leaped to his feet, and reached for his own blade. The other three reacted as well.

"We greet you, Creek," Rusog said, "and salute you as we send you to your ancestors."

"The Cherokee dog has a tongue," a Creek said, motioning to his fellows to begin an encircling movement.

"And teeth," Rusog added with a dangerous smile.

It was as spirited a fight as Renno had ever encountered. Creek warriors had been fighting for decades against the white men, the Chickasaw, and anyone else they found in their hunting grounds. The four who faced the two brothers were skilled and brave. Renno stood back-to-back with Rusog and met the first onslaught of the two warriors who faced him, blocking one tentative blow and feinting to check the reflexes of his opponents. In his left hand the Spanish stiletto gleamed in the late-afternoon sun. In his right hand his tomahawk made a swishing sound as he tried for a killing blow, only to have to abort the effort and block for defense.

Rusog drew first blood, killing a Creek neatly with a slicing blow aimed to cut jugular and windpipe without striking bone, and shortly afterward Renno disabled a warrior by cutting both tendons behind the right knee as the Creek whirled to escape a feint to his stomach. The odds were even now.

The warrior facing Renno was as good with the blade as any man he had ever faced. Time and again blows were launched and blocked with almost equal skill by the Seneca and his opponent. For a moment they stood only feet apart, eyes locked, both breathing hard from exertion. Behind him Renno heard the sound of blade striking bone, then a moan, and he turned his head quickly to see Rusog standing over the second of his opponents.

The Creek who now had one useless leg was trying to stand. Rusog, seeing that Renno had things in hand, moved toward the crippled man and said, "May the spirits welcome you," then ended the man's life with a blow to the neck.

"Who faces me?" the Creek asked Renno.

"Renno, of the Seneca."

"I know you not, nor do I know why a Seneca would be here, so far from his hunting grounds."

"No matter," Renno said. "I grieve for your death, Brother."

"Perhaps it will be *my* grief, not yours." The Creek leaped to the attack.

Steel rang on steel once, twice, and then, with a grunt of effort, the Creek put all his strength behind a blow aimed to force Renno's blocking tomahawk aside, leaving the follow-through to bury the blade in Renno's chest. Renno slipped a half step to one side, then surged forward, his left hand driving the stiletto up and deep into the chest cavity under the Creek's ribs. The Creek's tomahawk whistled past Renno's chest and fell to the ground from a limp hand, and it was over.

They hid the bodies in a ravine, covering them with brush and leaves. Scavengers would find them, and the smell of decay would soon alert any passing hunting party, but by that time Renno and the others would be well out of the area.

Both Renno and Rusog were subdued as they moved silently downriver. Soon they spotted the camp where El-i-chi, Se-quo-i, and Mandy waited. Rusog, always practical, had taken the forequarter of venison from the Creek camp, reasoning that dead men would have no use for it. It was still warm when they arrived in the camp and required only a few minutes' cooking to complete the job.

Now the character of the river changed, and El-i-chi, showing no signs of the easy fatigue that had plagued him since the fight aboard the barge, led the way at a warrior's pace. At the first obstruction there were definite signs of hard work but no sign of flatboat or renegade. As El-i-chi and Se-quo-i had feared, the various delays had given Atarho and his men time to portage the boat and its cargo past the shoals. There was plentiful evidence in the form of discarded items, such as an iron-bladed plow, that the task of portaging the vessel had not been completed easily.

Renno looked around, disgusted. He had no map, except in his mind. The river was now running westerly toward Chickasaw territory. The northern turn, which would take the river far north to join the Ohio near the Kentucky border, was days of travel away.

"I think we have a long trip ahead of us," Se-quo-i observed.

"There are other rapids that will slow them," Rusog said.

"But in between the rapids the water runs swiftly," El-i-chi said.

"Then we, too, must move swiftly," Se-quo-i said. He looked at Mandy with some doubt. "Now it is necessary to move at the warrior's pace. I hope you will be able to keep up."

That concern was in Renno's mind, too, as they set off downriver, making their way past some impressive white-water rapids. Renno was in the lead, with the shoals behind them, when he saw signs indicating the nearness of a Creek village. He halted the main party and, El-i-chi at his side, moved silently forward. It was late in the day, and the village was settling down for the time of the evening meal. All the hunters who were going to return had done so. The young ones had come in from their play and were gathered in small groups in the spaces between the Creek lodges. Women were singing over cook fires.

"We will have to circle far from the river to pass," El-i-chi said.

"Perhaps not," Renno replied. He led the way to the river's edge and moved along the bank, out of sight of the village. He found what he was looking for on a sandy bank—a dozen canoes pulled from the water. There was no sign of a guard. In the manner of the four warriors who had met their death farther up the river, those in the village felt secure in the heart of their own lands.

Renno motioned, and El-i-chi led the way back up the river. "We wait for darkness," Renno told their companions. "And then we will have a rest from running."

A waxing moon rose not long after darkness to give a silver sheen to the river and forest. The village sounds diminished with the passing hours, and soon the feel of midnight was in the air. The only sound from the village was the idle barking of a dog. Walking was easy and silent along the sandy brink of the river. Renno selected two canoes, which were soon afloat. El-i-chi and Se-quo-i were assigned to one. Mandy sat between Rusog and Renno in the other.

The dark masses of the canoes were clearly visible on the moonlit water as they were paddled out into the current and turned downstream. But no alarm was sounded, and soon the village was left behind.

El-i-chi, at the front of the lead canoe, had little to do. Se-quo-i steered the canoe easily with a trailing paddle, keeping to the center of the river. Gradually the dark shores began to rise and show rocky cliffs. The water was moving faster. "Easy," El-i-chi warned over his shoulder, using his paddle to try to slow the canoe. They allowed Renno's boat to come alongside. For some minutes El-i-chi had noted that a soft, rushing sound had been growing louder.

"I don't like this at all," El-i-chi said. "There's whitewater rapids ahead."

"And Creek behind who will miss their canoes at dawn," Renno said.

"So we face the rapids in the dark?" El-i-chi wanted to know.

"If the flatboat could navigate them, they can't be too bad," Se-quo-i suggested.

"I would rather face the Creek Nation," El-i-chi said, thinking of dark, cold waters that would begin to froth as they tumbled over rock.

"Stay behind me," Renno said, stroking with his paddle to pass El-i-chi's canoe.

The white water gleamed in the moonlight, allowing Renno and Rusog to steer the canoe to the deepest runs, and even then it was a thrilling ride as the small boats were lifted, twisted, and tossed by the force of the current. Now

and again Renno cast a look over his shoulder to see his
brother fighting the water with his paddle, his back bent,
body straining with the effort. And then they were past the
last, surging, twisting constriction of the river's flow and
into quiet waters. Renno knew that there would be other
stretches of white water, but he felt confident now, quite
unlike the way he had felt as he steered his canoe into the
top of the rapids. He would never have admitted it to
El-i-chi—or to anyone—but he, too, would have preferred
to face overwhelming odds in battle than to take that frail
canoe into the unknown, with the roar of cascading waters
sounding in his ears. But with a pounding heart, he had
done and he had won, and now the river could hold no
terror for him.

The same stretch of white water that had tested Renno's
courage had not been a formidable obstacle for the flatboat,
although had Atarho and Simon Purdy been able to see
ahead, they might have hesitated to enter the run. They
had come into the gorge before they could make a decision
to tie up and scout ahead, having drifted silently past the
Creek village in the night. Although the barge bounced and
soared, there was only one time when the hull glanced off
an exposed, smooth rock, and that without damage.

For days, and especially during the backbreaking work of
moving the flatboat and its cargo past Muscle Shoals, Simon
Purdy had been too busy, and too tired at the end of a day,
to think much about the pleasure that was in store for him
during the long trip downriver to the Ohio. It was enjoy-
able to anticipate it. In fact, the anticipation was so pleasant
that he was in no real hurry to get under way with his plans
to show the four captives what was in store for them. Just as
a colt had to be broken to the reins and the rider, the four
young girls would have to be trained, and it would be his
pleasure to do the job.

The late Colonel Brown had given his daughters pious
names. The eldest, who had turned sixteen during the early
days of the trip west, was Grace, and her physical appear-

ance matched her name. She was willowy and tall, and her hair was like cornsilk. Her movements were naturally smooth, lithe, and ladylike.

Hope, at fifteen, just ten months younger than her older sister, took after the women of her father's side of the family and was cutely plump, weighing twenty pounds more than Grace. Simon Purdy knew that Hope would be valuable, for most men liked women with a bit of meat on their bones.

Charity, fourteen, the youngest of the Brown girls, was a few months older than the bond servant, Tess, but looked younger, for her body had not yet begun to form curves. She was as slim as a boy, her breasts only small knots on her chest. Although a child physically, Charity had weathered the shocks of the days following the murder of her father on the flatboat better than her older sisters.

The four girls had stayed mainly under the canvas shelter while the flatboat was moving, and Purdy had set up a tent for them while the boat was being portaged past the shoals. Always under guard, the girls had, at first, suffered agonies by trying to withhold nature's urges, but eventually necessity had overcome modesty. The stoic Indians who kept watch over them showed no interest in any flashing glimpse of white flesh and, within a few days, all but Grace had become quite accustomed to being watched every minute, even while reaching up under their wet clothes while standing in the river to bathe their body parts.

At first Tess had feared for Grace, for the oldest girl had fainted dead away when Simon Purdy threatened to burn off Judith Brown's hair and had been unconscious when Judith died. Upon regaining consciousness, Grace had been vague, unconcerned, sitting alone under the shelter and lacing her fingers together into patterns while singing hymns in a soft, sweet voice. The sobbing had come later, and it came as a storm, with a violence that frightened the younger girls into crying with her.

The days passed, and nothing more had happened to them. They were fed well from the on-board provisions. None of them had been threatened, but Tess remembered

how Simon Purdy had told her to come with him right after
all the men had been killed. Then her sister had come to
her rescue. Mandy was gone now, and Tess was afraid that
she was dead. No other circumstance would have made
Mandy disappear, for Tess didn't think that Mandy could
have escaped, not even during the fight in the night that
was so frightening and confusing. Mandy might have been
killed during the fight or knocked overboard, but, Tess
believed, her big sister would never have abandoned her.

The barge was moving slowly, the river water wide and
calm and serene. The Indians were at the steering oars.
Simon Purdy came to stand looking down at the four girls.
Tess involuntarily reached to pull her skirt over her ankles.

"It's about time you ladies started earning your keep,"
Purdy announced. "You, Grace. You and your sisters git
over there and cook something."

"Our mother and Mandy did the cooking," Hope said.

"Do as you're told," Purdy ordered, kicking Grace on the
thigh with the toe of his moccasin. All three Brown girls
rose and scurried toward the cooking area. Tess rose and
started to follow. Purdy seized her by the arm. "I didn't tell
you to go."

"I know more about cooking than the others," Tess told
him.

"I think maybe you know more about a lot of things than
the others," Purdy said. "But if you don't, that's fine,
because I'm gonna teach you, and it's lesson time." He
dragged her toward the rear, to the spot where he had
taken Mandy, where they were out of the direct line of view
of the others. When he put his hands on her small, budding
breasts, Tess cried out and tried to pull away.

"Now we got a long way to go," Purdy said, "and I don't
think they's many clothes on this boat. If I have to, girl, I'll
rip 'em off you, and then you can run around naked if'n you
want to, but I think it would be best if you don't fight and
tear up your clothes."

When Tess continued to struggle, he hit her lightly with
his fist, and to his amazement, she went limp. She was only
partially conscious as he undressed her but she was brought

into full awareness by the pain when the unthinkable happened to her.

She was weeping softly when Purdy led her back to the shelter. When Hope Brown came to her, bringing food, she was still whimpering.

"What did he do to you?" Hope whispered.

Tess turned her head away. It was too shameful to put into words.

"Did he . . . did he—"

"Yes!" Tess sobbed.

"Oh, my God! You poor thing! Can I do anything for you?"

Hope's voice was soft and filled with concern, but it grated on Tess's nerves. She turned to look at Hope, wiping her face with the back of her hand. "Oh, you poor thing," Tess mimicked. "Do you think that he's not going to do the same thing to you?"

Hope's face went white. Obviously such a thought was alien to her. Things like that didn't happen to nice girls. To a bond girl, maybe, Tess thought bitterly. To a Brown girl? Never.

It didn't happen to Hope for two more days, for Grace was first, and then Charity. When Purdy came for her, she was screaming, and he had to half carry her.

Thus were the first lessons in Simon Purdy's training school for girls completed.

The flatboat was making excellent time. It had drifted out of Creek lands and into Chickasaw territory. The river had begun its northward turn. Atarho was greatly pleased. From that point on he had heard that the river was readily navigable, so that there would be no more hair-raising rushes down rapids. After some days of pleasant traveling the Tennessee would join the Ohio, and soon after the Ohio, the Mississippi. Then only a few days of drifting would bring them to New Madrid, where the boat and its cargo would earn them good money and the sale of the girls would make them very prosperous.

Atarho was keeping a close eye on Simon Purdy. Purdy

had begun to use the white girls. Atarho didn't care about that, so long as he didn't mark them or hurt them badly enough to damage their value. He was a bit surprised that the other Cherokee warriors had not washed off their war paint so that they, too, might enjoy the charms of the captives, but he was proud of them for not falling to temptation. They were, after all, still in the territory of the Chickasaw, and although there was peace between Cherokee and Chickasaw, that didn't stop the occasional war party from embarking on a coup-counting raid. The Chickasaw would certainly not take kindly to Cherokee renegades drifting downriver on a flatboat as if they owned it. The white girls themselves were the best reason for maintaining an alert watch, for they would be considered prizes by any Chickasaw party that might happen along.

So Atarho was always ready to repel boarders, just in case, and when he directed the barge to be tied up at night he set out sentinels. He had good men; he was confident; and he was counting his money in advance when the flatboat ran directly into the jagged, broken end of an underwater snag and began to sink rapidly. Atarho was too angered by the event to appreciate the irony of it. The boat had crashed its way down some wild rapids only to meet its end where the river was wide and calm.

The accident happened near the western shore. The water was shallow enough so that the deck was still above water, the cargo undamaged. The flatboat would not be going anywhere without being dismantled and lifted from the water for repairs, however, and none of the men had carpentry skills.

Atarho estimated that they were directly east of Chickasaw Bluffs on the Mississippi and thus considerably south of New Madrid. He could strike out overland to the northwest and reach the Mississippi somewhere in the vicinity of New Madrid, but he would be marching through the heart of Chickasaw lands. The chances of getting to the river and then across without losing the girls were slim. There was another choice: He could march brazenly directly to the Chickasaw capital at Chickasaw Bluffs and try to talk his way into river transportation to New Madrid. The more he thought about it, the more it made sense. After all, he had some trade goods in the form of the boat's cargo.

He explained his plan to his men. Purdy spent most of the time giving more lessons to the white girls as Atarho and his men offloaded the cargo of the flatboat and secreted it in a rocky cave. And then they all set out, marching directly west, not trying to hide their trail. When they first encountered a hunting party of Chickasaw braves, Atarho approached the Chickasaw arrogantly and demanded to be given a safe escort to meet with the principal chief, Oklawahpa.

"I have come from the north, from the great chiefs Blue Jacket and Little Turtle, with counsel for our brothers the Chickasaw and with great gifts for Oklawahpa." He didn't care if the warriors mistook the four white girls as the gifts he meant; all he wanted was free passage to the river. Once there he'd find a way to wrangle a boat so that he could go upriver to the Spanish at New Madrid.

Ah-wa-o's sense of direction had brought Egan Kirk and her to the Tennessee just at the point where it began its northward turn. Egan spent a morning moving up and down the river, climbing a tall tree now and then to be able to see to the next bend of the stream. He saw nothing. It was as if they were thousands of miles from the nearest human beings. There were no trails, no sign of passage, and no villages along the river for the three or four miles that they explored that first day after reaching the stream. They made camp. Both were reluctant to talk, each fearing that the flatboat had already passed or that Renno and his group had caught up with it to the south and east.

With the morning they moved north. "We'll find a high place where we can see a long way upriver, make a comfortable camp, and wait for a few days," Egan decided.

Ah-wa-o started toward a high ridge to the north that seemed to run directly alongside the river. The way led through a dense riverside thicket and into a stand of huge oaks and cottonwoods. She wended her way around huge

trunks, pushing aside underbrush. It was hot and still, and
the mosquitoes were hungry. She was uncomfortable and
eager to reach the ridge, climb to where she could feel a
breeze, and make a comfortable camp for some well-earned
rest. Thus preoccupied, she pushed into a tiny clearing and
stood face-to-face with a female black bear who reared on
her hind legs not ten feet away.

"Stop," Ah-wa-o whispered to Egan, behind her.

"Wha? . . ." Egan got no further, for the bear opened
her maw and roared an angry warning.

Ah-wa-o began to back slowly into the underbrush.

"Let me past," Egan said. "I have the musket."

"Back off, slowly," Ah-wa-o whispered.

Something stung Egan's neck painfully. He slapped in
quick reflex action, and a bee was squashed on his hand.
"Darn!"

Ah-wa-o was beginning to get the whole picture. The
bear was standing beside a dead cottonwood. Twenty feet
up the tree there was a black, seething mass—bees . . .
bees by the hundreds . . . bees by the thousands. The
bear was still watching Ah-wa-o carefully, but it was not the
girl, thank the manitous, that had the bear's interest. The
bear's sharp nose smelled honey, and Ah-wa-o knew that as
long as she didn't try to interfere with the bear's quest for
that honey, she would be safe.

It is not wise to crush a bee on one's skin when other bees
are nearby. In dying, the bee releases a scent that infuriates
other bees. Once again Egan was stung on the back of the
neck. He yelped, and the bear roared another warning.

"Move slowly," Ah-wa-o urged. "And be quiet!"

Soon they would be back in the underbrush, leaving the
bear to her honey tree. This strategy would have worked
well had not the bear decided to have a taste of that sweet,
good-smelling stuff in the hollow tree. She reared and with
a massive grunt of effort threw her weight against the tree,
which, long dead and rotted at its base, toppled slowly.

"Watch out!" Egan yelled as the tree seemed to fall
directly toward them. He leaped to one side, pulling
Ah-wa-o with him. His feet became tangled, and both he

and the girl went down. The tree crashed within three feet of them, and the swarming bees, having had their hive destroyed, soon found soft flesh.

Ah-wa-o could face a bear and had been taught from childhood to be calm in the face of danger, to be tolerant of pain, and to be stoically brave under all circumstances. Nothing in her training, however, had prepared her for being stung repeatedly by angry bees. She did not scream, but she was letting out little moans and yelps, sounds that were almost like those coming from Egan, as she scrambled to her hands and knees and plowed through the brush toward the river. When she could, she got to her feet and ran, with Egan right behind her, both fighting bees with their hands, both yelping as the bees struck time and again.

It seemed to be ages before she broke through the last barrier of riverside brush, her face and arms scratched by limbs in addition to being stung by bees. Ahead of her was the water, and she flew toward it at top speed, strong thighs exposed by her short skirt. She splashed into the water, crawled forward as she fell, then submerged herself. She came up spitting water and fighting persistent bees. Egan was nearby, making great splashes. She submerged again and swam underwater. When she came up there were no bees, but there was an odd sound. At first she couldn't identify it, and then she saw a buckskin-clad man standing a little way downriver. He was bent double with laughter.

"It would not be so funny if it was *you* with bee stings!" Ah-wa-o yelled indignantly.

And then the man, his face still contorted with laughter, stood straight.

"Renno!" Ah-wa-o called. "Oh, thank the manitous!"

The white Indian had happened upon the trail of a man and woman a mile or so back, and he had been nearby to hear the warning roar of the female bear and to see the headlong rush to the water to escape the bees. He had never met Egan Kirk and so could not recognize him, and he didn't recognize Ah-wa-o, mainly because her appearance was so totally unexpected, until she called his name. He waited on the bank as she waded toward him. He kept one eye on the white man, who was still swatting at a few bees.

"Ah-wa-o," he said. "*Ska-noh.*"

"*Do-ges,*" she answered, and then, in the next breath, "El-i-chi?"

Renno smiled. "All the noise that you and your friend have made should have him here any minute."

She threw herself into Renno's arms and squeezed him, saying, "Oh, my brother."

"Who is your companion?" Renno asked as Egan Kirk, having discouraged the bees with splashed water, came wading toward the bank.

"He came to help, Renno," Ah-wa-o said. "His family was killed by the same renegades you seek."

"And the others?" Renno asked, assuming that Ah-wa-o and the white man had not come alone.

"Just the two of us. Renno, we heard from Se-quo-i that El-i-chi was badly wounded. I had to know."

"And so you will," Renno said, for he had heard the sound of a barking fox, which told him that El-i-chi was near. He lifted his head and cried out in a strong voice. "Come out, little brother. I have a surprise for you."

"Oh, how I must look," Ah-wa-o said, fingers exploring the swelling bee stings on her face and neck.

"You will be as sweet in his eyes as the honey was to the bear," Renno consoled.

El-i-chi strolled out of the forest onto the sand of the river's bank, halted in stunned surprise, for he recognized the shape of her without even seeing her face, and then he was pounding up the sands to sweep her into his arms. Renno turned away to examine the face of the white man, whom El-i-chi did not even notice.

"We've been looking for you," Egan said.

"We will have to talk later about how my sister came to be alone with you in the forest," Renno said. "For now, your name."

"Egan Kirk." He held eye contact with Renno, waiting for reaction.

"So." Renno's blue eyes turned cold.

"I have a stake in this, Sachem," Egan explained. "Slim Tom killed my family."

"You have come far," Renno acknowledged. "I suggest that you gather some river mud and spread it on your stings."

El-i-chi, after a devouring kiss and a hug that drove the breath from Ah-wa-o's lungs, had seen her condition, and even as Renno gave Egan advice, El-i-chi was gathering mud and caking it on Ah-wa-o's face, neck, arms, and legs. Ah-wa-o began to sob. "It is not enough that you see me with my face all swollen, now I am to be covered in mud."

In spite of himself, El-i-chi laughed. She lashed out at him, her fist bouncing off the top of his shoulder. "First you worry me so, and now you cover me with mud."

El-i-chi's laughter was contagious. Renno, remembering the mad dash that he had witnessed, began to describe it to his brother, and soon the two warriors were rolling shamelessly on the sand, laughing so hard that they could not speak. Ah-wa-o, weeping and calling them brutes, animals, and louts, was dancing between them, kicking at them with her wet moccasins and flailing them with her fists until, at last, weak from laughter, El-i-chi rose, lifted her, and carried her off into the trees for a few moments of privacy.

At the camp, Rusog did not accept Egan's presence as calmly as had Renno. Rusog's square, dark face went sour as he heard Kirk's name, and his hand closed involuntarily over the handle of his tomahawk. "Have you come to murder more unarmed men?"

"I have come to murder those who killed my family," Kirk said.

Rusog turned to face Renno. "I know not what you and the others may say, but I will not march with this murderer."

"So," Renno acknowledged.

Just then El-i-chi and Ah-wa-o emerged from out of the trees. El-i-chi's face was red, flushed from Ah-wa-o's fierce kisses. Mandy and Se-quo-i went to greet them, while Rusog, without further words, walked swiftly to the north and disappeared. After Renno explained Rusog's behavior to El-i-chi and Se-quo-i, El-i-chi glared at Kirk, measuring him in a way that made Egan nervous.

"We have not heard the white man's side of it," Se-quo-i pointed out.

"I do not deny it," Egan said. "I have no way to defend my actions. I had seen my wife dead, her scalp gone, her body mutilated. I buried my boy in two pieces, and his head had been burned to nothing more than a skull. I am sorry for what I did. I know now that I killed innocent men, and I want to atone for that, in part, by killing those who are guilty."

It was, Renno admitted to himself, a touchy situation. Before he had time to think about it, he heard an urgent whistle from Rusog. He ran ahead, the others following. He found the Cherokee chief atop the ridge beside the river. There, two hundred yards downstream, was the Brown flatboat, sitting on the bottom near the opposite shore.

Rusog seemed to forget the presence of Egan Kirk as they scouted around. They found the cache of material from the flatboat and then the signs of passage of men wearing moccasins and the tracks of four women in heavy shoes. The trail led due west.

"They are making for Chickasaw Bluffs," El-i-chi decided. "The tracks are no more than three days old."

"We must travel swiftly," Se-quo-i said. "If they reach Chickasaw Bluffs, they will either sell the white girls to the Chickasaw or have them taken away."

"I do not march with this white man." Rusog spoke firmly.

"As long as I can walk," Egan said, although he could see death in the eyes of the Cherokee chief, "I will follow those who killed my wife and my boy."

"Brother," Renno said softly as Rusog made a move, tomahawk in hand.

Rusog paused.

"We have come this far for good reason," Renno continued quietly. "Not just to punish the guilty but, if possible, to rescue the girls. Fighting among ourselves will only delay us."

"I can go alone," Kirk offered.

"He loses his way on a day when there is no sun," Ah-wa-o told them.

"Please," Mandy begged. "You said you saw the tracks of four women. My sister is still alive, then."

Rusog spoke gruffly. "I suppose that it would be better to have this murderer with us, where we can watch him, than to have him wandering alone in the woods."

"There is another possibility," Renno suggested. "It is not good for both of us to be away, my brother Rusog, and there are many at home who will be concerned, for we have been gone for a long time already and will be gone for, I think, much longer. The girls could be taken back."

"By me?" Rusog asked, ready to flare in anger.

"Ah-wa-o goes where I go," El-i-chi said. "I am more sure than ever now that we should be together."

"Then *you* go," Renno told him.

"Under no circumstances," El-i-chi said grimly. "It was my skull that was almost broken."

Renno looked up at the sun. They were wasting time. Having Mandy and Ah-wa-o along offered one advantage: A party traveling with women would not be ambushed as a war party, for women were not taken along on the warpath. He understood the feelings of both his brothers, and he hesitated to urge either one to go back. He would have to smooth things over with Ha-ace upon their return, that was a certainty. "Then the girls will accompany us. We must travel swiftly, but first I think that it would be wise to find a different hiding place for the cargo from the barge."

"Why waste the time?" El-i-chi protested. "We have no way to carry it home with us."

"But the goods may prove of value to others," Renno pointed out.

It took half a day to find a new cave, transfer the cargo, and hide the traces of their movement.

Renno was now traveling through familiar country. He had fought over most of the land along the Mississippi, and he had crossed this land on the way to and from the far west in the company of Beth Huntington and her brother,

William. The trails were good. Mandy had already shown that she was made of stern stuff by keeping pace, and there was no doubt Ah-wa-o could do even better. Renno had to resist the urge to break into the warrior's run, however.

They made camp in a beautiful little glen with a clear spring bubbling up from a rocky slope. Although Mandy was tired, she and Ah-wa-o saw to the cooking after El-i-chi had bagged a young deer.

Egan came to Renno after everyone had eaten. Rusog sat beside Renno, his face stern. "Sachems," Kirk began, "I cannot beg your forgiveness for what I have done. I can ask only that you believe that I know that what I did was very wrong, the act of a coward and a madman."

"I think," Renno said, "that your last word describes the act best."

"You have lost loved ones, then?" Kirk asked. "You understand how I felt, how the world seemed to be not worth living for, how nothing mattered but to see the blood of killers?"

Renno remembered the murder of his father, the death of his wife. "We will see this through together, Egan Kirk. Afterward we will discuss what happened when you went into the cabin with Old Tassel and the others."

Chapter VII

Oklawahpa, chief of the Chickasaw, had not had so many interesting visitors in a long time—not since the Spanish governor in New Orleans had given up sending gifts and emissaries in the hope of enlisting the Chickasaw Nation in the continuing frontier war against the United States.

The second group of visitors was standing before the Chickasaw chief outside Oklawahpa's lodge. Two faces were very familiar. Seeing the Seneca Renno and his brother, El-i-chi, served to remind Oklawahpa of past events both unpleasant and pleasant. Once, the Seneca had been in the forefront of a spirited little war against the Chickasaw and Spanish cavalry. That had proved quite unpleasant. But

then—and this Oklawahpa remembered with pleasure—
Renno had passed through Chickasaw territory to and from
some far western land and on the return trip had brought
gold as a gift for the Chickasaw chief.

Now it was obvious that Renno had no gift—not unless he
intended to give Oklawahpa the white girl who was with his
·party, and Oklawahpa doubted that.

The formal greetings took some time, for there was a
great deal of protocol to be observed when three sachems
came together, so it was not until the visitors were seated to
Oklawahpa's left and right at a hastily organized feast that
Renno had an opportunity to broach the subject of concern.

"I would say, my old friend Oklawahpa, great chief of the
mighty Chickasaw, that you show statesmanship in your
present course of neutrality," Renno commended.

"When next Chickasaw warriors die in battle," Oklawahpa said, "they will die for Chickasaw reasons, not for
Spanish reasons."

Renno nodded. It seemed that the chieftain had matured
in his thinking since last they had met. "Oklawahpa shows
great wisdom. For too long have the tribes been used as
soldiers for the countries of Europe in their efforts to
maintain power here. As you know, my brother Rusog's
Cherokee and my Seneca also walk the path of peace with
the United States."

"Some do not," Oklawahpa observed.

"Ah," Renno said, smiling and spreading his hands, "my
Chickasaw brother drives to the heart of the matter."

"My Seneca and Cherokee brothers understand that
neutrality extends both ways," Oklawahpa said.

Rusog spoke gruffly. "The Cherokee do not ask the
Chickasaw to punish Cherokee wrongdoers."

Renno cleared his throat as a polite signal for Rusog, to
put it bluntly, to shut up. He had never been noted for his
diplomacy. "For my brother's Cherokee and my Seneca, I
thank Oklawahpa for his permission for us to pass through
his lands in pursuit of those who must be punished."

Oklawahpa's face showed no smile, but there was a touch

of humor in his voice. "It seems to me that Renno and Rusog obtain this permission only after the fact."

"Alas, that is true," Renno admitted. "Perhaps, my brother, we should establish better communications in the future, with a regular exchange of runners to keep each other apprised of events."

Oklawahpa, not quite ready for such cooperation, merely nodded. Renno gave his attention to an ear of freshly harvested corn that had been roasted and touched lightly with salt, and waited for Oklawahpa to speak.

"When last I saw the sachem of the Seneca," the Chickasaw said, "he had horses laden with Spanish gold, and he was generous with his friend Oklawahpa."

Renno nodded and smiled. As he remembered it, he'd had to be pretty quick on his feet to keep Oklawahpa from taking all of the Spanish gold. "This time, great Chief, alas, I came quickly, without gifts, but with friendship and a request for a favor."

"Speak, friend," Oklawahpa said.

"The favor comes in two parts: First, we would like to know the number of the Cherokee renegades whom we follow and the condition of their white captives."

"Atarho brought gifts," Oklawahpa said.

Renno looked surprised. "And yet he traveled fast and light."

"There are gifts nevertheless," Oklawahpa said.

Renno looked puzzled, and then he leaned forward and spoke earnestly. "If my brother speaks of the property of the white men who were killed by Atarho and his renegades, property that now, by right of inheritance, belongs to the young captives, my heart is heavy, for Oklawahpa has been deceived." As expected, his statement did not upset the Chickasaw. Renno and his party had crossed the trail of a large party of Chickasaw moving in the opposite direction, toward the Tennessee, obviously to retrieve the cargo of the flatboat.

"Atarho left the cargo not well hidden," Renno went on smoothly, "and to protect it from animals and, perhaps, discovery by a Creek war party moving north through your lands to join the Ohio tribes, we moved it and concealed it so well that discovery will be impossible."

Oklawahpa reached for an earthenware cup and sipped from it to hide his chagrin.

"I said, my friend, that we came without gifts, but under the circumstances, perhaps that omission can be corrected," Renno went on.

Oklawahpa looked up, his face blank.

"This one," Renno went on, indicating Mandy, whom he had coached, "will make you an offer."

"Speak, woman," Oklawahpa said.

"We desire only to rescue my sisters," Mandy said. "The great chief Oklawahpa is welcome to the cargo of the flatboat."

"Ah," the Chickasaw breathed.

Renno lifted a cup, saluted Oklawahpa, and waited.

"Atarho had with him eight Cherokee warriors and the white man Simon Purdy," Oklawahpa said. "The girls were in good health."

"It is my guess," Renno said, "that Atarho asked for water transportation so that he could join his masters, the Spanish. Is that true?"

"It is true," Oklawahpa confirmed. "Perhaps Renno will now tell his friend the location of the flatboat's cargo."

"Gladly," Renno agreed. "But let us speak of Atarho first."

"There was, here in Chickasaw Bluffs, a Spanish trader named Juan Cristobal," Oklawahpa said. "He dealt with Simon Purdy and Atarho for the white captives, offering a price in silver with the provision that Atarho and Purdy deliver the captives to New Madrid. That was accepted."

Mandy's face fell, and a tear escaped one eye.

"Do they travel by land or water?" Renno asked, watching Oklawahpa's eyes carefully. The old adage that an Indian cannot lie well to another Indian made him feel that Oklawahpa spoke truth.

"Atarho travels by land," Oklawahpa said, "on the eastern side of the Father of Waters."

Renno nodded. Egan Kirk and El-i-chi looked restless, eager to end the feast and get under way. Renno told Oklawahpa how to find the flatboat's cargo and, within the hour, was leading the way out of Chickasaw Bluffs, for at least three hours of light were left for travel, and the renegades had a good head start.

So far as he had spoken, Oklawahpa had told the truth to Renno. Atarho and his men were traveling north along the Mississippi by land. Atarho carried a leather pouch of silver, all that the trader Cristobal had had with him in Chickasaw Bluffs, but there was to be much more silver. The deal that had been made had taken a long time and much talk.

In the end Simon Purdy had accompanied Juan Cristobal on the Spaniard's small keelboat, which was overcrowded with the addition of Purdy and the four captives. Purdy would represent Atarho in New Madrid, collect the rest of the silver, then have a boat meet Atarho on the eastern side of the river. Because of the difficulty of river travel, those who traveled by land would arrive at New Madrid at approximately the same time as the keelboat.

Atarho had thought long and hard before entrusting the valuable merchandise to Simon Purdy, but he had been faced with a difficult choice: His men had been purified for war for a long time, and some of them were thinking about going home to their families, hoping that the furor over the murders of the Kirk family and the killings and kidnappings of the Brown party would have died down. Some believed that Slim Tom—or Atarho, as he now called himself—was the only one whose identity was known for a certainty.

In order not to lose his small cadre of fighters, Atarho promised his men that they would share in the Spanish silver. Then they could choose between accompanying him to the north to rejoin his mentor Hodano, who would reward the fighters with honor and with women, or taking the silver and going home to their Cherokee villages. After agreeing to travel by land, leaving the girls to Purdy and

Cristobal, Atarho had had to appease his grumbling men; to
that end he set a leisurely pace, stopping to hunt, eat, and
rest often. He could not imagine any possibility of pursuit;
even if one or both of the warriors who had attacked his
force aboard the flatboat had survived, even if the white girl
who had disappeared during the fight had lived, he had
covered many watery miles on the boat and now was
moving far north through Chickasaw lands.

Once or twice he sent men to the bank of the river, and
each time the Spanish keelboat was seen, struggling up the
mighty waterway. Even leisurely travel would keep him
ahead of the boat.

So it was that Atarho's overconfidence made it possible
for Renno to gain ground steadily as he moved his party
briskly. Even Mandy could match the warrior's pace.
Ah-wa-o ran lightly at El-i-chi's side without apparent
effort.

Day by day the trail was fresher, but Renno was puzzled
because there was no sign of the white women—no mark
from the heavy shoes that they wore. El-i-chi, Se-quo-i,
and Rusog also noted the lack of sign, but no one mentioned
the fact. Whatever had happened to the girls, their hopeful
rescuers had come too far to leave off the chase.

Without discussion it was agreed that the murderers
would be punished, and then attention could be turned
toward the whereabouts of the captives. El-i-chi suggested
that Oklawahpa had bought the captives and had hidden
them in his town, but Renno suspected that the girls had
been put aboard a boat on the Mississippi. If that was the
case, it would make any further attempt at rescue a major
undertaking.

There came a morning when, after an early start before
the sun, Renno and El-i-chi found campfires with still-
warm ashes. They waited until the others caught up.

"This day will see the finish of it," Renno announced.

Now it was the sachem and shaman running together,
legs pumping, all senses alert. The land away from the river

was as flat as a table and well treed, but with open areas of
tall grass. When Renno saw bent grass spring up from the
moccasin print of a warrior, he knew that the renegades
were very near. Obviously Atarho had chosen this route,
rather than the dense riverside thickets, for ease of travel.

Renno slowed the pace. Together the brothers crept
through a copse. Ahead the land sloped slightly to a little
stream that ran on a clean, sandy bottom toward the
Mississippi. They heard voices before they saw any renegades and then, lying in grass that hid them, Renno and
El-i-chi looked down the slight slope. The renegades had
killed a yearling buffalo and were in the process of butch-
ering it, taking only the tender internal organs for their
meal. The cook fires had already been started, the campsite
selected on the banks of the stream. It was evident that
they would travel no farther, although the hour was early.

Renno looked around carefully. There was no sign of the
captive girls. Oklawahpa had lied by omission.

El-i-chi held up both hands, fingers spread, mouthed the
number *nine*. Renno nodded. El-i-chi thrust his hand
forward, indicating his desire to attack immediately. Renno
shook his head and pointed backward. El-i-chi reluctantly
followed him into the trees.

"I know not which of them found my head with the flat
side of his blade," El-i-chi said. "If I kill half of them, there
is a good chance that he will be among them."

"We will wait," Renno said, grinning in spite of himself.
"Others have marched as far as we to be in on the kill.
Would you deprive Rusog of his opportunity to punish
Cherokee murderers? Or deprive Egan Kirk of the sweet-
ness of revenge?"

El-i-chi snorted. "I was thinking only of myself."

With the group together, Renno made his suggestions,
not presuming to give orders to his fellow chief, Rusog.
Rusog was content to have Renno plan the strategy, so he
merely nodded, indicating his agreement.

Egan was grimly seeing to the priming of his musket.
El-i-chi fingered the edge of his tomahawk and found it to
be sharp enough.

"Hear me," Renno said. "If we are to know the where-abouts of the white girls, we must keep Atarho alive."

Kirk growled in his throat. Renno looked at him, his piercing blue eyes burning. "*Alive*, for there is one among us, one who has traveled as far as any of us, whose journey would be for nothing if we do not obtain news of her sister."

"All right," Kirk said sourly.

"Take Atarho alive," Renno repeated.

Mandy and Ah-wa-o protested, but only mildly, when Renno chose a place of concealment and ordered them to stay here.

Renno gave one last instruction: "I have no desire to lose any of you or to have any one of us wounded. This is not an affair of honor but punishment for crimes. We will kill swiftly and from cover."

"I want them to know who kills them," Kirk growled. "I want them to watch me watching them die."

Renno considered for a moment. "So be it," he consented, understanding.

It was still light when the white Indian had his force positioned in the woods above the camp beside the stream. He had chosen to approach with Egan, lest the white man, in his eagerness, expose the attack prematurely. Rusog and El-i-chi were to the left, Se-quo-i to the right. Each had a musket ready. Renno slipped the English longbow from his shoulder, situated the quiver with arrows handy, and lifted his musket. Finally he nodded to Kirk.

Egan Kirk stepped out of the woods and stood, tall and straight, his face hidden by the long shadows cast by the setting sun.

"Slim Tom!" Egan called, in a loud voice filled with emotion.

Atarho spat out a mouthful of buffalo liver and leaped for his musket.

"I am Egan Kirk."

Chaos prevailed in the renegade camp as men lunged for their weapons. Renno's musket spoke, and a man was knocked violently backward into a fire. On either side of the

Seneca came other reports from muskets, and five men were down. Two broke and ran up the slope away from the campsite, and Renno's fingers drew the strong bow and let fly an arrow to pierce a renegade's spine. Two more arrows flew as swiftly, both catching a renegade in the nape of the neck just as he hurled himself over the brink of the slope.

Atarho, musket in hand, hesitated in choosing a target. First he had the muzzle of his weapon pointed toward the white man who had announced his name, Kirk, in a voice sounding like the trumpet of doom. But then Atarho saw the deadly effect of Renno's musket followed by the singing arrows, so his weapon wavered between the two attackers. Meanwhile, the last survivor other than Atarho—the man who had been wounded so severely by Se-quo-i aboard the flatboat—fired his musket at the white man, only to see his shot miss. Although he was healing, he had no real strength in his fighting arm.

Atarho could not assimilate all the action. So quickly his men were dead! Death faced him now in the form of the white man named Kirk, a man he now realized was the husband of the woman Simon Purdy had raped and muti- lated. With a howl of fear and rage he lifted his weapon and aimed it at Kirk, who, musket discarded and tomahawk in hand, was advancing on him. Renno saw the movement. Knowing that Atarho's musket was still loaded, he drew an arrow quickly and sent it winging on a straight, hard line to blunt its tip against the butt of Atarho's musket just in time to knock it askew and cause the ball to go harmlessly into the air over Kirk's head.

The man with the bad shoulder lifted his hands in the white man's signal for surrender, then remembered the carnage at the Kirk cabins and saw the darkness in the face of the white avenger. He knew that he was a dead man. He grasped a tomahawk in his left hand and rushed to meet Kirk, swinging awkwardly. Kirk didn't even slow down. He buried his tomahawk blade in the man's stomach, jerked it out, struck the back of the warrior's neck as he fell, and then rushed on toward Atarho.

"Kirk!" Renno roared as Egan ran for Atarho with his blade lifted for the kill. "Kirk!" he shouted once more as the distance closed, and it was evident that Egan was maddened by the sight of the face of the Cherokee who had professed friendship for the Kirk family before slaughtering them.

Renno realized that he would have to kill Egan Kirk before the man murdered Atarho. He had an arrow drawn and a bead on Kirk's exposed side when he saw El-i-chi in position to stop the young avenger. The sachem let the drawn bow go slack as the shaman threw himself in front of Egan, saw the glazed, maddened look, and shouted Kirk's name. Egan, in a red haze of hatred and blood lust, screamed out hoarsely and struck out at the man who was blocking his path to Slim Tom. The strength of the blow tested El-i-chi's defensive skill, but his blade clashed against Egan's and deflected it. The power of the blow caused Egan to stumble, and El-i-chi aided the process with a foot inserted neatly between Egan's legs. The white man sprawled full length on the ground only to start crawling toward the stunned and terrified Atarho.

Seeing that Rusog and Se-quo-i were closing in on Atarho to prevent any action or escape, El-i-chi whooped and threw himself onto the crawling man's back, straddling him, one arm under Egan's chin, trying to choke the white man into calmness. Egan was making a noise like a distressed boar, something between a grunt and a squeal.

"Kirk! Kirk!" El-i-chi continued to yell into Egan's ear as he applied pressure to the man's windpipe. He feared that he would have to crush Egan's larynx in order to stop him, but at last Egan's wild strength seemed to falter all at once. He collapsed to the ground, and El-i-chi leaped up and stood over him, saying his name softly.

Egan's eyes seemed to focus again. He shook his head, then he saw Atarho, standing defiantly with Rusog on one side and Se-quo-i on the other. Renno approached, his blue eyes striking fire. "You are lucky to be alive, white man. Thank my brother for saving your life."

"I—I don't know what happened," Kirk said, shaking his head. "I saw that murdering savage and—"

"Enough," Renno said. He turned to face Atarho. "I will give the living dead man a chance to speak."

Atarho snarled, trying to appear brave.

Renno looked around. "The renegade white man, Simon Purdy, is not among the dead. Where has he taken the four girls?"

"Where you will never see them again," Atarho hissed.

"Once more I ask," Renno said coldly. "Where are they?"

Atarho cleared his throat noisily and spat onto the ground. Renno nodded to Rusog and Se-quo-i, who seized Atarho's arms. Renno stepped forward, the Spanish stiletto in his hand. He drew a neat, straight line from Atarho's left eye down his cheek, curving it in toward the Cherokee's chin. Blood welled up.

Atarho was trying to remember some of the chants that he had learned from his mentor, Hodano, but with pain lancing down his cheek, his mind was a blank. Then Renno held the blade firmly against the renegade's throat. His intentions were clear.

"Where?" Renno repeated.

"On the river," Atarho said, sputtering in his eagerness to talk. "With the Spaniard Cristobal."

"In which direction?" Renno asked.

"The north, toward New Madrid."

"Tell it true," Renno warned, now placing the flat side of the stiletto's blade against Atarho's cheek. The feel of cold steel and the burning pain from the shallow cut almost loosened Atarho's bowels along with his tongue.

"I speak true," he blabbered. "Purdy will collect the balance of the silver that the Spaniard pays for the women. They will be kept in New Madrid for a little while, and then moved downriver to New Orleans, where the Spanish soldiers and the French bayou men will pay much money for their favors. I swear it is true. They have not been hurt."

"Bind him," Renno said.

"I say kill him now," El-i-chi put in.

"And I," Rusog seconded.

"And if we kill him him, what proof do we have that the murderers of the Kirk family and the Brown party have been punished?" Renno asked.

"In the name of the manitous, Renno," El-i-chi pleaded, "you don't expect us to haul this dog all the way back to the eastern frontier!"

"He is proof that the Cherokee have kept their faith," Renno said. "Rusog?"

"My brother is right," Rusog admitted reluctantly. "He is our only proof. He will go with us and be turned over to the white man's justice."

"Do you hear our decision, Egan Kirk?" Renno asked.

Egan nodded. "I myself will guard him every step of the way, praying that he will try to escape."

Atarho shuddered and submitted meekly as El-i-chi and Se-quo-i secured him to a tree with leather thongs.

"Now we must have a council," Renno said. "Se-quo-i, bring the girls to us."

Se-quo-i was back within a few minutes, Mandy and Ah-wa-o with him. Renno asked all to sit in a circle. He outlined the situation: The four white girls had been put aboard a boat to be taken to New Madrid, and then to New Orleans. Simon Purdy still lived and was with the girls on the river.

"We must return Atarho to the east, as proof that we Seneca and our brothers the Cherokee are sincere in our desire for continued peace. New Madrid is several days' march to the north and across the river. There is a Spanish garrison there. We are but five."

"Until they are all dead, I do not turn back," Egan vowed. "Simon Purdy lives."

"Egan, I hate to mention this," Mandy said, "but aboard the flatboat, Simon Purdy alone was not in a state of purification for battle."

Everyone understood; in all probability it was Purdy who had raped Mary Kirk before killing her.

"Although the man who almost split my head is probably

already dead," El-i-chi added, "there is the small possibility
that it was Purdy who landed the lucky blow."

"Se-quo-i?" Renno said.

"Although I hate to leave a job undone," the Cherokee
scholar said, "I will abide by the decision of my chief."

Rusog grunted. "Depending on the numbers and the
alertness of the Spaniards in the town, we may not be
able to bring out the white girls. In a trading-post town,
however, no one will notice a few more Indians, so we
should be able to deal out the punishment Simon Purdy
deserves."

Mandy's face had gone pale. Renno looked at her to speak
next. "You all have done so much," she said gratefully. "You
have risked your lives, and but for a stroke of fate, my sister
and the Brown sisters would be with us now. I can't ask you
to risk more, for surely to go into a Spanish town to try to
rescue my sister and the others would be far too dangerous." She lowered her head and began to weep quietly.
Ah-wa-o put her hand on Mandy's shoulder.

"If there is a way, it will be done," Ah-wa-o said. "If it can
be done without loss of life, I believe that these brave
warriors will do it. But it wouldn't do anyone any good for
our men to die in a hopeless cause."

"Yes, I understand," Mandy said weakly.

"We cannot, of course, bring the girls or Atarho," El-i-chi
said. "Who will stay to guard the dog and to keep watch
over Ah-wa-o and Mandy?"

For a few moments no one would meet Renno's eyes. He
chuckled. "I see only one way to resolve this. We will draw
straws."

Rusog, holder of the short straw, glowered as the others
prepared to cross the river. They had made camp in a
secluded spot a good distance from the crossing. Atarho was
in a seated position, bound to a tree, his legs stretched out
in front of him. Ah-wa-o, to lessen Rusog's disappointment,
was cooking rabbit for an early supper.

Renno wanted to time their arrival in New Madrid for
dusk. He led the group of four to the river crossing where

Quapaw and Chickasaw boatmen were preparing to settle down beside their fires for the night. One silver coin was enough to see them safely across the Father of Waters.

New Madrid had grown up around an Indian trading post. It was small, scattered along the riverbank, its log buildings often destroyed by floods. The original trading post had been rebuilt more than once, and now, of course, there were several business establishments. The Spanish fort, if it could be called that, was a log structure with a pointed log palisade fence.

Renno saw a couple of Spanish soldiers almost immediately after landing. The men were slovenly and unkempt, a sure sign of poor discipline in the garrison. No one challenged them. Many Indians walked along the streets and along the waterfront—Chickasaw, Quapaw, and an occasional Shawnee.

Three more Indians and a scurvy-looking young white man were not objects of special notice on the edge of the Spanish western frontier. They sauntered along the waterfront, mounted a log walkway, and heard the babble of voices from inside a log building with an open door. Renno smelled the strong aromas of rum and tobacco smoke. He looked inside and saw that they had arrived at a public house. He could hear smatterings of Spanish, English, French, Chickasaw, and another Indian dialect or two.

"It is best that we separate," Renno decided, "so that later we will not be immediately grouped together in the minds of our enemies. Se-quo-i, with me. El-i-chi, with Kirk."

Renno led the way into the smoky, dimly lit room, scanned the men here, spotted a table where three Spanish soldiers drank and talked, and worked his way toward it. He was rewarded with information immediately, for the three soldiers were complaining about their commander, Captain León Bocalos, who, it seemed, was in the process of buying four fresh, young white girls from the trader Juan Cristobal.

"Of course, he will not share such treasure with the common soldier," one man grumbled.

"Nor make them available at a price that we can afford," said another.

"Perhaps it is all someone's imagination, after all," the third remarked. "Who has seen these girls?"

"I," said the first soldier. "When Cristobal came in with them. They were disembarked along with a white man dressed as an Indian."

In order to hear better, Renno had edged close to the soldiers' table. A passing man bumped him from the rear, and he was pushed against a soldier's shoulder.

"Watch yourself, savage," the man growled.

"Excuse me, sir," Renno said in Spanish. The soldier looked up at Renno more carefully.

"This one," the soldier said, pointing at Renno and laughing, "parrots words of our language." The other two looked at Renno's blond scalp lock with curiosity.

"You speak Spanish?" one asked.

"No, señor," Renno said, deciding that it would be best to pretend to be the ignorant savage that he was in the eyes of the Spaniards.

"Oh, too bad," said a soldier. "I would love to have a servant who speaks our language instead of that stupid Quapaw I have now."

"This one does not have the air of a servant," the first soldier said, gazing at Renno, who let his eyes fall. "At any rate, I did see the white women. Cristobal took them to his place, behind the barracks."

Renno began to edge away, signaling to the others to follow. Outside, he reported what he had heard. "Se-quo-i and I will move toward the house behind the barracks. Stay well behind us, El-i-chi, but be ready to move quickly if I call."

The streets of the town were muddy, and it was quite dark. Occasionally the glow of a lantern or an oil lamp would escape through an open window to give a hint of light. Renno and Se-quo-i had walked only a short distance when he heard a sound like the excited warning call of a chipmunk. He did not look around immediately, but when he did, he saw that the three soldiers from the public house had come out and were following him down the street, walking swiftly, with purpose.

"You there!" the soldier called, drawing closer.

Renno chose the spot to halt, a dark area shadowed even from the dim moonlight by a cabin from which no light came. "Do you call me, señor?" he asked in perfect Spanish, carrying the accent of the Spanish aristocrat.

"I do," the soldier said. "I thought I detected a hint of Castile in the few words you spoke. And now, for one who does not understand Spanish, you speak very well."

"What has that to do with you, my friend?" Renno asked in a lazy, insulting manner.

"I think we'll take this one before the commander," the soldier said, drawing his saber. "Don't give us any trouble."

Renno didn't call for help; he didn't need it. It was only three against two, and the three Spaniards were half-drunk. "The one on the left is yours, Se-quo-i," he said in English as he raised his tomahawk, then darted under a wild swing of the soldier's saber and lessened the Spanish population of the New World by one with a suddenness that left the other two soldiers easy prey to Seneca and Cherokee blades.

In the silence that followed, Renno turned to see other soldiers moving swiftly down the street toward them. He called out his warning to El-i-chi and fell back, with Se-quo-i, into the darkness next to the cabin wall.

El-i-chi and Egan met four Spanish soldiers quietly. El-i-chi, who had faced long blades before, had little trouble making his first kill. Kirk, unnerved by the long saber, gave ground. Renno and Se-quo-i moved in from the rear, and soon only the Spaniard facing Egan was alive. El-i-chi rectified that situation quickly.

"When you face a long blade with a tomahawk," Renno told Egan, "the idea is to close rapidly and get inside. If you fall back, you surrender the advantage to your enemy."

"I hope I don't have to face any more long blades," Egan said, "but if I do, I'll remember that."

"What made them suspicious?" El-i-chi wondered.

Renno shrugged. "Apparently a Spanish-speaking blond Indian is a rarity here."

"We must accomplish our task quickly now," Se-quo-i urged.

Renno nodded, setting out once again toward the barracks.

A dim light gleamed from the windows of the barracks, which was nothing more than a long, low log shed with a sod roof. Past it was a neat-looking log house, and oil lamps gleamed brightly from its windows. Renno approached, bent low, and as he moved toward a window he heard a woman's laughter. The sound was joined by a man's deep chuckle. Renno lifted his head and carefully peered through the window. On a bed covered with trade blankets and cured skins sprawled a rather handsome Spanish man and a woman. Her back was to Renno, and she was a bit more than half-naked. The bulk of her told him at a glance that she was not Mandy's sister or one of the young Brown girls.

"Juan," the woman said, laughing, "you are so mean to me. Be a good fellow and open another bottle of wine."

Juan was a common Spanish name, but perhaps this was Juan Cristobal, who had purchased the girls from Atarho. Renno told El-i-chi and the others to wait, keep watch, and warn him if danger approached. He went to the front door, tried the handle, and found that the door was unbarred.

He entered the house quietly. The woman and the man called Juan were quite obviously drunk. Renno stood looking down on them before the man realized that he was no longer alone with his woman. He tried to stand, but Renno shoved him back, hard. The woman opened her mouth to scream, but he showed her the blade of his stiletto and hissed, "No sound." She sank onto the bed, her eyes wide.

"Now look here," the man objected, making a move to sit up again. He, too, was almost naked, wearing only a soiled white shirt that did not cover his genitals very well.

"Are you Juan Cristobal?" Renno whispered.

"Yes, I am. But there must be some misunderstanding—I don't even know you." Cristobal was a gentleman, his Spanish accent almost as aristocratic as Renno's.

"It does not matter who I am. What have you done with the four young American girls?"

"Girls? Girls?" He looked around, as if seeking help. "What have I to do with American girls?"

Renno moved his arm quickly. The blade of his stiletto was now pressed upward between Cristobal's legs. The Spaniard made a sobbing sound, for he felt the sharpness.

"I have no time for games," Renno warned.

"Please," Cristobal begged. "Not that. Not that."

Renno grinned. He had guessed correctly that a man who would buy and sell little girls would value his own sexual apparatus highly. "The girls."

"They're safe." Cristobal's words came in a rush. "They are under the protection of the Spanish army. In fact, just this evening, after I tricked the renegade Simon Purdy into handing the girls over to me, I delivered them to Captain León Bocalos. He was so excited at the opportunity to rescue four such beautiful maidens that he set out downriver immediately to take them back to their families. So, my friend, you are too late, but everything is all right! And now will you please remove your knife from, uh, that spot?"

"You may not be lying altogether," Renno said, "so a half lie will cost you only one." He put pressure on the knife, and Cristobal screamed.

"You win!" Cristobal said, weeping real tears. "I sold them to Bocalos! The rest is true. They are, even now, aboard a boat on the way to New Orleans. This I swear."

"That is the truth, Señor Indio," the woman confirmed. "This I know. Look, señor, I know that he is not much man, but he is all I have. Spare him for me?"

Renno removed his knife. "Well spoken, señorita," he said. "I leave this caballero in your tender care. But if either of you happens to stick your head outside the door or the window to yell for help in the next half hour, one of my men will send an arrow into your left eye."

"I will see to it that he stays here," the woman promised. Cristobal nodded vigorously.

"Señor," the woman said softly, "has it occurred to you that perhaps those you seek do not wish to be rescued?"

Renno's first action when he stepped outside was to bend and clean the blade of his stiletto by stabbing it repeatedly into the dirt.

Chapter VIII

Rusog was agitated. Mandy and Ah-wa-o sat beside the fire, but the Cherokee, unable to relax, would sit for a few minutes, then rise to circle the camp's circumference, listening and looking toward the river. Now and then he would bend to check Atarho's bindings. His disquietude came from knowing that he was going to miss some interesting action.

Atarho mistook Rusog's restlessness for nervousness. "I think you fear for your companions," he said with a sly grin.

Rusog merely grunted.

"You are justified in your worry," Atarho went on. He knew that if his mentor, Hodano, were ever to find himself in such a position, he could twist and turn the mind of one man so skillfully that soon he would be free and his captor dead. This one, this Cherokee, did not seem to have the intelligence of the group's leader, Renno. He would emulate Hodano and influence Rusog's mind.

"Soon you will be alone," Atarho said, "for the Spanish will kill your friends in New Madrid. They are not stupid, the Spanish."

"If you are not stupid," Rusog growled, "you will stop the flow of your words before I find it necessary to do so."

Atarho laughed. "You are far from home, Cherokee, and now you have only two women to aid you. Do you really expect to take me all the way back to Knoxville?"

"All or a part of you," Rusog replied. "All of you alive, or your scalp dead."

"I have friends among the Chickasaw," Atarho warned. "You will have to be very, very careful to avoid all Chickasaw, for if you encounter even one, you will be in trouble. They will free me and kill those who are against me."

"You trouble me," Rusog said sarcastically, but Atarho, misunderstanding, gloated. Rusog went to the fire and sat down heavily near Ah-wa-o. "He troubles me like the buzzing of a mosquito." He sat in silence for a few minutes. It was going to be a long, long trip back to his own land and then on to Knoxville to turn Atarho over to the whites. Largely because of Atarho he had been forced to stay behind while Renno and the others went off to adventure.

The Cherokee chief was wise in many ways, and yet he was a simple man. With Rusog things were either black or white, right or wrong, with few gradations in between. When the renegade called him, he rose, knelt beside Atarho, and loosed him from the tree. "Come," he said. He led the renegade into the bushes where Atarho answered the call of nature, then pushed the renegade ahead of him back to the tree.

"I have powerful friends to the north," Atarho whispered. "My friends would reward you well if you delivered me there instead of to Knoxville."

"Spare me your buzzings," Rusog growled, knotting the leather thongs quickly.

Atarho had tensed all his muscles while Rusog was tying him to the tree. To Atarho's delight, when Rusog went back to the fire, he found that the thongs were quite loose. He exulted. His talk had upset the Cherokee so much that the man had become careless in his haste to get away from it. Now Rusog was lounging at the fire, and he had foolishly left his musket leaning against a tree not ten feet from Atarho. Slowly the renegade worked to loosen the bonds. He watched as the girls spread their blankets, lay down, and fell asleep. The Cherokee nodded at the fire. Soon the idiot would sleep the eternal sleep of death.

One hand was free. Rusog had gone to lean against a tree, his face away from Atarho. Now the other hand was free, and hidden by the shadows away from the fire, Atarho quickly tore at the thong that secured his legs. Rusog was breathing deeply, obviously asleep. Atarho tensed himself, then hesitated. What if the Cherokee awoke before he could reach the musket? Rusog was a big man, a strong warrior. Yet Atarho knew he had no other choice.

He began to move slowly, slowly toward the musket, until he was but a leap away. He took that leap, had one hand on the musket, and was lifting it when, with a blur of movement, Rusog put his entire torso behind his right arm and sent his tomahawk winging to bury its blade in Atarho's forehead.

"You see," Rusog said mildly to Ah-wa-o and Mandy, who had jumped up at the sound. "You see that he had somehow escaped his bonds and was reaching for my musket."

"I see that Rusog was quite careless in leaving his musket so near the renegade," Ah-wa-o said with a hint of a smile. "And I think that Rusog may have been a bit careless with the bonds when last he tied them."

"Yes, perhaps," Rusog admitted. His face was set in serious lines. "But now we will not have to endure the buzzings of that mosquito. True?"

"True," Ah-wa-o agreed.

Mandy had to turn her head as Rusog took his proof for the Knoxville authorities, in the form of Atarho's scalp, that justice had been served. The Cherokee chief then dragged the body a good distance from the camp to dump it into an erosion gully. If the white men did not believe that the Cherokee had punished the Cherokee renegades, then so be it. A man can only be pushed so far before he takes action to remove an irritant from his life.

Seven Spanish soldiers lay dead in the shadows of the streets of New Madrid. Knowing full well that Juan Cristobal and his woman would, sooner or later, accumulate enough courage to sound the alarm, Renno led his group quickly toward the riverfront. There, at a wharf built of logs, he saw a bored Spanish soldier on guard duty at the door of a log warehouse. He approached, giving a friendly greeting in Spanish. The guard straightened and tightened his grip on his musket.

"I have sold my hides," Renno said conversationally, "and the money was soon gone."

The soldier laughed. "I have found myself in the same situation many times."

"I have not even the money to pay for a night's lodging," the white Indian continued, "and the riverboatmen do not work at night, so I cannot start my journey for home."

"Sleep there, on those bales of hides," the soldier said, showing sympathy. "You poor *cabrón*. You worked for an entire winter, probably, trapping in the cold and in the snow, and in only a little while the charms of New Madrid have seduced you out of your entire year's earnings."

"Your heart is good," Renno said. He laughed. "Well, perhaps it was worth it, after all. That woman, ah. Yes, she was worth the price."

"Which one was that?" the soldier wanted to know.

"I didn't ask her name," Renno said. He described one of the women, obviously a prostitute, that he had seen in the public house.

"Ah, *sí*, Rosita," the soldier said. "She is much woman."

"You know her, eh?"

The soldier laughed. "Now I know why your money went so fast, for Rosita does not come cheaply. But at that you are lucky to have found a woman who is affordable, if expensive. Those that the captain took downriver today—" He lifted one hand, made a curving sign in the air to indicate feminine charms. "The likes of you and me, my friend, will never be able to afford such ones as those."

"Were they so beautiful?" Renno asked.

"*Muy bonita*," the soldier answered. "Four of them. Young white girls." He sighed. "I envy the captain and the white man who accompanied him. The trip to New Orleans will be a long one, but I suspect, very pleasant for them." He sighed again. "Four little white flowers, and only two men. Ah."

Behind them, in the town, a man shouted out in alarm. The guard looked toward the sound idly, obviously accustomed to that occurrence. Renno said, "My friend, I thank you for the offer of a place to sleep. I will accept gratefully, but first I think that I will go back and take one more look at Rosita, even if I have no more money for her."

The guard nodded. He was preoccupied, for the shouts from the town were growing. Renno moved away quietly and rejoined the others in the shadows. "The white girls are indeed being taken downriver to New Orleans."

"I think that our handiwork has been discovered," El-i-chi remarked, inclining his head toward the growing clamor from the town.

"There are canoes," Se-quo-i said, pointing.

They took two canoes and pushed them into the water. The once-darkened town was now bright with light. Lanterns and torches bobbed about on the streets. But the canoes moved quickly into the dark, big waters and soon reached the eastern bank.

Rusog was dozing when he heard the sharp bark of a fox. He answered, yipping twice. He heard nothing then, so silently did Renno move, until the Seneca stood across the fire from him. The others followed, not as quietly. Egan's progress through the woods would have alerted any Indian within three hundred yards. Renno saw a fresh scalp drying on a stick thrust into the ground near the fire, and there was no sign of Atarho.

Rusog did not lie. "He loosed his bonds and tried to seize my musket."

"He did not succeed," Renno said.

"He did not," Rusog replied.

Renno nodded knowingly. "The night is far gone. We will talk in the morning." Within minutes he was asleep.

Hours later, they sat in council again, five men and two women. Renno spoke. "All but one of the renegades who broke the peace are dead. The one who lives is not Cherokee but white. Even now he travels down the Mississippi in a Spanish riverboat with Captain León Bocalos. Mandy, your sister and the other girls are on that boat, being taken to New Orleans. Bocalos travels, no doubt, with a crew, on a vessel with oars and sweeps. He will make good time. Should we decide to follow, I suspect that we will arrive in New Orleans days after Bocalos."

"Four young white girls would disappear quickly into the city's many houses of pleasure," Se-quo-i said grimly.

"I am reminded of something that the woman who was with Juan Cristobal in New Madrid said to me," Renno mused.

"Tell us what she said," Ah-wa-o requested, for Renno seemed to be lost in thought.

"She said that perhaps the girls did not wish to be rescued," Renno said quietly.

"That's nonsense!" El-i-chi erupted.

"I think I know what she meant," Mandy put in. "By now Tess and the others have been used by men. We can't even guess by how many. The girls might be so degraded by what has been done to them that they would not want to be brought back among decent people and have their shame exposed."

"There could be circumstances where a woman felt so dishonored that she wanted only to die," Ah-wa-o agreed.

"These are young girls," El-i-chi said. "Two of them are no more than children. No matter what has been done to them, they will want to live."

"What do *you* think, Mandy?" Renno asked.

She waited for a long moment before replying. "You all

know that aboard the flatboat I was . . . dishonored by Simon Purdy. While it is true that I feel shame, Purdy's touch has long since been washed away from my body by water, by sweat, and by time itself."

"May I speak?" Egan asked.

Renno nodded.

"My mission has not changed. Simon Purdy lives. He is the last of those who killed my family. You—Renno, Rusog, all of you—have done your duty. You have punished the Cherokee renegades, as you had promised to do. Let me pursue the last of them. I swear to you that you will not see my face again until Purdy is dead."

"One man could not hope to locate four girls among the pleasure houses of New Orleans," Se-quo-i said. He looked at Renno. "Sachem, we have traveled far, you and I. We have seen the lands between our mountains and the Atlantic. We have sailed the oceans, and we have braved the jungles of Jamaica together. And yet we have never seen the length of the Father of Waters."

"It would make sense," Rusog suggested, "to use the canoes to travel back to Chickasaw Bluffs. There Egan Kirk can make his good-byes if he goes on to New Orleans."

"My brother, then, has no intention of visiting New Orleans?" Renno asked.

"My task is done," Rusog said. "I will lay Atarho's scalp before the whites in Knoxville and reunite with my people . . . as should you, Renno."

"As always," the Seneca sachem replied, "my brother is wise."

In order to begin the trip by water it was necessary to wait for darkness. It was a simple matter for El-i-chi and Se-quo-i to obtain another canoe from the camp of the Quapaw boatman. It was a moonlit night. Three canoes moved out into the current, three dots lost on the broad, muddy belly of the Father of Waters. El-i-chi had as his partner the little Rose, Ah-wa-o. He sat in the stern and used his paddle to keep the canoe's prow aimed in the proper direction. It was not strenuous travel, for the river did the work.

Renno and Rusog were in a canoe together, leaving
Se-quo-i to team up with Egan Kirk. Mandy had chosen to
be the midcanoe passenger in Kirk and Se-quo-i's canoe for
a reason that did not become clear until well into the
second day's travel. Until that time the conversation had
been largely small talk, comments on sights on the shore,
the weather, and on the might and volume of the great
river.

"Mr. Kirk," Mandy said, "are you truly determined to go
on to New Orleans?"

"I am," Egan replied. He was taking a turn at steering. In
the bow of the boat Se-quo-i was lost in his own thoughts,
muttering the often odd sounds of the Cherokee language
to himself under his breath.

"I would like very much to go with you," Mandy
proposed.

Egan thought for a few moments. "I don't think that
would be wise."

"If we were wise, we'd be back east somewhere working
at a job in some nice, safe town where a constable walks his
rounds regularly," she said. "Think about this, Mr. Kirk.
Where have I to go? If I return with Renno and the others,
I can go into Knoxville, where, for a while, I will be treated
with sympathy. But sooner or later I will have to find a way
to earn money, and I know two ways to do that—one is to
do the drudge work of others."

Egan was a young man. He flushed red when he slowly
realized the second way that Mandy knew to make money.

"Tess is all I have," she went on. "Even if I find her
working in a house of ill repute, she is still my sister, and I
will always know that she did not choose her fate, that it was
forced upon her." She turned and focused her large, brown
eyes on Egan's. "Please."

He had to look away. Her anguish was too much for him.
"Let me consider it."

The contour of the riverbank became familiar. When
Renno signaled to the others to head toward the eastern
bank of the river late one evening, he knew that Chickasaw

Bluffs was just around the next bend of the river. He felt it would be best to land there early the next morning so they would not have to endure a night of Oklawahpa's sometimes doubtful hospitality.

The evening meal, fat ducks taken by arrow, was begun in moody silence. El-i-chi's usually hearty appetite seemed to have failed him as he nibbled without enthusiasm at a drumstick.

"Sachem," Egan said, breaking the silence, "as you know, I am going on to New Orleans. Mandy has asked that I allow her to accompany me."

Renno, chewing on a slice of breast meat, raised his eyebrows.

"So, what do you think?" Egan asked after a long pause.

"I think that although she is young, Mandy is a woman," Renno said, "and thus capable of knowing her desires."

El-i-chi sighed. "So we are to let the task be completed or not by a white man and a woman."

"Should you catch Simon Purdy and kill him," Rusog said, "it would be good to know."

"I'll get word to you, Rusog," Kirk said. "I owe you that, at least."

"You owe me nothing," Rusog replied. "Your debt is to the spirits of Old Tassel and the others you have killed."

"And so we do not see the great city at the mouth of the Father of Waters," El-i-chi said, looking at Se-quo-i as if searching for support.

Se-quo-i let a smile play on his face for a moment. He knew El-i-chi's feelings exactly, and so he spoke. "Sachems, while it is true that the leaders of our two peoples should be at home to administer their responsibilities, there is no pressing need for my presence." He was looking at El-i-chi out of the corner of his eyes now, watching for reaction to his next words. "I seem to be the only one free to accompany Mandy and Kirk, since our leaders have obligations, and El-i-chi must escort Ah-wa-o home."

"Now hold on," El-i-chi said quickly, then, with a glance at Ah-wa-o, he fell silent. He had no right to take her into further danger.

"I, too, would like to see the great city," Ah-wa-o said. "And it is true that a group traveling with women attracts less suspicion. If El-i-chi feels that his duty takes him to New Orleans, then I am with El-i-chi."

The shaman beamed. She was, his little Rose, a woman among women.

"The spirits have touched you all," Rusog said, but there was amusement in his voice. "Even my brother Renno has that far, far look in his eyes. Do you deny it?"

Renno shook his head ruefully, for Rusog knew him well, knew that the next hill, the next valley, the far horizon, had always held an irresistible attraction for him. "I confess."

El-i-chi gave a whoop of joy. "You speak Spanish better than any of us."

"We will have no problem with the Spanish," Se-quo-i said. "They befriend any Indian who sides against the United States. A sachem of Renno's stature will be met with great courtesy in New Orleans and will be given gifts in the hope that he and his tribe will cast their lot with Spain."

"We will try to make this a private visit," Renno said, already thinking ahead. "I don't think we'll have any trouble moving about in New Orleans, for, as you say, Se-quo-i, the Spanish have many Indian allies. And I'm sure that the city draws its share of long hunters and frontiersmen, so Kirk will not stand out. Mandy can pass as Kirk's wife—or woman, since many frontiersmen make a union with a woman without benefit of a marriage ceremony."

"I think," El-i-chi said, "that we will need better transportation than canoes."

"We will pay a visit to Oklawahpa," Renno said. "Spanish traders visit Chickasaw Bluffs often. If the manitous are with us, such a visitor will be there now."

El-i-chi grinned. "With a very comfortable riverboat, which he will be happy to lend to us for such a worthy cause."

The manitous were with them. As they rounded the last gentle bend in the river before Chickasaw Bluffs, the white Indian saw a neat, freshly painted keelboat tied up at the trading dock at Oklawahpa's town. Renno led the way to land near the dock.

The arrival of the party caused some little excitement among the Chickasaw, and soon Oklawahpa himself was coming toward them. After formal greetings, as if it had been years since they had last met and talked, Oklawahpa commented, "The scalp tied to the muzzle of my brother's musket looks familiar."

Rusog nodded, lifting the musket to allow Oklawahpa a closer look. "The Cherokee renegades who broke the peace have been taught the law."

Oklawahpa grunted. "Not all of them."

Rusog grunted in return. "The one who lives is not Cherokee."

"True," Oklawahpa said. "The dress of the Cherokee that he once wore has been discarded. Now he is once again a white man."

Rusog frowned with sealed lips, not willing to give Oklawahpa the satisfaction of making him ask questions.

Renno had no such pride. "You have seen Simon Purdy, my brother?"

"Four days past a keelboat stopped here briefly," Oklawahpa answered.

"Aboard were Captain León Bocalos, Purdy, the four captive white girls, and a small crew." Renno's intentions were to deflate Oklawahpa a bit, to make him realize that his information was not all new.

Mandy, who had not been given leeway to address the Chickasaw chieftain directly on this visit, whispered to Renno, "Ask him how the girls looked, if they were in good health."

"This one, whose sister is among the captives, wishes to inquire about the health of the captives," Renno said.

Oklawahpa turned his gaze on Mandy. Her dress, taken from a dead woman many weeks and many miles past, was the worse for wear. Only one thin shift was under the dress, and her womanly hips and breasts were evident. Her hair was coiled carelessly atop her head. Her skin had darkened from the sun. "I did not examine the captives closely,"

Oklawahpa said. "I saw them from the shore only, but they seemed to be in goood health."

"Thank you," Mandy said.

"This one," Oklawahpa said. "I will give you horses for her, so that your journey to the east can be made easily."

Egan's hand tightened on his musket. Renno grunted lazily. "Twenty horses would not buy this one, for she is a good cook."

Twenty horses was so far beyond the number envisioned by Oklawahpa, he did not even try to bargain. He merely grunted. He had had white women. No woman, much less a white woman, was worth twenty horses, no matter how well she cooked.

"So," Renno continued, "now we make our farewells to our brother Oklawahpa and leave him with the wish that the manitous give him long life."

They marched together to the east. When back checks showed that no Chickasaw trailed them—with the Chickasaw, one never knew—they paused and took leave of Rusog. The lure of far travel and the call of the great city of New Orleans held no attraction for him. He would report the death of the renegades, then go home. He had a great urge to hold Ena in his arms and to watch his twins at play.

"I know you will return," he told Renno, clasping his arm in the warrior's salute.

"And I know that you, Brother, will keep things well in order with our people," Renno replied.

Renno led the group north, and then back to the river at dusk. The keelboat was still tied at the dock. Stacks of pelts lay near the boat, but apparently the trading had not been completed. When darkness came, a lantern was lighted aboard, and one man could be seen moving about on deck. In a Chickasaw town there were always widows who were free, by custom, to entertain visitors. The trader and the crew of the boat were, most probably, somewhere in the town in good company.

"Se-quo-i," Renno decided.

El-i-chi started to protest, but Renno put a hand on his

arm. "I want you with the girls and Kirk, to be sure they come aboard quietly."

El-i-chi agreed.

Renno and Se-quo-i crept down the riverbank, keeping to the shadows. When they were just above the keelboat, they waded into the water, having left their muskets concealed on the shore, and swam silently to the side of the vessel that lay toward the river. Renno drew himself up slowly, until he could peer over the boat's low rail. The guard was sitting on a crate at midships strumming chords on a guitar. He hummed a melancholy tune, and the sound of his voice and the stringed instrument covered the only noise made—the dripping of water from Renno's clothing— as the white Indian lifted himself onto the boat and moved in one swift flow of motion to stand behind the musician.

The safest and the simplest thing for Renno to have done would have been to slit the guard's throat quickly, and, indeed, that had been his intention; but the man was singing of home, of Spain, and of a girl, and the song had a sincerity and a simplicity that made Renno think it was the man's own composition. He put one hand over the man's mouth, held his stiletto at the throat, and whispered, "Total silence and quick obedience will allow you to live, my friend."

The man nodded eagerly. Renno turned and saw Se-quo-i come aboard. "This one sings too sweetly to die," Renno said. "Give the signal."

Se-quo-i sent the prearranged signal by covering and uncovering the lantern three times. They waited in silence. Night sounds came from the Chickasaw town. Small wave-lets muttered against the side of the keelboat. Renno stood tirelessly, his hand over the Spaniard's mouth, the knife still at the man's throat. When he heard splashings, he whispered, "Move to the rail ahead of me. Be silent."

"I have no wish to die here," the Spaniard whispered when Renno removed his hand.

"Help them aboard," Renno said.

El-i-chi was surprised to find that the hand that helped first Ah-wa-o, then Mandy and Kirk onto the boat was that of a Spaniard. He whispered to Renno, "Have you found an ally?"

"He lulled me into mercy with his singing," Renno admitted.

"I am not so much a lover of Spanish music," El-i-chi said. "Shall I be the one to still his voice?"

"I have told him that he will live," Renno said. "Quickly now, the lines."

"There are three," the Spaniard told him. "Bow, stern, and spring lines."

"Thank you," Renno replied. "Show me how to loose them, for we will have need of them."

The Spaniard, moving with the grace and quickness of youth, soon had the lines freed from the shore. El-i-chi and Kirk used the sweeps to push the boat from the dock. There was a feeling of motion as the current caught them. The keelboat moved downriver not far from the eastern shore.

"Señor," the Spaniard said, "there is an eddy filled with snags just ahead of us."

Renno peered into the darkness. The moon had not yet risen, and all he could see was dark water.

"You must pull hard for the center of the river," the Spaniard went on, "and take the downriver bend near the western shore."

"I see no eddy," El-i-chi said. "Is he trying to trick us?"

"Señor, I cannot swim well," the Spaniard said. "I beg you to put men on the sweeps and pull for the center of the river."

"Quickly, then," Renno ordered.

As it was, the keelboat was caught in the outer edge of the strong eddy, and it was a muscle-straining task to pull her out of the odd current toward midstream.

"You spoke true," Renno told the Spaniard.

"Only God knows why I am on the river," the Spaniard grumbled. "All my life I have disliked the water, especially when it is dark."

"Then I won't do as I had planned to do," Renno said. "I had thought to let you swim ashore and make your way back to the town."

In the dim glow of the lantern he saw the young man shudder. "Perhaps, señor, you will put me ashore farther downriver."

"All right," Renno agreed.

"Now you must go nearer to the western shore," the man directed, "and when the river straightens again, pull once more for midstream."

"You seem to know the river well," Renno observed.

"I have been twice to St. Louis," the Spaniard responded. "And now it seems that I will not go there the third time, no?"

"No," Renno said. "We go to New Orleans."

"Perhaps it is God's will to get me off this river before she claims me with her dark waters. If you will have me, señor, I will guide you, for the river can be dangerous."

"And then he will give the alarm when we reach New Orleans," El-i-chi muttered.

"We left New Orleans on high water," the Spaniard said. "We were no more than two weeks on the river when we were caught in a great whirlpool. The floods had uprooted huge trees, and we became entangled in the dead branches of one. At that time I promised my God that if He would return me to New Orleans in safety, I would never set foot on a boat again. Put me ashore above New Orleans, if you doubt me."

A splendid day dawned, a day that held a hint of change, the smell of autumn. On the far, western shore a brushfire burned, adding the tang of wood smoke to the freshness. Overhead a V of huge, fat geese winged south.

For the first time Renno had an opportunity to see the face of the Spaniard. He was a mere boy, younger than Egan Kirk. He was darkly handsome and delicate. His name, he announced with fine, rolling "r's" and some pride, was Teodórico de St. Gothard y Peronne. He had been brought from Spain by his father, a soldier, at a very early age and left alone when his father was killed on an expedition to the western areas of New Spain.

"Teodórico is a mouthful," Egan said.

"I am called Teo by my friends."

"That's better," Egan approved, then made introductions all around.

"Is there food aboard?" El-i-chi wanted to know.

"We had not yet loaded any fresh vegetables or meat," Teo told him. "There are dry provisions—beans, rice, flour, and sugar. When we tie up at night, it is easy to catch fish. If you are hungry, Señor El-i-chi, I had cooked a large pot of beans with peppers for myself last night. It can be warmed quickly."

El-i-chi waited impatiently while the cook fire was rekindled and a huge, iron pot suspended over it. Soon delicious aromas were drifting over the keelboat. El-i-chi's hunger forced him to sample the beans before they were more than lukewarm. He dipped a generous helping into a bowl and spooned a huge mouthful. He chewed for a moment, and then his eyes went wide. He rushed to the rail and spat the mouthful into the water. He turned, eyes watering, mouth open.

"This Spaniard has tried to poison me!" he roared.

"No, no," Teo protested. "It is only the peppers. Only the peppers."

Renno chuckled. He tried the beans, and they were delicious and filled with fire.

"Perhaps if you eat them with bread?" Teo suggested helpfully.

The bread made it only marginally possible to eat the beans, delicious though they were. Renno had to mop sweat from his brow. El-i-chi, watching Teo spooning beans eagerly into his mouth, told everyone that if the Spaniard could eat the fiery food, so could he.

"Good," Egan gasped, looking at Mandy, who was bravely eating one or two beans at a time, taking huge bites of bread with them. Ah-wa-o, after one sample, said that she would wait for something a bit less flavorful before she ate.

The keelboat, guided by the sweeps, drifted slowly but steadily down the great, muddy river. Now Renno was

traveling a path that was new to him. On either bank, he
saw lands that looked intriguing, forests that seemed to go
on forever. These were rich lands, Indian lands, and it was
evident that over the aeons the Father of Waters had left its
deposits of rich, black soil. But nothing attracted the white
man more than rich loam. One day, Renno realized, a
traveler on a boat would see many white man's towns along
the banks, and lands cleared of trees for the growing of
crops.

While there was still light to hunt, he directed the boat
to the western shore, where Teo secured it for the night.
El-i-chi and Ah-wa-o took to the forest, and within a half
hour the people on board heard the bark of El-i-chi's
musket. Soon the hunters were back with a yearling deer.
Teo, meanwhile, had set out fishing lines baited with salt
meat, and he soon had a five-pound catfish flopping on the
deck.

With full bellies, they sorted out sleeping arrangements.
Ah-wa-o and Mandy would be below, in the small cabin.
The men situated themselves at various places on deck.
Renno said that he would take the midnight watch and
rolled himself in a blanket from the boat's stores and was
quickly asleep. He awoke when he felt the boat shift and
raised himself to see El-i-chi coming aboard. The shaman
moved to the spot where Teo had placed his blankets and
kicked the boy on the thigh. Teo, jerked into wakefulness,
sat up.

"I hope, boy, that you give me reason to kill you,"
El-i-chi threatened, and there was no doubt in Teo's mind
that he meant it.

"What have I done?" Teo asked fearfully.

"Three times now your poison has sent me to the woods,"
El-i-chi said.

Teo laughed in spite of himself. El-i-chi's hand went to
his tomahawk. Renno came to stand beside his brother. He,
too, had been to the woods earlier in the evening, and he
understood why his brother was angry and why Teo was
trying to contain his laughter. But El-i-chi's face was so

dark, his manner so serious, that Renno could not resist joining in the laughter.

"What have I missed?" Egan asked, coming from his blanket.

"It depends," Renno gasped, laughing harder now, "on whether or not you have been to the woods."

"I see nothing funny," El-i-chi grumbled.

"But you ate more of Teo's beans than any of us," Renno managed through his laughter.

"Señor Renno," Teo said, "perhaps I should have warned everyone that good Louisiana hot peppers speak twice, not only when they are eaten."

"Let me kill him," El-i-chi begged, his anger growing, for now everyone was laughing at him.

"Your own gluttony is no cause to kill," Renno said, at last controlling his laughter. "Go, Brother. Sleep. You will live, that I promise you. I will take the watch."

With fresh meat and fish aboard, the keelboat drifted south, swinging with the current around slow and graceful bends in the river, passing on the eastern shore a bustling Choctaw village. Men and boys, fishing from canoes on the river, waved at them.

Teo often played his guitar, and even El-i-chi came to enjoy the music, which could be soft and languorous, plaintive or sad, joyful or thunderous, depending upon how Teo's fingers flew over the frets and strings. And he sang the songs of Spanish gypsies in his clear, tenor voice.

"Is it difficult to play the instrument?" Renno asked one afternoon as the boat drifted down a wide, straight stretch of river requiring only one man at the steering sweep.

"I have been playing since I was a boy," Teo said, handing the guitar to Renno. "I will show you a few simple chords, and then you can judge for yourself." He taught Renno how to hold the instrument and positioned Renno's fingers on the frets. The first sounds were discordant, but as Teo showed Renno how to hold down the strings and just how to strike them with the fingers of his right hand, the sounds became musical. Renno was fascinated. Thereafter, for several hours each day, Teo instructed him. His fingers, toughened by his life in the wilderness, still became surprisingly sore, but then began to form calluses on the tips. He learned a simple Spanish song, and Teo sang with him as he made the chords and strummed. And then he asked Teo if he knew a certain old English melody, a song that Beth had loved, a song about a lady whose dress had green sleeves. Teo knew. He showed Renno the plaintive, minor chords, and soon Renno was singing "Alas, my love, you do me wrong," much to the delight of Ah-wa-o and Mandy.

"With practice, Renno," Teo said, "you can become a good player."

"I fear that my life does not ordinarily give me as much leisure as we have here," the Seneca confided.

He sat alone on the stern of the boat in darkness. The others were asleep. He cradled the guitar, played it softly, so softly, and whispered the words. "And who but my la-a-dy Greensleeves," and it was as if Beth Huntington were near. He could smell the perfume she favored, could almost taste the full lips that had been his. They had loved, yes, but their love was not true enough on the part of either to overcome the obstacles that life had placed between them long before they met. He hummed the sweet, sad old tune and remembered her as she had been on the trip to the mountain of gold, aboard her ship, in Jamaica, and in England where he had told her good-bye. She had come to him to fulfill a prophecy by the manitous, and her going from his life had also been foretold.

"Manitous," he whispered, "you have not spoken to me with regard to this venture."

Nor did they. A cold front moved across the river from the northwest bringing a light but raw rain. He put Teo's guitar under cover in the cabin and wrapped himself in a blanket, keeping the watch well past time to awaken Se-quo-i. In a chill dawn he still sat at the stern of the boat, his eyes studying the forests along the bank and the surface of the river as the growing light made them visible. Again he was wandering, and his children and his family—his people, as well—were at home without a sachem.

"Manitous," he whispered, "am I wrong? Am I presuming beyond my responsibilities to think of total revenge? Is it desirable to rescue the young white girls or, as the woman in New Madrid hinted, would it be best to leave them to their fate?"

Chapter IX

~~~~~~

El-i-chi and Ah-wa-o sat on blankets at the stern of the
boat. The centrally mounted cabin hid them from the
view of the others. El-i-chi had found a delightful way to
pass the slow hours as, day after day, the keelboat drifted
down the endless river. Had he counted the number of
kisses per mile, he would have strained his limited ability to
do sums. Ah-wa-o became a smoldering, sensuous presence. The intensity of the passion engendered on the
blankets behind the cabin was carefully controlled according to tribal custom, although tribal custom had not,
perhaps, envisioned a situation where a young man and his
beloved had long, hot, lazy hours to be together in privacy
every day. The steamy intensity of the young couple's love

was at times almost embarrassing for Renno and Egan, men who had loved women, and puzzling for Mandy, whose one experience had been violence at the hands of a rapist.

"My love, you dizzy me," Ah-wa-o murmured, pushing feebly against El-i-chi's chest.

"And I soar on wings of eagles," El-i-chi whispered. He pulled away for a while, for it *had* been getting rather intense here in the shade of the cabin with the sun low in the west. He sat with his hands clasped around his knees for a long time before he spoke. "As shaman I can perform the ceremony of union."

"Yes," she cooed.

El-i-chi pounded his fist against the planks of the deck. "They have no right to deny us! Had we come to love before Ha-ace married my mother—"

She giggled. "I would have been a girl-child with no breasts. You would not have loved me."

El-i-chi chuckled. It was true that he greatly admired Ah-wa-o's firm, young bosom. "You know what I mean. Nothing would have stood in the way of our marriage."

"I would not like to hurt Toshabe and my father."

El-i-chi snorted. "Taboos are laid down by old women."

"And yet they mean much to the old ones who follow the traditions."

"If I say that I would perform the ceremony of union right now, would you refuse?"

She pulled herself close and clung to him. "I could never refuse you anything."

There were more kisses. He thrust her away in desperation. "So," he said angrily. "We will continue to observe their cursed customs, but when we have returned to the village, a decision will be made immediately."

"And if the decision is against us?" she asked fearfully.

"How could it be?" he demanded. "It would be against all reason. Our love is too strong to be denied." He reached for her again.

"No, no," she said, "for I am molten inside, and it is time to begin the evening meal. Look, even now Renno steers for the shore."

El-i-chi grinned and clasped her tightly. "Let them prepare the meal themselves." But after a few more passionate
moments, he released her. She stood, smoothed down her
buckskin skirt, took several deep breaths, and swept out
onto the open deck trailing—or so it seemed to Renno
and Kirk—tangible evidence of passion behind her. Renno
looked toward the sky and rolled his eyes. He would be
very much surprised if his brother had the patience to wait
for the decision of the matrons before becoming one with
his little Rose.

The men aboard the keelboat took turns at the steering
sweep, although Teo often did more than his share. Their
days began with the sun and ended while there was still
light to find a good place to tie up for the night. When there
was a need for fresh meat, Renno would direct the boat to
the shore early enough to allow for a couple of hours of
hunting. In that rich wilderness the hunter was often back
with fresh venison before half the allotted time had elapsed.

Renno knew that the river passed through lands populated by one of the more numerous southern tribes, the
Choctaw, to the east, and yet it was seldom that they saw
another human being. A few Choctaw towns were sighted
on bluffs along the river, and near those villages they saw a
few canoes; but for the most part it was as if they floated on
the only river in the world, a river that ran through a land
populated only by animals and birds. Their world consisted
of a few square feet of deck in the midst of a brown flood,
a sweeping forest, and a vast sky that was mostly sunny but
occasionally convulsed with sudden thunderstorms.

Renno cared for his weapons, and never had his blades
been sharper. He also found a supply of buckskin clothing
on board, which he parceled out to his companions. He
spent time in thought and meditation, reliving good memories and praying to the manitous for a good future for his
children and his people. He worked with Teo and Teo's
guitar daily. In the evenings, when the group was gathered
around an open fire on the bank of the river or on the deck
of the keelboat, he took his turn at story-telling. Mandy
gasped in horror as he told of the mass human sacrifices in

Benin, the City of Blood. Ah-wa-o especially liked to hear of the leopard that had been Renno's companion and had saved his life.

Egan found that those sessions of talk were therapeutic. At first he would not participate and would only listen as the others told of their lives and their experiences. When Egan first spoke of his wife and his son it was an emotional moment, for his voice thickened and he had to stop talking. Later on he could tell of the time that his Mary was treed by a wild boar and how he and his father had worked without rest to clear their acres and make their home in the Cumberland wilderness.

Mandy spoke of life in town and her gentle mother, then of her sister, Tess, as a baby and as a mischievous young girl. Teo sang and described his country, warm-blooded Spain, and so vivid were his accounts that everyone seemed to walk the streets of old Valencia, hearing the music that was a blend of Moorish and Spanish influences, seeing the dark-eyed señoritas in their elaborate skirts and head-dresses.

No one thought of Teo as an enemy anymore, for his cheerfulness, his music, and his willingness to do more than his share of the work had endeared him to all, even the fiery El-i-chi, who had never harbored affection for any Spaniard. No longer did any of them speak or think of distrust where Teo was concerned. Teo's plans were to find employment on one of the plantations in the New Orleans area.

"There I will take myself a wife," he said, "as lovely as you, Mandy, and as shapely as you, Ah-wa-o, and have ten children."

Ah-wa-o laughed. "I am glad that I am not going to marry you. Ten children?"

"Well, maybe not so many," Teo decided.

Renno wondered about the land to the west of the river. He had traveled west through the lands of the Comanche and the Apache but had not been as far south as their present latitude. On the way to and from the far southwest he had crossed three great rivers: the Arkansas, the Ouachita, and the Red. Only one of them had joined the Mississippi by that point.

He had no way of estimating distances as the boat drifted around bends, turned lazily in eddies, or drowsed in the sun on long, straight stretches of river, but he knew that they had come far. The feel of the air was different now: Often in the mornings a mist hung low over the river, giving evidence of the moisture that made the midday air heavy and hot.

There was also a difference in the lands on either side of the river. Often low floodplains extended far away from the banks, and the huge trees were festooned with a gray-green moss that, Teo said, had taken its name from his people, Spanish moss. The moisture in the air seemed to breed thunderstorms, which came with continuously rumbling thunder and spectacular lightning. The storms arrived almost as if by clockwork at midafternoon. First the clouds would build, then the white, fleecy, towering pillars would turn deep gray and sweep toward them in a wall of rain and darkness.

If it were possible, Renno would steer the boat to the nearer bank and ride out the thunderstorms tied up to a stout tree.

At midmorning, with the thunderclouds building high in the west—earlier in the day than usual—the boat began to be a bit contrary, as if a current pushed it from the west as well as from the north. Renno noticed the mouth of a large river, soon to join the Mississippi.

"The Ouachita," he told El-i-chi. He could not know that he was wrong, that the Ouachita had joined the Red to the west. The juncture that the boat was now passing was formed by the Red River. The Mississippi was very broad now, and the currents created by the union of the two rivers made for challenging steering. El-i-chi was taking his turn at the sweep, and his muscles bulged as he tried to correct the boat's course in the confused currents.

"Teo," he called, "how much longer will the river not know its own mind?"

"Soon," Teo said, coming to stand beside the shaman.

"Soon she will begin a gradual turn toward the east, and when that turn is complete, we will be in New Orleans." He put his hands on the sweep to aid El-i-chi, and the shaman did not protest.

Preoccupied with the swirling eddies, marveling at the different colors of the two rivers and how, for a long time, the two waters did not mix, no one paid any particular attention to the unusual buildup of clouds. The morning sun still gleamed brightly, but a wall of darkness had formed to the west, roiling and moving rapidly. As the boat moved past the mouth of the Red River, the weather front sent its advance messenger. Wind hit the boat in a solid wall of force. She heeled before the sudden blast. "Ho!" El-i-chi yelled in surprise as the boat tried to spin away from her course down the middle of the river. The wind had sprung from a gentle breeze to a gale within seconds. The surface of the muddy river was whipped into small whitecaps.

"Steer with the wind," Teo advised. "Make for the eastern bank."

Mandy and Ah-wa-o had been airing clothing and sleeping gear. Blankets were hanging on lines running from the top of the cabin to the bow of the boat and on the sides of the cabin.

When rain followed the sudden hammer blow of the wind, Mandy ran to gather the blankets. Ah-wa-o, too, leaped into action, snatching coverlets off the sides of the cabin. On the foredeck Mandy grabbed a quilt and jerked it off the line only to have a huge gust of wind catch the bedding like a sail and push her backward toward the rail. She cried out once as she felt herself being lifted, and then she was falling.

Water closed over her head. Her arms were tangled in the quilt. She could use only her legs. She kicked in panic, got her face above water for a moment, and took a quick, gasping breath. She fought against the constricting, wet tangle of the blanket and managed to free one arm. The boat was moving away from her, pushed by the powerful,

steady wind. Raindrops pelted into her face painfully, so
strongly were they blown by the wind.

"Help!" Mandy cried. "Help me!" She had extricated her
arms from the quilt, but now it was wrapped around her
legs. She took a mouthful of muddy water and gagged.

Only two men had seen Mandy go overboard. At the
sweep Teo shouted to El-i-chi, "Hold her straight!" He ran
to a point amidships and dived over the rail. El-i-chi could
not turn loose of the sweep.

"Renno! Ho!" El-i-chi yelled.

Egan had also seen Mandy go overboard, the blanket
acting like a sail to lift her feet from the deck and send her
flying into space. He was at the bow. Before he jumped
feetfirst into the water, he peered into the rain and saw
Mandy's head surface. She was struggling, obviously in
trouble. The wind was sending the boat rapidly past her.
He jumped in, came up snorting water out his nose, and
swam powerfully toward Mandy. He looked for Teo but saw
nothing. He heard Mandy call out for help and put more
power behind his strokes.

"Mandy!" he yelled as he neared her. She was struggling
to keep her head above water. Something seemed to be
pulling her down. He put his hand in her hair, and she
raised one hand to seize his wrist. "Just relax," he shouted
over the roar of the wind and water. "Don't fight me."

"Quilt." She gasped. "Weighing me down."

She relaxed, lay back, her hair in his grip, and using both
hands, pushed and tugged at the blanket until she had one
leg free, then both. "I can swim now," she told him.

"We'll have to make it all the way to the bank," Egan
said.

The boat was lost to sight amid the heavy rain that
slanted almost horizontally across the surface of the river.
Not even the banks were visible through the solid sheets of
rain.

"Don't fight the current," Egan said. "Let it carry us
downstream. We'll just take our own sweet time, not get
too anxious."

Now they swam side by side, Egan holding the back of

Mandy's clothing. Slowly, slowly, they made progress. After what seemed to be ages the wind began to abate and the rain to lessen. They saw the darkness of the eastern bank, far away, so very far away.

"I don't know if I can swim there." Mandy choked on the muddy waters.

"I'll be with you. If you tire, relax and float. I'll pull you along."

After another age, the shore seemed nearer, and then Egan's feet made contact with the bottom. Clinging to each other, Mandy and Egan waded to a muddy bar and collapsed to rest. When the young man had his breath, he rose and looked up and down the river. He didn't know whether the boat had made shore upstream or down from them. Mandy, still trying to catch her breath, pulled herself into a sitting position. Her tangled hair and buckskins clung to her wetly.

"Thank you," she said, "for coming in after me. I was about to go under for the last time when you reached me."

Egan cleared his throat. "Well . . ."

Mandy looked around. The darkness brought by the storm was passing. "Where, do you suppose?"

He knew that she was asking about the boat. He shook his head. "I think the best thing we can do is sit tight and let them find us. If I had to guess, I'd say that they made shore upriver. I figure if we wait awhile, they'll come drifting down." He patted his wet clothing. "Sure wish I had the makings of a fire."

Renno had hurried to the stern to give El-i-chi a hand with the steering sweep. Se-quo-i manned one of the side sweeps, and slowly the boat came around so that its stern was to the wind. The cabin and, to a lesser extent, the boat's low sides acted as sails, and soon, even through the rain, they saw the dark outlines of the eastern bank. There wasn't much choice of a landing spot. Renno let the boat touch where it would, which happened to be on a muddy bar with huge oak trees not far up the bank. Se-quo-i leaped off the boat and secured lines so the boat was steady, pinned to the bar by the strong wind from the northwest.

It was only then that Renno learned that Teo was not the only one missing. El-i-chi had told Renno how Teo had, to the shaman's amazement, run and dived over the side. El-i-chi himself had not seen Mandy being blown overboard, but it was evident that Teo had gone into the water to try to rescue someone. What had happened to Egan no one knew.

"I'm sure they all made it to shore," Ah-wa-o said.

"We'll build a large fire on the bank," Renno decided. "I think it's best to stay here and let them come to us, since we don't know whether they're up or downriver from us. With just four of us, we're not going to move this boat too far upstream."

Soon a fire was burning, the damp wood giving off satisfying amounts of smoke. When twilight came, and with it a glorious sunset of reds and greens, El-i-chi lit all the boat's lanterns.

Egan saw the smoke from the fire billowing into the sky to the north of them. It seemed to be quite far upriver, but then he had no way of estimating how long it had taken for Mandy and him to battle their way to shore, not able to swim directly at right angles to the current but angling slowly in toward the bank.

"It's they," Mandy said. "I know it is."

"But that's a mile or more away."

"I don't think we have any choice," Mandy said. "We either spend the night here in wet clothes or start walking."

"I guess we start walking," Egan said.

They stayed on the riverbank, and at times they had to struggle through clinging mud. The heat had returned after the violent storm, and sweat ran into their eyes, making them sting, while a host of hungry mosquitoes took advantage of two mobile feeding stations. The sun came out through lessening clouds, low in the west. Tired, steamy-hot in their soggy clothing, fighting the voracious mosquitoes, neither had eyes for the glory of the western skies; they had no strength for the appreciation of beauty. Their one thought was to keep going, to reach the signal fire and the boat.

It was Mandy who saw the body first. She was ahead of Egan, struggling through another area of deep, black, sucking mud, having to lift her feet high. Each step required all-out exertion. Egan had his hand on her shoulder, helping to push her along.

"Oh, God," she moaned as she spotted what she recognized immediately as Teo's fine silken shirt. She halted, and Egan pulled up even with her. He moved forward to wade into the water.

"I don't think you'd better see this, Mandy."

Teo's body was in about three feet of water. He was lying beside a waterlogged, barkless section of tree trunk from which protruded water-hardened, jagged remnants of small limbs. When Egan first saw him, it appeared that Teo was embracing the tree trunk. On closer examination he saw that Teo was pinned to the trunk by a rock-hard limb with a jagged end that, protruding from his back, held small, whitened bits of flesh among its splinters.

In spite of Egan's warning, Mandy waded out into the water and stood beside him. Her eyes were wide, and she was chewing on the knuckle of her forefinger.

"Poor little devil," Egan whispered.

"Get him out from under it," Mandy begged urgently. "We have to get him—"

Egan turned and put his hands on her arms. "You go to the bank. I'll do—"

"No, I'll help."

As it was, the task required both of them, for the waterlogged trunk had rolled partially atop the boy. Egan tugged and pulled until Teo's body rolled upward. Mandy, closing her eyes, put her hands on her dead friend's shoulders and pulled. She fell backward with a splash when the hardened limb jerked out of the body. The body landed across her legs, and for a moment she panicked, clawing at the muddy bottom, trying to kick the weight off her legs. Then Egan was there, hauling the body toward the shore. The length of weathered trunk, relieved of its anchor, angled lazily and drifted slowly into the current, submerged except for two or three jagged limbs extending above the surface.

Egan tugged the body from the water and onto the muddy bank to stand over it, breathing hard. Mandy waded out of the water, averting her face. "Dear God," she whispered.

"He must have landed right on it when he jumped out of the boat," Egan said in a quiet, small voice. "Punched right through his stomach and came out beside his spine."

"Oh, God," Mandy said.

"Sorry," Egan said. "Look, it can't be too much farther to the boat. Maybe I'd best stay with him—"

"All right," she agreed.

"Let's see if they can hear us," Egan said as Mandy began to walk. He cupped his hands around his mouth and called, "Hallooo."

"I'll go," El-i-chi offered after answering Egan's shout. He met Mandy about fifty yards downriver. She pointed downstream.

"Who's there?" he asked.

"Teo's dead," she said. "Egan's with him."

"You're near the boat," El-i-chi told her.

"I'll go back with you."

"If you wish," he said.

It was fully dark and another thunderstorm was moving toward them across the wide river when El-i-chi reached the boat, Teo's body across his shoulders. Teo had been a small fellow, weighing less than some of the deer that El-i-chi had carried in the same way.

They buried Teo on a fine autumn morning with a pleasant hint of coolness in the air. When the grave was dug and Teo, wrapped in a blanket, was lowered respectfully into it, Renno said "Hold" and went back to the boat for Teo's guitar.

"Renno," Mandy said quietly, "I think he'd like you to have it."

Renno stood silently, the instrument in his hand. Since Teo had loved the guitar so, it had been Renno's intention to bury it with the little Spanish musician.

"He would want you to keep it," Ah-wa-o agreed.

Renno nodded. He looked at Mandy. "Will you talk to the white man's God on his behalf?"

Mandy lowered her head and closed her eyes. "Lord God, look down on Teo, one of your children. He was a good man, Lord, a gentle man, and now we ask you to clasp him to Your bosom, to take him in. He was young, Lord, and far from his home. He bravely sacrificed himself with the hopes of saving another. We know that this lonely grave is not his destination, but that he is now with You and not lonely."

Ah-wa-o wiped away tears.

"Add his voice to those of the angels, please, Lord," Mandy said, "for You will like his sweet singing, as did we all."

Later, as the boat moved toward midriver, leaving the grave behind, Mandy stood with Egan at the stern, looking back. "He was so afraid of the river," she said, "afraid that it was going to get him."

"And so it did," Egan replied sorrowfully.

Mandy began to weep silently. Egan could not find words of comfort, so he put his hand on her shoulder and squeezed lightly. She made no attempt to move away from his touch.

"He was trying to save me," she whispered.

"Mandy, don't blame yourself. He could have been caught off balance when the big wind hit. He might have fallen overboard."

"It's still my fault," she said. "I wouldn't listen to Rusog or to Renno. I could only think of finding Tess!"

"It's no more your fault than my own," he said. "*I* was the one who wouldn't give up. I insisted on going after Simon Purdy."

Renno, standing nearby, had overheard. He came to join them. "One who takes a bath in regret emerges more soiled," he said. "It was Teo's time. His God called, and Teo answered. That is all."

Captain León Bocalos had been in the provinces of New Spain for almost a score of years. He had served in Mexico before being sent to head the Spanish military in New Orleans, to take responsibility for supply and relief of the various Spanish garrisons on the Mississippi. The trip to the settlements on the upper river during which he met Simon Purdy and came into half ownership of four lovely young American girls had been his first upriver journey, and he was happy to have it almost over.

Bocalos, son of a Córdoba merchant, had come to the New World with high hopes, but it seemed that the conquistadores had already looted all the gold and silver. Quick riches and a triumphant return to Spain had eluded Bocalos for almost twenty years. Now, at the age of forty, his choices had been reduced to only a few, all equally undesirable: He could return to Spain and live on a very small pension earned as a twenty-year officer; he could accept a land grant from a grateful king and become a farmer or a rancher in New Spain, but the land grants were often in areas where a man spent most of his time fighting Apache Indians and was considered rich if he still had his scalp; or he could stay in the king's service and wait for some entrenched administrator either to die or steal enough money to be able to afford to go back to Spain. In that last event, Bocalos could only hope that his long service would outweigh the bribes of a newcomer in the struggle to obtain the vacated administrative office.

Opportunity, large or small, had come seldom to Bocalos. Thus, when he saw the white renegade land in New Madrid with the trader Juan Cristobal in possession of four white girls, he leaped at the chance to improve his financial condition. In New Orleans, the girls would provide a very good living or a quick source of profit. Very soon he learned that Cristobal had not had the ready capital to satisfy Purdy's selling price for the girls. Cristobal would have to sell them in New Orleans to meet Purdy's demands, but that would not be so convenient; Cristobal had his own woman in New Madrid, plus his trading post. Thus, when Bocalos offered to relieve Cristobal of the girls, the trader was immediately interested. So it was that Bocalos left New Madrid with no money, Cristobal had a good profit from the transaction, and Bocalos, like Cristobal before him, had a partner.

Bocalos had offered to send Purdy's money back upriver on the next boat, but Purdy looked wary. "It's a long river, Captain, and I've never seen it. I think I'll just tag along and keep an eye on my half of the property. Then you won't have to worry about getting the money back to me."

The boat left New Madrid with a crew of four, in addition to Bocalos and Purdy. Purdy had used some of the money he had received from Cristobal to buy white man's clothing in New Madrid. He had cut his hair and now looked quite presentable. He had a thin face, sharp black eyes, and a body hardened by his life among the Indians. It was evident to Bocalos, who considered himself to be a gentleman, that Purdy would as soon kill a man as not.

Bocalos had one half of the cabin. His quarters were separated from those assigned to the four girls by a thin partition. On the first night out he heard Purdy among the girls, and he burst angrily into the small space to find Purdy embracing the youngest, thinnest Brown girl while the other three sat together quietly, faces turned.

"Here, now!" Bocalos said sternly. "You must not do that."

Purdy's eyes seemed to bore into those of the captain. His voice was low. "Seems to me, Cap, that I own half of this here merchandise, and it ain't up to you to tell me what to do with it."

Bocalos considered calling the crew to tell them to kill the man, but he was concerned about the crew, for they, too, had eyes for the girls.

"It's going to be a long trip, Cap," Purdy added. "You might as well enjoy it. Have yourself one. Hell, take two, they's small." He laughed and pinched the little girl in his lap on the rump.

Bocalos looked at the girls and felt desire begin to simmer.

"Customers likes 'em broke in," Purdy said.

Bocalos examined the three girls. The plump one was out; his mother had been short and fat, and his sisters had taken after their mother. Even the girl whom he had kissed a few times before leaving for the army had been a fat and sweaty armful on warm, humid nights. He had sampled the wares of various Indian women in the New World, and almost all of them had been fat. He liked the one called Tess. He pointed to her and said, "Come."

"Take another one," Purdy invited. "It's crowded in here."

Bocalos pointed to the oldest girl, Grace Brown.

"Cap," Purdy said, "you might give this a thought: You're going to have four angry crewmen on your hands. They's going to see and hear us having ourselves a time, and they's going to be a little mad about that. What do you think about letting them have this here chubby one?"

Bocalos considered. It was, he felt, a sensible idea. He said, "You two, go to my cabin and wait."

Plump little Hope Brown, fifteen years old, had been used, to that date, only by Purdy. The thought of being handed to the four dirty, smelly crewmen brought a wail of anguish from her, and she struggled as Bocalos seized her arm and dragged her toward the deck. The other girls started weeping. Purdy turned Charity, the youngest sister, over his knee and popped her a few times on the rump. "None of that. Hush your mouth, or we'll let you take on the crew."

Hope had very little sleep that night. Meanwhile Bocalos was discovering that one girl was quite enough for him, after all. So it was that the next morning he told the crew that the tall one, the oldest, Grace, was also available to them.

After Purdy, Tess found the captain to be a gentle man who, in spite of his hateful desires, treated her almost with kindness. She spent her days and nights in the captain's cabin, seldom going on deck. She was afraid that Bocalos would tire of her and pass her to the crew. Each night she heard the raucous laughter, the shouts, and the quarrels as the four crewmen vied for their turns with poor Grace and Hope.

To secure what she considered to be her favored status as the captain's cabin mate, she began to do things voluntarily that had been forced on her previously.

"Ah, yes, little one," Bocalos would whisper. "I think perhaps I will keep you forever."

That hope filled Tess's thoughts. She had heard the talk between first Purdy and Cristobal and then Purdy and the captain, and she knew that the plans were to put all of them in houses of ill repute. The thought of being imprisoned in some horrid place, of being on call for any man who had enough money, inspired Tess to cling to Bocalos, do those things for him that, at first, had been soul rending. And when Bocalos was lovingly tender with her, she came to know little by little the pleasures of womanhood and to feel her blood turn to fire.

It was quite different for Hope and Grace Brown. The four crewmen had orders not to damage the merchandise on pain of death, but they were naturally rough men. Both girls were bruised, sore, soiled, filthy, and so filled with shame that they could not face Tess and Charity, the lucky ones who got to stay in the cabin with only one man.

Hope lost count of the days, but it seemed that months had passed. It seemed that she never could get enough sleep. The men kept her awake far into the night and often one of them came to her where she slept, huddled in a blanket on the deck, to awaken her and subject her to more torment.

The demands made by the crewmen seemed to be endless, and she could find little sympathy from her older sister, Grace, who had withdrawn into a type of madness and spoke only seldom. Grace seemed not to be aware of what was being done to her repeatedly. Worse, Charity,

Hope's younger sister, seemed ashamed to speak to her; and from the captain's cabin she often heard sounds from Tess that made her think that the shameless wench was actually enjoying the attentions of Bocalos. Hope prayed to God for deliverance and then quit praying, for it seemed that God did not hear.

On a steamy, endless night when the lust of the crew seemed to reach new heights, each of them using her at least twice before, at last, she was left alone, Hope Brown came to a decision: she had been violated by five men, and from what she could understand, that would be a very small number compared to those who would buy her time in a New Orleans house. There, said the crewmen, it could be as many as a dozen in one night, every night, until she died of the Spanish disease or grew old and ugly. Hope knew she could not face that existence.

Now alone—but not for long, she knew—she eased herself over the rail of the boat and into the water. It came to her knees, for the vessel was tied up close to the bank. She moved very quietly, careful not to splash or fall. She went around the stern of boat. The river, flat and dark in the dim moonlight, stretched far and away toward the other shore. She waded forward slowly, and just before her head went under, she remembered something her father had preached: she who took her own life would burn forever in hell. Somehow that seemed amusing, for she didn't think that the real hell could be any worse than the hell she was experiencing. She struggled a bit when the water burned its way down into her lungs, but then her splashings quickly died away, and there was only the dark, muddy, mighty flow of the Father of Waters moving her limp body southward as it sank down, down, down.

Purdy was still sleeping, his arms around the naked, childish body of Charity Brown, when Bocalos called to him that one of the girls was missing. Purdy came out of the cabin pulling on his shirt, a pistol in his hand, another at his belt.

"What have you done with the girl?" Bocalos demanded of his crewmen.

"In truth, Captain," a man said, spreading his hands, "last time we saw her she was on her blanket, sleeping."

Purdy jumped down into the shallow water and examined the muddy bank. "No tracks," he called up to Bocalos. "She didn't go into the woods."

"Which one of you harmed her?" Bocalos demanded, thinking that one of the men, in the throes of passion, had killed the girl and tossed her body overboard.

All four men denied having done anything to the girl. Grace Brown sat up from her blanket, unconcerned that she was nude.

"You," Bocalos said to her, "do you know what has happened to your sister?"

Grace smiled beatifically and began to weave patterns with her intertwining fingers.

Purdy climbed back aboard. "She's in the river for sure."

"All right, then," Bocalos said, lifting a pistol to give weight to his words. "I have been generous with you. I have shared the women with you, and this is my reward. For the balance of the trip you will not touch any of the women."

"Now, Captain," one of the crewmen said. "That isn't fair. We can't help it if the girl fell or jumped overboard during the night. We think you had better leave us the other one."

"Are you questioning my orders?" Bocalos asked.

"If it comes to that, Captain," said another man, lifting the muzzle of a musket.

Beside Bocalos, Purdy's pistols spoke. Two men fell, one tumbling over the rail into the water. Bocalos, seeing the remaining two move indecisively, panicked by the threat and by the sudden deaths, shot one man, and a Cherokee tomahawk whizzed from Purdy's hand to kill the last.

"We're only a couple of days out of New Orleans," Purdy said. "We didn't need them." He quickly dumped the bodies into the river and loosed the lines, getting the boat under way.

Bocalos had been very impressed by Purdy's swift and decisive action. There had been times in the past when he would have been glad to have Purdy at his side. Since it was a violent world, there would undoubtedly be times in the future when a man who could kill so easily and so quickly would prove valuable to him. As the boat drifted slowly toward New Orleans, he began to consider ways that he could keep Purdy with him, either as a hireling or ally.

Chapter X

La Nouvelle Orléans had been built on land created by the Mississippi River. It occupied the east bank of a crescent bend a hundred miles north from the river's mouth. The site had been chosen by the Frenchman Jean Baptiste le Moyne, sieur de Bienville, for its access by water from the Father of Waters and from the lakes to the north. As Renno and his friends approached the city, their keelboat having drifted through a lengthy series of sharp bends that eventually turned toward the east, the torrid summer had moderated into a season viewed by older residents of the city—French, German, and Spanish—with mixed emotions. The temperature was pleasant, but autumn was the season of storms. The soft, cooling breezes that came from the Gulf of Mexico could grow into the fury of *huracán*.

Floods from the mighty river had taken their turn in nature's attempts to return the Isle of Orleans to its original state, and disease—fevers and the dreaded cholera— plagued the city.

With the Treaty of Paris in 1763, France had ceded to England all the territory east of the Mississippi with the exception of the Isle of Orleans, which, along with all of Louisiana west of the river, had been given in a secret treaty to Louis XV's cousin, Charles III of Spain. As a result, New Orleans was, in spite of its mixed populace, a Spanish town ruled by Governor Esteban Miró.

Esteban Miró had one burning ambition: He wanted to see the flag of Spain flying not only over all of the vast lands west of the Mississippi River, but on the eastern bank as well. Spain, Miró believed, had a right to those lands extending all the way to the mountains marking the western boundaries of the United States. It was Miró's policy to be generous in supplying weapons, ammunition, and special inducements to any Indian tribe, and to any war chief, who would use those weapons against the settlers on the western fringe of the United States.

As the sachem of the southern Seneca neared his city, Miró was entertaining one of his most powerful Indian allies, Alexander McGillivray, the Creek who was by blood more white than red. McGillivray liked the sophistication of New Orleans' social life. He was quite often in the city, and he divided his time here between the social salons of the powerful, and the debauched, sensual pleasures of his favorite house of prostitution.

The morality of the city had been established in its earlier days, when there were few women of good character among the French settlers. Although New Orleans was no longer a primitive settlement, it was far removed from the mainstream of European life. There were three levels of society: The bottom layer, of course, was made up of the poor. Legitimate society—among whom moved the governor, French plantation owners, prosperous merchants, and the

lowly developing class of artists—centered around the
salons of matrons who were, in most cases, the daughters or
granddaughters of the *filles à la cassette*, the "casket girls."
This interesting moniker came about because the French
government had given them small caskets of clothing and
linens when they left their homes in 1727 to cross an ocean
and become brides of worthy New Orleans Frenchmen.

Not so legitimate but accepted was the gay life in the
salons of the madames, some of them, too, daughters or
granddaughters of the casket girls. Many of the houses and
the salons outshone the homes of the more moral matrons.

Miró and McGillivray had concluded their business in an
amiable manner in a private room in the establishment of
the premier New Orleans *fille de joie*, Laure Beyle. The
business, as usual, had had to do with guns, powder, shot,
daggers, axes, a bit of whiskey, and war against the United
States along the exposed borders of the state of Georgia.
Both men were satisfied with the outcome of their bar-
gaining—McGillivray, because he had squeezed more long
rifles out of the Spaniard, and Miró, because he had got off
so cheaply this time. McGillivray rang for service and
ordered a roasted duck with fresh asparagus, two bottles of
fine wine imported all the way from Spain, and an assort-
ment of sweets for dessert.

"I take it then, my friend," Miró said, "that you will be
leaving us shortly. I'm sure you're eager to get back to your
warriors and, with these new arms, to strike a swift blow
against our enemy."

McGillivray raised one eyebrow. He did not look kindly
on Miró's efforts to treat him condescendingly, as if he were
nothing more than an ignorant Creek war chief. "I have
traveled quite a distance, Governor. Would you have me
rush away before I enjoy the hospitality of this beautiful
city?"

McGillivray spoke perfectly accented Spanish. Miró was
reminded, once again, not to forget that this king of the
Creek had been born to a wealthy white family and that he
had been welcomed into the highest levels of English

society as the result of his undying enmity for Americans in
general and Georgians in particular.

"Of course not," Miró assured him, pulling out his fa
pocket watch and frowning. "Unfortunately, my friend,
must take my leave of you now. Duty calls, you know."

Alone, and pleased by Miró's departure, McGillivra·
rang for the black serving maid and told her to request the
presence of Laure Beyle. He pronounced her name prop
erly, not "Low-ray," as the Spanish would have said, o
"Laura" as in English, but "Lor."

Laure Beyle swept into the room with a smile on her full
square face. She was dressed splendidly in silks, the gow·
showing an astounding amount of cleavage. Her perfume
filled the air.

"Ah, madame," McGillivray said, "each time I see you
you are more beautiful."

Laure showed fine, white teeth in a smile, but her eye·
did not join her lips in the expression. "My dear Alex
ander," she cooed.

"The governor did not help me with the wine," Mc
Gillivray said. "If I drink both bottles, I shall be too
intoxicated to meet the new lady you have promised me."

"We mustn't let that happen," Laure said, seating hersel·
with ladylike posture and accepting a glass of wine.

"Of course, Laure," he said, "if you yourself would joir
me—"

She laughed, but her cold gray eyes lashed him. "Alas,"
she said, "my responsibilities—"

He knew that Laure had long since graduated from doin·
her time in one of the cozy, nicely decorated rooms on the
second story of the cypress-plank house, and although she
was beautiful, he was not serious in his invitation. He had
heard that the new one was no more than sixteen.

Thus, he was not offended that Laure limited her time
with him to ten minutes. He knew she had other guests,
some of them more important than a man who was a friend
and a guest of the governor. When she rose, McGillivray
leaped to his feet to bow and put his lips to within a fraction
of an inch of the back of her gloved hand.

"Liza will show you to the room," she said, then was gone with a swirling of skirts.

There was a full bottle of the fine, Spanish wine left. McGillivray carried it with him up the stairs and down a long hall past doors from which came sounds of revelry or passion. When the black maid opened the door to a private room and stood back, he entered with much anticipation.

The girl was sitting on a chaise. One arm was elegantly arranged along the back of the seat, the other hand rested demurely in her lap. She wore a flowing, lacy, black creation of the night that showed her fine young body well. Her cornsilk hair had been brushed to a lustrous sheen, and she wore only enough makeup to accent her youthful grace.

"Ah, my dear," McGillivray breathed, hurrying across the small room to fall to his knees, to seize the languid hand from the girl's lap and press his lips into the palm. Once he had taken such a girl, a young white girl, during a raid on a poor settlement on the frontier, and his time with her had been sweet, for she had fought him fiercely, and her struggles, even after he had beaten her into accepting him, had added to the joy of it. This one would not struggle, he knew, but she would remind him of that fine, long night on blankets under the stars.

He could not be patient. His hands began to explore. The specially designed garment fell easily to the floor when he lifted the girl from the chaise and directed her toward the bed. He did not notice, not for a long time, that the girl did not speak, nor did her eyes ever seem to focus on his face.

Renno always carried a few small gold coins, for one never knew when the white man's money would be needed. But he did not have enough money to pay for lodgings and food for the entire group. He did have one asset available in the form of the keelboat. One boat looked much like another, and no ownership papers were required. He let it be known among the dockworkers that the boat was for sale, and soon he had an offer.

"The boat's worth more than that," Egan grumbled.

Renno shrugged. He had not come to New Orleans to

haggle over the sale price of a boat but to find five people—one to kill, the others to rescue. He accepted the offer, which provided enough money to take rooms for his group in a boardinghouse, with plenty left over to flash as he and Egan visited various houses of pleasure in search of Tess and the Brown girls.

On the face of it, it seemed that it would be easier to find the girls than it would be to find Simon Purdy. Once the girls had been found, they might have information about the renegade. Renno spent some money on clothing for Egan and himself. In frontier buckskins they could not have gotten past the front door of some of the finer establishments, and it seemed logical that the white girls would not be found in the type of house that catered to rivermen and frontiersmen.

It was a simple matter to get the names and locations of the city's fancy bordellos. Every man who worked on the riverfront knew them, even if he couldn't afford to frequent them. Egan was all eyes as they entered the first of the houses, where well-dressed gentlemen and ladies talked, drank, and played cards in a room as big as a Seneca council house. The grandeur of the decor intimidated Egan, who had never been inside anything fancier than a Knoxville log cabin.

Renno did the talking, speaking smoothly and in perfect Spanish to the serving maid who brought two tall, cool glasses containing something very alcoholic with just a trace of mint. Renno touched the glass to his lips. The white man's alcohol had been almost as effective in the conquest of Indian territory as had the white man's muskets. Renno had no use for it. Egan, on the other hand, drank eagerly.

Now it was the hostess herself who came to their table and greeted them in accented Spanish. Renno replied in French, and the woman's face brightened. She was not young, but with her makeup and her expensive silk garments, she was an attractive woman.

"Ah, handsome one," she purred, "you speak the language of love, the language of beauty."

"Ah, but doesn't everyone?" Renno asked.

"In this city everyone used to speak French," the madam said, "but now—" She sighed, her ample breasts heaving. "But you are young and handsome, and I have just the girl for you."

"I have heard that there is a new American girl here," Renno said, lifting his glass casually. "Young and tender."

"Americans," the madam said. "What do they know of the arts of love? I have for you, handsome one, Carlota, with the fiery blood of Spain. And for the strong, silent one—" She put her soft hand on Egan's shoulder. "Well, let me think."

Renno let a touch of anger enter his voice. "Then you save the young and tender American for others?"

"*Chéri*"—the madam pouted—"you hurt me. Would I deny such a handsome one as you anything? You will fall in love with Carlota. This I promise."

Renno stood. Egan, who was still working on the tall drink, looked up in puzzlement.

"If I cannot have the woman I want," Renno said, "then I will take my business elsewhere." He was halfway to the front door before Egan could gulp the last of his drink and leap to his feet.

The same scene was repeated, with minor variations, three more times. At each house Egan had finished the drink that Renno had ordered him, and as they walked around a square toward still another fine house of pleasure, he had a desire to sing a little bit. Renno suppressed a smile.

"Unless you can sing in Spanish," Renno said, "I think it's best that you whistle."

Egan puckered up, but for some reason he couldn't get any sound to come.

The house that they entered was the most grand they had seen. Fine Persian rugs covered the polished, wide-plank floors. The furniture was French, and luxurious in rich, plush colors of velvet. Handsome, slim, black serving maids circulated, one of them bowing before Renno and Egan the second they sat at a little table. The white Indian ordered the same drink that he had ordered at the other places and, while he waited, looked around. Four musicians were playing an elegant melody. One couple was dancing, the girl powdered, regal looking in a fine gown, the man slim, tall, dressed in Spanish finery.

There was something about the man that seemed familiar to Renno, but the dancer's back was to him. His attention was diverted as a stunning woman approached the table with a smile and greeted them in Spanish. Once again Renno replied in French.

"Monsieur," the woman said, "I, Laure Beyle, welcome you. I have not seen you here before, have I?"

Egan was finding that the tall, minty drink was getting more delicious all the time. He had, in fact, gulped his own drink down. Now that Renno's attention was on the woman, he quietly exchanged his empty glass for Renno's full one. After all, it was a shame to waste such delicious stuff, and he'd noticed that Renno hardly ever touched his drinks.

"My lovely lady," Renno said, standing to bow to the madam, "I have not had the pleasure of visiting your fine establishment previously."

"We shall try to make your first visit so memorable that you will want to return," Laure said.

"You can, if you have, as I have heard, a new girl, a young and tender American."

"Ah," Laure said, "so the word spreads. Good, good. Yes, monsieur. Her name is Grace, and you will find, I promise you, that she lives up to her name. But I must ask you to be patient, for she is very popular. When the girl is free, I will send a maid to fetch you. Now, the other gentleman?"

Egan looked up, a placid smile on his face. His head seemed to be too heavy for his neck.

"My friend is celebrating in another manner," Renno said. He waited for the madam to leave, then bent to put his lips close to Egan's. "She has a young American girl. The name is Grace."

"'S go get 'er," Egan mumbled. "'S Grace Brown, sure as Dan'l Boone. I'll bet the others are here, too."

"We'll see," Renno said.

He glanced around the room again. He spotted at least

two men who were not participating in any activity. They stood with their backs against the wall, one with his arms crossed over his chest. After a while a movement in the darkness of a curtained archway told Renno that there was yet another strongman. There could be others. The two visible ones looked strong and confident. Renno was intent on examining the other men in the room when a shadow came between him and the light from a chandelier.

"Renno, by God!" erupted a male voice in Spanish. "I thought it was you."

He looked up into the eyes of an old friend who had not always been a friend. Once he had crossed blades with this slim, tall man who stood grinning before him. He stood and extended his arm for the warrior's clasp. "Well, Adan, we are well met," he said with genuine pleasure. "But you? In a Spanish port?"

Adan Bartolome, onetime pirate, brother of the wife of William Huntington, Lord Beaumont, laughed. "I might ask the same question of you."

"I will tell you gladly, but not here."

"I was wondering about that." Adan grinned slyly. "Since I am Spanish," he whispered, leaning close, "I decided to put it to good use. As far as they know here, my ship is out of Veracruz, not Wilmington."

"So," Renno said. Adan captained one of Beth Huntington's ships.

"Look," Adan said, "there are questions I want to ask. Is your business finished here?"

"No, but it can wait," Renno decided.

"Come, then. We'll go to the ship. Does this American come with us?"

Renno nodded. If Adan could so easily spot Egan as an American, perhaps it was time to remove the young man from public display. He bent, whispered, "Come, we go."

"We ain't got Grace and the girlsh," Egan said, his words slurring, his voice loud enough to cause a few people at a nearby table to turn their heads.

"No more talk," Renno said sternly. "On your feet."

Egan tried to rise but fell back unsteadily into the chair.

Laure Beyle chose that time to glide gracefully toward the table.

"Monsieur," she said, smiling at Renno with her lips while her cold, gray eyes swept swiftly over Egan and Adan, "if you will come with me."

"A thousand pardons, madam," Renno apologized, with a courtly bow. "I must beg you to forgive me and ask you to expect to see me again soon. My friend has become indisposed, and I must take him to his bed."

With Adan on one side of Egan and Renno on the other, they made their way toward the front door, swaying now and then as Egan lost his balance.

It was but a short walk to the waterfront. Adan's ship was a new three-master, sleek and well maintained. As they approached her, helping Egan along the dock, Renno could make out her name, lettered ornately in Spanish, *Nuestra Señora*.

"Not exactly original," Renno commented.

"In numbers there is safety," Adan said cheerily. "She is one of perhaps a dozen with the name of *Our Lady*. But under the nameplate there is another, *Jamaica Belle*. She's the newest ship in the Huntington fleet, and a true lady."

Renno grunted. There had been a time when all of Beth's ships had been named, one way or the other, for him, such as *Seneca Warrior* and *Seneca Chieftain*. So quickly had things changed after his good-bye to Beth in England.

Egan made no protest when, once they were aboard, Adan called on two of his crewmen to help the big American to a bunk. Adan faced Renno in the well-appointed captain's cabin.

"By God's grace, Renno, it is good to see you."

"Truly," Renno agreed.

"Now, I am consumed with curiosity as to why the sachem of the Seneca is in a New Orleans bordello."

Renno smiled. "Not, I think, for the same reason Adan Bartolome was there."

"No, I think not," Adan conceded with a grin.

"Have you seen a young American girl there called Grace?"

"I have heard others speak of her. She is pretty, but as I have heard it, not many are willing to pay her price a second time." He spread his hands. "This girl has brought you?"

"She and three others drew me to New Orleans, and a white man named Simon Purdy."

Adan saw a look in Renno's eye that did not bode well for the man called Simon Purdy. "I have not heard the name," the Spaniard said. "But I do have some contacts with traders and merchants. I can inquire quietly."

"Thank you, my friend. What do you hear from your sister?"

"Ah," Adan said, smiling broadly. "Estrela seems content to be wife and mother. When last I had letters from her, she was again with child." He flexed the biceps of his right arm. "She tells me that she will stimulate the tired, old blood of England with Spanish vitality from the New World."

Renno was silent. As if sensing his thoughts, Adan said, "Forgive me if I touch on a sensitive subject, but I would like to express my regrets about you and Beth."

"It was the will of the manitous," Renno said. "Is she well?"

"Quite well." He considered for a moment, then decided that Renno had a right to know. "She has announced her engagement to a fellow named Jowett. Seems that he's a man of some influence in the king's court."

Renno was silent. In all truth, Beth's place was in England. Her beauty and wit would make her a favorite in that exclusive society centering around King George. And yet he could remember her astride an Apache pony or keeping pace with him as they moved swiftly in the north woods to avoid an enemy war party.

"May she find happiness," he said.

"Estrela doesn't like this Jowett fellow," Adan confided. "And there's no indication as to when she'll return to Wilmington. Meantime, Moses Tarpley is running the firm. The trade deal with the British islands in the Caribbean has not lived up to expectations. Billy the Pequot and his *Seneca Warrior* handle the Caribbean trade, and this new ship would be idle if I hadn't come up with the idea of turning her into a Spaniard. This is my second trip to New Orleans. I'm loading mainly myrtle wax for candles. I can buy it cheap here and sell it dear in Wilmington. It brings a better price in England, though. This time I'm buying a new product that should become a staple of trade. A gentleman named Jean Etienne Boré has found a way to turn sugarcane extract into a granulated form."

Renno wasn't really concentrating on the details of Adan's trading. He was thinking of Beth, and for a few moments he missed her as he had not missed her since leaving England.

"Tell me about the girls you're looking for," Adan said.

Renno gave him the story in brief. Adan shook his head. "If they are indeed in Laure Beyle's house, it's going to be difficult to pry them out. A young white girl is worth roughly her weight in gold over a period of time if she does not become diseased early. Madam Beyle's house is under the protection of the governor himself. At any given time there are six to eight competent men-at-arms circulating in the house to prevent disturbances. And if you should get the girls out of the house, you'd have to move swiftly to spirit them out of New Orleans. What are your plans for escape once you'd done what you came to do?"

Renno shrugged. "Overland, through Creek and Choctaw lands."

"All Esteban Miró would have to do is speak to his great friend the king of the Creek, and the entire Creek Nation would be hunting for you."

Renno shrugged again. It would not be the first time he had been in hostile country with overwhelming numbers of the enemy seeking his death.

"There is another possibility," Adan said. "I should have my cargo loaded within a very few days. Once I loose my mooring lines, you will be safe. We'd sail into Bayou St. John and then the open Gulf. We will show the Spanish flag until we pass safely around Florida into the Atlantic."

Renno nodded. "Thank you, my friend. That would be the fastest way home."

"So be it, then," Adan said brightly. "Now we have only

to find the girls, timing it so that they will be put aboard ship just before we're ready to sail."

"And Simon Purdy," Renno said.

"To find one man in this city will not be easy." Adan rubbed his chin, which, at that late hour, was showing a darkness of beard. "We need access to Esteban Miró. His people watch and report all comings and goings. If this Purdy came here with four young white girls, he would not have gone unnoticed by Miró's spies. I think that you must go to Miró. As an important sachem, you will ignite his interest, and if you give him the idea that you might take the Seneca into the war against the outposts of the United States, he will do anything you ask, within reason, to buy your loyalty."

Renno laughed and fluffed the white, lacy sleeves of his shirt. "If you were the Spanish governor and I came to you dressed like this, with white skin, would you believe that I am sachem of the Seneca?"

"You have a point," Adan said. He snapped his fingers. "But you are not the only sachem who dresses in finery and has white skin. Tomorrow night, at nine, we will go back to visit Madam Beyle. There we will meet a man who will then introduce you to the governor."

El-i-chi and Se-quo-i were still awake and about when Renno returned to the boardinghouse. They had been out in the town.

"We saw many Spanish soldiers," El-i-chi told his brother. "This is a beehive of people. If we can find Simon Purdy, we can kill him, but to steal away four young girls—of this I am not sure."

Alexander McGillivray had not chosen to visit the distracted young white girl again. He had spent the early part of the evening with an active young woman of some twenty years who claimed to be the disgraced daughter of a French nobleman. Her ancestry had not interested McGillivray, but her other qualifications had been most suitable. Now he was seated with two Spanish cavalry officers and a ship's captain, discussing the political situation as it existed between Spain and England, when he looked up to see two well-dressed young men approaching. It was the dark one who spoke.

"Chief McGillivray," Adan said, "forgive me for intruding. May I have a moment of your time?"

McGillivray waved a hand languidly in permission.

"Alexander McGillivray, war chief of the Creek Nation, may I present my friend Renno, sachem of the Seneca," Adan said, bowing.

McGillivray's eyes narrowed as they examined Renno's dress, his face, his stance. Then the Creek rose and extended his arm for the warrior's clasp. "Sachem," he said, "I have heard much about you."

"And I of you, great Chief," Renno said.

McGillivray had his doubts, but he would soon see if this blue-eyed young man was, indeed, the Seneca whose name and prowess were known throughout the United States and up and down the frontier. He turned to his companions. "Gentlemen, please excuse me." He took Renno's arm and led him away from the table to a private room, told a serving maid to bring food and drink, then turned to hold Renno's eyes in a steady gaze. "You are far from home, Sachem."

"Yes."

"I trust that you are enjoying the pleasures of this city?"

"I did not come for pleasure," Renno replied coldly.

"Ah," McGillivray said, "nor did I come strictly for pleasure, but one must seize the opportunity for enjoyment when it comes." He motioned Renno to a chair, then sat down himself, crossing his legs. "Among the Ohio tribes Renno is known as a great warrior and as the man who, through his family connections with the Cherokee, could bring thousands of warriors to join our cause."

Renno smiled. "You broach the issue in the manner of a white man."

McGillivray answered Renno's smile. "If you and I were in the wilderness with our brothers, with village chiefs and war chiefs of the various tribes, it would be necessary to preface any serious discussion with much oration. Do we need that now?"

"No," Renno said.

"I don't believe you came idly to New Orleans, to the city of the Spanish governor. And I beseech the spirits that I am right in suspecting that, at last, the Seneca and the Cherokee tire of the duplicity of the United States."

Renno spread his hands.

McGillivray leaned forward. "Sachem, the Spanish population of the vast territories they control—or hope to control—is sparse and scattered. And yet the king of Spain wields great power. My friend Governor Miró is a most generous man. He understands the desire of the Indian to reclaim the lands stolen from him by the United States, and he will distribute the gold and silver of Spain to aid that effort."

"And if the Indian succeeds with the aid of Spain? I have found little difference between white men, be they Spanish, English, or American."

"Ah, but you don't know Miró," McGillivray said, "or the Spanish philosophy. It is their desire to have a buffer state, an *Indian* state, between the Mississippi and the mountains. That is why we can coexist with Spain, Sachem. Their appetite for land will be sated by the vastness beyond the Mississippi. If we fight together *now*—Creek, Seneca, and Cherokee, with the Ohio tribes to the north—we can push the white man back across the mountains in your area and back to the sea in mine. Then we can live in peace under the flag of Mother Spain."

"Aha," Renno said.

"Tomorrow I will take you to Miró, and you will find that he is an honorable man."

"I will speak with the governor," Renno agreed, using his most impassive Indian expression.

"You have seen what the Spanish do when they conquer an Indian tribe," El-i-chi protested when Renno told of his plans. "You saw the mummified remains of Indians who cooperated with Spain in the caves of the mountain of gold.

You saw how, in Jamaica, the Spanish exterminated an entire people."

"Trust me, Brother," Renno said.

"It is the Spanish, and any who walk with them, that I do not trust," El-i-chi seethed.

"Together we have fought British soldiers, Spanish soldiers, Tory renegades, and enemies from many tribes in our land and others," Renno told him. "I have long since chosen those with whom I will run. I have no desire to change my alliance." He chuckled. "Come with me as shaman of the Seneca. If you sense duplicity, tell me."

McGillivray nodded in approval when Renno appeared in front of the governor's house with a Seneca warrior in buckskins and paint. He knew that the defiant gaze and sturdy stance of the warrior would impress Miró. McGillivray had arranged the appointment with the governor for midday, for the Spaniard's staff served a good meal. Thus it was that four men sat at the table, Miró at one end, McGillivray at the other, with Renno and El-i-chi at the governor's right and left.

At first the conversation was informal, with McGillivray reinforcing Miró as he spoke of the power and loyalty of Spain for her allies. McGillivray managed to talk for a long time, bringing into his conversation much information about one Alexander McGillivray. The Creek stated that he was in great demand, courted by the king of England, respected by his enemies in Georgia, and acknowledged as a grand ally of Spain.

McGillivray's self-serving talk led El-i-chi to sneak a look at Renno, who sat impassively until McGillivray ended with a final flurry of name-dropping.

Renno spoke in his most effete British accent, and El-i-chi had to control himself to refrain from smiling. The simpering, lisping accent was used only when his brother was about to pull someone's leg. Renno talked for a long time, as McGillivray had done, and managed to do it without saying much—certainly without making any commitment. To El-i-chi's amusement, Renno matched McGillivray in name-dropping and without lying, for Renno could toss out names such as Lord Beaumont in all confidence.

"When does Indian lie to Indian?" El-i-chi asked when they were alone.

"How did I lie?" Renno demanded with an amused twist of his lips.

"Not in words," El-i-chi admitted.

"Well, then?"

"In your accent, in your posture, in every action you lied."

"But not to an Indian brother," Renno said, "for this so-called king of the Creek is more white than Indian."

"Can you condemn him for his white blood, Brother?" El-i-chi lifted his own arm to place his bronzed, white skin before Renno's eyes.

"If he were Creek in his heart," Renno said, "I would not condemn him at all."

Esteban Miró sent a man to intercept Renno and El-i-chi as they were returning to their boardinghouse after the sumptuous meal, requesting that Renno return to the governor's office for a private talk. Renno motioned to El-i-chi to come with him, and when they were shown into Miró's office, the governor looked at El-i-chi in disapproval.

"My brother, shaman of our tribe, shares any secret that I hold," Renno said stiffly.

"I wanted to correct any wrong impression that my good friend and ally, McGillivray of the Creek, might have given you, Sachem," Miró began.

Renno raised an eyebrow and waited.

"While the Creek are our loyal allies," Miró went on, "and are valued highly, one would think from hearing Chief McGillivray speak that it is the Creek who decide policy and not myself." He laughed lightly. "That is not the case, I assure you. In the territories of New Spain, the tail does not wag the dog."

Miró took a seat behind his desk and tented his hands. "I am aware that not only the white neighbors of the Creek

Nation have reason to fear the Creek's willingness to fight. While we encourage our Indian allies to make war on the United States whenever and wherever possible, we do not—and I repeat, do *not*—condone raids on other Indian tribes by Creek warriors. I assure you, Sachem, that all the power of Spain, which is significant, would be brought against the Creek should they extend their love of war to a friendly neighbor."

"I hear," Renno said.

"Good." Miró smiled. "If you have any questions, Sachem, any needs, please feel free to call on me. And when you have, in your wisdom, decided to seek the umbrella of Spanish strength as a haven for your people, we will speak of the aid that I can give you. I trust that will be soon."

"Soon you will know," Renno agreed.

"That man lies with a smile," El-i-chi said in disgust once they were on the street again. "He would have us think that he would stand with us against the Creek. And as he makes this promise to us and to others, he is promising undying loyalty to McGillivray's Creek."

"I think, Brother," Renno said, "that his true attitude was expressed inadvertently when he said that in New Spain the tail does not wag the dog, thus assigning the entire Creek Nation to an insignificant position."

"We did not come here to become involved in politics," El-i-chi said fiercely. He would have said more had Alexander McGillivray not stepped from the shadows under a canvas awning to confront them.

"Sachem," McGillivray said, "I thought that you might like to have a cup of tea with me in my lodgings. And you, as well, Shaman."

El-i-chi wondered why Renno nodded in assent. He followed the two sachems to the guest house near the governor's mansion, accepted a hot cup of tea into which he put enough sugar to make the tea fit to drink, and listened as Renno and the Creek sparred politely with words for some time. McGillivray was insisting on an immediate decision on Renno's part. The white Indian said that there was plenty of time for a decision, and there it stood.

"Perhaps, Sachem, I am not communicating my thoughts properly," McGillivray insisted, looking slightly flushed. "I will now impart to you information that is of a highly confidential nature to prove a couple of points. One is this: I am not so much interested in extending the domination of Spain up the Mississippi as I am in securing inviolable homelands for the various tribes. I understand that you have said that the best chance for survival of the Indian is assimilation into the United States, and I say, in all respect, that such talk is talk of death. If we are smart enough, quick enough to react when the time comes, we can stop the white pressure on our hunting grounds forever."

El-i-chi was the first to speak. "To do that would require magic a hundred times, a thousand times more powerful than any magic that I hold."

"Your magic is strong, Shaman, but now I will tell you all about the magic that the white man works against himself." McGillivray leaned back in a chair and made himself at ease. As he spoke the Creek leader gave an outer impression of calm confidence, but Renno did not have to look twice to see the fire raging in McGillivray's eyes.

Chapter XI

In the capital city of the new United States of America, Congress was still concerned with the first problem that it had faced upon convening in the spring: revenue. Money. The men from the thirteen states represented almost four million Americans, not counting almost a million black slaves. The nation stretched from the dark northern forests of Maine to the marshy coastline of Georgia, over a thousand miles and, in theory at least, three thousand miles westward on certain east-west bands. The original colonial charters of Massachusetts, Connecticut, Virginia, North and South Carolina, and, significantly in that year of continued crisis, Georgia, were "sea-to-sea" grants, giving those states control of the land all the way to the Pacific.

In reality, of course, only a few men dreamed of such a westward extension, for beyond the Mississippi were the Spanish, a few of the French, and numerous warlike tribes of Indians. If one considered only the land area of the thirteen original colonies and those portions of the western frontier peopled by white settlers, such as Kentucky and the Cumberland Gap region beyond the Smoky Mountains, the United States was still larger in area than most European countries. Old England and all her adjacent isles could have been set down inside the boundaries of the state of Georgia, with thousands of square miles left over.

Yet in spite of the vast and rich lands with their wealth of natural resources, the United States was almost bankrupt. So it was that money was the prime concern of the Congress, and so it was that early on, the gentlemen of the two bodies of the legislative branch of government created the Treasury Department. To head the Treasury, President George Washington had chosen a man who had been one of his more efficient aides-de-camp during the War for Independence, Alexander Hamilton. Treasury soon became the largest of the executive departments being formed, with thirty clerks and over a thousand customs collectors. In contrast, the Department of State, in charge of foreign relations, standards of weights and measures, coinage, patents, and other interior affairs, was allotted four clerks, a messenger, and a secretary; and the War Department consisted of five clerks and Secretary Henry Knox.

Washington had chosen an old friend, fellow Virginian Thomas Jefferson, to head the State Department. When talking with trusted friends such as Hamilton, Washington confided that Jefferson's sanguine view of Shays's Rebellion, a minor crisis in Massachusetts, had convinced him that Jefferson was the man to conduct relations between the United States and the old powers of Europe. Daniel Shays, protesting the fiscal policies of the state of Massachusetts, had disrupted a session of the state supreme court, inspiring a panicky Congress to authorize an army of thirteen hundred men to deal with the rebellion.

Washington showed Hamilton a letter written by Jefferson from France in 1787, in which Jefferson had commented on the minor uprising."

"What country can preserve its liberties if their rulers are not warned from time to time that their people preserve the spirit of resistance? Let them take arms. What signify a few lives lost in a century or two? The tree of liberty must be refreshed from time to time with the blood of patriots and tyrants. It is its natural manure."

"A man who can so calmly accept the death of citizens," Washington told Hamilton, "could be relied upon to remain serene under any threat."

"Unlike our friends in the Congress," Hamilton agreed.

But that minor crisis was in the past as Washington gathered his primary cabinet advisers Jefferson, Hamilton, and Knox to discuss a threat that was, in his mind, much more serious than any other that plagued the young nation.

"I will ask Secretary Jefferson to acquaint you with certain facts," Washington said.

Jefferson put aside a glass of wine—Washington served only the finest. "I assume, gentlemen, that we are all aware of a specific act of the Georgia Legislature regarding an area of land along the eastern bank of the Mississippi and the southernmost bend of the Tennessee."

Hamilton and Knox nodded. Knox spoke. "The legislators sold land—Indian land—to speculators."

Jefferson continued. "The area in question consists of twenty-five million acres presently occupied by three major Indian tribes: the Creek, the Choctaw, and the Chickasaw. The area is also claimed by Spain. It is, of course, far beyond the present extension of settlement in Georgia. At first, as you know, we considered the sale to be nothing more than a cynical attempt to force the central government to come to the aid of Georgia in regard to its western land claims."

"Odd people, the Georgians," Hamilton muttered.

"Thus," Jefferson went on, "the Georgia Legislature would bring the United States into direct confrontation not

preserve the right of this country to develop to the west. The average, unsophisticated citizen is concerned only with his own cabbage patch."

The possibility of war between Spain and England was also the topic of discussion hundreds of miles away as Renno and El-i-chi sat across a small table from Alexander McGillivray.

"The state of Georgia has generously sold twenty-five million acres of Indian lands to speculators. Can you guess what was paid for our lands?"

Renno shook his head.

"Five-sixths of a cent per acre," McGillivray said in disgust. "Less than one penny per acre. It is a desperate act by the weakest member of the United States, clearly intended to draw the central government into war with the Creek Nation. And if that happens, so be it, for then the Spanish would be forced to enter the war, with most of their forces concentrated in the south, against Georgia. With all Spanish forces committed alongside my Creek warriors, we can wipe the state of Georgia off the map."

"And leave the entire Mississippi Valley in Spanish hands," Renno said.

"Not necessarily, my friend," McGillivray countered. "For war has already begun between Spain and England on the far Pacific Coast. Soon the soldiers of the two nations will be contending for the Mississippi Valley, and in the confusion we will clear our lands of white settlers. The United States will no doubt side with England; Spain will lose the war; and then two old enemies—the United States and England—will be content to accept an Indian nation from the Mississippi to the mountains. Such an independent Indian nation would serve as a buffer zone. The British would be content to make their expansion to the west of the Mississippi. The United States would be effectively bottled up east of the mountains, and the tribes would be at peace from the Great Lakes to the Gulf of Mexico."

"And so once again we hear the name of that worthy gentleman of Kentucky," Henry Knox said ruefully.

"There is a family connection between George Rogers Clark and the director of the company that has purchased rights to the land being sold by Georgia," Jefferson said. "Dr. James O'Fallon has recently married Clark's fifteen-year-old daughter."

"And now Clark is up to his old tricks," Knox said, frowning. "He's still trying to establish an independent principality in the Mississippi Valley."

"If Clark were to lead an army of Kentucky volunteers into the lands claimed by Spain, the United States would find itself at war with Spain and three major Indian nations," Jefferson pointed out.

"While I would consider it propitious to see Spain driven out of the Mississippi Valley," Washington said, "we are not in a position to protect our settlers on the frontier, much less to go to war against Spain and her Indian allies. We must do everything within our power to prevent Mr. Clark from leading an armed force southward from Kentucky." He paused and sighed. "Without, of course, rousing the ire of the independent-minded men of the frontier."

Jefferson laughed. "What you're asking for, sir, is a miracle."

"I expect no less from you, Thomas," Washington said, his thin lips curving slightly.

"Does it concern us and our Cherokee brothers that Spanish soldiers have fought Englishmen at some faraway point on the western shores?" El-i-chi asked as he and Renno left the conference with McGillivray.

"Yes, because a war between England and Spain would be fought at the frontier of the United States," Renno answered.

"But mostly at sea, and far away," said El-i-chi.

"My brother," Renno said, "the prize is here." He gestured to indicate the vast areas to the north and west. "English troops would move down the Mississippi from Canada. Would you like an English presence along the Mississippi in our own backyard?"

El-i-chi growled.

"Neither would the United States. If war came between Spain and England, I think the United States would have to side with one sooner or later. And if the United States goes to war, we will fight with them."

"Now, O great sachem who deals in matters concerning the great powers of Europe—"

Renno raised one eyebrow and answered El-i-chi's sarcasm with a slight smile.

"—would it be possible to get back to our business?"

"Very possible," Renno said. "Tonight we will visit the house of the charming madam Laure Beyle."

"Thank the manitous," El-i-chi muttered.

Egan Kirk, Mandy, and Ah-wa-o had been seeing more of New Orleans than any of them wanted to see, having walked miles along the waterfront and around the city. They had asked many people without success if they knew or had heard of one Simon Purdy. The group was at the evening meal when Renno and El-i-chi returned to the boardinghouse. The two brothers had just been seated and were being served when Adan came sweeping in, very cavalier in high boots and ornate Spanish silks.

He declined an invitation to dine, removed his plumed hat, bowed, and flashed a smile at Renno. "My inquiries have borne fruit."

Renno tensed, his eyes narrowing.

"I must admit that I was growing less hopeful," Adan said. "Inquiry after inquiry produced not one word of an American named Simon Purdy. It was as if he did not exist or, at best, had never arrived in New Orleans."

"Adan," El-i-chi asked plaintively, "can you get to the point?"

"Certainly, my friend. And so it might have continued, without success, had I not suddenly remembered that the man you seek—"

"Adan," El-i-chi said.

"—did not come to New Orleans alone, but in the company of a Spanish officer."

"Ah," Mandy said.

"Ah, indeed," said Adan. "So I simply inquired of my friends in the Spanish customshouse about Captain León Bocalos and—" He paused, hands spread, eyes flashing.

"Adan," El-i-chi threatened, "if you don't tell us what you've discovered—"

"Of course," Adan said. "What I discovered was that Captain León Bocalos has left New Orleans."

El-i-chi groaned.

"Purdy." Renno's serious expression brought Adan to the point immediately.

"Bocalos has been promoted. He has been named governor of a remote province in lower Mexico. A white man who answers the description you gave me of Purdy was with him."

Mandy's mouth was open to ask a question. Adan pointed a finger at her and said, "Two young white girls were members of the Bocalos party when it embarked."

"Oh, God," Mandy moaned. "We have come so far."

Egan, seeing her bitter disappointment, walked over to put a hand on her shoulder.

"Do not be discouraged," Adan chirped cheerily. "Now we know for sure where three of the missing girls are."

"And tonight we will have one of them," Renno promised.

"I am ready," El-i-chi said.

"Hear me, then," Renno said. "This is how we will do it. . . ."

Juan Martez was a common soldier with a common name. He had been in the New World since he was a mere boy and was content with his sergeant's rank and his light duties as a member of the New Orleans garrison. As a veteran of New World service, he was given certain latitude. As a married man—his wife had come from one of the less ornate houses of pleasure to give him three fat babies and a love that pleased him well—he was not content to live on the small pittance that was his army pay. Thus he was seen each evening to *montar la guardia*, to take his place at the entrance to the rich house of Madam Laure Beyle. For this he was paid more for a few hours' work each night than for his long days as a sergeant, and as a result he was able to afford a small house with a garden kept blooming with various flowers by his wife.

Martez was in a splendid mood, bowing and nodding cheerfully to the gentlemen who entered Chez Beyle, looking forward to the hour when he could leave his post and make his way to his cozy bed where all the women he would ever need awaited him. It was a busy night, so traffic into the house did not slow until after ten. Finally Martez could relax and light a cheroot. He was leaning against the wall in the shadows just to one side of the lighted entrance when he felt a strong hand close over his mouth. His heart pounded as a keen blade pressed against his throat. And then there was a calm, deadly voice in his ear.

"I know you not, Spaniard, and so I do not desire your death. Whether or not you die depends on you."

Juan slowly lifted one hand and tapped gently with his forefinger on the hand over his mouth. The hand relaxed. "Señor, I have no wish to die. What do you desire?"

"A few words," El-i-chi said. Juan nodded carefully. "How many guards keep order inside the house?"

Juan paused for only a second. He was thinking of his wife and his three children. "Seven, señor. Four on the lower floor, three upstairs."

"And outside?"

"Only one other than myself. At the back entrance."

"How can I be sure you're not lying?" El-i-chi asked.

"I have a plump, happy woman who awaits me at home," Juan said, "and three children who, it is said, look like me. Here I own nothing, nothing worth my life."

El-i-chi was feeling amazed at himself, for he had had every intention of slicing the Spaniard's throat. And yet, as he had watched the man, saw how he smiled to himself now and then, saw him smoking his cheroot happily, his hand had stayed itself as if of its own accord once he had his knife in position.

"Your name?" El-i-chi asked.

"Señor, I am Juan Martez, at your service."

"I think your plump and happy wife will see you again, after all. I hope she will have a remedy for your headache." After all, the man was a Spaniard, and mercy and trust could be extended only so far. After the flat side of the blade of El-i-chi's tomahawk thudded down, the shaman pulled the limp Juan Martez to the cover of some dense shrubbery.

El-i-chi moved silently to the corner of the house, hooted like an owl, and watched Se-quo-i silently glide from the shadows. "As we thought, there are only two outside guards."

Se-quo-i held a knife in his hand, and in the moonlight, there was a darkness on the blade. "Now there are none, since there is no longer any guard at the rear entrance." That Spaniard had not fared as well as Juan Martez. Se-quo-i bent to clean the knife's blade on the grass. El-i-chi nodded. He saw no reason to let anyone know that he had not killed the man at the front door.

The Seneca led the way to the back. First there was a hallway, dimly lit, which passed by a kitchen where three black women worked, sweat glistening on their skin. He led Se-quo-i to a curtained entrance to the main salon, and here they waited.

Renno, Adan, and Egan had entered the house an hour earlier. They sat together at a table, drinks before them. Only Adan had sampled the contents of the glasses; Egan had learned that the drinks came strong in a New Orleans bordello.

El-i-chi notified Renno of his arrival with one quick, shrill whistle that went unnoticed except by Renno and Egan. Adan, meanwhile, motioned to a serving maid. The shaman fidgeted as the minutes passed. Se-quo-i was looking over his shoulder, examining the luxuriously appointed salon.

As prearranged, Renno flicked a glance toward the three guards: Two leaned against the wall; another stood in a curtained alcove. El-i-chi nodded understanding to his brother and watched as Laure Beyle came to the table, spoke for a few minutes, then left. It had been decided at the boardinghouse that Egan would request the Brown girl, go into her room, and bring her out.

"How much longer must we wait?" El-i-chi whispered to Se-quo-i just as a black maid approached the table and made a bow. Egan Kirk rose, looked around the room, and followed the maid to the stairs.

"It begins," Se-quo-i said.

They watched as Renno let three minutes elapse, rose casually, and sauntered toward the stairs. In his Spanish clothing he looked very much the city man. His weaponry was limited to his stiletto and a brace of pistols in his belt under his jacket. He did not look back at El-i-chi or Se-quo-i as he mounted the stairs.

Then Adan finished his drink and walked around the room, arms clasped behind him, until he came to lean one elbow on the newel post of the stairway.

"I will take the man on the right," El-i-chi said, nodding in the direction of the two visible guards. "The first to finish goes after the one behind the curtain."

"Agreed," Se-quo-i said, changing his grip on his tomahawk.

Grace Brown had recovered enough from her vagueness, from the disassociation that had protected her sanity, to know what was happening to her. She had found that by feigning willingness it was possible to accelerate the events that occurred each time a man came into the room. When the door opened and a strong, tall man whose skin was whiter than that of all the others came in, halted, and closed the door behind him, she rose, dropped the lacy wrapping to expose her firm, slim body, and walked toward the bed.

"Are you Grace Brown?" Egan asked.

She froze in midstep and looked at him, her eyes going wide. "Grace Brown?" she whispered.

"Yes. Are you Grace Brown?"

How he had come to know her name she did not know, but the mere fact that he knew it, caused her face to burn with shame.

"Damn it," Egan said, listening for fighting to erupt downstairs, "answer me."

"No, I am not," Grace whispered.

Egan moved quickly, seized the fallen wrap, threw it around her naked shoulders. "Why do you lie? If you are not Grace Brown, who are you?"

She couldn't answer.

"Where are your sisters? And where is Tess?"

She gulped. "Dead. Gone. I know not."

"None of the other girls are here in the house?"

Tears scalded her eyes and wet her cheeks. "Hope died on the river. Charity and Tess—I don't know, and no one will tell me."

"Have you any clothing?"

"No," she said, her shoulders shaking with sobs. Could it be true? Had this young man come to save her?

Egan jerked a blanket off the bed. "Wrap up in this. We're leaving."

Renno had located two of the men who kept guard on the second floor of the cypress-plank house, one at each end of the central hallway. He walked casually from the landing into the hall. The guard nearest him jerked into alertness, came toward him.

"Here," the guard said, "where do you think you're going?" It was standard procedure for a client to be escorted to a room by one of the colored maids. One of the guard's duties was to be sure no man came upstairs alone without having paid the tariff.

"I know where I'm going," Renno said, vaguely in answer to the guard's question. He stood in a relaxed position, his lips forming a smile that was belied by the coldness of his eyes.

"Get back down the stairs before I have to throw you down," the guard warned, his small, close-set eyes glaring, his face looking as if he hoped that Renno would resist.

"I pray," Renno said, "that you are ready to meet your God."

"Huh?" the guard grunted, and a smile distorted his face

as he drew back a fist, preparing to see if he could knock the cold sneer from Renno's lips. The guard's smile altered suddenly to horror as the Spanish stiletto entered his body just below his diaphragm and thrust upward, deep into his heart. He died with nothing more than a muted hiss.

Renno jerked the stiletto free and whirled in time to see the guard at the other end of the hall lifting a pistol. He threw himself to one side and heard the ball from the Spaniard's weapon pass close by his ear. His own pistol spoke, and the ball found its target, slamming into the Spaniard's chest with enough force to knock him backward as he fell.

When El-i-chi heard the two shots in rapid succession from upstairs, he nodded at Se-quo-i and surged forward. The loud reports had alerted the two visible guards. El-i-chi's target was reaching for a pistol at his belt when he saw the blur of motion coming toward him. He tried to cry out as he began to lift his weapon, but El-i-chi's tomahawk silenced him. Even as the Seneca struck he heard an unmistakable sound—tomahawk smashing into bone. Se-quo-i's man was slumping, blood surging up from his split skull. El-i-chi leaped toward the curtained alcove only a split second ahead of Se-quo-i. The guard who had thrust the curtain aside to extend a pistol pointed toward El-i-chi was now presented with two targets, causing him to hesitate. The pistol wavered from El-i-chi to Se-quo-i as the two ran side by side. Unfortunately for the guard he pulled the trigger in panic while his weapon was pointed at empty space between the two buckskin-clad Indians. It was the last mistake the guard ever made as El-i-chi and Se-quo-i vied for the kill. Two tomahawks almost met as Se-quo-i struck from the left and El-i-chi from the right. As the guard fell, his head wobbled feebly, supported only by the central spinal column at the neck.

The fourth guard, who had sneaked into the kitchen

to coax a little snack, now heard pistol shots, women's screams, and men's shouts. He ran up the hall, his mouth full, and burst into the room to meet two balls, fired almost simultaneously by El-i-chi and Se-quo-i.

Egan opened the door to Grace's room and cautiously looked out into the hallway. He saw Renno with two pistols in hand—one of them smoking—and he saw two guards on the floor. He pulled Grace into the hallway and started toward Renno.

The third upstairs guard had been taking advantage of one of the perquisites of the job. Laure Beyle had no objection to a guard's taking a few minutes off to sample the merchandise, as long as his fellows were vigilant and a girl was not wanted by a client. The last guard had just started to dress after a very pleasant interlude when he heard the gunshots. Made nervous by the apparent emergency, he fumbled with his clothing.

Egan and Grace moved rapidly toward Renno at the head of the stairs. Shots sounded from below, so Renno looked down, where El-i-chi and Se-quo-i had the situation well in hand for the moment. He looked up just in time to see a door burst open and a guard emerge, his clothing in disarray.

"Down, Egan!" Renno cried, for Kirk and the girl were between the Spaniard and him. The white Indian leaped to one side and raised his pistol, but the guard's weapon spoke first, and with a muted cry, Grace pitched forward. Egan felt her hand go limp in his grasp and looked down as Renno's second pistol fired. Blood was oozing at the nape of her neck. The shot had effectively severed Grace's brain stem, and her body did not even twitch as it slumped to the floor.

"*Nooooo!*" Egan roared, lifting his own pistol, but there was no need for it. The third upstairs guard was already dead.

Renno knew from the way Grace Brown fell that there

was no hope for her. One quick look at the position of the wound confirmed that she was dead. "We will have to leave her," he said.

"It is not fair to have come so far, to have found one of the girls only to have her killed just as she was being freed," he moaned. "My God, Renno, at the very least she deserves a decent burial."

"I think that Laure Beyle will give her that," Renno said. "I can't say the same for us should we delay our departure." He led the way downstairs on the run. He saw a well-dressed gentleman standing behind a decorative pillar, a pistol in his hand. The paying clients and the serving maids were in various stages of surprise and fear. Some women were screaming; some of the male clients, familiar with the sound of gunshots, had sought protection by diving to the floor behind chairs and tables.

Adan, looking quite calm, leaned on the newel post at the foot of the stairs, pistol in hand, his eyes sweeping the room.

"El-i-chi! To your left," Renno called as the man with the gun reached around the pillar, preparing to fire. The tomahawk flew from El-i-chi's hand and struck the Spaniard on the bridge of the nose just as he pulled the trigger. The pistol jerked up as bone fragments were pushed directly into the Spaniard's brain. The ball smashed into the chandelier, a pretty arrangement of crystal oil lamps. As the shaman ran to retrieve his weapon, a lamp fell with a smash, and fire blazed up from the spilled oil. A woman cried out, while three Spanish gentlemen worked up enough nerve to get up off the floor. They had knives—in a civilized city like New Orleans not many carried firearms during a social outing.

"I don't think you want to stand in our way," Renno warned, advancing on the three formally dressed Spaniards.

Se-quo-i and El-i-chi appeared at Renno's side, tomahawks bloody. The three gentlemen lowered their knives and backed away. Renno heard the crackle of flames behind him and smelled the tang of wood burning. Men were bellowing orders. He turned and faced the room. The spilled oil had pooled and run. Flames climbed an ornate wall hanging from its lower fringes.

Laure Beyle stood on the lowest step of the stairway, pointing an ornate, silver-plated pistol at Renno. His weapons were not loaded, and she was across the room, too far to be disabled with his stiletto. He watched the pure hatred grow on her face, guessed the moment at which her finger would tighten on the trigger, and leaped to one side. Her shot thudded into the wall beside him. He made a slight bow. Laure's face was eerily illuminated by the rapidly spreading flames. She had to know that she would lose everything to the fire, and in a rage she hurled the silver-plated pistol with all her strength. It clattered to the floor and skidded to within a few feet of Renno. He picked it up. It was a beautiful weapon. He brandished it toward Laure and shouted, "Thank you."

El-i-chi and Se-quo-i led the way into the street. A half block away, uniformed Spanish civil guards ran toward them.

"Hold!" Renno said to El-i-chi and Se-quo-i, who were preparing to meet the policemen with arms. He ran toward the advancing Spaniards, crying, *"Fuego! Fuego! Incendio!"* He pointed frantically toward the house. Already smoke was pouring from windows, and the occupants were jostling each other to get out the doors. The guards ran past to investigate.

Adan, who had not been called upon to participate in the action inside the bordello because it had all happened so fast, said, "Soon every guard and soldier in town will be here. We'd best get to the ship." He turned into a dim street and the others followed, walking swiftly but not running lest they attract attention.

The crew was already aboard the *Nuestra Señora*. Several men stood at the shoreside rail, watching for the captain. Mandy and Ah-wa-o were already on deck. Ah-wa-o, confident that the fighting ability of the man she loved would bring him back to her, was nevertheless pacing anxiously until she recognized El-i-chi as he emerged from the dark shadows of the warehouses along the waterfront.

Adan was first on board, giving orders in a quiet voice. Men scurried; lines were loosed; a longboat was lowered. There was no wind to move the ship, so she would have to be towed by the longboat, a slow, backbreaking task. The ship began to move with creaks and groans as the men in the longboat bent their backs to their oars.

It was Egan who told Mandy and Ah-wa-o of the ironic fate of Grace Brown. He spoke in a quiet voice, blaming himself for not being more careful.

"Oh, poor Grace," Mandy breathed.

As dawn neared, a fortunate breeze began to blow. Adan ordered sails and hoisted the longboat aboard. The *Señora* began to gain headway in the calm waters of the large lake that would take them to the Gulf of Mexico.

Renno stood at the stern of the ship. The horizon over the city glowed red, and plumes of smoke billowed into the lightening predawn sky. New Orleans was a wooden city, cypress being the prime building material. And now she was burning. The roofs of all but the richest, finest houses were formed from cypress bark, the walls and floors of cypress planks. The fire that had started in Laure Beyle's salon had spread. It was obvious from the intensity of the flames and from the towering pillar of smoke that a large section of the city was aflame.

Renno had not wanted that; the people of New Orleans were not his enemies. But it had not been his direct actions that started the fire. He could only think that the blaze was the will of the manitous, for he had come to New Orleans on a mission of justice and honor.

The next day the *Señora* sailed into the Gulf of Mexico on brisk, favorable winds. Smoke from New Orleans rose high into the western sky. In spite of the beautiful day, bracing sea breezes, and the swift, mile-covering motion of the ship, an air of gloom hung over those who had gathered in the captain's lounge for breakfast. Only El-i-chi and Ah-wa-o seemed cheerful.

"Have you seen the smoke?" the shaman asked. "I think

that the Spanish know that we have been in New Orleans."
He looked around. Renno had begun eating, his eyes on his
plate.

Egan waited until everyone had finished eating. "I
haven't told you something that I learned from Grace.
Hope, the middle sister, was lost on the way downriver."

Mandy bowed her head and said a prayer for both Hope
and Grace.

"So only two are left," Egan said.

"I fear that it must be God's will that we do not find my
sister," Mandy said, her voice low and sad. "Each time we
have thought that we were close to her, we have found that
she has been taken farther from our reach. I have prayed for
her soul, and although it grieves me, I have accepted God's
will."

"He has not spoken to me," Egan said. "Simon Purdy still
lives."

"And has sailed away for some unknown place in Mexico," Mandy replied. "And *you*, Egan, are aboard a ship
sailing for the United States."

With a muted curse Egan leaped to his feet and stormed
out of the lounge. Adan raised one eyebrow. "I think the
boy is upset."

"I understand how he feels," El-i-chi admitted. "I, too,
regret leaving this affair unfinished."

"Perhaps it *is* God's will that Mandy's sister and the other
child remain with their captors." Adan smiled. "But perhaps not. Mandy said that Purdy had sailed away for some
unknown place in Mexico. That is not true."

Renno, who had been thinking of home and of his
children, lifted his head in interest.

"I know exactly where Purdy and the Spanish captain
have gone," Adan said.

Ah-wa-o reached for El-i-chi's hand and squeezed it.

"Bocalos was appointed governor of a province called
Yucatán. It is a peninsula that extends northward from
lower Mexico. The capital is Córdoba, near the northeast-
ern point of the peninsula near Cabo Catoche."

"You're certain of this?" Renno asked.

"It is a matter of public record," Adan replied.

"And Purdy is with him?" El-i-chi asked, his blue eyes blazing with new excitement.

"Purdy left New Orleans with Bocalos and the two girls. It would seem logical that the captain and he had a common destination," Adan said.

"How far?" Renno asked.

"A few days' sailing, no more," Adan replied. "Unless, by some chance of fate, one of the autumn storms rises." He spread his hands. "There is no sign of *huracán*. The skies are clear."

"What do you know of Yucatán and Córdoba?" Renno inquired, and his interest pleased El-i-chi, who glanced at Se-quo-i and nodded.

"I have not been there. It is a place of dense jungle. I would imagine that there would be only a token population of settlers."

"A garrison?"

"Perhaps, but few in number."

Renno mused for a few moments. "I have no right to ask you, my friend, to take your employer's ship into danger."

"I'm sure that if Beth were here she would want to make an effort to find those girls," Adan said. "At any rate, I have full authority aboard this vessel as long as she is at sea. If you would like to pay a visit to Córdoba, you have only to say so."

"I say we go," El-i-chi stated emphatically.

Renno let a quick smile cross his lips. "How soon would we have to decide our course?"

Adan went to the chart bin, came back with a large chart, and spread it on the table. "We are presently sailing southeast, making for the passage between the Florida Keys and Cuba. To go to Yucatán we turn almost due south. There is time for you to make your decision, my friend."

"So," Renno said, rising.

The white Indian went to the stern of the ship and stood there watching the wake. Again he was faced with a decision between two duties. He raised his face to the sunny western sky. Fleecy white clouds, good-weather clouds, dotted the blue. "Manitous," he whispered. "Ah, manitous, advise me."

He knew that George Washington should be told of the talk with Alexander McGillivray as quickly as possible, for the situation in Georgia was a dangerous one, which could lead the United States into war. It would be, however, a matter of long weeks before the *Nuestra Señora* made port in Wilmington, and the President would be in New York. That meant more weeks of travel. By the time Renno could arrive in New York or send letters, what was going to happen could already have happened.

His other duties lay to his people, and to his brothers the Cherokee. Not all of the renegades had been punished for breaking the fragile peace. Two young girls were still captive. He sighed, lowered himself to the deck, and sat cross-legged, his eyes staring at the northern horizon.

"Manitous," he whispered.

As darkness came El-i-chi saw his brother in the same position he had assumed early in the morning, and he knew that Renno was seeking advice from the spirits.

"We will leave him alone," he told Ah-wa-o and the others as they gathered for the evening meal. "And with the morning I think that we will know our course."

Chapter XII

Mandy leaned against the bow rail and let salt spray mingle with the salt of her tears. The snapping of the sails before a brisk wind, the hiss of the prow, the slap of waves, the beauty of the day, all were lost on her. Poor, chubby Hope Brown was dead, likely having chosen the river in preference to being the plaything of men. At the moment of her rescue, Grace had been killed. Of the four, only two still lived. In view of recent events, those two seemed destined to live on in captivity, perhaps to end their days in some terrible place far, far worse than Laure Beyle's house in New Orleans.

A soaring bird drew her eyes, but Mandy's thoughts were of Tess. She would observe her fourteenth birthday soon.

By that time she would have been used by men for months.
If Renno made the decision to travel south, how would Tess
react to being rescued? Mandy had been raped only once
and by only one man—but even so there were times when
she awoke in the middle of the night with sweat pouring off
her body, with her very soul crying out at the horror of it.
With her friends—and she considered all of the group to be
so—she had ceased to redden with shame; but during the
time they were in New Orleans walking in the streets to
look for Simon Purdy, she had felt that dark-dressed
Spanish matrons, their faces modestly hidden behind veils,
had looked at her with sure knowledge that she had been
dishonored, that she was no longer worthy of walking the
streets in their presence.

If she felt this way, how must poor Tess feel? How had
Grace lived through being handed from man to man in the
bordello? Had *she* been thrust into such a desperate
situation, Mandy knew that she would have found some
way to end her life. And yet life was sweet. Perhaps she was
wrong. Perhaps hope of solution would never die. Perhaps
it had never died in Grace, not until the Spanish pistol ball
had smashed into her spinal column.

Mandy started in fright and uttered a small sound when
a hand fell on her shoulder. She swiveled to see Egan
standing beside her; the sound of his approach had been
hidden among the sounds of sail, wind, and water.

"You frightened me," she said.

"Sorry." He leaned on the rail, letting his eyes sweep
over the emptiness of the gulf. "It seems, or so I have
concluded from listening to El-i-chi and Se-quo-i, that the
fate of your sister and Charity Brown will be decided by the
spirits." He said the last word with contempt.

She said nothing. She had talked with Ah-wa-o about
God and had exchanged beliefs. She had always been
taught that Indians were heathens doomed to everlasting
fire, but after talking with the girl who had become a good
friend, Mandy wasn't so sure. The Master of Life in
Ah-wa-o's belief sounded very much like the one God of the
Jews. The fact that other spirits were involved in the

Seneca belief seemed no more heathen to her than worship of the Trinity. At first when Ah-wa-o had said that the Indian had difficulty understanding the white man's God with three heads, Mandy had been shocked, but then she had considered the Christian saints. Perhaps Ah-wa-o's spirits—manitous—were no more confusing than the many saints who were grouped around the Christian God.

"Whatever they decide," Egan said now, "I will continue my search for Simon Purdy."

"But if the ship sails for Wilmington—"

"There will be other ships."

"You would be alone, traveling into Spanish lands. You don't even speak the language."

"I can learn."

"Egan, I've been doing a lot of thinking. I don't understand why God allowed all of this to happen—"

"A God who would allow to happen what happened to my wife and baby is not my God," he said bitterly.

"But evil comes not from God."

"He allowed it," he retorted.

"There's evil in the world, too," she said. "Perhaps, since He gave man self-determination, He expects us to fight against evil. Perhaps we must not depend on Him to do it all."

Egan muttered an oath under his breath. He was remembering vividly how Mary had looked. "At least, thank God"—he said the words totally unaware of the contradiction with his previous statements—"she did not have to live with the shame of what they did to her."

Mandy flushed, her heart sinking. She was well aware of the total irrationality of men, and many women, regarding women who had been taken by Indians. It had been the case since the first settlers landed on the shores of America: A woman who had been kidnapped and used by Indians was rejected as totally soiled and unfit to live again in white society. Men felt that it was better for a woman to kill herself than to submit to an Indian. As Egan stood there gazing into the distances, her anger grew.

"Are you saying, Egan, that if they hadn't killed your wife

but only raped her, that you would have wanted her to kill herself?"

His face darkened. His mouth opened, but no words came.

"I was raped," she said. "Do you think I should kill myself?"

He still could not speak.

"Well?" she demanded.

"It's different with you," he said.

"Why? Because I'm not your wife or because the man who raped me was not an Indian?"

"I don't like dirty talk," he said gruffly. "I came out here to tell you that I'm going to find Purdy, even if it takes my lifetime, and to tell you that you can go with me if you're still interested in finding your sister." He had recovered his composure. "I can forgive you for—"

The quick rush of color into her face was not from shame but from anger. "Oh? You can forgive me for having been forced to come west into the wilderness? You can forgive me because Colonel Brown let himself be deceived by the renegades? You can forgive me because my strength was not enough to kill Purdy or myself?"

"Now don't get crazy on me."

"I pity you," she seethed. "Perhaps it was best that your wife was killed, for you, in your sanctimonious self-pity, would have considered what they did to her—no matter how painful, how shameful to her—as something done directly to you." She whirled.

"Now listen," he called after her. "You're in no position to be so high and mighty."

She turned. "You can go to hell. And I'm sure you will unless you learn how to be a real man."

The *Nuestra Señora* sailed into a night perfumed by tropical air. Renno was not present at the evening meal; he was still sitting in the same position on the stern, his body rocking with the movement of the ship. The stars, the lights of the night, spread themselves over the inky blackness, winking through the moisture-saturated air. At home the

leaves of the deciduous trees would have been painted with
the colors of autumn. The squirrels would be making one
last rush to store nuts for the winter. At night, fires would
be burning in the longhouses to ward off the chill. He
yearned to be there and sent his thoughts winging northward in an effort to envision what Little Hawk and Renna
were doing at that exact moment.

He had felt thirst during the heat of the afternoon, but
now, as the cooling breeze of the ship's movement dried the
day's perspiration on his body, he knew neither thirst nor
hunger—only a longing to know, to be advised. His low,
rhythmic chants occasionally rose in volume so that the
sailors on watch could hear and feel a shiver of dread or
respect for things that they did not understand.

A pale, late moon lifted above the eastern horizon, and
for hours he watched it as it rose, passed the zenith, then
began to fall. She came in the late hours of morning,
pale-haired, dressed beautifully in beaded, embroidered
buckskins—his Emily. She seemed to hover over the water
just past the stern rail, but her eyes were on him, and a
smile was on her face.

"*Nyah-weh ska-noh*, Wife," he whispered, his heart
pounding with joy at her beauty.

"*Gayan-da-sey*, Husband," the manitou responded.

"I am troubled," Renno confessed.

"One day you will no longer wander," the manitou said,
drawing so close that Renno believed he could reach out
and touch her. "But to the strong, many duties are given."

There was a silence. The spirit faded. Renno reached
out, crying, "No, no! Advise me!"

As the spirit of Emily faded there came to his ears—or his
mind—words that seemed to fade in and out of his awareness. For long moments he sat, his arms outstretched
toward the empty air, his mind trying to put the words
together, to make sense of them. And then they seemed to
echo in his ears.

"Against danger, draw on the strength of the ancient
ones."

* * *

All eyes lifted from the breakfast table in the captain's lounge when Renno entered. El-i-chi saw only the signs of strain around his brother's eyes. "Eat," the shaman said simply.

Renno sat, and Adan's black mess boy quickly served him. Egan had stopped eating and was staring at the white Indian, a fork held in midair as he waited for Renno to speak. When there was a long silence, he recovered and lowered the fork.

"Captain Bartolome," Renno said at last, "if you are still willing, it would be considered a great favor if you would alter your course to the south, for Yucatán."

Adan's white teeth flashed. He jumped to his feet and hurried out the hatch. Soon those in the lounge could hear the thumpings and clatterings of the sails being given a new set.

Twice, as the *Nuestra Señora* sailed directly across the sea-lanes running from Spanish Cuba and the Atlantic to the various ports in New Spain, sails were sighted. But the *Señora* sailed under a Spanish flag, so when one ship passed within hailing distance, Adan sent out greetings, and the two ships sailed on. Once the balmy weather worsened, but not with the dread *huracán*. The squall was soon over, and the rain had served to cool the sun-heated deck of the ship and had replenished the supply of fresh water. When landfall came, there was only a smudge of darkness on the horizon.

Upon approach, the barrenness of the shoreline was a surprise to them all, for Adan had expected and had led them to expect dense tropical jungle. Instead there was sparse vegetation, sunbaked open spaces, and no sign of human habitation.

The *Señora* had come to the peninsula of Yucatán west of Cabo Catoche, so she now sailed easterly along the shore. The semiarid shore sent forth land smells that were welcome after the time at sea, especially when a shower came with tropical suddenness and sent rivulets of muddy water scouring the landscape.

"This is an example of how little we know our world,"

Adan said, "and of how many places are still not well-known to us, for the maps show this area to be jungle."

The *Señora* sailed carefully into a passage between the mainland and the offshore island of Cabo Catoche, then moored off a sordid-looking little village. It was late in the day. A fire was lighted on shore, but Adan signaled that no landing would be made before morning.

"We can get this over quickly," El-i-chi said, "by going ashore in the longboat after dark."

"And we would be as blind men," Renno said.

"My friends," Adan pointed out, "we are not invading Yucatán. We are a Spanish vessel on a peaceful mission of trade. Tomorrow morning I will go ashore—"

"And I," Renno said.

"I was about to say with Renno," Adan continued. "This Captain Bocalos, the new governor of this province, knows neither of us. We will be able to talk with him with ease." He chuckled. "Even though the new governor has been here only a short time, from the looks of the place he will welcome visitors. And I'm sure he'll welcome a case of good Jamaican rum."

León Bocalos had been in Córdoba long enough to realize that fate had played him a cruel trick. When he had been called to Governor Miró's house in New Orleans to be rewarded for long and loyal service to Mother Spain by being given an important post, his chest had swelled. For a time he had felt young again, vigorous, and confident that the future held promise, after all. Then he had seen Córdoba. In contrast to Córdoba, New Madrid had been a metropolis, a golden city.

In Córdoba it rained. As if to give the lie to the brown and sere landscape, the skies opened and dumped a downpour that rivaled the biblical deluge of forty days and forty nights . . . but in Córdoba the Lord set no forty-day limit.

"It is only the rainy season, Señor Governor," he was told. "When it is over we have endless months of sun."

The *indio* population of the town and surrounding areas

grew a few gritty crops during the rainy season, then in their efforts to trade their produce for strong spirits, they cluttered the deeply rutted streets of Córdoba, which billowed dust in the dry season and became a sea of mud when it rained. To Bocalos the natives were a filthy lot, vermin ridden, totally without pride, stupid, dull, and uninteresting. The Spaniards on the Yucatán peninsula were not much better; authorities in several New Spain cities had dumped their misfits and drunkards into the garrison at Córdoba. The very few settlers who had come to the peninsula, lured by expectation of lush, rich, tropical plantations, were either doing all within their power to leave or had abandoned all hope. Some men had gone native and lived in thatched-hut squalor with broad-faced, broad-bodied *indio* women who brought into the world flat-faced, dark-skinned babies at intervals of one year or less.

The garrison overlooked the strait between the mainland and Cabo Catoche. It was a poor structure of logs, mud, and thatch. The strength of the Spanish force was listed at twenty-eight men and one officer, but the constant fevers kept the duty list at two-thirds or less at any given time. As for the officer, he was a lieutenant. His lowly rank, his age, and his time of service quickly told Bocalos the caliber of the man. The reason for Lieutenant Cirilo Pelayo's lack of advancement in the army was evident: He was drunk the first time that Bocalos saw him, and in spite of orders, he had not been totally sober since Bocalos and his companions were dumped quickly onto the soggy shore by a ship that did not even anchor, so eager was her captain to sail away from Córdoba.

At first only one thing made life bearable for Bocalos—his *solterita*, his *moza de fortuna*, the young American girl. She filled his nights with delight, for he had been gentle with her and had taught her well.

Bocalos had brought a generous supply of rum and a few bottles of Spanish brandy that was almost worth its weight in gold. He found himself seeking solace in the bottles as the weary, water-logged days passed and he told himself that he must be strong, or he would soon become like Lieutenant Pelayo and the other Spaniards who had settled in Córdoba.

Brandy caused the first flare-up of hostility between the governor and the lethal Simon Purdy. One full bottle of the precious brandy had disappeared, and after a heated search, Bocalos found the bottle, empty, in Purdy's quarters.

"Señor Purdy," Bocalos said, trying to control his unreasonable anger, "you have stolen from me. If that is how I am to be rewarded for befriending you—"

"Hold on, Guv," Purdy said, with a laugh that left his eyes slitted and cold, "who befriended who? Didn't I bring you your little *puta*?" Purdy, who had been lounging on a filthy bed with Charity Brown, rose lazily to his feet. He wore only a flimsy loincloth. His brown body was quite hairy. Sweat beaded on his muscles. "And you have to remember, Guv, that you still have not given me my split for selling the older girl to Laure Beyle."

Bocalos felt the urge to draw his pistol and kill the presumptuous savage. For long moments they stood face-to-face, eyes locked. "I have given you position, weapons, food, lodging, and, not least, my friendship, and you chide me?"

"Gold," Purdy said evenly. "That was the agreement."

There was a bit of gold, but Bocalos had spent more than half of the price of the older girl equipping Purdy and himself for what he had thought would be a fine assignment as a provincial governor. In addition to his own gold he had been given a small amount of money to run his office. He was still angry, but he became a bit more cautious. "Can you spend the gold here?"

"I just like to look at it now and then," Purdy said.

"But it is safer in the strongbox in my office."

"There it is *yours*. In my hands it would be *mine*."

Bocalos decided that strategic retreat was advisable. "We will talk of the gold at another time. Now we speak of my personal property, which you have taken without my permission."

A mocking smile twisted Purdy's lips. "Accept my plea for forgiveness, Señor Governor," he said, bowing slightly. "*I* am insulted that you expect me to drink the slop that is available here."

"I had the foresight to bring my own brandy, while you spent all the money in your pockets on fine wines and food in New Orleans." Bocalos felt belittled, arguing with a hireling. He turned and stalked out of the room.

Purdy turned to Charity. She cringed away from him, for she had seen that look of hatred on his face before, and it had resulted in pain for her. Purdy, however, did not re-join her on the bed. He dressed and went into the office of the governor's chief clerk and stood before a map mounted on the wall. He, too, had found Córdoba to be a miserable place. He had envisioned opportunity as the governor's right-hand man, but here in this poor place there was opportunity only to sweat away one's life. He studied the map closely. Most of the Yucatán was trackless jungle once one left the immediate north and northwest coasts. The only settlements other than Córdoba were to the south, Chan Santa Cruz on the east coast, Campeche on the west.

The man who showed Purdy the charts was the governor's chief clerk and a rarity—an *indio* with a missionary education. He had an odd, almost unpronounceable name, Tzotzil. He dressed in cool, thin, cotton fabrics in gay colors, a mixture of traditional Mayan style and Spanish comfort. His overblouse was striped red on white. When he left his office, he donned a wide-brimmed, round-topped hat of woven straw decorated with a tassel of brightly colored ribbons.

Tzotzil had served under no fewer than three Spanish governors, and he was still a young man of only thirty years—as measured by his Spanish masters. By the long count of his ancestors, he was living in his second *katun*, which was a passage of 7,200 days, having counted more than thirty *tuns*, or three hundred sixty days. He was considered by most members of his race to be a rich man, for the sum he received for his job in the governor's house would have supported most Mayan families in what would be, to them, a regal fashion. But Tzotzil, having seen Mexico City and the strong, permanent houses built by the conquerors and having tasted the fine wines of Spain and Mexico, had dreams. Of late he had begun to think that he had accumulated enough money—through careful living and saving that had been a constant sacrifice—to consider leaving Córdoba to become a part of that exciting world in Mexico proper.

Toward that end he had chosen a wife. He was not inexperienced with women, for one small coin would buy the favors of a girl from an outlying village; but he had never taken a mate. He had chosen the daughter of a minor craftsman, a worker in clay. Her name was Coba. She had a huge mass of inky-black hair, which she wore in the ancient style, and she dressed demurely in a white cotton blouse embroidered with flowers of brilliant colors. Her underdress featured horizontal, multicolored stripes, a true work of art and an indication that she was a hard worker, a woman of talent.

Tzotzil looked up with a blank face when the white man asked, "Have you seen Campeche?"

"I have, sir," Tzotzil answered.

"Tell me about it," Purdy said.

Tzotzil was silent for a long time, collecting his thoughts. "It is larger than Córdoba."

"Do ships call there?"

"They do."

"More often than here?"

"More often."

Purdy chewed on a hangnail on his left thumb as he examined the map before him. "If a man wanted to see some of the interior, what could he expect?"

"It is not advisable for a white man to go into the interior," Tzotzil said.

Purdy turned to face the clerk. "When I ask you a question, Indian, I want information, not advice. Tell me about the interior."

Tzotzil shrugged. "*Malo. Peligroso.*"

"Why dangerous?"

"Not many miles to the south, the jungle begins—reptiles, insects, the jaguar. But the dangers of nature are the least of it. There are men there who have not seen a white man. Their arrows are dipped in poison that causes a painful death."

Purdy sat in a chair in front of Tzotzil's desk. "Suppose a man wanted to travel into the interior. Let's say, maybe, he wanted to do some exploring and end up in Campeche. Could he make it if he had guides, and guns to fight off the *indios* and the animals?"

Tzotzil was becoming more interested in this conversation. The white man had something in mind, and when a white man had plans, they usually centered around profit, around gold. "Perhaps."

"Where would I find *indios* who know the jungle?"

"That would not be difficult." Tzotzil risked a question of his own. "May I ask, sir, why you are considering such a dangerous and strenuous journey?"

Purdy laughed. "How long have you been in Córdoba?"

"For over ten years."

"And you have to ask?"

"Córdoba is all right," Tzotzil said. "Better than the jungle."

"But worse than Tampico or New Orleans," Purdy said. "Actually, I'm just making talk. Restless, is all. But it might be interesting to take a look at the interior. If there are places where no white man has been, hell, I might get famous as an explorer."

"More likely, sir, you would find your head mounted on a post outside the hut of a jungle *indio*." He had a feeling that Purdy was up to something. "The *indios* of the interior guard the sacred cities of the old ones, and any man who comes seeking gold does not live." He had chosen his words deliberately, and he had watched Purdy's eyes carefully when he used the word *gold*. He saw the expected light of interest and surprise on the man's face.

"Cities? Gold?"

Truly, the white man had not known of the legends of the

ancient ones, their cities, and the great treasures hidden in the sacred stones, Tzotzil thought.

"Think not of that, señor," Tzotzil warned, "for there lies death."

"No, I wasn't going treasure hunting," Purdy said. He chuckled. "But if I stumbled over a nugget or two, I wouldn't kick them aside."

For the first time Tzotzil's face showed emotion as he smiled. "Nor would I, señor. Let me consider the matter. Perhaps there are those who would act as guides."

Purdy rose and fumbled in his pocket. He had two coins, a gold and a silver. He hesitated a moment, drew out the gold, and carefully placed it in front of the Indian. "I don't have anything to hide, but I'm a private man. I'd like for our little talk to remain with us. Understand?"

Tzotzil picked up the golden Spanish coin. "I understand fully."

Only two days had passed when Tzotzil appeared at Purdy's door. He had checked to be sure that the governor was in retirement, in his suite with his white *puta*. Purdy had been drinking the vile but strong beer brewed in the barracks by Lieutenant Cirilo Pelayo. When he saw Tzotzil, he turned to Charity. "Get some clothes on."

Charity Brown scrambled into Mayan cottons.

"Go for a walk," Purdy told her.

"It's so hot and sticky outside," she whined.

"You heard me," Purdy growled, taking a step toward her and lifting one hand. She ran from the room, turning sideways to slip past Tzotzil. She was, Tzotzil saw, only a child. His Coba, by contrast, was a mature woman with firm breasts the size of his clenched fist, and with spreading hips. "Come in," Purdy told him.

"I have considered your desires," Tzotzil said as he accepted a cup of the potent beer. "If you are serious about exploring the interior, I can arrange it." He had done some thinking. He had his savings. He did not have access to the governor's strongbox, but he could get his hands on a small

amount of silver, which was used for the payroll. It was not
a fortune, but it would augment his savings a little.

"Good," Purdy said.

"Although I have leave time coming from my position,"
Tzotzil said, "I would not care to cause the governor worry,
which he would feel, I suspect, if he knew that we were
going into the jungle."

"Ah," Purdy said, a light of awareness going on inside his
head. This *indio* had reasons of his own for wanting to go
into the interior. "Very thoughtful," he muttered.

"We will need supplies," Tzotzil continued.

"Can't we live off the land?"

"When we reach the jungle, there will be fruits and nuts
and meat, true. But we will need weapons, salt, water
containers, and some other things—not many. I can pur-
chase all we need—and guns, as well—and hire men to
carry everything with only a few more coins like the one
you gave me."

"How many is a few?"

"Ten, no more."

Purdy winced, then nodded.

"Fortunately, we are past the time of the heaviest rains,"
Tzotzil said.

"You couldn't prove it by me," Purdy growled.

"The dry season will come as we travel," Tzotzil assured
him. Now that he had made his decision to leave, he was
eager to act. Realistically, he didn't need the white man; he
could travel faster and in greater safety with only Coba as
his companion. But he suspected that Purdy had secret
reasons for leaving Córdoba and assumed that the man
would carry additional gold and silver in his pack. The
jungle hid more death than this white man could imagine,
and if a snake, a cat, or the fever didn't kill him, the jungle
would hide one more violent death easily. Then Tzotzil's
pack would be heavier with the white man's treasure.
Perhaps, with Purdy's gold, Coba and he could live in the
splendid style of the Spanish in Mexico, in a comfortable
house of brick, with *indio* servants to tend their every need.

"I will take the money now," Tzotzil said.

Two nights later Tzotzil was once again in Purdy's quarters. He told Purdy that all was in readiness.

"I will need clothing suitable for the jungle for the girl," Purdy said.

Tzotzil had not imagined that Purdy would be foolish enough to take such a frail girl into the jungle. "She will not live long," he warned.

"I don't know, she's pretty tough. At any rate, she's going."

"It is your decision," Tzotzil said.

"We will leave in the darkness of the night," Purdy said. "I need tomorrow and at least a portion of tomorrow night. Be ready at any time after midnight."

Tzotzil nodded and told Purdy where he would be waiting just outside the town.

Purdy had not mentioned his plans to Charity. She had become friendly with some of the servants of the house, and she often talked with Bocalos's *puta*, Tess. She wasn't exactly a font of wisdom, and he didn't want to risk her letting the cat out of the bag.

Actually, it was not the day Purdy needed; what he had in mind couldn't be done by daylight. He was ready, except for one thing. He set about accomplishing that by having dinner alone with the governor. Bocalos was feeling generous and broke out a bottle of rum. Purdy drank just enough to keep Bocalos from being suspicious, but the governor was soon quite merry and did not object when Purdy continued to fill his glass. It was near midnight when Bocalos, with one last belch, fell asleep in his chair. The rest was simple. Quickly Purdy bound the man and stuffed a cotton cloth into his mouth, securing it with a silken scarf.

The door to Bocalos's office gave way to gentle pressure. The safe offered only slightly less resistance, its padlock yielding to three blows of a hammer. The gold and silver inside the safe was a disappointingly small amount, but it would have to suffice—at least it was more than Bocalos owed Purdy for his share of the girl who had been sold in New Orleans.

With the money in a leather pouch, Purdy went back to check on Bocalos. The governor was still unconscious. Purdy was going out the door when he heard a sound and turned to see Tess standing in the doorway. She was dressed in a skimpy cotton shift, and he felt his blood stir, for she was more curvaceous than his Charity.

"What? . . ." Tess asked, rubbing her eyes sleepily. Then she saw the bound governor and opened her mouth to scream. Purdy was on her in a leap, his fist contacting her temple. She crumpled. He stood for a moment looking down. The cotton shift had pulled up to reveal her well-developed thighs. So it was that when Bocalos was discovered the next morning by the household servants—his hands and feet swollen and painful from the tightness of his bonds, his eyes wide and full of panic because he was having difficulty breathing—it was found that the money in the safe was not the only possession that Purdy had stolen.

An hour later, when Lieutenant Cirilo Pelayo, a small group of men—most of them suffering from the excesses of the previous night—and Bocalos found the trail of a party of six men and two women, they followed it south to a point where the trees became taller and the undergrowth greener. The jungle soon erased the traces of passage. Within a few miles the jungle closed in, smothering Bocalos with its rank dampness. When Pelayo said that it would be stupid to try to penetrate that jungle, that five times the number of men available could not catch the thieves, Bocalos was almost eager to agree. He had only one desire: to get out of that place of stench and wet and claustrophobic closeness.

As luck would have it, it was only a matter of days before a Spanish ship arrived offshore late in the evening and anchored for the night. The ship would be able to take word to the Spanish authorities that a trusted clerk and another employee had robbed the safe and disappeared into the

jungle with the only possible destinations being either
Chan Santa Cruz or, more likely, Campeche, there to take
ship and escape with the gold. Bocalos could hardly wait for
the morning, when he could set in motion events to bring
back the traitorous Tzotzil and the man who had betrayed
his friendship.

Chapter XIII

$\mathbf{R}$enno and Adan left the *Nuestra Señora* at eight, long after the sunrise. As the longboat neared shore Renno saw a reception committee: A slim, rather handsome Spaniard in an ornate uniform stood stiffly before a formation of soldiers not nearly so splendidly uniformed.

"It looks as if the whole town has turned out," Adan said.

Ragtag Spanish civilians, mostly men, preempted the best vantage points around the ramshackle dock. Indians in colorful dress stood in the background.

Adan directed the men at the oars to bring the longboat to the end of the dock. Renno leaped up first, then turned to give Adan a hand. It was a walk of some fifty paces to shore, where the local governor stood in formal readiness.

Adan swept off his hat and made a polite bow. "Your Excellency," he said, "His Royal Spanish Majesty's ship *Nuestra Señora* requests permission to visit His Majesty's port at Córdoba."

"Welcome to Córdoba," said Governor León Bocalos. He turned and barked an order, which was repeated with only a slight slurring of words by Lieutenant Cirilo Pelayo. The honor guard of soldiers hoisted their muskets into the air, and there was a ragged blast of shots. From the jungle, nearby birds screamed back a protest of the noise.

Adan introduced himself. "And this is Señor Renno, supercargo of the *Nuestra Señora*."

Formalities finished, Bocalos said, "Captain, gentlemen, you will, of course, take lunch with me. Now, if you will be so kind as to come to my office, I will be pleased to hear news from the outside world and to discuss the business of your visit to Córdoba."

Renno made a surreptitious but careful inspection of the town and its defenses as they walked to the governor's house. He had not only seen evidence that many of the soldiers in the honor guard had been drinking, he had smelled it. The sloppy condition of the soldiers' uniforms and, above all, their weapons, had told him that discipline was slack in the Córdoba garrison, and where there is no discipline, men fight poorly. He estimated that the barracks could not house more than forty men.

Bocalos, in the hope of having his investment returned multifold, offered his visitors some of his precious brandy. Adan accepted. Renno held up his hand in polite, smiling refusal. Bocalos smiled for his own reason—not having to share the brandy with Renno.

"And so," Bocalos said, "what can we here at this poor post do for you, Captain Bartolome?"

Adan shrugged and smiled. "Governor, we have cargo for Chan Santa Cruz and will be returning this way with our hold empty. We had been told that indigo plantations were being developed in the northern Yucatán, and so we hope for a cargo from Córdoba."

"Alas," Bocalos said, "development of such plantations

has not proceeded as swiftly as had been planned." Actually, work on the indigo plantations had ceased long ago, and the jungle had reclaimed everything. Bocalos knew that Córdoba had nothing of value, nothing to offer in trade. But he knew that there might be rum on board that Spanish ship or perhaps brandy and a case or two of good wine. He was thinking desperately. He brightened. "However, Captain, we can offer you some valuable goods that won't take up too much room aboard your ship."

Adan nodded and tried to look interested.

"Jaguar skins," Bocalos suggested. "And charmingly colored cotton cloth made by the local *indios*."

Although Adan was not in Córdoba for trade, he feigned interest. "For such I would pay in gold."

"Gold would, of course, be welcomed, but it is not required. Here in Córdoba we lack many of the small luxuries that men in the outer world take for granted."

"What then?" Adan wanted to know.

"Spirits," Bocalos answered. "In this place a snifter of good brandy, a sip of wine, that is all that keeps a man free of the fevers."

Adan smiled. He always kept a good store of spirits aboard his ship not only for trade but for his own moderate consumption. "Done. When may I see these trade items you mention?"

Sweat poured down Bocalos's back. "Señor Captain, not having advance knowledge of this opportunity, I will need a few days to gather it, for the cloth is made by the *indios* in scattered locations. The jaguar hides are also taken and cured by *indios*, some of them at great distances."

"I will make this proposal," Adan said. "We will continue our course for Chan Santa Cruz and, on our return, stop here. That will give you time to gather your materials." He had quickly given up on the idea of making a profit on the hides and native clothes, for he knew that the ship would not be here long enough for Bocalos to contact the Indians and make his deals. And certainly the ship would not be coming back.

A feeling of desperation came over Bocalos. Soon he

would be reduced to drinking the vile beer brewed by Lieutenant Pelayo. He opened his mouth, but nothing came. Adan, seeing the governor's distress, said, "Of course, Governor, to show our good faith we will deliver a percentage of the items you ask in trade before we sail."

Bocalos's face lit up. "As it happens, Captain, I have men available to move the, uh, items today."

Renno caught Adan's eye and winked. It was evident that Bocalos was eager to have his spirits.

"Governor," Adan said cheerfully, "since I have my boat at the shore now, I will go to give orders to my men to start offloading. What say you to two cases of French brandy?"

Bocalos was thunderstruck. French brandy? Heaven had come to sodden Córdoba.

"And a few cases of assorted wines, plus a case or two of Jamaican rum?"

"Ah, very good," Bocalos breathed, almost tasting the French brandy.

"If you'll excuse me, then," Adan said, looking at Renno with raised eyebrows, seeking a clue to Renno's wants.

"Perhaps the governor will be good enough, Captain, to show me his town while you attend to business," Renno suggested.

Bocalos groaned inwardly. There was nothing to show except squalid huts, verminous *indios,* and mud. And it was moving toward midday, when the heat would reach a peak before the predictable afternoon shower turned all into a steam bath. "With great pleasure," he said.

Renno and Bocalos walked first along the waterfront, past the garrison. No guard was mounted; there was no sign of activity. A few soldiers, uniforms open in an effort to ease the suffocating heat, sprawled in the shade of trees.

"I see no cannon," Renno remarked.

"There is no need for guns here," Bocalos explained, thinking that only the Spanish would be foolish enough to want the Yucatán. "There are no enemies worthy of cannon. We are too poor to attract buccaneers, and even though the eternal disputes with England continue, we are so far off the beaten sea-lanes that an English ship would have to be lost to arrive here."

"There is no threat from the native Indians?"

"None. Oh, in the interior there are *indios* who protect their jungle haunts with poison arrows." He laughed. "Once, they say, a great civilization flourished here, but I think that is a fable. How could civilization arise in such a place?"

"So it is not necessary to maintain a large garrison?" Renno asked.

"Not at all. Actually, we are overmanned with thirty-eight enlisted men and one officer," he revealed easily.

"I almost envy you, Governor," Renno said, by way of getting Bocalos talking. "It is so peaceful and relaxed here. Even though we are a merchant ship, we must carry cannon for protection. The *Nuestra Señora* mounts twelve guns, and our men are well trained to use them. Here, I would imagine, one escapes the stress and pressures of daily life in an idyllic surrounding."

Was this fool talking about Córdoba? Bocalos almost had a coughing fit, trying to stem the urge to roar with laughter. "There is," he managed, "a certain serenity."

Renno nodded.

They had turned onto a muddy, narrow street. On an open porch a soldier, his tunic removed, was dallying lazily with a fat, giggling *indio* girl.

"And to have the luck to be amid people who are so friendly, eh?" Renno said, winking at the governor. "I do not understand the concern of those in Spain regarding *fraternidad*. After all, the *indio* is a source of cheap labor, is he not? And the fruit of this *fraternidad* is *indio*, is it not, just as the fruit of jackass and horse is mule, regardless of the pedigree of the mare."

"Indeed," Bocalos said, "I do not try to interfere with the, uh, social life of my men."

"And you, Governor," Renno pressed on, "I imagine that you are a married man, being a mature gentleman and in a position of great importance."

Bocalos chuckled. "To date, señor, I have not been cornered by a wife."

"Ah, well," Renno said, "there is always the *indio* girl, eh?"

"For some," Bocalos replied. "Not for me, señor. I said merely that I was not married, not that I do not have a woman."

"Ah," Renno said. "And you, Governor, would settle for nothing less that the most beautiful of New Orleans' women."

Bocalos had seen all of Córdoba that he wanted to see. Sweat was dampening his linen. "Come with me, señor, and I will present you to my little love." He sorely regretted having lost his Tess to Purdy. Charity Brown, who had been left behind, would not make as good an impression.

Renno made no protest. Soon they were in the governor's house. An *indio* servant provided cool, damp towels to wipe sweaty faces, then nodded when Bocalos ordered her to fetch the *mujer joven*.

The white girl with only buds for breasts, small hips, and child's legs, was dressed in Mayan cottons. She entered the room shyly, cast one quick, fearful glance at Renno, and then lowered her eyes to the floor. "*Chiquilla*," Bocalos said, "this gentleman came from across the seas. Señor Renno, I present my little one, my *chiquilla*."

"*Con mucho gusto,*" the girl said.

"Go, go," Bocalos said, making a shooing motion. He turned to Renno and smiled, but the smile faded quickly, for he had surprised a cold glare of disgust in Renno's blue eyes.

"A pretty child," Renno forced himself to say.

"Come," Bocalos said, "we will see if your captain has returned, for it is almost time to eat."

The meal was an interesting one, with dishes made of yams, jungle fruits, and goat meat. When it was finished, Bocalos made no protest when Renno said that it was time for him to get back to the ship. The cases of spirits had been delivered and were stored snugly in the governor's office.

Bocalos told the two visitors of plans to protect the cases with locks, reinforced doors, and barred windows.

The population of Córdoba turned out to watch the *Nuestra Señora* sail away. She disappeared around a jungly point. There was no one to see as Adan directed the ship into a cove and lowered anchor.

El-i-chi, Se-quo-i, Egan, and Adan listened with great attention as Renno explained the layout of Córdoba. "We will land there in three boats," Renno said. "Our force will be divided into two units. You, El-i-chi, will take the smaller unit to the governor's house. Se-quo-i and I will lead the other force against the barracks."

"I'll go with you," Adan offered.

"I'm sorry, my friend," Renno said. "Any man can fight, but not many have the skills to sail a great ship. You must stay aboard."

Adan started to protest.

"If it becomes necessary to use the ship's guns, Adan, you have to be aboard," Renno said, and the young captain subsided glumly. "We know that one of the girls is in Córdoba. Although neither Adan nor I saw any man who looked like an American, we can only assume that Simon Purdy is there, with the other girl. It is your job, Brother," he said to El-i-chi, "to rescue the girl from the governor's house and to keep your eyes open for the second girl and for Purdy."

El-i-chi nodded, absently touching his tomahawk.

Renno paused for a moment, then continued. "There are twenty-nine soldiers. There may be guards, but if so, they will not be alert. They have been lulled into laxness by the heat of this place and by its isolation. I think we will find most of them inside the barracks. A few may be sleeping with their women in the town, so we will have to watch our backs."

"Why not wait until the town is asleep and bombard the barracks?" Adan asked. "In that way none of our people will be risked."

"If we could be assured that all could be killed with the first few shots," Renno said, "I would agree, but bombardment would serve to alert the men, to scatter them, and then we'd have to seek them out in small groups or individually. No, we will surround the barracks."

"You'll be outnumbered," Adan warned.

"But we will have surprise working for us," Renno said. He did not say that he expected the garrison to be confused, disorganized, and of little value in a fight, for he did not want to make Adan's sailors overconfident. Even a man who is half-drunk could get lucky and place a ball in a fatal spot. Or, as Roy Johnson had once said, "Even a blind hog can find an acorn occasionally."

El-i-chi had Egan and four sailors in his vessel when the three longboats set out from the ship by the light of a tropical moon. Renno's two boats held five sailors each, with Se-quo-i in the second boat. The late-afternoon shower had accentuated the dank, musty smell of the jungles, but the night sky was clear as the boats neared Córdoba and landed close together between the dock and barracks. El-i-chi led his men off toward the governor's house.

The barracks had only a front entrance, but there were windows at the back. Renno, working slowly and silently, positioned Se-quo-i and three men at the rear, with orders to prevent the escape of any soldiers through the windows. He soon had the balance of his force positioned around the front, each man assigned a field of fire. There was a guard, but that man had brought a stool to his post at the front of the barracks and was seated, his head leaning back against the log wall.

Renno was carrying all of his favorite weapons—musket, pistol, stiletto, tomahawk, and the English longbow—and had changed from his Spanish dress into the breechclout of the Seneca warrior. His face was painted for war. He walked openly toward the entrance and had to shake the guard to wake him. The guard came awake with a groan, mumbling a protest, and then his eyes went wide and he opened his mouth when he saw the fierce-looking face near his. Before he could yell he felt the pressure of a sharp knife at his throat, so there emitted from his mouth only a grunt and a gulp.

"How many are inside?" Renno asked.

"I don't know," the guard said.

Renno increased the pressure on the stiletto until the skin was parted and a trickle of blood ran to join the sweat on the guard's neck.

"Please," the guard begged. "Almost all, maybe a dozen are sleeping in the town."

"And the officer?"

"He sleeps in his own house."

"Good," Renno said. "Go inside, wake the men, and tell them that if they surrender, they will be allowed to live. Tell them to light their lamps and toss their weapons out the windows, and then lie down quietly on their beds."

"Sí, señor," the guard said.

"Go, then."

The guard ran into the dark barracks. Renno retreated a few steps and hid in shadows.

As soon as the guard was inside, he turned, peered out into the dappled moonlight, raised his musket, and fired, although he had no definite target. Shouts of alarm broke out in the barracks. A lamp was lit, then quickly extinguished. Shots came from the windows. Renno's men, obeying orders, were holding their fire until they had a specific target.

There was movement at the entrance. Slowly a man stuck his head out and peered around, then shouted to those behind him. Men began to pour out the door. The first, running eagerly, died with a steel-tipped arrow in his heart. One, two, three times, Renno fired, bringing the arrows from his quiver in a smooth, quick motion, drawing the powerful bow, and sending the arrows flying with deadly accuracy. Around him muskets crashed, and the first rush of men sprawled on the muddy ground.

Lieutenant Cirilo Pelayo, his senses dazed by the evening's beer consumption, struggled from the bed of his Indian wife. He fell twice as he tried to thrust his feet into the legs of his trousers and finally rushed out of the hut without his shirt to see the flash of gunfire near the barracks. Lights began to glow in the town as people were awakened by the shooting. He dived back inside, pushed a pistol into his belt, seized his musket, and ran toward the sound of firing. Before he could cross the short, muddy distance the gunfire ceased.

Cirilo, thinking that the gunfire was the result of a drunken fight among his men, was angry. He began shouting as he closed the distance, calling the men every profane name he had learned in his years of army service. He ran directly into the arms of two strong men who stripped him of his weapons and pinned his arms. A ghostly thing with a painted face spoke. "Do you die tonight, my friend?"

Cirilo gasped. "What? Who?"

"You wear the trousers of an officer," Renno said.

"Yes," Cirilo said, fear beginning to clear his head a bit.

"Go inside, Lieutenant," Renno said. "Some of your soldiers are already dead. The barracks is surrounded. Tell your men to toss their weapons out the windows so they might live."

Cirilo looked around and saw only sailors and the one painted Indian. "This I will do," he agreed, but he had other plans once he was with his men. He walked stiffly across the open area and disappeared into the barracks.

The firing broke out from the rear after about five minutes as Cirilo ordered men to go out the open windows and circle around to face the unknown foe at the front. Four men died quickly under the muskets of Se-quo-i's men. A fifth refused to leap out the window. Cirilo decided to change his tactics. "There are a handful of sailors out there, probably English privateers. We are Spanish regulars. Can we not handle a few brigands?"

He felt that he was in good voice, that his impassioned words of courage were inspiring his men. They grouped behind him, weapons in hand, as he led the way to the front entrance. "All together," he exhorted, "all as one. We rush them, close with them, and give them a taste of Spanish steel with our bayonets." With a shout of daring, he ran from the door to meet not one but two musket balls. He died instantly and was knocked backward into the following man.

The rush was instantly aborted. A hail of musketry killed two more men huddled in the entrance before the others could scramble back to safety.

Renno called out, "Enough have died! Throw your weapons out the windows, and you will live."

"We surrender!" a man yelled, and muskets began to fly from the windows to plop into the muddy ground.

El-i-chi posted the four sailors under his command outside the governor's house to watch the exits. With Egan at his back he entered the front door, which was unlocked. The house, small and crudely constructed, was dark and quiet. El-i-chi stood just inside the door to try to orient himself to the layout. Suddenly firing broke out at the barracks, and there was a shout from the rear of the house.

"I think His Excellency is awake," Egan whispered.

El-i-chi moved toward the sound. A flare of match light came from an open door, and then the glow of a lamp.

León Bocalos hurried from his bedchamber into horror. He carried the lamp with him, the upward light distorting his face and spreading outward to show him the visage of a painted demon. He cried out like a woman, his voice gone high and shrill, and almost dropped the lamp.

"Put the lamp on the table," El-i-chi ordered. He saw no reason to leave Córdoba as they had left New Orleans, in flames, so he didn't want the governor to drop the lamp. Bocalos obeyed with shaking hands. "Egan, check the other rooms."

Egan ran eagerly, hoping to encounter a white man, an American, Simon Purdy. Instead he startled the *indio* couple who lived in the lean-to shed attached to the back of the governor's house and frightened a cowering, mangy dog at the back door.

The girl, moving slowly and fearfully, came out of the bedroom with a blanket wrapped around her. When she saw Bocalos standing stiffly, she silently moved toward him, only to halt with a sharp cry as she noticed El-i-chi's war-painted face and naked torso.

"You will not be harmed," El-i-chi told her. "I suggest that you get dressed."

"León, who is this man?" the girl asked.

"Do as he says," Bocalos said in a hushed, frightened voice.

Egan came stomping back, his face showing his disappointment. "There's an old Indian couple out back. That's all."

A new burst of firing came from the direction of the barracks. El-i-chi turned his head toward the sound. He made a quick decision. "Bring the governor," he said. "Tell the girl to get dressed and wait here."

Before Egan could protest, the shaman was out the door and running toward the barracks, the four sailors following.

Renno counted the muskets that had been tossed out the windows and counted the dead in front of the barracks. The numbers did not come out right. Several men were not accounted for, either by body count or weapons count. Obviously, some soldiers inside the barracks were still in possession of muskets. He kept to the shadows so as not to offer a good target and yelled, "You men inside! Come out one by one by the main door, and you will not be harmed."

As the first man came out, hands held high, El-i-chi joined Renno.

"One girl, no Purdy," El-i-chi said, giving all the information Renno needed, then turning his attention to the men exiting the barracks.

"Unless many were sleeping in the town," Renno said, "there are eight men inside with weapons."

The lack of action at the governor's house had not pleased El-i-chi. "When a raccoon holes up in a hollow tree, one must drag him out." He started toward the barracks. Renno called out harshly, and he halted.

"One against eight?" Renno asked.

El-i-chi's teeth showed white in the tropical moonlight.

"I'm not selfish, Brother. You may have one or two of them if you wish."

Renno had something else in mind to clear the holdouts from the barracks, something that involved fire. But when he saw El-i-chi's fierce smile in anticipation of battle, he felt his blood surge. "Se-quo-i!" he called, and held El-i-chi's arm until Se-quo-i was with them. "My brother's blood calls for battle. I will share this call with him."

Se-quo-i volunteered by lifting his own blade.

El-i-chi led the way. He darted into the barracks, threw himself to the floor, and rolled as two muskets spoke. The balls splintered planks behind him. He saw movement in the darkness, and his pistol's bark brought a cry of agony.

Renno edged into the room, taking advantage of the confusion. Se-quo-i was behind him. As another musket fired, Renno aimed at the flash and heard a satisfying thud as a body fell. And then he was moving swiftly down a wall, stepping into and over the rows of crude beds.

"Where are they?" a voice cried in panic. "I don't see them." The man who spoke saw no more as Se-quo-i's pistol fired with accuracy.

A shadow moved near Renno, and he froze.

"There," whispered a Spaniard. "See him?"

The shadow that was Renno moved faster than the two men could react, his tomahawk slashing in the darkness. A hoarse scream sounded, and the second man near Renno fled, only to be overtaken in one quick bound by a nameless, faceless terror of the night. His death was swift.

"I surrender!" a Spaniard screamed in terror as he saw other moving shadows.

"That opportunity has passed," El-i-chi said as he lunged forward, his tomahawk descending. The Spaniard heard only the first two words before blackness became forever for him.

At the far end of the long main room of the barracks two men, hearing their comrades' death, jumped through the windows and ran into the waiting guns of the sailors outside.

A grim silence descended upon the dark barracks. Renno

hooted and heard two hoots in return. He stood still and quiet, and there was no sound. Then there was the scratch of a match and a glow of light. Se-quo-i lit a lamp. A glance around the room told Renno that it was empty, save for his friends.

The soldiers who slept in the town had surrendered and were now seated on the ground, hands held behind their heads, the guns of two sailors trained on them. Renno heard a hoot that sounded more like a white man than an owl and watched two figures come near.

"Here's His Excellency," Egan announced.

"The governor and I have met," Renno said, answering as Egan had spoken, in English.

Bocalos, feeling certain that the raiders were English, knew that he had been wrong about Córdoba being so remote and so poor that it would not be a worthy target for a British buccaneer.

"Señor Renno," Bocalos said, "have we not had enough death?"

"We have," Renno agreed, "save one. Where is the American Simon Purdy?"

"*Madre de Dios*," Bocalos said. "Is this, then, about Simon Purdy?"

"Purdy and the two girls," Renno answered.

"And that's all you want?" Bocalos asked, dumbfounded. "All you want are Purdy and the two American girls?"

"That's all," Renno said.

From the moment he had first faced a war-painted Indian in his salon, Bocalos had expected to die. Now he dared to hope, and the relief was overwhelming. He felt dizzy, and he could not keep from bursting into laughter.

"What's so damned funny?" Egan demanded, punching Bocalos with the muzzle of his musket.

"All this for two little *putas* and Purdy," Bocalos gasped through his hysterical laughter. "You are not here to sack our poor little town. You are not after Spanish blood—only two little girls and Purdy. *Madre de Dios*."

Renno, realizing that the man was almost crazy with fear and relief, waited patiently. Gradually the governor gained control. "Señor," he said, "I can give you one-third of what you want. There is the girl in my house. As for the others, Simon Purdy has stolen my *puta*, the provincial treasury, and the monthly payroll for the garrison and disappeared. He may have had the help of my chief clerk, an *indio*, for he vanished at the same time."

"Where?" Renno demanded, and the tone of his voice told Bocalos that he was in grave danger if he lied.

"On the veil of the Virgin," Bocalos confessed, "I do not know. We followed them into the jungle, but we gave up when the jungle ate their trail. Is my second in command, Lieutenant Pelayo, dead?"

"He is," Renno said.

"Pelayo," the governor said, crossing himself, "guessed that Purdy was trying to make it to Chan Santa Cruz or to Campeche—most probably Campeche, since ships call there more often. At any rate, it was impossible to follow their trail. There were four men and two women."

"Two women?"

"Two," Bocalos said, and he began to laugh again, for the fates had been so unfair to him: first his disappointment with his new posting, then betrayal, and now ignominious defeat. But the most amusing thing of all was that the theft of the provincial treasury had not satisfied Simon Purdy. In leaving, Purdy had taken with him the *puta* chosen for himself by Bocalos, leaving behind the poorly developed girl-child, Charity Brown.

In the east the night was dimming. Renno ordered the men to put the Spanish soldiers back inside the barracks. While that was being done, he told Egan to return the governor to his house and wait there with the girl. Another man was sent to light a signal fire on the waterfront.

With the dawn the *Nuestra Señora* was anchored off-shore, and Renno could see that Mandy was in the ship's last longboat as it was rowed toward shore. He met them on the dock.

"Is Tess here?" Mandy asked anxiously. "Is she safe?"

Renno smiled ruefully. "There is one girl here. I must

confess that in the excitement it seems that no one has asked her her name."

"It went well?" Adan asked. "Did we suffer losses?"

"None," Renno said.

"Thank God," Adan breathed.

"Renno, where is she?" Mandy implored. "Take me to her, please?"

"Come," Renno said.

A few sailors were outside the governor's house, comparing notes about the battle and looking quite self-satisfied as they saw the American girl approaching with Renno.

"Well, miss," yelled out a sailor, "I pray that you will find your sister well."

Renno let Mandy enter the house first. Egan was sitting on the edge of a heavy Spanish chest, his musket leaning against his knee. Bocalos was seated. He looked up as Renno and Mandy entered.

"Where is she, Egan?" Mandy asked.

"I think she's a bit shy," Egan said, pointing toward the bedroom.

"Hold," Renno said as Mandy started to run toward the bedroom door. She turned. "I want to see her, too. We have come a long way for her."

Egan uncoiled from his perch on the chest and went to the bedroom door. "Little miss," he said, "please come out now. There is someone here to see you."

Mandy's heart was pounding as she waited. She lifted one hand to her mouth and bit down, hard, on the knuckle of her forefinger to be able to bear the suspense.

"Oh, God," she whispered as Charity Brown appeared in the doorway. "Oh, merciful God." Blood rushed to her stomach, and she slumped. Renno leaped to catch her before she hit the floor.

"Damn it, woman!" Egan roared. "This is no time to faint, not before we know." He turned to face the child. "Your name, girl?"

"Brown. Charity Brown."

A wave of sympathy flooded Egan so strongly that he was astounded. He fell to his knees and lifted Mandy's head from Renno's lap. "Ah, Mandy," he whispered. "You poor Mandy."

Charity, her eyes wide with fright, seeing before her two Indians much like those who had killed her parents, scurried to the chair where Bocalos sat and threw herself down beside him, reaching for his hand. "León," she whispered, her voice quavering, "who are these people? Why is my family's servant with them?"

Mandy opened her eyes. The first thing she saw was Egan's concerned face, then she sat up and looked to see Charity clinging to Bocalos. "Charity, where is my sister?"

"Gone," Charity answered. "Simon Purdy took her, thank God, instead of me."

"Charity," Renno said, speaking softly, "do you know where Purdy has taken Tess?"

"No," she said. "He's very mean. He hurt me. León doesn't hurt me. He is kind and gentle."

Mandy was helped to her feet. She walked toward Charity, extending her hands, but the younger girl cringed away, clinging to Bocalos's arm.

"We've come to take you home," Mandy told her.

"León?" Charity said in a small, sad voice.

"Come," Mandy encouraged.

"No," Charity croaked, tears forming in her eyes. "I have no home. I want to stay with León. He is nice to me."

"You can't stay," Mandy pleaded. "You mustn't stay and be this man's—" She could not bring herself to say the sordid word.

"León," Charity begged, "don't let them take me, please. I want to stay with you."

"The choice, Little One, is not mine," Bocalos said.

"I won't go," Charity declared heatedly. "You can't make me go. What would I do? I have nothing to do with this bond servant and these savage Indians."

"Mandy, take the girl to her room," Renno requested.

Charity jerked away from Mandy's hand and, sobbing, ran into the bedroom. Renno looked at Bocalos, who spread his hands.

"Lock the governor in his office," Renno told Egan.

The conference was held in the governor's salon. The jungle's humidity came into the room though the open windows.

"She's only a child," Mandy said. "Fourteen years old. She can't make such a choice on her own."

"Mandy, if we take her, what will become of her?" Egan asked gently. "Do you see the way Bocalos looked at her? I think there was a certain fondness here."

"He bought her," Mandy protested. "She was obviously left to him when Purdy took my sister."

"She has become a woman in function if not in years," El-i-chi pointed out. "Should she not have a choice?"

"Bring Bocalos," Renno said.

The governor entered the room, looking from face to face apprehensively.

"Mandy, please wait outside," Renno said, and Mandy left reluctantly.

"You said that Purdy took Mandy's sister, abandoning this one for you," Renno said.

"It is true," Bocalos admitted. "However, in the short time since, I have become fond of the girl. If you are to let me live, Señor Renno, it would please me to have this girl. You heard her say that I have been gentle with her, and so I have, unlike Purdy."

"What guarantee do we have that you will not tire of her and sell her?" Egan wanted to know.

"Señor Renno," Bocalos said, directing his answer to the white Indian, "you have seen this place. I can assure you that unless by some stroke of fate I should become rich enough to go back to Spain, Córdoba will be my post until I die. You have seen it, and you have seen the Indian women. This girl would be my lifelong companion."

"Have you a priest here?" Renno asked.

"Father Paul travels between here and the jungle villages. He is due to return."

"Then you will marry the girl," Renno said.

Bocalos smiled. "Why not?" His smile broadened. "In a way it is fitting, the glorious climax to my career, to marry an American waif who was not a virgin when she came to me. Yes, it is most fitting."

There was one other decision to be made before the *Nuestra Señora* sailed from Córdoba. Actually, whether or not to go after Purdy was a foregone conclusion, considering how far they had come, Egan's determination to find and kill Simon Purdy, Mandy's heartbreak at finding that once again fate had taken her sister beyond her reach, and El-i-chi's reluctance to abandon a job before completion.

As it happened, before Renno led members of his party into the jungle, the priest returned from his evangelizing in the Indian villages and performed a simple but rather beautiful ceremony of marriage.

Three of the kidnapped girls were now accounted for: Two were dead, one was the wife of a minor Spanish governor.

Chapter XIV

After the priest, Father Paul, performed the marriage of the governor to a young American girl, he turned his attention to the blessing of the dead, while Renno took Bocalos away. The governor, thrilled to be alive and pleased that he was going to be allowed to keep Charity as his wife, was eager to cooperate with Renno. So it was that he found a local Indian who was familiar with the country to the south, including the jungle, and who would be willing, for gold, to guide a party to Campeche.

Mandy remained behind in the governor's house with Charity while the men made their preparations. Charity acted as if Mandy were still her bond servant, ordering her to prepare a plate of fresh fruit. Mandy wanted information, so she obeyed. She stood as Charity nibbled on the snack.

"Well, you don't have to stand here watching every bite I take," Charity said. "Sit."

Mandy sat in a mildewing, massive wooden chair.

"You're hanging around because you want to know how it was for your snippy little sister," Charity said.

"I'd appreciate anything you can tell me about her," Mandy said mildly.

"I can assure you that Little Miss High-and-Mighty got hers." She laughed nastily. "And she'll get much more, some of it not so pleasant, from Simon Purdy. Oh, we could hear her, the little slut, in León's cabin while we were on the riverboat, moaning and crying out, enjoying it. What she was doing was obvious. She thought she'd be better off with the captain, a real gentleman, so she was playing up to him."

Mandy closed her eyes in pain.

"Yes, she thought she was so smart, having been chosen by León. She stuck her nose up at Grace and Hope, who had been handed over to the crew, and she even looked down on me because Simon Purdy had me." Her eyes narrowed. "She knew Simon, you know. He had us all before we got on the boat with the trader to go up to New Madrid. He didn't play favorites. He just took us aside, one by one, and your sister cried and moaned and begged just as hard as Grace and Hope and I did."

"Oh, dear God," Mandy whispered.

"And so now she's Simon's again," Charity said.

"Is he so cruel?" Mandy asked.

"Dog mean," Charity said with a smile of satisfaction. "Especially when he's drinking. And he told me he likes variety. He never stays with any one woman for long. He'll get tired of Tess and sell her to a bordello in the first town he reaches—if they don't get killed by the *indios* in the jungle and if they don't die of snakebite or the fevers. León says no white man can live in the jungle, especially not a white girl."

Mandy was silent, an ache in her breast.

"I wonder if I shouldn't tell León I want to keep you,"

Charity said. "After all, you were my father's property, and I'm the only heir."

Mandy was secure in the knowledge that Renno and the others had thoroughly defeated the Spanish garrison. She would not be staying in Córdoba; Renno would not allow it.

"Charity, are you sure you know nothing about Purdy's intentions?"

"I told you," Charity snapped. "Are you calling me a liar?"

"No, no," Mandy said quickly. "I had just hoped you might remember something that had been said, some little hint."

"No," Charity said.

"There's still time for you to change your mind and go home with us."

"Home? Are you mad? I know how people feel about a woman who has been kidnapped and raped. Besides, what do I have in the United States? My father put everything he owned into that boat and the cargo. I have no close relatives. What would they do, put me in a workhouse or an orphanage?"

"You could live with me," Mandy offered. "I'll find a job."

"Ha!" Charity exploded. "I? Live with a bond servant? I have a nice house here. I have position, servants, and a man who is nice to me. No, thank you very much."

Mandy took her leave of the governor's new wife, feeling a bit angry but mostly sad. Charity was, after all, only a child. She hoped that things would work out well for the surviving Brown girl, that her life with Bocalos would make up for the tragedy she had known.

While the men were making their plans and preparations, she went back to the ship, rested, prayed, and had a tepid bath. She watched as the longboats brought Renno and the others back.

From the longboat in which he was riding, Egan Kirk saw her standing on the stern of the *Nuestra Señora*. She was still there after he had cleaned up a bit, snorting and splashing in a washbasin. A pleasant evening breeze was blowing, discouraging the voracious mosquitoes that were a plague when the air was still, even aboard ship, two hundred yards offshore. When he joined Mandy and leaned his elbows on the rail, she looked up to give him a quick, polite smile.

Egan pointed toward the Córdoba cemetery, a clearing just to the east of the town, where the survivors of the garrison were still busy burying the dead. "Hot work," he remarked.

"I would imagine," she agreed.

The sky to the west was purple and red, like a bruise. The birds were using the last light of evening to claim their territory with strange squawks and chattering.

"Hope this breeze keeps up," Egan commented. "If it does, it'll make for good sleeping."

"Lord, it does get hot," Mandy said.

"I picked up some thin cotton net in town," Egan said. "You tent it over your bed, and it keeps out the mosquitoes, or most of them."

"*Um*," she said.

"I got one for you."

"Thank you. That's very nice."

"Bocalos found us a guide," he continued. "Little fella, short and thick. Name's Kanam. He says there's only one main track through the jungle, and it isn't much—just a path used by the Indians. Grows over when it's not used."

"I don't see why all of you don't stay with the ship and go to Campeche. If Purdy is really headed there, you'd be there to wait for him."

"Well, that's just it, you see. We're not sure he isn't going the other way, to this place called Chan Santa Cruz on the east coast. It's closer than Campeche, but Bocalos says that one time Purdy and he were looking at a map of the province, and Purdy was asking about places. Bocalos remembers telling him that it might be a whole year before a ship comes to Santa Cruz, so we're all betting that Purdy's heading for Campeche. The only way we can be sure we don't miss him is to follow him. This Kanam says that the passage of a party with a white man and a white girl would be noted by the jungle Indians. Kanam's from out there somewhere, has relatives in one of the villages, so even if we can't pick up a trail, we'll find out Purdy's direction when Kanam talks with his cousins and such."

"Charity says that Bocalos thinks they'll both die in the jungle," Mandy said.

"Well, that's a possibility," Egan said frankly. "And we wouldn't know, would we, unless we follow them. We might go over to Campeche and wait months and they'd never show and we wouldn't know if they were dead or in Chan Santa Cruz."

The sun had disappeared, leaving behind the heavy, livid coloring. Then even that spectacular light began to fade as the tropical night fell rapidly.

"That Charity's a nasty little girl, isn't she?" Egan asked.

"Don't you think she has good reason?" Mandy retorted, a bit of anger in her voice. "She's a fourteen-year-old child, and she's had, in the past months, some good teachers in how to be cruel."

Egan frowned. "Put my foot in it again, didn't I?"

In the fading light his woeful expression touched Mandy. She laughed. "Well, you're only a man, after all."

"I've been thinking about what you said, about how people seem to blame a woman who is, uh, taken, more than they blame those that did it. I reckon you're right, Mandy."

She was silent.

"We'll be leaving in the morning, and I didn't want that between us," he said. "I'm asking your forgiveness." He chuckled. "'Cause I'm just an insensitive man, I guess."

"Thank you," she said, turning to look into his face. "Perhaps I was insensitive, too, thinking only of myself. You also have suffered a great loss."

"What I saw at the cabins when we came back from the hunt will be in my gut until I die," he admitted softly. "Mandy, I can't even think of Mary and my boy the way they were before, but only the way I saw them last." His voice choked, and tears came to his eyes. "God *damn* them, all of them! They took not only my wife and son but the memories I had of them."

Touched, she put her hand on his arm. "Egan, what you saw was not your wife and son but only their earthly remains. They're looking down on you now, from heaven, and I think your Mary would be weeping for you—not for herself but for you."

He jerked away from her hand and turned his back.

"Pray to God, Egan. Pray that He will help you wipe the terrible images from your mind and leave you only the memory of your wife and son as they once were."

He turned back to face her. "Can *you* forget? If your sister dies out there in that jungle, will you be able to forget? Can you forgive God for letting your sister be used by who knows how many men? Can you forget Simon Purdy's touch?"

"No," she confessed, "I won't forget. But I won't let it ruin or control the rest of my life."

Resentment and hopelessness raged within him. "Well, you can believe that others won't forget. You'll be an old maid because no decent man would want you after you've been touched by that animal."

"Then so be it," she said quietly. She turned and, hurt once more, started walking swiftly forward. He caught her and held her by the arm.

"I'm sorry, Mandy. I didn't mean to say that."

"Don't let it bother you," she said stiffly, twisting her arm from his grasp. "Because you will never be asked to want me. And if I ever meet a man who does, and I want him in return, I won't lie to him."

Egan's mood was black, as black as the night that stretched toward the south and infinity. Amid the blackness was a certain confusion, for in the months of traveling with Mandy, he had not been blind to her kindness, her cheerfulness in the face of pain and danger, or her calm, womanly presence. He had to deal with his guilt, too, for being aware of another woman with his wife not long dead. But mainly there was hatred for those who had killed Mary and his son and for the man who had forever soiled the

pretty, considerate girl who was walking away from him
with her head high, her back straight.

El-i-chi and Ah-wa-o did not join the others for the
evening meal. They remained on deck under the stars, she
clinging to him silently, praying to the manitous to bring
him safely back to her.

El-i-chi paused in a maize field on the slight rise behind
Córdoba. He lifted one hand, for he could make out the
doeskin color of Ah-wa-o's dress as she stood at the ship's
rail. The *Nuestra Señora* lay at anchor, her spars bare.
Because she would be able to sail around the peninsula and
reach Campeche long before Renno and the others could
reach that west-coast settlement through the jungle, Adan
had decided to wait for Bocalos to gather the promised
cotton cloth and jaguar skins. Even with the wait the
Señora would be in Campeche long before them, to stay no
longer than two months from the time that Renno's party
left Córdoba.

El-i-chi turned after one last look at his love, then
plunged into the scrub after the others. At first the trail was
well used. Kănam, the Mayan guide, set a torrid pace. The
two *indio* bearers began to complain almost immediately,
and Kanam, short, thick-chested, stern of face, spoke to
them harshly in the Mayan language.

The first night was spent in Kanam's village, only a few
miles from Córdoba. One of Kanam's requirements was
satisfied when Renno gave him half the agreed-upon sum of
money for his services, to be delivered to his wife. Egan
remarked to El-i-chi that this did not bode well; if the
native wanted to be sure that his wife was taken care of in
case he did not come back from the jungle, then there must
be dangers ahead that Egan could not begin to imagine.

For several more days the trail was clear. Then the land
changed, the trees growing taller and the vegetation
thicker. So quickly did the jungle begin that it seemed
supernatural. Now Kanam was often forced to clear new
growth from the trail with the broad blade of his machete.

As he worked sweat poured down his face, beading on the smelly, yellow grease that he used to repel mosquitoes. Progress was maddeningly slow, and Egan was concerned. "Renno, I know that we couldn't hope to pick up a trail after several days, but if Purdy had come this way, wouldn't the trail be more open? Surely this stuff can't grow so much so soon, even if it has rained every day."

"You hear," Renno said to Kanam.

The Mayan was definitely not a talker. His conversation consisted mainly of single words or at best two or three strung together. "There water." "Eat, good." Now he nodded. "Two, three trails. We take shortest."

"But we might miss Purdy then," Egan said.

"All trails lead to stones of the giants," Kanam explained. "Tzotzil leads Purdy. Go through villages of his clan, there." He pointed toward the west. "We come here—" indicating an easterly direction. "From the stones of the giants one trail leads then to Campeche."

The jungle closed in, wet and green. Even the dim light filtering through the canopy of vine-covered trees was greenish. Water dripped constantly from the rank, overhead growth, so they remained drenched with the moisture and their own sweat. Thorns tore at them, and insects attacked in what seemed to be the millions. As the party pressed forward, the only sounds were the slashing of Kanam's machete, the slap of a hand that killed half a dozen mosquitoes, the squish of wet clothing.

From the beginning, Renno and El-i-chi had covered their exposed skin with foul-smelling black mud, a practice adopted quickly by Se-quo-i. Egan Kirk, nauseated by the stench of the mud, waited until his arms, face, and the back of his neck were red and swollen from insect bites; then he gave in and became, as he said without amusement, a mud man. He did confide to El-i-chi that the mud was preferable to the rancid grease used by Kanam as an insect repellant.

The direction of travel was southwesterly. On a straight line, as measured on the maps in Governor Bocalos's office, they had over three hundred miles to travel, all of it through dense jungle.

At times they moved through mist as thick as the smoke of a forest fire. The mist seemed to mute the squawks and clatter of the ever-present birds, leaving only the sound of their movement and the *whish-whish* of Kanam's machete. In the middle of an afternoon turned into a steam bath by a shower, Renno was directly behind Kanam. The Mayan was slashing his way through new growth. The trail was discernible only with difficulty as a less densely tangled area. The going had been difficult since morning, and it was obvious to Renno that Kanam was very tired.

"Kanam, hold," he said. The Mayan turned. "Give me the machete."

"Difficult work. You have no experience." Kanam's pride was touched. He had been hired as a guide; a guide leads the way.

"Come," Renno said, holding out his hand.

"You need eyes used to seeing jungle dangers," Kanam said.

"Kanam," Renno said, "I have seen jungles."

With an expression of doubt Kanam handed Renno the machete. Renno began to move forward, slashing at the thorny vines that clogged the trail. It was hot, brutal work, requiring tremendous effort. Kanam, just behind Renno, was impressed as one hour, then another, passed. He remarked dryly that the white man who called himself an Indian did not tire.

Renno lapsed into a meditation and willed his aching arm and his body into a kind of numbness, even though his eyes searched the foliage ahead of him. One danger was, he knew, snakes. They had seen many snakes, mostly in the trees and mostly, according to Kanam, harmless boas. They seemed to come in two principal colors, emerald green with an orange underbelly, and brownish tan with light and dark patterns. Although the boas were nonpoisonous, they had a startling habit of falling from the trees—a behavior that had surprised members of the party.

Renno missed seeing the snake that fell down from a point directly over his head, but he felt the brush of the dry scales down his sweaty back, turned quickly to see Kanam leaping frantically backward.

"*Palanca!*" Kanam shouted, reaching for the knife at his belt.

In a fraction of a second Renno saw that the snake that reared its head not six inches from his left leg was no harmless boa. He had never seen such a snake, but it looked deadly and evil. For split seconds that saved Renno's life, the reptile's attention was held by Kanam's frantic movements. And then, as its head turned and cocked for the strike, Renno swung the machete with a force driven by more fear than he had ever known. The snake's head was severed; it sailed to the ground where it writhed, forked tongue lashing.

"*Palanca,*" Kanam said, bending to pick up the writhing, headless body. "One bite, no hope."

"Nasty-looking devil," Egan said, cringing. "What did you call him, Kanam?"

"*Palanca.* Spanish name, *barba amarilla.*" He turned to Renno, obviously impressed by the white Indian's swift strike. "Eyes must see jungle danger."

"Would *you* have seen the snake?" Renno asked.

Kanam shrugged. When Renno took the lead again, he made no protest.

"It is not the snakes that worry me most," El-i-chi confided that night in camp. He had spent a long time getting a fire started with damp wood, and the smoke was trailing up through the dense canopy, causing some excitement among a flock of colorful, chattering birds.

Egan was scanning his arms and torso for ticks, found one, took a burning twig from the fire, and held the glowing, red end close to the tick until it loosed its tenacious hold and crawled away to be seized between Egan's fingers and tossed into the embers.

"At least you can spot a snake most of the time and avoid it," El-i-chi continued. "These things—"

"*Garrapatas,*" Kanam defined.

"Whatever," Egan grumbled.

"Mosquitoes," El-i-chi continued, batting at a persistent one, "gnats, fleas."

"Tomorrow or next day we reach village," Kanam said.

"Good," Renno said. "Your clan, Kanam?"

"Cousins. Get food."

"And ask about Purdy, of course," Egan put in.

"Ask," Kanam agreed.

The party owed much to Egan, who had discovered that the *indios* of Yucatán used the light cotton netting to keep away mosquitoes at night. Each member of the party had been supplied with a net, so each man slept with the fabric tented over him on sticks driven into the soggy jungle floor.

Kanam offered no protest the next day when Renno volunteered to take a turn in the lead. The guide's respect for this man from a faraway land was obviously growing. Now, when Renno asked a question about the jungle, Kanam no longer answered in one or two words. For example, he tried his best to explain why his people valued the bright, long feathers of a particular bird over all others. When Renno spotted the tracks of a jaguar at a watering hole and followed them into the jungle, Kanam was pleased.

"Keen eye," Kanam approved.

The incident that cemented a friendship between the Seneca sachem and the Mayan guide came in midafternoon with Renno once more in the lead, slashing through a thick patch of tall ferns. Since the encounter with the *barba amarilla*, he had been giving more attention to the foliage overhead. So it was that he was looking upward when he slashed twice and dropped his eyes to look directly into the blank, staring eyes of a huge, dark spirit towering over him.

He exhaled with a *whoof* sound as he reached for his pistol with his left hand and brandished the machete with his right. The face, taller than Renno's, seemed to grow from the ground in the midst of the jungle. It took him only a moment to realize that it was not alive, that it was stone, but his surprise had not been lost on Kanam. The Mayan burst out laughing, pointing his finger at Renno. He motioned El-i-chi forward, pointed at the stone face, pointed at Renno, and reenacted Renno's reaction.

"Our Mayan friend thinks that you are very funny," El-i-chi said with a grin.

"*Whoof*," Kanam said in imitation.

"I'm glad *I* didn't see that thing first," Egan said. "Mean-looking bugger. It might have taken all three of you to catch me."

Kanam was still laughing, and the laughter became infectious. Renno joined in, waving his hand at the stone giant.

Se-quo-i, ever curious, moved to circle the head, marveling at the work that had been expended to form it from a huge boulder.

Kanam had laughed himself out.

"Who has made this thing?" Se-quo-i inquired.

"The ancient ones," Kanam replied.

"Mayans?" Se-quo-i asked.

"When the world was young," Kanam said, "there were giants with great strength and magic. You will see."

Kanam moved ahead, and soon the little-used track through the jungle joined a wider, cleared trail. "One hour, no more, to village," Kanam said.

The footing changed suddenly, becoming more solid. Renno halted, bent to use his tomahawk to scrape away detritus. Underneath the debris were cut stones laid as a road.

"What's this?" Egan asked.

Se-quo-i began to clear a larger area. "Each stone is finished," he marveled. "Smooth, even. Not like the cobblestone streets in Wilmington."

"The magic of the ancient ones," Kanam explained.

The trail curved sharply and left the stone roadway.

"Where do the stones lead?" Renno asked.

"Sacred place," Kanam answered.

"Renno," Se-quo-i said, "I would see this place."

"Is it forbidden?" Renno asked Kanam.

Kanam thought hard for a moment. "To disturb the rest of the ancient ones is forbidden."

"But to look?" Renno asked.

"Come," Kanam said, starting to hack a trail leading at right angles away from the traveled track. A half hour later he halted. "We are here."

Renno looked around but saw only the dense greenery, vines, and trees. The sun was low in the west. The always dim, greenish light was fading. At first he saw nothing, then he spotted a protruding stone—a tall, squarish shape that was not of natural origin. He took Kanam's machete and cleared vines from the wall to see, carved into the stone, the stylized form of a giant serpent.

Movement was difficult, but it soon became evident that the jungle had hidden beneath its creepers several massive stone structures. Renno tried to see a pattern, but the buildings were too well covered with growth. He had moved a few paces from the others—only a short distance—but he felt very much alone. He could hear the voices of his companions muffled by the dense greenery, but he could also hear something else—something unfamiliar, an emanation rather than a sound. He turned at a rustling, and El-i-chi joined him.

"The spirits of these ancient ones are strong here," El-i-chi breathed.

"I also have felt and heard them," Renno agreed.

"What manner of men could build with stones so massive?" El-i-chi asked in awe. "If we could only see—"

"Renno," Kanam called, "we must go. We must not be here when the night comes."

They made camp near the hidden city, and even at a distance Kanam seemed subdued and a bit nervous.

"Spirits are there," Renno said.

Kanam nodded, his dark eyes searching outside the circle of light from the fire. "Had darkness not come so quickly, we would have traveled to be safe, away from the place of ghosts, and nearer the village of my clan."

"Who were they, Kanam?" Se-quo-i the scholar asked. "Who built the city?"

"I know only that they were great magicians, giants with the strength of ten men. They built temples and shrines to honor the gods—the gods of rain and of wind, the crops, and the ancestors. Here the spirits of the ancestors guard their tombs."

Egan said softly, "I'll bet there's treasure here."

Kanam jerked his head to glare at Egan. "In such thoughts lie death," he warned.

"Hey," Egan said, "I was only making a comment."

"Even now we are being watched," Kanam whispered.

"By spirits?" Egan asked.

"By those who guard the sacred places," Kanam replied. "My clan has long been entrusted with keeping the peace of this place."

"If it's members of your clan who are watching, why don't they make themselves known?" Egan asked.

"As yet they know us not," Kanam responded. "There is nothing to fear—only if we disturb the ancient ones."

"Maybe we'd better mount a guard tonight," El-i-chi suggested.

"No," Kanam said. "The fire will keep away the jaguar. That is our only danger."

Nevertheless, El-i-chi had difficulty falling asleep. The familiar jungle sounds now seemed threatening. When he sensed movement near him, he eased himself into a sitting position, tomahawk in hand. It was Renno; his brother was disappearing into the blackness beyond the firelight. El-i-chi left his mosquito tent as quietly. The other men and the porters were sleeping soundly, one snoring loudly.

El-i-chi halted to allow his eyes to adjust. The blackness was so complete, however, that it deceived his eyes into seeing little dots of brightness. He felt his way along the trail that had been cut from the city and softly made the sound of a cooing dove. Renno's reply came from only a few feet away. El-i-chi moved forward and, sensing Renno's body heat, reached out his hand. Renno said nothing but began to move along the trail, feeling his way with both hands extended to contact the uncut growth.

In that stygian blackness El-i-chi's imagination was hard at work. Each time something brushed his legs, he thought, *snake*. From a long distance away came the grunting call of a jaguar, a sound that they had heard several times before. The shaman had his hand on Renno's shoulder, and the white Indian moved steadily into the heart of the city, where they had cut the greenery away from a stone wall.

Renno, being honest with himself, had to admit that he was glad for his brother's company. He had been unable to sleep, for each time he closed his eyes an odd sensation came to him, something felt but not heard, a beckoning. It was weak but persistent, and it stayed with him as he led the way through the blackness with an assurance that he knew was not his alone.

When he halted, El-i-chi was silent for a long time. Then the shaman said, "If I guess correctly, we stand near the wall that we cleared."

"Yes." Renno had been orienting himself, uncertain of which way to go. Then he saw it clearly in his mind: a solid wall of green that slanted away toward the treetops. "Come." When he reached the wall he began to climb, clinging to thick vines. El-i-chi followed.

As they ascended what seemed to be narrow, stone terraces, there were times that Renno had to force his way through dense vines and other growth. Several times he had to hack away with his tomahawk at the growth. Then, after what seemed to be hours, he pushed his way through thick limbs and saw the glowing light of a full moon. The terraced stone slope continued past the top of the forest canopy and into full moonlight. The brothers paused to rest; looked around and saw the moonlight reflecting off the top of the jungle. The effect was eerie. It was as if they looked down on a dark sea that sparkled with dim light. Their vantage point was the top of an ancient pyramid that sloped sharply down on four sides. The entire structure was shrouded in its jungle coating.

The dark sea that was the jungle's canopy spread outward on all sides with a levelness that emphasized the nearby protrusions of what could only be other buildings or structures.

"Our longhouses are only temporary dreams compared to

these things of stone," El-i-chi whispered. "These people built for the ages, and now there is only jungle and the spirits."

"Once the people who built this city must have numbered in the thousands," Renno remarked, his own awed tone matching that of El-i-chi.

"What happened to them?" the shaman wondered. "This cannot be blamed on the white man."

"Only the manitous know," Renno said.

A breeze was blowing here above the canopy of the jungle. Gradually Renno's body cooled, and the perspiration brought by the difficult climb dried. There were no mosquitoes. Overhead the moon continued its path toward the zenith. El-i-chi sat on a raised platform of stone covered only lightly by vines, musing over the power of the jungle to climb so high, to obliterate the works of those men who had labored so mightily and so long ago to build this lost city.

Renno stood looking at the setting moon, his face tilted upward. By chance or by the guidance of the spirits he had chosen the tallest edifice in the jungle-shrouded city, so now he looked down on the peaks of other buildings that extended above the level of the treetops.

"Spirits, old ones," he sang, chanting a Seneca invocation. "Tell me of your joys. Tell of the time of your lives on this earth. Speak to me, manitous."

He knew from experience that the manitous of the Seneca seemed bound to their own traditional lands. In Jamaica, and in far Africa, he had been unable to summon the spirits of his own ancestors. But in each place he had had spirit communication. Now, in this place of great sadness, this city that once had rung with the sound of human voices, he sensed a presence, fragile, far away, as weak as the wind generated by a butterfly's wings.

El-i-chi sat in silence, Renno's chanting rising and falling in his ears. What sort of people had been the old ones who constructed the city? Had they fierce, dark faces like the giant stone visage in the jungle? And where had they gone?

"They are here," Renno whispered. "Do you feel the presence of the spirits?"

"I do," El-i-chi answered.

"They whisper," Renno said, "like the wind in the rushes of the lakes in our original homeland, but I cannot understand."

The sun burst up over the eastern horizon of green. Below them in the tangled mass of the jungle's canopy, birds greeted the day with a din of varied noises. El-i-chi led the way down the steep, vine-covered sides of the pyramid. They met Se-quo-i on the trail to their camp.

"Kanam is sure the spirits have devoured you," the Cherokee said.

Renno turned, took one last look toward the lost city, and felt a tug of contact with something—but that bond was quickly broken.

Chapter XV

Coba, mate of Tzotzil, had known from the first time that she entered Tzotzil's bed that she was a fortunate young woman. Because she was comely, she had not lacked suitors in her native village not far from Córdoba. When she continued to refuse all pleas for her company and the months passed, her mother told her that the spirits of the jungle had entered her head and made her giddy.

Coba had not really known what she was waiting for, but when it came, she knew immediately that the old gods had been looking out for her, that they had turned her stomach and heart against all suitors—however handsome, however tempting—to save her for Tzotzil. He came to the village dressed in suitor's feathers, an open statement that he was seeking a wife. In one fashion or another all the nubile girls of the village managed to parade themselves before him, for it quickly became known that he was a man of importance, the secretary to the governor of the province in Córdoba, thus, a man who had Spanish coins in his pockets.

In her pride Coba did not parade herself. In her pride she felt that it was not up to her to display herself, that if the gods had intentions for her, they would create an opportunity. She made no overt attempt to avoid the distinguished visitor, but their paths did not cross until the very morning that he was preparing to leave Coba's village. She was walking toward the well with a gaily decorated water jug on her head, not even thinking about the visitor, when he stepped around a hut and blocked her path. For an earth-shaking moment she looked into the man's eyes and then, modestly, let her own eyes fall.

"I have not seen you," Tzotzil said.

"I have seen you," she said.

"Your hair is worn in the style of the maiden."

"It is so," she confirmed.

Tzotzil looked at her, saw the flare of her hips and the narrowness of her waist—not at all like the thick waists of most Mayan women. He saw high, proud breasts, and when she raised her face to look into his, he saw two things he liked very much: pride and a bit of defiance.

"I have a fine house in Córdoba," Tzotzil said. "The woman who becomes mine will have a house servant. She will wear the fine fabrics of the Spanish and sleep on sheets. She will feast on cakes made with honey, and the meat of Spanish cattle."

"And she will, no doubt, become fat," Coba said, moving to push past Tzotzil. She did not look back.

Tzotzil was seated with her father in front of her family's hut when she came back from the well. Her father looked at her without speaking.

Her mother came to take the water jug and whisper, "Daughter, the man of wealth from Córdoba has asked for you."

Her father stood, Tzotzil following suit. "Daughter, I

have given you to this good man. You will accompany him, and our hearts will go with you, to Córdoba."

"And what of my courtship?" Coba demanded, her eyes sparkling in anger. "Am I to be cheated of the right of every maiden to be honored in the eyes of the people of her village?"

"Coba," Tzotzil said, "my time is short. I must return to Córdoba."

"Then you go without me," Coba snapped, running into the hut.

Thus it was that Coba's courtship began with gifts of feathers and cloth. True, it was a brief courtship, but it was an ardent one, and the gifts that came to Coba and her family showed that her mate-to-be was indeed a rich man.

She had never regretted not having the full-term courtship, and it was not only because she lived a good life in Córdoba. Tzotzil gave her love, respect, good-humored teasings, and sometimes a rollicking game that took her back to her childhood. When her husband came to her and said, "Tomorrow morning we leave for the south," she did not question. Where Tzotzil went, Coba went. Whatever would come, Tzotzil knew best.

Coba was surprised to find that they traveled not only with porters but with a white man and a white girl. She was a bit scornful of the white man's morals when he took the reluctant girl to his bed on the first night out from Córdoba and made noises like a rutting jungle boar, noises so loud that everyone could hear. But Tzotzil merely laughed, held one of her hands in his, and touched her cheek with the other. "Be patient," he whispered. "We will not have to endure this man long."

Coba did not think too much about the possible meanings of Tzotzil's statement. They were traveling fast, as if Tzotzil feared pursuit. He did not relax until they had crossed many miles and were in the depths of the jungle.

Now that the danger of pursuit was over, Tzotzil began to turn his thoughts toward the future . . . which did not include association with Simon Purdy. Tzotzil, however, was not yet a murderer. Although he professed to scorn the teachings of the white missionaries regarding their God and the Blessed Virgin, those good fathers had left their mark, for he had decided to let the jungle do the work for him. He did not fear the Spanish, for if they ever caught him, he would be killed for stealing the gold and silver as quickly as for killing a white man. But he was certain that fever or a snake would eliminate Purdy and his white girl.

Coba sometimes walked with Tess and learned that the girl had been Governor Bocalos's lover and had been stolen away by Simon Purdy. The fiery young woman asked questions, and Tess, pleased to have a female to talk with, even if her own Spanish was still spotty, told Coba all—from the time Mandy and she were forced to indenture themselves, through the massacre on the Tennessee River, and all subsequent happenings.

"This poor child," Coba told Tzotzil, "has had her share of the displeasure of the gods. It is not right for that *cabrón*, Purdy, to misuse her so. He treats her like an animal, forcing her to serve him at the end of a long day's march, then using her body when she is so tired that all she wants to do is sleep."

"She is his," Tzotzil pointed out.

Coba lifted the keen-bladed knife that she always carried in her sash. "It would be a pleasure to see how loudly I could make him gasp as my blade enters his belly."

Tzotzil smiled grimly. "I have told you that he will not be with us always. Let the jungle take him."

To the surprise of both Tzotzil and Coba, the two white people were alive and healthy when Tzotzil led the way past the first place of the stones of the ancient ones. Tzotzil carefully avoided the village of the protectors, for they were not of his clan. Ordinarily one could travel at will, provided that he observed the rules of the stranger, but the heavy burdens of the porters offered too much temptation to men who were not of his blood. He would not place temptation before members of another clan.

The village that was the southernmost settlement of

Tzotzil's clan lay in the midst of fields that had been slashed and burned and cleared from the jungle. Here Tzotzil was honored and feasted. Women of the village prepared maize, beans, and squash all seasoned so liberally with chilis that although they ate their share, Purdy and Tess drank large quantities of water and stuffed chewy yam bread into their mouths to cool them. In the evening there was a dance of maidens, followed by the more energetic dance of the warriors.

As the evening progressed and the strong local beer began to have its effect, the short, thick-chested warriors of the village began to show more interest in Tess. She had bathed with Coba and a few of the young women of the village in a pool in the nearby stream and had washed out her Mayan cotton garments so that they were clean and fresh. Her skin, bronzed by white standards, was a pale curiosity to the jungle dwellers, many of whom had never seen a white man, much less a white woman.

When a warrior reached out a grimy hand to touch Tess's face, she pulled away. "Don't be so damned jumpy," Purdy snarled. "These people could kill us and eat us, and no one would ever know. Be friendly."

Tess cringed a bit as the warrior rubbed her cheek lightly, saying things in his odd language. Only a few villagers spoke any Spanish at all.

Purdy was most interested in the decorative items that hung around the necks of the people of position. Several men and a few of their women wore carved jade ornaments. Far more exciting to Purdy were the gold pendants. The headman of the village wore a stylized bird fashioned nicely of gold. Another had a golden frog on a thong around his neck. The young man with the frog seemed more fascinated than the others by Tess, coming back time after time to stand close, to speak to her in his odd language, to stroke her arm or touch her cheek.

Purdy motioned to Coba as she walked past with some of the village girls, and she came to look at him indolently. "This fellow," Purdy said, "ask him where he got his ornament."

"He will tell you that he found it on a jungle path," Coba said, for that was the standard answer from any man who owned a piece of the yellow metal of the ancients.

"Why is he so interested in Tess?"

Coba shrugged. "Why is any man interested in a woman?"

Purdy chuckled. "Ask this young chief if he would trade his ornament for an hour with the girl."

Coba flushed. "You are more vile than the scum that forms on a stagnant pool." She turned and stalked away.

Purdy caught the attention of the young warrior who was admiring Tess. He pointed to the golden frog hanging around the man's neck, then to Tess. He then made certain unmistakable motions that were understandable to any man regardless of his language and indicated time by sweeping his hand across the arc of the heavens and dividing the arc into small portions. The young Mayan mused for a while, fingering the golden frog. He went through the motions himself, to confirm the agreement. Purdy nodded eagerly.

"Simon, what are you doing?" Tess asked anxiously.

The Mayan nodded, removed the frog, handed it to Purdy, and reached to seize Tess's hand.

"No, leave me alone!" she cried, jerking away.

"Be nice to him, girl," Purdy threatened.

The Mayan buried his hand in Tess's hair and jerked. She cried out as she was half dragged toward a hut.

Coba saw, and her heart went out to the girl. Then she looked away. It was not her place to tell the white man what he could do with his woman. It was not her place to make a scene in the village of her husband's clan. At any rate, what happened to the white girl did not matter, for soon both she and Purdy would be dead.

To that time, Tess had known only two men, Bocalos and Purdy. She had seen Grace and Hope Brown handed over to the smelly crew of the flatboat on the Mississippi as if they were objects, and she had been told that Grace had been sold into a bordello, where she would serve all comers. Now it was happening to her, and in a way that was worse than anything that had happened to the Brown girls. She had been given to an Indian who reeked of the yellow grease that warded off mosquitoes. For a moment she fought but soon learned that the Mayan was a man of small patience and heavy hand.

All things, except death, are over soon. Then she was running from the hut and into the arms of another Mayan. She screamed. Behind the Indian Purdy said, "Take it easy, girl. You're earning me more money than the finest whore in New Orleans."

Purdy was very pleased. In less than three hours he held three golden objects and two finely carved pieces of jade. He went in search of Tzotzil, leaving Tess to service two more young Mayans who wanted to know how it felt to possess a white woman.

"Gold," Tzotzil confirmed when Purdy held out the frog that had been given to him by the first Mayan.

"Look," Purdy said, "I'm told that these young bucks find these things of gold and jade lying around on the floor of the jungle."

Tzotzil smiled grimly. "It has happened that way perhaps once or twice."

"And the rest of the time?"

"Let us say," Tzotzil said, "that the taboos against disturbing the sleep of the ancient ones are not taken as seriously by this new generation as they once were."

"Meaning," Purdy said, "that the young men go into the old tombs, eh?"

"I fear so," Tzotzil verified.

"You told me once that if you stumbled onto a few nuggets, you wouldn't kick them aside," Purdy said.

Tzotzil nodded.

"Look," Purdy continued, holding up the golden frog. "Where this came from, there's more."

"They would kill you if you tried to break into a tomb in the old city," Tzotzil warned.

"But I don't intend to. We let *them* do the work."

"I see. And what do we trade to them for the gold?"

"They've taken quite a shine to my little whore," Purdy said.

Tzotzil grimaced with distaste.

"Don't be so fine mannered," Purdy said. "I wouldn't let her go for, say, less than a quarter of her weight in gold. Half of it would be yours. Talk to 'em, Tzotzil."

Tzotzil knew that gold was scarce in the dead, lost cities. Jade was more plentiful, but first one had to find the tomb of an ancient king. However scarce it was, there was gold; and jade objects of antiquity would bring a high price in Mexico. Judging from what he had seen in the village, protection of the old tombs was lax, for many of the young warriors wore objects that were obviously ancient.

"I will speak with some of them," he said to Purdy.

During the march from the lost city to the village where Kanam was welcomed as a brother, the whispers of the spirits remained with Renno. They came to him at random times . . . distant . . . faint . . . confused. It was as if multitudes did not rest.

The feast of welcome gave the party fresh vegetables, a fine roasted wild pig, and speeches and dances to honor them. During the evening Kanam questioned the warrior who was, this season, in charge of keeping guard over the city of the dead. "Yes," the warrior said, "others have passed near, not more than ten days ago. A Mayan of the Jaguar Clan with his woman, bearers, and a white man with a white girl."

"We are far behind them," El-i-chi moaned.

"They will rest before marching into the swamps between here and the coast," Kanam consoled. "There have been festivities in the village of the Jaguar Clan that lies to the west."

"Kanam, my friend," Renno said, "we would leave as quickly as you think it is possible without insulting the hospitality of your cousins."

"They will understand," Kanam said. He turned to the village headman and spoke rapidly in Mayan. The headman nodded and bent forward to look at Renno.

"The clan lord of the village wishes you to see the sign of the blessings of the ancestors," Kanam said. "It is the pride of his people."

Renno and the scholarly Se-quo-i followed the headman to the western edge of the village and passed through a band of undisturbed jungle. Here spread a clearing about fifty yards in diameter. The fact that such a place existed without being planted with crops testified to its importance, for it required much labor to keep the area free of jungle encroachment. At its center stood a tall pillar of stone, a stele squared on four sides, tapering toward the top, which reached at least ten feet above the jungle floor. Deeply carved designs and patterns covered the stone.

"Long ago, when the sun was young, our ancestors placed this great magic here," the headman explained. "Now it protects our village. We do not build our houses near it but leave it in its own place of honor."

"Chief," Se-quo-i said, "the carving consists of both pictures and symbols that are obviously letters. Can any among you read the writings of the ancients?"

"Alas," the headman said, "that magic died with them."

The evening brought another feast, more dancing, and singing. Men made plaintive music from instruments carved of wood while young women sang. Se-quo-i tried to make melodious sounds with one of the flutes but gave up quickly, laughing at his unmusical efforts. Renno briefly regretted having left his guitar on board the *Nuestra Señora*.

The white Indian had eaten well, adhering to Indian custom—storing food against future shortage; once they were marching again, there would be no delicious fresh vegetables, no well-cooked, seasoned meat. He sat with his own, idly watching the faces of the dancers. A vague feeling of melancholy brought him thoughts of home and family, and an underlying sadness that puzzled him. Feelings of loss and regret became more powerful as the plaintive songs continued. The voices that he had first heard at the old city were whispering, whispering, in the background of his thoughts. He rose quietly and left the circle of firelight without anyone's noticing and walked toward the jungle clearing where the stele of the ancients occupied its place of honor.

Moonlight reached the floor of the clearing and highlighted the pillar of stone. He walked to it and placed his palms on it, fingers splayed.

"You have tried to speak to me, spirits," he intoned. "I am open to hear."

He felt anew the poignant sensation of loss and deep sadness, of blood and death and broken peace. He knew of the pain of the death of thousands and of hunger. He would not have been able to put into words how, but he could feel the anguish of knowing that a world was ending, so slowly that only he knew that a great dynasty, a majestic civilization, was writhing in its death throes. He felt fear until he realized that it was not his world that was to end but the world of the whisperers, the world of the ancient ones who had carved their words and thoughts on this stone, which seemed to give warmth to his palms.

A glow emanated from the stele. It was strong enough to overpower the moon and illuminate the clearing. The surrounding jungle faded and was replaced with a scene of wonder: A magnificent city of stone spread before him, temples with shining towers pointing toward the sky, the buildings brightly painted as gaily as the cloth costumes of the people who walked, laughed, and traded in the city's squares. He saw the great structure that El-i-chi and he had climbed. It was resplendent, and the temple at the top was filled and surrounded by priests who chanted to the gods.

A single voice came to him: *"We are brothers."*

Renno chanted a short hymn of praise to his manitous. And then he said, "We are blood, for in the dawn of the world our ancestors gave birth to all tribes."

"But the end comes to all," the single voice said.

Renno's vision widened, and he was a hawk, soaring high, observing all, seeing in the jungle the clearings of many fields, wondrous systems of canals and raised plots for growing, and other cities connected to this great city by an incredible network of stone-paved roads.

"The end comes to all," the sad voice repeated, and in the city green shoots sprouted between the cut stones in the plazas. The gay paint of the buildings was fading, and only a few priests chanted at the top of the temple. The clothing of the people was tattered and patched, and their eyes were haunted. War and savagery prevailed, and no men kept the jungles from overtaking the clearings . . . no men removed accumulating debris from the canals that drained the fields. Around the city the houses of the laborers, the hunters, and the woodcutters were deserted. Birds' nests spilled over from the niches of the buildings. Water from the reservoir was cloudy with silt and rank with slime.

And then slowly, even as he watched, things changed. The chants of the priests faded. One last gaunt, starving man stood before him in a driving tropical downpour. The great plaza was empty save for that one forlorn figure. The priest raised his empty hands to the gods in supplication, but his prayers did not alter events. The jungle surged, its growth accelerated for Renno's eyes.

"The end comes to all," a voice said from a great distance.

"And yet the Mayan live on here in the jungle," Renno said.

"To allow their young ones to desecrate the tombs of the ancients," the voice whispered.

A feeling of outrage poured over Renno in a deluge from many sources, and for a while the whispering voices thundered in his mind, protesting ravagement and sacrilege. Another city was before his eyes, vine covered and steaming in the jungle sun.

"The end comes to all," the voice said, *"but the dead have the right to peace, the right not to have their slumbers disturbed."*

"Help us, Brother," came a chorus of voices, and then the distinct words merged and blended to become a diminishing, plaintive keening.

With the morning the group was moving again. Renno sought out Kanam. "There is a city," he said, "there." He pointed toward the west, their direction of travel. "In it there was, is, a central plaza overlooked by three temples, none as grand as the one in the place you called Chichén Itzá."

"Yes," Kanam said. "It is Uxmal."

"Your clan protects the stones of the ancients. Others do not do their duties as well."

"Perhaps that is true," Kanam said. "I myself do not believe that the ancient stones are cursed or that those who enter the old tombs will perish." He laughed uneasily. "But you do not see me breaking through the stones, searching for a tomb of an old one. There are some who do, I fear, search for the treasures of our ancestors."

"Some do, there, at Uxmal," Renno said.

"How can you know?" Kanam asked. Then he shrugged. "At any rate, Uxmal is under the protection of the Jaguar Clan and is none of our affair."

"We are all of the same blood," Renno said. "We will go to Uxmal."

"It is two days' travel off our trail," Kanam protested.

"We will go to Uxmal," Renno repeated.

Kanam made a small bow. He didn't understand why Renno, not of Mayan blood, was so concerned with the right of the long dead to their peace, but in his heart he sang praises to the bronzed warrior from far away. If such a man from the outside world cared about the dignity of the ancient dead, Kanam could do no less than fight at his side.

El-i-chi and Se-quo-i, noting that Renno spent an unusual amount of time with his weapons that night, followed the white Indian's example and saw to their own blades. As Kanam had predicted, it was two days' travel to Uxmal. Late on the second afternoon Kanam motioned for silence, indicated that the others should wait, and called Renno to follow him. The sachem did not choose to follow. When advancing toward danger, he wanted his eyes to be the first to see, so he pushed past Kanam. Soon he heard voices and the ringing sound of metal striking stone.

"It is as you said," Kanam whispered in awe. "Someone works to break through the protecting stones."

Renno crept forward, edging around a vine-covered

stone wall until he could look into a partially cleared area in what seemed to be the city's central plaza. One of the first things he saw was a white man. The sachem had never seen Simon Purdy, but in his heart he knew that it was the man, that the long search for the last surviving renegade was over. To confirm that the white man was Purdy, a white girl sat beside an attractive Mayan woman on a cleared ledge of stone at the base of a pyramidal temple. The white girl's face showed the swellings and marks of insect bites, but she seemed to be in good health otherwise.

Renno turned his eyes to the workers. He counted fifteen Mayans, all young and strong, battering through a stone wall. The results of their labors lay among the browning vegetation that had been cleared away from the stone structure, some of the building blocks broken in twain by the fall. Other Mayans came and went. Renno held his position long enough to know that there were at least thirty Indians with Purdy, one of them a proud-looking man whose clothing was not soiled with labor, a man who seemed to have authority. That, he thought, would be León Bocalos's secretary.

He signaled Kanam to go back, then followed him. Kanam suggested a campsite farther from the city, but Renno shook his head. "We will have business in the city tonight."

Something in Renno's voice made the Mayan shudder and thank the old gods that he was not among those who were working to rob the tomb.

Tzotzil had cleared the vines and growth from a stone platform in the plaza of the old city, and here he made a bed for Coba and himself. Simon Purdy and Tess had settled not far away but out of sight around a vine-covered building. The Mayans, brave and arrogant during the day, were subdued as darkness came. They clung together in small groups around their fires. Purdy sneered and said to Tzotzil, "Look, the brave warriors fear ghosts."

Tzotzil nodded. "Perhaps we should all fear them, for the spirits are here."

"The hell you say." Purdy laughed. "Well, you and these brave ones stay awake and watch for the ghosts. I'm going to sleep."

One by one those who camped in the plaza slept, for it had been a long, strenuous day for the warriors who worked to break through the stone wall into the darkness of the tomb.

And with the moon that sent tendrils of pale light downward through the rampant growth, to make pinpoints of brightness in the plaza, death came to Uxmal.

"Egan, my friend," Renno said, putting his hand on the young man's shoulder. "You are brave. There is no question of that. But you are a white man—"

"With feet bigger than those of a grizzly bear and twice as heavy," El-i-chi interrupted. "Any Indian in the city would hear you coming from half a mile away."

"Renno," Egan said earnestly, "I'll pull off my boots. I can walk quiet barefooted."

"Until you step on a thorn," El-i-chi remarked.

"This is work to be done quietly," Renno said. "There will be work for you with the morning's light, after we have evened the odds against us. Limit your kills. We are not at war against the Mayan Nation. We want only to discourage the looting of the sacred tombs, and perhaps finding ten men dead in their camp will send the others home. We will then take Purdy in our own time."

"And if they stay to fight?" Kanam asked.

"We will be five against twenty," Renno said.

"Seven." One of the Mayan porters volunteered. "We both are men who honor the gods and our ancestors."

"Seven, then," Renno agreed.

Four young Mayans who had camped as near the edge of the city as possible without leaving it were the first to meet their death. Renno, leading the way through the dark jungle, feeling his path very, very slowly down the trail cut by the defilers of the city, heard the sleepers' deep, even breathing.

With the quietness of the ghosts themselves, El-i-chi and
Se-quo-i drew abreast of him, and the three stood while
their eyes sorted out the tumbled, dark shadows. Renno
touched each of his companions on the shoulder, sending
El-i-chi right, Se-quo-i left. He himself crept to hunker
beside a sleeping warrior and at the same instant that his
hand pressed down hard on the sleeper's mouth, his stiletto
sliced through skin, tendon, flesh, and arteries. The only
sound was a wet gush of blood, and then the sachem was
moving on to repeat the deadly performance as Se-quo-i
and El-i-chi finished and stood facing him.

Two Mayans sleeping together, hammocks swung between two trees, made easy work for Renno and El-i-chi.
Six men were dead, and only a quarter hour had passed
since the three entered the city. It was now to become
more difficult, however; the six who had died so quickly
were the exceptions, for the remainder of the Mayans were
grouped closely in a cleared area of the main plaza, sleeping
back-to-back as if for mutual courage and protection against
the spirits that frequented the city by night. To approach
the sleepers, the three warriors had to cross the area that
had been slashed partially clear.

They converged from three directions. Renno was able to
see El-i-chi and Se-quo-i now and again as they moved
wraithlike through a patch of mottled moonlight. He
himself moved forward slowly but carefully, and under his
feet not even the browning, cut vegetation protested his
passage with sound.

El-i-chi reached the circle of sleeping Mayans first and
selected his victim. He saw Se-quo-i get into position and
waited only a few seconds, for he knew that Renno could
take care of his end of the job and more, if necessary. The
shaman's hand closed over the mouth of the sleeping man,
and his blade accomplished its bloody work. He stiffened as
he heard a grunt from the direction of Se-quo-i.

The Cherokee had let his hand slip off the sleeper's
mouth before his blade severed the man's voice box and
arteries, so the dying man had had one chance to utter a

sound. It came out as a startled, protesting cough. Se-
quo-i's hand closed over his tomahawk. He prepared
himself to meet the danger, assuming that the rest of the
warriors were now alerted; but there was nothing but the
jerking of the dying warrior's legs. Se-quo-i put his hands
on the man's knees and leaned forward, lest the drumming
of the victim's feet accomplish what his death grunt had
failed to do.

Silence. El-i-chi breathed again. He crawled on hands
and knees to the next man, and once again blood flowed.
And then the Seneca was carefully retreating. He located
the other two in the darkness by clicking his fingernails
together until he heard Renno's answer, and then they
were making their way back down the trail in silence. At a
distance from the edge of the city Se-quo-i said, "And so
their strength is cut by ten."

"Eleven," El-i-chi corrected.

Renno patted his brother El-i-chi on the back. "Good.
Now we will face one fewer should they decide to stay and
fight."

Kanam and Egan were waiting anxiously when the
threesome reached the camp. Renno left it to Se-quo-i and
El-i-chi to tell the details of the night. He found his blanket
and was asleep before El-i-chi, making the most of a good
story, had described the demise of the first four men.

Tzotzil, too, slept well, for before retiring he had made a
decision: He had been wrong to participate in the desecra-
tion of the tombs of the old ones. He had let the white
man's greed for gold influence him. "I have no taste for this
robbing of the dead," he had whispered to Coba.

"Nor I," she had agreed.

"We will leave this place tomorrow." Tzotzil's head was
clear. He wanted the gold that Purdy carried, and that
would be simple. He slept, Coba's warm body close to his.
Soon they would be in Campeche, and only the worst
luck—such as a Spanish ship having arrived unexpectedly
in Córdoba within days of their departure to carry the news

to Campeche by sea—would prevent them from taking a ship to a Mexican port, there to disappear and live a life of comfort.

Tzotzil was now awake with the sun. He sought out the leader of the young warriors who smashed at the ancient tombs. "My brother, you work hard and invade the tombs of the ancients for that which you can possess at any time."

The young man looked at him questioningly.

Tzotzil slashed across his throat with his forefinger. "Speak to the white man thus, and the girl is yours."

"The white man was never intended to leave this city alive," the warrior informed Tzotzil.

"I would that you do it now."

The warrior's lips twisted nastily. "Who are you to order me? How do you know that *you* will leave the city alive?"

Tzotzil moved with the swiftness of a striking snake, wrenching the warrior's arm behind him, and had his blade at the warrior's throat. "I know," he seethed into the startled man's ear, "because if you try to stop me, you may join the old ones in the eternal sleep."

"Great one," the warrior croaked, "I spoke in jest."

Tzotzil released the man in a harsh shove. "I would that you kill the white man now, for he has something that is mine."

"The girl is ours."

"Yes, yes. I want only the leather pouch that he keeps beside him at all times."

"So be it," the warrior agreed. "I will go now and relieve the white man of his ghost."

At Renno's orders, his small force stepped into the cleared area of the central plaza of the ancient, jungle-shrouded city in a line, shoulder to shoulder, each man a few feet from the next. Kanam sent his voice roaring through the plaza, and the Mayans, just emerging from the dullness of sleep, their thoughts confused, were frozen by the royal Mayan battle cry. As they recovered and leaped to their feet, seeking their weapons, Kanam shouted, "Brothers, we do not want your blood! Go now!"

"What the hell?" Simon Purdy yelped. He had just awakened. He grabbed his pistols and ran toward the plaza. He turned the corner of a vine-covered temple in time to see two arrows fly quickly from the bow of a bronzed man in the dress of a North American Indian.

Renno's arrows started it. Seeing two of their number die so quickly, the Mayans shouted their calls to battle, and those on their feet cried out hoarsely to those who were still sleeping. It was then that they discovered that of the men who had slept in the plaza, five were dead, the blood from their slit throats having drained out to clot and draw flies.

"The ghosts, the ghosts of our ancestors!" a young man screamed in panic as he looked down on his brother, dead, the eyes cold and staring.

"These are not ghosts," another yelled, advancing to meet the charge of the seven men who had appeared so suddenly.

Simon Purdy's pistols fired almost simultaneously, but because of his surprise at seeing a force led by three North American Indians—one of them definitely a Cherokee—he missed cleanly, turned, and fled back toward the spot where Tess sat with his gold, ammunition, and powder, to reload his pistols.

Tzotzil heard the first screams of surprise and ran to see what was happening. He saw two men die with arrows in their chests and then watched the charge of the oddly mixed group of Mayans, a white man, and three darker men in odd clothing. He wanted no part of a battle. He ran forward and found Purdy and the white girl. Purdy was working swiftly to reload his pistols, so Tzotzil was able to approach unnoticed and thrust his own pistol into Purdy's back.

"Now we say farewell," Tzotzil said.

"What? What's this?" Purdy demanded. "There's only seven of them. We can kill all of them."

"Fight as you will," Tzotzil said, grasping Purdy's pistols and tossing them into the undergrowth. Then he took Purdy's leather pouch, satisfyingly heavy, and backed away.

"Here, Tzotzil," Purdy whined. "We're partners, aren't we? We've come a long way together. You wouldn't take my gold and leave me here with these Indians."

"Wouldn't I?" Tzotzil asked. He backed around a corner. Purdy ran after him. Tzotzil, still reluctant to have the white man's blood on his hands, fired so that his ball pinged off the stone near the man's head.

"Now we'll see," Purdy snarled, drawing his scalping knife.

Tzotzil knew that he had made a serious mistake. Now he would have to kill the white man with his knife. He put the gold down, drew his weapon, and crouched.

"Simon Purdy!" a voice called harshly from behind Tzotzil. The Mayan whirled. A white man stood there, tomahawk in hand.

"I have no quarrel with you," Egan Kirk said to Tzotzil. "Get out of the way."

Tzotzil eagerly seized the pouch of gold and ran. Behind him he heard the shouts and clash of battle as he seized his own gold and Coba's hand and disappeared into the concealing jungle, his wife at his side.

Chapter XVI

With Renno at the center, two Seneca and a Cherokee brought to the ancient city of Uxmal the style of battle that had made the League of the Ho-de-no-sau-nee feared from the Great Lakes to the Mississippi Valley. Each roared his own war cry. Renno's tomahawk struck first, meeting the forehead of a Mayan who had lunged with his short spear only to see Renno dodge to the side and escape the thrust.

On either side of him Renno saw his companions at work, El-i-chi's lips parted in a grim smile, Se-quo-i all serious-ness, his brows knit. Renno, busy with a man very profi-cient with a machete, did not notice Egan break through

285

the ragged line of Mayans and run toward the center of the old city. He did see Kanam dueling with a Mayan, each man with his short spear, but then El-i-chi moved quickly to Kanam's aid and dispatched the Mayan with a whoop and a swing of his bloody tomahawk.

Simon Purdy had not survived for thirty-odd years by being a coward. From the time that he had fled Pennsylvania justice after having killed a man who had dared to look down on Purdy's family, he had faced adversity. His life among the Indians—first the Miami and then the Cherokee—had taught him the value of an expressionless face. Among the Indians, one hid his emotions. Thus, even as the voice of a white man told him several things in one flashing moment of revelation, he seemed to be totally calm.

The voice calling his name told him the reason for the presence of a white man and three Indians, one in Cherokee dress. It was incredible, but it was true. They had followed him all the way from the valley of the Tennessee. That had taken some doing.

"Purdy!" Egan yelled as he lifted his tomahawk. "My name is Egan Kirk. Does that mean anything to you?"

So that's it, Purdy thought. The Kirk family. This young stud was probably the husband of the one he'd enjoyed so much.

"Means nothing to me, friend," Purdy yelled back. "What's the problem? Why do you want to fight me, a fellow American?"

Egan was walking slowly forward, his tomahawk at the ready. Purdy had retrieved his pistols but had not been able to complete their loading.

"It does no good to lie, Purdy," Egan said. "The others are dead—all the Cherokee renegades—but they didn't die before telling me about you. I'm going to keep you alive while I slowly unravel your guts."

Purdy considered the situation. Behind Kirk he saw that the Mayans were faring badly. He made up his mind: To fight would be the less promising of two possibilities, for if he killed this big, overgrown boy, there would be others to fight. Flight was his only chance. He turned quickly and ran to seize Tess. Holding her in front of him, his tomahawk poised at her throat, he said, "I don't know what you're talking about, Kirk, but I don't intend to stay here and find out. If you or anyone else tries to stop me, I'll kill the girl."

Tzotzil, meanwhile, had gathered up one of his porters and was moving away with Coba through the dense jungle as quickly as he could chop a path. He circled the old city until he struck a well-used trail that led roughly eastward. "Who were they?" Coba asked when at last Tzotzil stopped the headlong flight for a brief rest. "Were they from Governor Bocalos?"

"Not from Bocalos," Tzotzil said, "for the white man told me to leave. He was interested only in Purdy." He had an odd look. "I told you that we would not have to endure Purdy's company for long."

"That poor little girl," Coba said.

"Perhaps the white man will look after her," Tzotzil suggested. "Now we must move on. We have far to go before we have the comfort of a good bed. Perhaps we will board a fine ship and sail to Spain."

Three Mayans fell to Renno's tomahawk. Others felt the blades of El-i-chi and Se-quo-i. The brave porters sparred with the enemy with spears but failed to kill, leaving that to the three North Americans. Now only two Mayans stood, for the others were dead or fleeing into the jungle. El-i-chi and Se-quo-i had the situation well in hand, engaging the last two survivors. Even as Renno heard a shrill scream from behind a vine-shrouded pyramid he saw first one, then the other Mayan leap back, throw down his weapon, and bow his head in surrender. Renno ran toward the scream as it was repeated.

He skidded around the corner of the pyramid and jerked to a halt as he saw Simon Purdy backing toward him, holding Tess in front of him. Egan was following, his face terrible and distorted with rage.

"Where do you go, Purdy?" Renno asked quietly, having waited until the man was only ten feet away.

Purdy jerked his head around, saw Renno, and looked back in desperation toward Kirk. A dense wall of jungle lay to his right; the steep, angled side of the pyramid was to his left.

"It's over, Purdy," Renno told him. "We have come for you. Now you will pay for what you and your renegade friends did to the Kirks and to the Brown expedition."

"Oh, please," Tess moaned, getting over her shock and her amazement to hear the odd man in Indian clothing speaking English. "Don't let him hurt me anymore."

"If you care about her," Purdy said, "you'll get out of the way."

"I wonder," Renno said, raising his pistol and aiming it at Purdy's head, "if I could hit you in the right eye without harming the girl."

"I'll kill her, you bastard!" Purdy yelled, stooping to put his head directly behind the girl's.

The pistol blasted. Purdy let out a startled yelp.

Tess screamed, "No! Please!"

"Only the ear," Renno said regretfully.

Purdy lifted his hand, the hand holding his tomahawk, and brushed the back of it against his ear. It came away bloody.

"You're crazy," he yelped. "You don't give a damn about this girl."

"Not really," Renno said mildly. "I believe I can get a little closer to your eye with this." He lifted his other pistol.

"Renno!" Egan yelled, coming closer. "Don't kill him. He's mine."

"Crazy," Purdy said, moving until his back was pressed against the lower level of the pyramid. He leaped to sit on the ledge and lifted Tess upward quickly into his lap. "Stay away," he warned. "I'll kill her."

Renno motioned to Egan to stay back as, level by level, Purdy climbed the pyramid. Soon he was past the area that had been cleared by the Mayans and was struggling to push Tess upward over the verdant growth.

"Let him go," Renno said.

* * *

Sweating, panting with effort, Purdy reached the top of the pyramid. The sun beat down on him. The air seemed to be as thick as the steam issuing from a fiercely boiling caldron. Tess had slumped to the vine-covered platform and was weeping silently. In the newly cleared area below he saw the dead and the living, and not one of his group was on his feet. Purdy found a protruding stone and sat to finish the reloading of his pistol. As he worked he considered his situation. He stood and walked to a point where he could look down on Kirk and the Indians.

"Kirk!" he called. "Listen to me, Kirk! Your little wife—Slim Tom told me her name was Mary—she was sweet and tender. She was very good, Kirk. Too bad you couldn't have been there to see it."

Egan lifted a pistol and fired, but Purdy had ducked back. "I'm going up there after him," Egan seethed, on the verge of sobbing.

"Yes," Renno agreed. "I will climb from the rear."

Purdy looked upward at the sun. He knew that the heat would be worse with midday, and then the afternoon. Down on the ground were more men than he could hope to kill. "Well, Simon," he mused aloud, "looks like this is where it's going to happen." He had often wondered where and when he would die. He had picked up some Indian stoicism regarding death. It came to all men, and one measure of a man, in the Indian's view, was how well he faced death. Purdy would have preferred to have postponed his appointment, but here it was, climbing toward him on two sides of the pyramid. He had one ball in his pistol, and then it would be hand-to-hand, tomahawk against tomahawk, unless the Indian chose to use the longbow slung across his shoulders.

"Kirk," he called out, peering over the edge carefully to see Egan halfway up, "let's make it just you and me. How does that sound? I've got nothing but my blade, boy. My tomahawk. Want me to demonstrate on you how I killed your wife?"

A howl of anger drifted up, and Purdy chuckled as Egan increased his rate of climb. *Good,* he thought. *The boy will be winded when he reaches the top.* He'd take the boy quickly with his tomahawk, saving his one shot for the Indian, who would most probably be a more formidable adversary. That way he'd take two of them with him to hell. And if the ones on the ground came at him one or two at a time, maybe he'd be able to take a few more with him.

He sat down, tucked his pistol in his boot, grasped Tess's wrist, and waited. He saw Egan peer carefully over the top of the pyramid, and sure enough, the boy held a pistol.

"Not man enough to face me with just a blade?" Purdy challenged. He let go of Tess.

Egan climbed up and stood facing Purdy. "Not enough to give you a fair chance because you're not deserving of it. Just enough to give me a chance to cut you up piece by piece, to see you hurt. To see you realize that I've just pulled your guts out into the open."

"Like I did to your wife," Purdy said, smiling pleasantly as he advanced on his foe. "It's an interesting feeling, having a woman's guts in your hand."

"Come on, you son of a bitch." Egan made a low, animallike sound, crouching, clutching his pistol in two trembling hands.

"Watch out!" Tess yelled as Purdy hurled himself forward and knocked Egan's pistol from his hands and over the pyramid's edge.

Purdy drew his own pistol and pointed it at Egan's midsection. "Too bad, Kirk," he said, laughing. "I'm going to take one more Kirk with me to hell. Any last words?"

Renno had reached the top of the pyramid and looked over the last level to see that Egan had fallen into a trap. The white Indian had his own pistol in hand. The problem was that Tess stood directly between him and Purdy. Her back was to him, so he could not gain her attention and motion her aside. He began to move sideways, careful of his footing, while Purdy taunted Egan. He was lifting his pistol again when, with a shrill scream of desperation, the girl threw herself at Purdy, her momentum and weight throwing the man off balance. Renno readied himself for a shot, but he had no chance as Purdy grunted in surprise, fought for his balance, and then, clutching Tess, tumbled over the side of the pyramid.

Only Purdy screamed as the two bounced from level to level, their rate of fall increasing.

Renno heard the scream and moved to look down. Purdy was clinging to the girl, and the two entwined bodies bounced off the steps of the pyramid, rolled down the vine-clad, steep slope, bounced once to fall freely through the air, and thudded on stone where the vines had been cleared away. There was no movement.

El-i-chi and Se-quo-i raced forward, reaching the bodies at the same time. Purdy's neck was twisted at an unnatural angle. His eyes were wide and staring and were taking on the glaze of death. The girl lay atop him. She was breathing.

"He is dead," El-i-chi said.

Se-quo-i carefully lifted the girl and carried her to a shady spot, placing her on a cushion of vines. She moaned. Her eyes flickered and opened.

"Tess," Se-quo-i whispered. "Your sister, Mandy, sends her love."

"Mandy."

"Yes," Se-quo-i said. "She's well, Tess. Soon you'll be with her. We've come for you."

She lapsed into unconsciousness.

El-i-chi began to run his hands over the girl's body, feeling each limb in turn. He put his head to her chest and listened as he put pressure on her ribs. "Nothing seems to be broken."

Egan fell and rolled the last few feet down the pyramid, but he rolled on vines and was only scratched. He ran to fall to his knees beside Purdy. "Don't die yet, you son of a bitch," he begged. "Not yet, not until—"

Renno put his hand on Egan's shoulder. "It's over," he

said quietly. "The girl did it for you, Egan. And when it comes down to it, I suppose she had as much a right to kill him as you."

Egan's anger began to fade. He got to his feet and looked around as if in a daze. "Where's the girl?"

"I don't find any broken bones," El-i-chi said when Kirk and Renno joined him, "but only time will tell if she has injuries inside."

"She saved my life," Egan said in awe. "Purdy had a pistol—" He looked down at Tess. Oddly enough, he did not think of her as being the whore of men like Simon Purdy. He was looking at a young girl who had been cruelly mistreated, and his heart went out to her. For once, and for the first time in a long, long time, he was not thinking of Mary and his dead son but of another human being, Tess. He knelt, took her hand, and whispered her name over and over.

Tess opened her eyes.

"Thank you, Tess, for what you did up there. You're going to be fine. We're going to take you to your sister."

"Vile," Tess whispered.

Egan wasn't sure he understood. He put his ear close to her lips and said, "What did you say?"

"Vile," she whispered. "I am so . . . vile."

"No, no, you're not, little darlin'," Egan said. "What happened is not your fault, and you're going to be with your sister again and—" He fell silent, for she was unconscious.

Kanam and the party's porters were being assisted by the two surviving members of the looters in removing the dead. Kanam said that those who desecrated the tombs of the old ones deserved no honor in death, so their bodies were dragged a couple of hundred yards away to a deep, overgrown *cenote*, a sinkhole with green, stagnant water at the bottom, and dumped in.

On the way back to the plaza, after disposing of the last body, Kanam heard a rustling in the jungle and, after careful investigation, brought home the bacon in the form of an adult iguana. Soon the meat was roasting over a fire, and all ate heartily.

"Why," El-i-chi asked, "does fighting make a man so hungry?"

No one answered immediately. Kanam said, after a long silence, "Perhaps, my friend, because the spirit is so happy to be still alive, it cries out for food as proof that the body still lives."

"Too deep for me." El-i-chi grunted. "I am very hungry after love, as well."

"El-i-chi," Kirk called out, "you'd better come over here."

El-i-chi rushed to Tess's side. Kirk was holding up her head. She had vomited blood in great, clotting masses, and now she was breathing with difficulty. El-i-chi looked at Egan and shook his head.

"We can't let her die," Egan pleaded, "not after all she's gone through."

As if she had heard the words, Tess opened her eyes and her whisper was weak but clear. "Tell Mandy not to weep. I'm glad—glad—" She spoke no more, but her expression was peaceful.

"Is she dying?" Egan asked.

El-i-chi had once seen a Cherokee warrior who died thus, after having pulled a Spanish cavalryman and the Spaniard's horse down atop him. The Spaniard had died first, the Cherokee's tomahawk buried in his chest, but the victor died shortly afterward, after vomiting huge quantities of blood.

"I fear so," El-i-chi said.

"How will I tell Mandy?" Egan moaned, once again more concerned with the pain of others than his own.

The sound of the male voices seemed to be coming to Tess from far, far away. Now no one would ever know the things that had been done to her. No one would ever know that she had been sold for gold and jade to more than a dozen Mayans who stank of rancid grease and unwashed bodies. Only God would judge her, and He was merciful. She

*became interested in a light that moved closer and closer,
and then there was a figure in the light and—*

*She smiled. Her lips opened, and for a moment she was
just a little girl, smiling happily.*

"Hello, Mother," she said. "I'm so happy to see you."

"It is fitting," Kanam said as the Mayans and he placed
the white girl in an ancient tomb. Around her, still arrayed
in their death gifts of jade and a few pieces of gold, the old
ones slept. Renno and El-i-chi knelt before the opening
that had been forced through the rock wall by the would-be
looters and chanted a song of the dead. Kanam and the
other Mayan returned the stones to their place as best they
could, resealing the opened tomb. Soon the jungle would
return and hide all signs of the tampering.

Kirk began to look forward to reaching Campeche. For
the first time since the death of his family, he felt free—free
to examine the jungle around him as if he had never seen it
before and to wonder at the building skills of the men who
had constructed the old city. Mostly, however, he thought
of Mandy, of the pain he must give her when he told her of
the manner of her sister's death. But perhaps he could also
help to ease that pain.

Renno was eager to resume the journey. It began at first
light, with Kanam in the lead and Renno directly behind
him. The pace was a fast one, for they moved on good trails
before turning toward the coast. The last battle, they felt,
was behind them. Their mission was complete, and only a
stretch of wet, marshy jungle lay between them and a swift
passage home on the *Nuestra Señora*. El-i-chi filled his
waking reverie with the face of Ah-wa-o.

Se-quo-i was musing on the ways of the gods—or the
manitous, or God if one accepted the views of the white
man: Five white girls had been taken by the renegades on
the Tennessee River near Muscle Shoals. Now only two
lived, one as the wife of a provincial Spanish governor. The
other was aboard the ship, with nothing more in life than
the friends she had made among her rescuers. It was

indeed odd. His thoughts shattered with the sound of a pistol report.

The dart that came hissing from the jungle to bury its tip into Renno's back was not large. His first thought was self-reproach for having been so complacent, for having believed that the battle was over. He crashed through the undergrowth after his assailant, pistol in hand, and fired at fleeting movement. The sound of the pistol was answered by a scream of anguish as the Mayan who had put the dart into his back died.

He made his way back to the trail, the dart still in his flesh. He presented his back to El-i-chi and said, "Please remove that small irritation, Brother."

Kanam's face was grim as El-i-chi pulled the dart from Renno's back. Renno removed his shirt. The wound was a small one, not more than half an inch deep.

Kanam had gone into the jungle and now returned with the dead man's quiver. He drew out a small arrow, sniffed it, then motioned to El-i-chi.

Renno felt a bit dizzy. He sat down, puzzled. He had experienced far worse wounds but had never felt so weak.

"My friend," Kanam whispered to El-i chi, "I am sorry."

A cold shiver ran down El-i-chi's spine.

"The dart that penetrated your brother's back was tipped with a poison so virulent that death is a certainty. It is only a matter of time—a very few minutes."

Alexander McGillivray did not ordinarily participate actively in the Creek attacks on white settlements along the Georgia border, but driven by frustration, he joined a small war party as he traveled southwestward on his way to New Orleans. It was a disappointing raid, for the cabin chosen for the attack proved to be occupied by only a single white man—no women, no children. McGillivray was a man who knew history and thus understood a bit of how humans behaved. Terror, he knew, was a weapon, and there was more impact for the living when women and children were raped and scalped than when one crusty old settler took three Creek braves with him to his death. McGillivray knew that such "victories" had reduced the Indian tribes from their former greatness. At a three-to-one kill ratio, the whites could wipe out every living Creek and all other Indians and still have numbers enough to swarm over the entire continent.

McGillivray was frustrated because absolutely nothing had happened in the months since he had visited Governor Miró in New Orleans and since he had briefed a Seneca war chief on the land speculation in the Yazoo Territory. He had read newspapers that had been printed in Savannah weeks before, and no mention was made of an English-Spanish war or of an invasion of Spanish lands south of Chickasaw Bluffs by Kentuckians.

Although he had been allowed the honor of taking the old white man's scalp when the settler had finally been overcome by numbers, his spirits were still low when he reached New Orleans and went directly to his favorite place, Laure Beyle's new house. In the great fire, nineteen squares of the carefully laid-out city had been destroyed. Eight hundred fifty-six houses had been gutted. Laure Beyle's new bordello was not nearly so grand as the one that had been lost, but the company was as good. There were two new girls, half-Indian, half-Spanish, who seemed to enjoy the company of the king of the Creek.

It was almost midnight when Governor Miró arrived. He was ushered without fanfare into McGillivray's private parlor. McGillivray rose and shook hands as if he was the English gentleman his dress purported him to be. He had retained the two new girls for the evening, and as he had suspected, Miró was quite taken with the younger.

They talked business during pleasure, Miró in a distracted manner, for he was busily watching the girls dance.

"My dear McGillivray," Miró said, "not even I claim to understand all of the Crown's decisions in faraway Spain. I know only that the local commander who sent troops to board British ships in Nootka Sound was reprimanded and ordered to deliver a formal apology to the British authorities there." The governor shrugged and returned his attention to the younger girl. "So it seems, McGillivray, that there will be no war."

"And what of the buffer state promised by O'Fallon, of the Yazoo Company, that state to be half-Spanish, half-independent, and not at all American?"

Again Miró shrugged. "It seems that O'Fallon preferred the dubious friendship of the British. But let us forget these dull things, my friend, and concentrate on the matter at hand."

To McGillivray, that seemed to be a worthy suggestion.

Thomas Jefferson had a more detailed explanation of what was not the end but the beginning of the end of the Yazoo affair. At George Washington's nod he briefed the small, intimate gathering in Washington's office.

"Dr. James O'Fallon—who, by the way, claims to be descended from Irish kings—miscalculated," Jefferson explained. "He had the cooperation of Miró, the Spanish governor, and apparently had promised Miró that the independent state to be created in the Yazoo lands would be pro-Spanish, a sort of buffer between the American and Spanish frontiers. Our information is that the colony of ex-Americans was to have a city to the north of Natchez as a center for trading slaves and for trading with the Indians."

"Meanwhile," said Knox, the secretary of war, "he was telling us, here in New York, that he deserved American support for his attempt to create this colony because he was making fools of the Spanish."

"Miró must have realized that O'Fallon was trying to play both ends against the middle," Jefferson said. "The governor withdrew his support, thus infuriating O'Fallon, who told the Spanish that he had enough power—through his marriage to the daughter of George Rogers Clark—to take the land in question whether or not he had Miró's sanction. This threat of invasion from Kentucky was the possibility that so concerned the President.

"Oddly enough, events in France became the factor of decision: When the mobs took to the Paris streets, it became apparent that France, in the throes of revolution, was rendered impotent on the international scene, unable to assist Spain in a new war with Great Britain. Suddenly Spain had to back down abjectly, and so the war clouds faded more rapidly than they had formed. Our friend Dr. O'Fallon found himself in an uncomfortable position: He had alienated the Spanish by his arrogance; he had shown contempt for the United States. So he now faces opposition from Spain, the United States, and all the Indian nations."

George Washington lifted a finger, which was all that was needed to have Jefferson defer to him. "Just this afternoon I received a letter that concerned the fate of Dr. O'Fallon, Thomas," Washington said. "It seems that James Wilkinson of Kentucky has convinced the stockholders of the Yazoo Company that the good doctor is no longer capable of directing the affairs of the company."

"I suspect," Alexander Hamilton said, "that the Yazoo Company will retreat in good order and leave the field to the Indians."

Jefferson sighed. "We are gaining experience in the art of managing crises, gentlemen. Each emergency seems to present the ultimate threat to national unity and then fades. Yet we are all still here, nervously awaiting the next blow of fate to our young government."

"We are thankful that God is with us," Washington said.

"Amen to that," the others agreed.

For a moment El-i-chi could only stare at Kanam. He could not believe that his brother was dying or that there was no hope. But one look at Renno told him the truth more eloquently than Kanam's words. Cold sweat beaded on Renno's face and forehead, and his skin was ashen. His eyes stared into space, and his facial muscles were slack.

"Manitous!" El-i-chi whispered, falling to his knees beside his brother. He began to chant a supplication to the spirits, but his voice faded into silence when Renno began to speak without his lips moving. El-i-chi bent close, for the words were faint. The language was one that he had never heard—harsh, guttural, rhythmic. The voice was Renno's; the words were not.

Kanam heard and made the sign of appeasement of the spirits, for Renno was speaking Mayan but with an accent and using words that made it difficult for Kanam to understand. He finally realized that Renno was repeating himself, saying a list of common jungle plants and herbs. Kanam leaned close and committed all the names to memory. The other instructions were simple. Kanam leaped to his feet and disappeared into the jungle to search frantically for the things named by Renno's voice.

Renno knew that death was near. He tried to lift his head, and the effort was beyond him. He could only move his eyes to see the blurred features of his brother. His own body seemed to have elongated. His hands and feet were still attached but were aeons away, so far that he could not move them. And in his soul and mind a soft, gentle numbness grew slowly, so that his breaths seemed to be hours apart, his heartbeat only every hour or so.

When, in this dazed and comfortable state, he saw the face and form of his beloved Emily, he rejoiced, for she was there to welcome him to the land of his ancestors who had gone before him to the Place Across the River. He tried to lift his arms to her, but his efforts were in vain.

"Husband," Emily said, her voice as sweet as fresh honey to him, "warrior of great heart who knows respect for all men of goodwill, you are indeed brother to all, even the ancients."

Something was wrong. She was not coming closer. He tried to reach out to her.

"All eternity is contained within a second," she said, "although the passage of time will seem long to you, Husband." Then she was gone.

He grunted in protest and called out to her, but no sound crossed his lips.

Kanam knelt in front of Renno, frantically pounding into a pulp the plants specified by the words that had come from the white Indian's mouth. The Mayan stuffed a generous helping of the pulp into Renno's mouth and told El-i-chi to make Renno chew.

El-i-chi put his hands on his brother's face and under the chin, working the jaw, forcing Renno to chew. Then he rolled the sachem onto his side so Kanam could smear some pulp over the tiny puncture left by the poisoned dart. Now El-i-chi stroked Renno's throat, causing him to swallow.

The white Indian coughed feebly. Then once more they heard his voice but ancient Mayan words: "Our brother lives, for his heart is great."

"No man has ever survived the poison," Kanam said in wonder as Renno stretched, yawned, and lay back to sleep comfortably, his breathing now even and strong. "The antidote he has given us through the spirits of the old ones will save many lives." He concentrated on remembering the ingredients of the pulp that he had prepared for Renno. "First there was—" He paused, and his eyes widened. "God of the winds," he whispered in despair, "you have swept the memory from me." Indeed, he could not name a single ingredient of the magical cure, and examination of the pulpy paste on Renno's back offered no clues.

With the morning, Renno was the first one awake. He walked a small distance into the jungle and lifted his hands. He praised the manitous, for he knew how close he had been to death. He remembered with satisfaction that he had felt peaceful and happy. There was also a bit of regret that he was not in the Place Across the River with Emily. Then he envisioned his children, his people, and his mother, and the urgency grew in him to be at home with all those he loved.

Soon waterways interrupted the march so often that Kanam negotiated with the Mayan in a riverside village for canoes. The trip's pace was increased hugely as the native rowers sped them toward the coastline. The villagers were vocal about their surprise at having two traveling parties traverse their isolated area within days.

"The governor's secretary," Kanam guessed. "Perhaps we can overtake him."

"We have no quarrel with him," Renno said.

Curiosity led Renno to direct his paddlers to shore near the point where two canoes were beached. His rowers hailed the camp where a cooking fire burned and were answered. "Men of our village," they reported.

Renno approached the fire. Tzotzil and Coba greeted him politely, extending both hands to Renno. The Mayan knew that if these men from far away wanted to kill him, they could do so easily. "Great warrior," he said, "my wife and I saw you in Uxmal, and you know that we did not fight you."

"Yes," Renno confirmed, "although you traveled with the man called Simon Purdy."

"And now Purdy is dead?" Tzotzil asked.

Renno nodded.

"The little white girl?" Coba asked.

"She, too, is dead," Renno answered.

Coba's face stiffened.

"Not by our hands," Renno said.

He told the story, crediting Tess with saving Egan's life. When he finished, Coba was weeping quietly.

When the governor's secretary was questioned, he spoke truthfully. He made no attempt to hide the fact that the two large bags contained gold and silver coins—the province's treasury, the garrison's payroll, and Bocalos's gold from the sale of Grace Brown. If he was to be robbed of it all by these newcomers, so be it. He wanted to live to be with his Coba, and if he had to be poor, then he would make the best of it. When he had finished telling how he had taken the money from Bocalos and the provincial government, Renno laughed.

"Neither of us has love for the Spanish," Renno said.

Tzotzil began to look hopeful.

"But there is one survivor of the killings and kidnappings of Simon Purdy," Renno went on. "It would seem fair to me to see her repaid—as far as money can repay the loss of a sister and the loss of her maidenhood. What say you, Tzotzil?"

Tzotzil smiled. "I say, warrior, that this woman is entitled to the gold taken by Simon Purdy."

"My friend," Renno said, "you are a sensible man. You may give Purdy's portion to this strapping young fellow here, who is able to carry it and who, I suspect, will be happy to deliver it to the recipient."

Tzotzil nodded, handing the large leather pouch to the young white man. "The fates and the gods are kind," he said. "There is more than enough in the half you are allowing me to keep to afford a comfortable life on good land with my Coba."

Campeche sat on the ocean side of a gently rising valley of verdant, fertile soil. Three ships were moored offshore, one of them the *Nuestra Señora*. Ah-wa-o was standing at the rail, waving, as the longboat brought El-i-chi and Se-quo-i to the ship. Renno and Egan were in the next boat. To El-i-chi, Ah-wa-o, his little Rose, was the most beautiful of all creations of the Master of Life, and his heart sang when she was in his arms.

Mandy was searching the faces in the second boat eagerly for sign of her sister. Because El-i-chi was occupied, Mandy took Se-quo-i's arm, looked at him imploringly.

"I'm sorry," Se-quo-i said. "Your sister is dead."

"I will ask how later," Mandy said, her voice choked. "I need to be alone." She walked to the stern of the ship. She wore a sailor's blouse and trousers, for her own clothing had been weakened and made threadbare. She had already shed her tears when Egan came to her. She turned to face him.

Egan put the leather pouch with its gold and silver coins on the deck. "This is yours."

"What is it?"

"It was Purdy's. Now it's yours. You and Charity Brown are the only ones left, Mandy. Charity's all right—a governor's wife. You thought you had been left with nothing, but

now that's not true. There's enough here to take you back to
Philadelphia and set you up in a nice little shop of some
kind or to interest a man in you, if you want to have a
husband."

Mandy nodded, her eyes downcast. "How did she die?"

"Your sister was very brave," Egan said. He told Mandy
how he, in his eagerness to kill Simon Purdy, had exposed
himself to Purdy's pistol and how Tess had pushed Purdy off
the pyramid and had fallen with him. When he paused,
Mandy was very quiet. Se-quo-i had joined them, standing
behind Egan, in time to hear Egan end his story.

"There's one thing more that you should know, Mandy,"
Se-quo-i said. "Tess lived for a while, and she spoke."

"Tell me," Mandy said.

"I think she wanted to die, Mandy, because of what had
happened to her." He held up his hand to halt Mandy's
angry protest. "I know. She deserved to live, and we
wanted her to live. After all, we did not follow Purdy over
two countries just to kill him. We failed miserably with the
other captives. Now there's only you and Charity. I don't
want to burden you or to hurt you, but I think you should
know that toward the end, Purdy sold your sister to a
number of Mayan for gold and jade. She was shamed, and
she wanted to die. Remember that she gave her life to save
another, and that she is now in the heaven of your God."
Se-quo-i reached for her hand, squeezed it, then left them.

Alone with Egan, Mandy gave way to tears. She did not
protest when Egan put his arms around her, held her close,
and patted her shoulder.

The *Nuestra Señora* sailed through the Florida Straits,
past Cuba, then headed along the Florida coast with
favorable winds booming her northward.

Wilmington, North Carolina, was, in Renno's eyes, un-
changed since his last visit. His distant cousin Nate Ridley
greeted him with pleasure and feasted the group in his
home. Nathan told Renno that there had been a little
flare-up between the Spanish and British out on the west

coast of the continent and some talk about a land scheme along the Mississippi that had not amounted to anything.

Renno wrote down the things that Alexander McGillivray had told him. The letter would go to George Washington with the next northward-bound ship. There no longer seemed to be an emergency to force Renno to travel to New York to talk with the President himself. He was free to make the long, long journey across the width of North Carolina to the mountains, over them, and home. He lost no time in preparing to set out.

"Well, Mandy," he said, "Nathan will arrange passage for you on the first ship to call in Philadelphia. He'll also help you turn the Spanish coins into United States currency and transfer the funds to a Philadelphia bank."

Mandy looked uneasy. Nearby, Egan Kirk examined the knuckles on his left hand.

"You have been a friend to me, Sachem," Mandy said. "I will be grateful to you always." She turned. "But I can't say the same for this big lunk."

"Huh?" Egan snorted, surprised at the attack.

"How so?" Renno asked, hiding a grin. During the voyage north Egan had spent much time with Mandy, and Renno suspected that the young man had wanted to speak his heart to her. Even now, when preparations were being made for her to go out of his life forever, he clearly was miserable but was saying nothing.

"I've done everything but throw myself at him," Mandy said, "and he does nothing but stammer like a schoolboy."

"Huh?" Egan asked. He moved closer, cocked his head. "Are you saying what I think you're saying?"

"I don't know what you think I'm saying," she said tartly, "but I don't want to go to Philadelphia. I have no one there. I don't want to buy a husband with the money you all have given me."

Ah-wa-o saw Egan's mouth work, but no words came. She moved to Egan's side. "Shall I translate those strangling sounds for you, Egan?" Ah-wa-o asked with a smile.

He nodded eagerly.

Ah-wa-o crossed her arms over her breasts, made her face impassive, lowered her voice, and said, in pantomime of some Easterners' picture of an Indian: "Ugg. White man say to white squaw this—he say he no want white squaw go Philadelphia, either."

"Is that true, Egan?" Mandy asked in a soft voice.

"True," Ah-wa-o confirmed. "White man whose tongue cat got say he want white squaw go with him, with all us."

"Really, Egan?" Mandy asked, smiling.

Egan, face flushing, nodded eagerly. "Thank you, Ah-wa-o," he said, laughing. "I think I can take it from here. Mandy, I'm often a fool, and I'm a man of the frontier. I wouldn't be comfortable in a town, but I'm not gonna ask you to live out there where Mary and my boy were killed."

"Marry me, then, and you'll be a man with a little nest egg. We can buy land anywhere we choose."

"Now dag-bone it, Mandy, the man is supposed to ask the woman to marry him."

"Well," Renno said, "do it, so we can start home."

Little Hawk and Renna sat in their father's lap. A very satisfactory meal was over, and the adults were waiting for Renno, Se-quo-i, and El-i-chi to enliven the evening with a recounting of their adventures. First, however, Renno had gifts for his children. They had come from the bag that had belonged to Simon Purdy. Mandy had given them to him, and Renno accepted them not for their monetary value but for their beauty: jade and gold ornaments to be worn around the neck.

"Far away to the south, in the jungle," he said, "the Mayan Indians, our brothers by ancient ancestors, built cities that reached to the sky. For reasons that only the spirits know, the manitous deserted the Mayan, and their cities are covered by the jungle. These things are to remind you, Little Hawk, and you, Renna, that even great cities can die and that we live by the will of the manitous and the Master of Life."

He gave Little Hawk the small, delicately fashioned frog.

It gleamed with the reddish color of ancient gold. To Renna he gave a carved jade stone. Renna liked the color and laughed happily when Renno lowered it over her head.

"Now," said Ha-ace, "since I have kept the tribe intact for you by preventing young Tor-yo-ne from naming himself sachem"—there was a general laugh—"I think I have earned the right to hear a story."

Here is an exciting preview of Book #19 in
the WHITE INDIAN series:

FALLEN TIMBERS

Coming in May 1990, wherever Bantam Books
are sold.

Prologue

The presidential mansion on Market Street near Sixth had drawn its share of gawkers on a pleasantly balmy day and, with the coming of darkness, presented glowing, lamp-lit windows to those few Philadelphians who were still curious enough to stroll past. Of course, there was no hope of catching a glimpse of the man whom some called "King George." The first president of the United States was not a man to go about after dark.

There were those who resented the mansion, for Washington had received numerous offers of hospitality from wealthy Philadelphians, each of whom would have been honored to house the president without fee when the government was moved from New York to the city of Benjamin Franklin in 1790. But Washington had said that the head of the nation should be no man's guest and had rented the finest house available.

The president issued forth occasionally to visit the gleaming new buildings that had been erected for Congress and the Supreme Court near the Pennsylvania State House. He rode in a cream-colored, French-built coach decorated with cupids and flowers and drawn by six prancing horses of the purest pedigree. Outriders and lackeys accompanied the coach, and they wore the finest livery.

The president was fond of wearing black velvet suits with many gold buckles. His hands sported yellow gloves. Under his cocked hat topped by an ostrich plume his hair was powdered in the style of the still-hated British gentry. His ensemble was made complete by a fine sword in a white leather scabbard. At public functions he shook no man's hand, preferring to acknowledge greetings with a stiff, small bow. He had offended a few well-wishers by announcing that due to a proliferation of callers he was limiting access to his person—except for a weekly informal reception presided over by Martha Washington—to those who had made an appointment. His table was no longer open to all. He invited members of Congress to dine at the mansion on a rotation basis, served fine wines and elaborate menus, and was criticized by some for making the meals too coldly solemn.

In this nation made up of thirteen dissimilar states, each more intent on its own welfare than on the general good, the house on Market Street had come to be called "King George's Court." Dissension, Benjamin Franklin had once said, is both the blessing and the bane of democracy.

Blessing or bane, there was dissension. It extended even into the president's cabinet. It was evident in the stilted politeness that characterized the relationship between the regal Virginian secretary of state Thomas Jefferson and the sometimes brash but usually practical-minded New Yorker secretary of the treasury Alexander Hamilton. Arriving together at the door to Washington's private office, Hamilton, the younger, bowed Jefferson into the room first.

"Ah, gentlemen," Washington said. "I do pray that you will forgive me once again for tearing you away from your hearth." He had risen and now indicated chairs for the two men upon whom he leaned most heavily for support and advice. A liveried black man entered on silent feet and poured a fine port into three crystal glasses. Both Hamilton and Jefferson waited for the president to speak. Washington's first words were a long time in coming, and the frank appraisal of his hard eyes made Hamilton stir uneasily in his chair. Jefferson, however, returned the president's stare with a slight smile.

Washington was thinking, *Thank you, Lord, for these two excellent men*. And he was remembering how Hamilton and the company he had raised had prevented Cornwallis from crossing the Raritan to attack the main army. In the years that followed, Hamilton had become one of his most trusted aides-de-camp and envoys. Yes, Hamilton was a rock, the rock upon which Washington was fashioning the fiscal policy of the new nation. But Jefferson was a man to be valued, too, even if his dependability had been proven in a different arena, far from the battlefields of the War for Independence. *Ah, what a waste to have these two at polar extremes*.

"Mr. Hamilton," Washington said, having finished the port. "At long last I have managed to digest your quite literate and, I might add, highly technical report on the public credit. I have taken the liberty of giving Mr. Jefferson a copy, as well."

Hamilton waited, offering only a sidelong glance in Jefferson's direction.

It was Jefferson who spoke. "An excellent piece of work, Mr. Hamilton, I must say. However—" The elegant Virginian looked at Washington. The president nodded at Jefferson to continue. Washington could handle differences between men. "I fear, Mr. Hamilton, that you're going to have difficulty getting your proposals through Congress."

"I anticipate no great problems," Hamilton replied stiffly. Washington's self-consciousness about his bad teeth did not prevent him from smiling into the hand that he raised to his mouth. *Odd*, he was thinking, *how great men can be petty and so obviously contradictory*. It had come to his ears that Jefferson had disparaged the secretary of the treasury as a "foreign-born adventurer whose financial policies are based on attitudes engendered by childhood poverty." Truly, Hamilton had known poverty when his mother and he were deserted by his father. Truly he was foreign born, a son of the island of Nevis in the British West Indies; and he was, perhaps, overly sensitive to slurs on his origin, for his mother, a French Huguenot, had lived with his father, James Hamilton, before her divorce from her first husband was official. But in the past Hamilton had been quick to point out that his lineage was good. He had once said, "My blood is as good as that of those who plume themselves upon their ancestry." After all, his father had been of the Scottish nobility, the fourth son of the Laird of Cambuskeith.

The president recognized that the political rivalry between Hamilton and Jefferson had deep roots and was fueled by personal considerations, for Jefferson was of the Virginia aristocracy and had married into one of the most influential colonial families, the Randolphs. Even though the Jefferson plantation was not in the aristocratic Tidewater area of Virginia, and even though the young Jefferson had, as a result, been exposed to influences more democratic than those of the Tidewater, he was, from Hamilton's viewpoint, only a shade removed from British gentry and suspect for it.

"There are those who say," Jefferson continued, "that your motives are political more than economic, that you plan to tax the poor to pay off debts to the rich merely to bind men of wealth and influence to the national government."

Now the president rolled his eyes heavenward. Hamilton had stated publicly that England had the best government in the world and thought that the government of the United States should be modeled after the England of

George III. Yet Hamilton was suspicious of Jefferson without realizing that Jefferson was the true republican, not Hamilton himself. Washington was certain that one or perhaps both of these men would, in all likelihood, follow him into the office of the presidency. And each of them thought of himself as the true man of the people. Who was right? Washington thanked God that he would not have to be the one to decide that question.

"Are you saying, Mr. Jefferson, that you will be unable to support my proposals?" Hamilton asked.

"In their present form it would be difficult for me." Jefferson looked into Washington's eyes. "For this, sir, I am sorry."

A grim smile twitched Washington's lips. "A man must support his convictions, Thomas." He made a motion with his hand, and the liveried black man poured more port into his glass. "However, gentlemen, perhaps there is a solution to our dilemma." He knew that a serious clash was inevitable between his two advisers. Already the sides were forming: Jefferson and James Madison were working together to form a political party based on democratic-republicanism; Hamilton, with his followers, believed in a strong federal government managed by men of means and property.

The two cabinet officers waited again as Washington sipped from his crystal glass.

"I have seen a preliminary draft of an interesting act that is being presented in Congress," Washington began.

Jefferson straightened his shoulders, obviously suspecting what was coming.

"This act," Washington said, "would establish the temporary and permanent seat of the government of the United States. I think you know of this act, Mr. Jefferson?"

"I do," Jefferson answered.

"I am considering sending a message to Congress stating that I have selected a site," Washington said.

Long moments of tense silence followed. Whatever Washington wanted, Washington got; it had been that way since Valley Forge. When the electors gathered to choose the first president of the new nation, only one name was considered—no other man was even mentioned—and that name had been George Washington's.

The president continued. "Mr. Hamilton and I are, of course, aware of your predilection to have the new capitol of the United States situated on the banks of the Potomac."

Jefferson took a deep breath and held it.

"This presents—as does your disagreement with Mr. Hamilton's, and my, financial policies—some difficulty to me, Mr. Jefferson. If I support a site on the Potomac, I can be accused of being partial, for I am, after all, a Virginian."

Jefferson nodded. This was a valid concern.

Washington leaned forward. "Thomas, I believe in Mr. Hamilton's policy. We need your support."

Jefferson nodded. "I think, Mr. President, that the banks of the Potomac would make an excellent location for the seat of government. The site would be centrally located and accessible to sea transport."

"Philadelphia has the same attributes," Hamilton pointed out, "although it is less accessible from the south. And my own state, New York, has a rightful claim, as well."

"Each faction can cite its own merits," Jefferson allowed.

"With my financial policy we would have a way to raise money to build a new capital," Hamilton said.

"I have talked at length with Major L'Enfant," Washington said. "He is enthusiastic about choosing an unencumbered site, and he promises to build a city that will testify to the future greatness of this nation." He shrugged, a gesture seldom seen. "However—"

Jefferson looked at Hamilton, and his face relaxed into a smile. "I think, sir, that I am being stretched a bit, as if in the rack."

"It will only be painful for a moment," Hamilton said, answering Jefferson's smile.

"Actually," Jefferson said, "I feel much better already. I am no dewy-eyed idealist when it comes to politics and compromise. What, exactly, would you like me to do in support of your economic plans?"

"That can be discussed at a later date," Washington said. "So. I have prepared a message to Congress, asking for authorization to have a plot of land surveyed on either side of the Potomac. I will leave it to the Congress to determine the exact size of this territory." He added, with true modesty, "I trust that Congress will give serious consideration to my proposal."

Hamilton laughed. "Congress will approve anything you propose, and public opinion will follow immediately."

"So that's settled, then," Washington said. "More port, gentlemen?" Both men accepted a refill of their glasses. "There is another matter that is giving me pause. I welcome your contributions and efforts." He looked at the ceiling. "I fought with and led good men to their deaths, not for love of war but for love of peace, and it seemed that peace came at Yorktown in September of 1781." He sighed. "But where is that peace now? Today the British are enforted at Niagara, Detroit, and Mackinac, on lands officially ceded to the United States by the treaty that you, Thomas, helped to define in Paris. The governor general of British Canada has promised arms and aid to the Indians of the northwest—we have this in writing from reputable authority. There are Spanish garrisons at St. Louis, Ste. Genevieve, Natchez, New Orleans, Mobile, and Pensacola. These two European powers—with the aid of those French who still exist in some numbers—control our western waterways. The Spanish are arming the Indians of the south, the Creek among them. And as you may know, the northwestern tribes, led by the Shawnee and the Miami, have declared that the Ohio is their last frontier, that they will fight to the death before retreating farther."

Washington paused and searched the two faces before him for reaction. "We promised our veterans land, gentlemen, and there was no land to give them. We told them to take their lands in the northwest, and many of them did just that. Now they are dying. We have sent them, our people, into a dispute that is claiming more lives than many battles of the great war. Our thirteen states are only now beginning to recover from the exhaustion of the war, and their main aim seems to be to cling not only to independence from England but independence from each other. We have no army. You, Mr. Hamilton, advocate a strong central government, but what does this government do to protect the people on the frontiers?"

Hamilton shifted in his seat.

"The frontier is ablaze, gentlemen. War parties roam from the far south to the Great Lakes, and those settlers who have survived the Indian raids have to contend with attempts by land merchants and lawyers to grab their property. These western settlers, you must remember, are, in many cases, Englishmen, Scotch-Irish, German, and Dutch. Before the war they were loyal to the Crown and had the Crown's protection. They had seen little from us, from this government, to gain their loyalties. One could hardly blame them—as their women and children are tortured or kidnapped, as their hard-won settlements are burned—if they turned to Spain, France, or England for protection—"

"Which is exactly what the foreign agitators want," Hamilton grumbled.

"I have been among them," Washington said, "and although I have had only scanty reports from the northwest of late, I think I know the settlers' state of mind. I tell you this, gentlemen: The shape and the future of this nation will be decided in the northwest. The northern tribes, nited, will be a most formidable enemy. A coalition of hawnee, Wyandot, Delaware, Mingo, Ottawa, Potawatami, Chippewa, and Miami have declared war, and they have he support of the British and the Spanish. I am thankful hat the Spanish are too far away, in the Floridas, to help much—except with arming the southern Indians to spread ur defenses thin."

"I have forwarded protests from the State Department o the government in London," Jefferson said.

"This matter will not be settled in London but in the orests north of the Ohio," Washington told him. "War is going on now, and it will grow more intense. These Indians have known nothing but war for hundreds of years, nd in recent decades they have had excellent instructors n the art of war. They come closer to being professional oldiers than any body of troops we could muster. They ave learned military skills and strategy from their fathers nd their grandfathers who fought under Frontenac, Vaudreuil, Montcalm, Abercrombie, Forbes, Amherst, Pontiac, and Bradstreet. And they have studied the lessons aught by that most successful coalition of Indian tribes in he history of this land, the League of the Iroquois. In act, Iroquois war chiefs and warriors are already among hem, bringing with them the great martial tradition of the roquois League."

It was Jefferson who broke the silence.

"Should the Indians, with the aid of the British and Spanish, be able to hold our line of expansion at the Ohio, hat means that our western boundary will forever be the Appalachian Mountains."

"Indeed," Washington agreed.

"And those vast and fertile territories between the mountains and the Mississippi will become a patchwork of foreign enclaves, Indian strongholds, and perhaps a small, ndependent state or two if men like George Rogers Clark prevail," Jefferson said.

Washington nodded. Thomas had a keen mind. H waited, but neither Jefferson nor Hamilton spoke.

"It would not take very much to turn the western set tlers away from us," the president continued. "This w must not allow. Mr. Hamilton, I would like an estimate o the cost of raising an army, equipping it, and sending i into the Northwestern Territories."

"Yes, sir," Hamilton said.

"To do so, as you know, sir, risks war with England, Jefferson put in.

"But that's the choice, isn't it, Thomas?" Washingto asked unhappily. "To give up territory that is legally our or to risk war?"

Jefferson nodded grimly. He rose. "Shall I tell the Brit ish ambassador of your resolve, sir?"

"No, not just yet," Washington answered. "Thank you gentlemen, for coming." He rose and nodded, satisfied "I think this has been a most productive session, do yo agree?"

"Indeed," Hamilton said, and Jefferson nodded ruefully

Alone, Washington finished his wine. The servan entered and stated quietly that Mrs. Washington had re quested the general dress for dinner. Washington wave the man away, reached into a drawer for paper, and dippe a quill pen in ink.

My dear friend Renno,

Some time in the past I penned a request to you, a request that I had no right to make, other than that the content was of importance not only to this new nation but to your people as well. Perhaps, in the confusion, the letter was lost, and so I address you again. It is of vital importance I have intelligence of

conditions in the territory north of the Ohio River. I
know of no man more qualified to make such a survey
for me.

He wrote more, signed with a flourish, closed the letter
in an envelope, and applied his individual wax seal.

Chapter I

The last surge of spring growth had provided a shade
canopy of green for the soft floor of the northwester
forests. To the eyes of the lone white man, the wilderness
seemed to be the last place for death and war. Roy John
son had traveled for weeks without coming face-to-face
with another man, although he had occasionally gone ou
of his way to avoid a hunting party or a secluded village
He had traveled northeast from Knoxville, then north
westerly to see the thriving little town of Boonesborough
in Kentucky, and to hear the concerns of the rugged
individualists who had braved the land west of the
mountains.

A musket, a knife, and a bag of corn gave him all he
needed to live well. Game was plentiful and could be
taken easily, most often by snare or stealth without wasting
shot and powder. His camp, in a thicket of brush, was the
ultimate of simplicity: a fire made as smokeless as possible
by the use of dry twigs, a bed of leaves on which to spread
his one blanket, a hare roasting on a spit. While he
waited for the meat to cook he chewed moistened cor
and let his memories flow. Here, in solitude, in the peace

ful forest, he was beginning to see things clearly, and the sorrow of losing a beloved wife was no longer a pain in his chest equal to that of a severe wound. Nora was dead, God bless her, gone with the angels to join a beloved daughter, their Emily, and he was alone in the world save for his grandchildren, Emily's son and daughter. They—the grandchildren—were the basis of his only regret at being so far from home.

Around him the night sounds began: the hoot of an owl, the scurry of small rodents in the leaves, a sigh of wind in the high treetops. It was thus, he was thinking, with the long hunters, those men who first penetrated beyond the mountains. Their stated purpose had been to collect hides and furs, but, he suspected, it was the forest itself that attracted them, drew them to a freedom unlike any other, based on one's own ability to cope and stay alive in a land that could be hostile.

He himself had journeyed to the north with a purpose—supposedly to see for himself the conditions in the Ohio lands. But the real motives behind his long trek were to learn to live with his grief and his new loneliness; to see ground that he had never seen before and to place, perhaps, the first white foot on some of that land; to live with a fullness made sweet by the certain knowledge that at any given moment he might lose his scalp. He had become one of the restless ones.

He had seen and listened to men much like himself in Kentucky. Ever-restless, they were their own law, men who scorned any vestige of authority except that of their own sinews and weapons. Those men who settled Kentucky had come first to hunt and then—in order to enjoy that one ingredient of life without which a man is not whole, a wife and family—to build their poor huts, to clear their three or four acres, and then to guard them against Indian raids and the rapacious land companies and lawyers who seemed to appear on the frontier as a natural consequence of settlement. Roy had heard settlers' complaints: They had no kind words for the federal government or for those bewigged and powdered men back in New York and Philadelphia who spoke of a great new nation and talked of taxes while the frontier flamed and westerners died under the blades of Indian tomahawks.

Roy Johnson would have a few words to report to George Washington. He would tell the president that the narrow belt of so-called civilization east of the mountains was but a tiny part of this vast continent . . . that the true riches of the land lay beyond the first natural frontier . . . and that those who had pushed westward were Americans, too. But they might not remain so unless that much-vaunted federal government either provided some protection in the new lands or forced the states to live up to their responsibilities.

Roy's task was just beginning, but already he could see the complexity of the problem. There were men in Kentucky such as George Rogers Clark, who realized that the true potential for the nation lay in the west. He had met and talked with Clark in Boonesborough and he had pieced together a picture of disillusionment. Clark dropped real hints that he just might cast his lot—and the lot of Kentucky—with any power that would come to the westerners' aid.

**FROM THE PRODUCER OF WAGONS WEST
AND THE KENT FAMILY CHRONICLES—
A SWEEPING SAGA OF WAR AND HEROISM
AT THE BIRTH OF A NATION**

THE WHITE INDIAN SERIES

This thrilling series tells the compelling story of America's birth against the equally exciting adventures of an English child raised as a Seneca.

☐	24650	White Indian #1	$3.95
☐	25020	The Renegade #2	$3.95
☐	24751	War Chief #3	$3.95
☐	24476	The Sachem #4	$3.95
☐	25154	Renno #5	$3.95
☐	25039	Tomahawk #6	$3.95
☐	25589	War Cry #7	$3.95
☐	25202	Ambush #8	$3.95
☐	23986	Seneca #9	$3.95
☐	24492	Cherokee #10	$3.95
☐	24950	Choctaw #11	$3.95
☐	25353	Seminole #12	$3.95
☐	25868	War Drums #13	$3.95
☐	26206	Apache #14	$3.95
☐	27161	Spirit Knife #15	$3.95
☐	27264	Manitou #16	$3.95
☐	27814	Seneca Warrior #17	$3.95

Bantam Books, Dept. LE3, 414 East Golf Road, Des Plaines, IL 60016

Please send me the items I have checked above. I am enclosing $_____
(please add $2.00 to cover postage and handling). Send check or money order, no cash or C.O.D.s please.

Mr/Ms _____

Address _____

City/State _____ Zip_____

LE3-9/89

Please allow four to six weeks for delivery.
Prices and availability subject to change without notice.

★ WAGONS WEST ★

This continuing, magnificent saga recounts the adventures of a brave band of settlers, all of different backgrounds, all sharing one dream— to find a new and better life.

☐	26822	**INDEPENDENCE! #1**	$4.50
☐	26162	**NEBRASKA! #2**	$4.50
☐	26242	**WYOMING! #3**	$4.50
☐	26072	**OREGON! #4**	$4.50
☐	26070	**TEXAS! #5**	$4.50
☐	26377	**CALIFORNIA! #6**	$4.50
☐	26546	**COLORADO! #7**	$4.50
☐	26069	**NEVADA! #8**	$4.50
☐	26163	**WASHINGTON! #9**	$4.50
☐	26073	**MONTANA! #10**	$4.50
☐	26184	**DAKOTA! #11**	$4.50
☐	26521	**UTAH! #12**	$4.50
☐	26071	**IDAHO! #13**	$4.50
☐	26367	**MISSOURI! #14**	$4.50
☐	27141	**MISSISSIPPI! #15**	$4.50
☐	25247	**LOUISIANA! #16**	$4.50
☐	25622	**TENNESSEE! #17**	$4.50
☐	26022	**ILLINOIS! #18**	$4.50
☐	26533	**WISCONSIN! #19**	$4.50
☐	26849	**KENTUCKY! #20**	$4.50
☐	27065	**ARIZONA! #21**	$4.50
☐	27458	**NEW MEXICO! #22**	$4.50
☐	27703	**OKLAHOMA! #23**	$4.50

Bantam Books, Dept. LE, 414 East Golf Road, Des Plaines, IL 60016

Please send me the items I have checked above. I am enclosing $_____ (please add $2.00 to cover postage and handling). Send check or money order, no cash or C.O.D.s please.

Mr/Ms _____

Address _____

City/State _____ Zip _____

Please allow four to six weeks for delivery.
Prices and availability subject to change without notice.   LE-9/89